CHILD OF A
DEAD GOD

CHILD OF A DEAD GOD

BARB & J. C. HENDEE

A ROC BOOK

ROC

Published by New American Library, a division of
Penguin Group (USA) Inc., 375 Hudson Street,
New York, New York 10014, USA
Penguin Group (Canada), 90 Eglinton Avenue East, Suite 700, Toronto,
Ontario M4P 2Y3, Canada (a division of Pearson Penguin Canada Inc.)
Penguin Books Ltd., 80 Strand, London WC2R 0RL, England
Penguin Ireland, 25 St. Stephen's Green, Dublin 2,
Ireland (a division of Penguin Books Ltd.)
Penguin Group (Australia), 250 Camberwell Road, Camberwell, Victoria 3124,
Australia (a division of Pearson Australia Group Pty. Ltd.)
Penguin Books India Pvt. Ltd., 11 Community Centre, Panchsheel Park,
New Delhi - 110 017, India
Penguin Group (NZ), 67 Apollo Drive, Rosedale, North Shore 0632,
New Zealand (a division of Pearson New Zealand Ltd.)
Penguin Books (South Africa) (Pty.) Ltd., 24 Sturdee Avenue,
Rosebank, Johannesburg 2196, South Africa

Penguin Books Ltd., Registered Offices:
80 Strand, London WC2R 0RL, England

First published by Roc, an imprint of New American Library,
a division of Penguin Group (USA) Inc.

First Printing, January 2008
10   9   8   7   6   5   4   3   2   1

ROC REGISTERED TRADEMARK—MARCA REGISTRADA

LIBRARY OF CONGRESS CATALOGING-IN-PUBLICATION DATA:
Hendee, Barb.
Child of a dead god: a novel of the noble dead / Barb & J.C. Hendee.
p. cm.
ISBN: 978-0-451-46187-2
1. Vampires—Fiction. I. Hendee, J. C. II. Title.
PS3608.E525C48 2008
813'.6—dc22   2007025720
Set in Adobe Garamond
Designed by Alissa Amell

Printed in the United States of America

PUBLISHER'S NOTE
This is a work of fiction. Names, characters, places, and incidents either are the product of the author's imagination or are used fictitiously, and any resemblance to actual persons, living or dead, business establishments, events, or locales is entirely coincidental.
    The publisher does not have any control over and does not assume any responsibility for author or third-party Web sites or their content.

For J.P.
Our sibling by choice

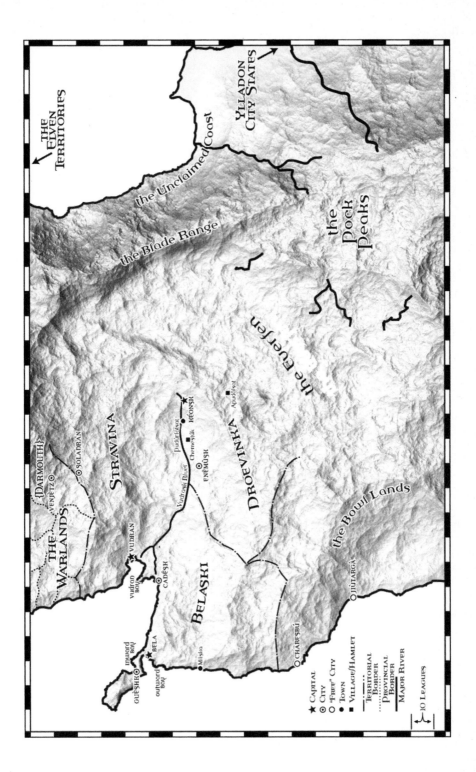

THE ELVEN TERRITORIES

the Unclaimed Coast

YLIADON CITY STATES

the Blade Range

the Pock Peaks

the Everfen

STRAVINA

{DARMOUTH} VENJETZ

SOLADRAN

THE WARLANDS

VUDRAN

vudron Boy

CADÉSK

Bucklefsot

KEONSK

Chernefkii

Abachfol

ENFMÜSK

DROEVINKA

the Bowl Lands

inward Boy

BELA

outward Boy

OUÉSHK

Milſia

BELASHI

OJUNARGK

CHÁRESBÚ

★ CAPITAL
◉ CITY
○ "FREE" CITY
● TOWN
■ VILLAGE/HAMLET

–·–·– TERRITORIAL BORDER
·········· PROVINCIAL BORDER
──── MAJOR RIVER

10 LEAGUES

CHAPTER ONE

Chane stood in the hidden mountain gorge amid the Crown Range. Light snow drifted down around him as Welstiel's mad shout rose into the night sky.

"No more! I am finished with you! Go back to where you hide. Find another toy . . . to cheat!"

Chane lifted his eyes to the dark expanse. The winter storm's cloud cover left the sky black but for one small space that exposed the stars.

Welstiel stared upward, his eyes filled with hate. His disheveled dark hair almost hid the white patches at his temples. Finally he lowered his head, and Chane followed his manic gaze to a switchback path leading up along the gorge wall.

One lone building stood halfway up, cut straight into the ancient stone. A small flicker of light traveled up the path's last leg, and then a figure stepped out of the structure's narrow door. Dressed in a pale blue tabard over a dark robe and full cowl, it lifted a torch high to greet two similarly attired figures ascending the path. All three went inside.

"Lock them all in," Welstiel whispered. "Feed if you must, but leave them alive . . . for now."

For too many days, Chane had fed only from Welstiel's life-conjuring cup. At the promise of fresh blood, he dropped his baggage and trotted toward the switchback path.

As he rounded the last turn, dim light spilled from the crack beneath the weathered front door. He slowed and crept quietly up to listen.

More than three voices sounded within. At first he couldn't follow the words, then realized they spoke Stravinan—of which he knew enough to understand simple conversations. Only the smell of life beyond the door mattered, and he gripped the cold door latch, senses widening. In one fluid move he squeezed it and shoved the door in. It clattered against the inside wall.

Three men and one woman in dark robes and blue tabards stood before a narrow hearth within a small room. All stared dumbly at him. One more elderly woman sat upon a long bench to the left, frozen halfway through pulling off her soiled boots. They took in the sight of him, tall and long limbed, with red-brown hair beneath a hooded wool cloak, and a long-sword's sheath tip peeking from beneath its soiled hem. He was clearly no mountain dweller.

Chane rushed them before he even distinguished their faces and lashed out with both fists.

A woman and a man went down before anyone could flee, and he found himself toe-to-toe with a cowled old man. Tufts of cropped gray-white hair stuck out above a deeply lined face. Then the last of the standing four darted for a stairwell.

Chane had not seen these steps from the entrance. He lunged after the slight figure, grabbing the robe between the shoulders as the man cried out.

"Help! Bandits are upon us!"

Chane braced a foot on the second step and jerked back hard.

The frail young man shot across the entry room. His head and shoulders struck the far wall among cloaks and coats hanging from wooden pegs. He slid down and tumbled off the bench, flopping motionless upon the stone floor. The elderly woman who had been sitting there was gone.

Chane twisted around the stairwell's partition wall.

Welstiel stood inside the open front door, holding the woman by her throat. His eyes roamed the entry room. Clipped choking sounds rose from the woman's gaping mouth as she fought for air. She pulled at Welstiel's grip, but he didn't notice. She grew weaker with each incomplete gasp, until her hands dropped limply to her sides.

As she sagged in Welstiel's grip, he released her. She fell, and her head smacked sharply against the stone floor. Chane turned back to the elderly man.

The old priest, monk, whatever he was, watched him with horrified fascination and lifted shaking fingers to his mouth. Chane realized what the old man was truly looking at, and stretched open his jaws, displaying sharpened teeth and elongated fangs.

The old man stiffened, eyes round in his wrinkled face as the scent of fear thickened in the room. It smelled so good that Chane almost felt it on his skin.

"Lock them up," Welstiel said quietly.

Chane whipped around. "I . . . you . . . said I could feed!" he rasped.

"Too late, too slow," Welstiel whispered. "You wasted your chance."

Chane took a quick step toward Welstiel. Pounding footfalls echoed down the stairs from above.

A crowd of people in dusky robes and blue tabards gathered at the top of the steps. One young man backpedaled at the sight of Chane, and then tripped and fell against two others behind him. A clattering of wood filled the entry room as Welstiel slammed the front door shut.

"Finish this!" he snapped, and kicked the crumpled old woman.

The impact lifted her from the floor. She landed across the room atop the bodies of her unconscious companions, and the old man backed away.

Chane looked up the stairwell. He could not count how many were huddled there. When he lunged upward, the tangled mob fled amid panicked cries. Chane crested the stairs before the last one bolted beyond his reach.

Old wooden doors lined the upper passage, each opening into a small stone chamber. He drove the shrieking robed figures before him, and though they struggled to escape, not one struck at him. These mortal cattle would not even fight him for their lives, and Chane grew more spiteful and brutal with each one. He wrenched and flung them into the small cells, their fear-scent making him nearly manic to be finished.

All he could think of was the taste of terror-seasoned blood tingling down his throat to fill him with euphoria. Not for release from hunger but for the pleasure of feeding.

He heard Welstiel's footfalls behind him, and the cracking of wood. When he pulled the last door shut, and shoved back a figure trying to emerge from the previous door, he was shaking with a wild appetite.

Welstiel carried shards of thick wood in his hands. He shoved one through each door's iron handle and braced its end against the stone frame. Anyone who tried to pull a door inward would need enormous brute strength. Welstiel passed his gaze over each door along the passage's sides.

"Seventeen candidates," he muttered, absorbed in thought. "Adequate . . . since we had no opportunity for a more studied selection." He lowered his head. "There are several still below, incapacitated. Drag them up and lock them away."

Chane wanted to snarl, but didn't. Instead, he pushed past Welstiel for the stairs, numbly following orders.

By his second trip down, only two priests remained in the entry room— the elderly woman and the young man Chane had thrown aside. Welstiel knelt on the floor by the latter, unpacking his little brass cup.

"Take the woman," he said. "Leave the man."

Welstiel refused to feed directly on blood, preferring his arcane methods to draw concentrated life force. He began chanting softly.

Chane snatched up the woman, dragging her limp body up the stairs.

By the time he returned, Welstiel had finished. The young priest was a desiccated husk, and the cup brimmed with red liquid so dark it looked black in the entry room's low hearth light. But Welstiel did not drink. He poured the cup's contents into a brown glass bottle and pressed a cork soundly into its neck.

"You will remain here, out of my way," he said.

Welstiel headed for the stairs, but he paused at the first step. A shiver ran through his back. He lifted his head, staring up the dark stone staircase for a long moment, and then resumed his ascent.

Resentment could not stifle Chane's curiosity. He drew close, watching.

Welstiel climbed in a slow, forced gait, as if bearing a weight that grew with each step, until he slipped into the upper passage beyond sight. A door creaked above, followed by a dull thump.

Chane's suspicion sharpened, but he felt compelled to follow Welstiel's orders not to pry—at least for now. He scanned his surroundings.

A passage ran along the building's front from left of the front door. The stairs were set farther back on that same side and ran upward in the same direction. An old bench stood against the opposite wall, with three cloaks and a long-haired goatskin coat hanging on wooden pegs. In the rear stone wall, between the small hearth and the stairwell's base, was an opening leading deeper into the structure.

Chane was in no mood for poking about, but he did not care to just stand there, waiting, so he stepped through the rear opening.

The passage immediately turned left, ended in a right turn, and spilled into a wide chamber behind the entry room. A lantern on the nearest table offered enough light for Chane's hunger-enhanced sight.

Bundles of drying leaves, flowers, and branches hung from cords strung loosely across the ceiling. Below the dangling harvest, pottery and glass jars sat atop wooden tables along with rolling pins stained from long use, polished marble pestles, knives, and other instruments. It was the priests' workshop.

Chane stepped back and retreated down the passage, and as he reached the entry room, a muffled clatter sounded from above.

He looked up the dark stairs, wondering again what Welstiel was doing. Curious, he climbed until he was high enough to peer over the last step. He saw the doors along the upper passage. A sharp squeal of panic came from somewhere behind one of them. Silence followed, and Chane crept farther up. He smelled the rich, salty blood even before he saw it.

Smeared trails led from a dark pool at the passage's far end to the second door on the left. Chane's longing began to build as he stared at one door after another, trying to discern which cell Welstiel was in.

The wood brace was missing from the second and third doors on the left.

The third door jerked inward and Welstiel emerged.

His cloak, shirt, and sword were gone. He braced one hand on the door frame and gagged with his mouth tightly shut. Fresh blood seeped from between his clenched lips and ran down his chin to drip upon his bare chest.

Welstiel had been feeding, while Chane had been denied a chance to do so himself.

Welstiel's eyes rolled up, and his clear crystal pupils vanished, leaving white orbs. He faltered, wavering near collapse, then turned back to heave something from the cell's floor. Welstiel dragged a young priest to the first door on the left, and kicked it open.

The dead youth's eyes were frozen wide in astonishment above the red mess below his chin.

Welstiel tossed the corpse in and jerked the door shut, not bothering to reset a wood shard in the door's handle. Instead he staggered away until his back struck a door on the passage's opposite side. Small startled whimpers answered from within that cell.

Chane took a step, unable to hiss even one resentful word, and then Welstiel stumbled.

He fell to his hands and knees and crawled to the passage's far end. His back arched as he vomited out blood, heaving violently. Finally, in a shadow of living habit, Welstiel drew a breath into his dead lungs and toppled.

He tried to fall clear of his own mess, but there was too much blood. It spattered across him as he landed, convulsing in the pool spreading down the passage floor. Finally, he crawled into one far corner and propped himself up against the walls.

Chane couldn't fathom what was happening. His mind was too clouded by the smell and sight of the red trails creeping down the passage, as if seeking him out.

"One . . . mine!" he rasped. "One should be mine!"

"Get out," Welstiel whispered and lifted a hand to hide his face. He recoiled at the crimson running down his bare arm.

"No," Chane answered. "No more drinking from your filthy little cup! I want one of them . . . now!"

He bolted for the door across from where Welstiel had tossed the dead priest. Before Chane's fingers touched the handle, Welstiel was there, and his hand closed in a crushing grip on Chane's wrist.

"I said *no*," Welstiel growled.

Chane lashed out for his throat.

Welstiel's head twisted aside like a serpent weaving upon its coiled body. He heaved on Chane's arm, turning it back and behind, and pulled it taut with a crack.

"Already twice raised"—Welstiel hissed at him—"in your first year of death!"

A fist struck the back of Chane's skull. His head snapped down, driving his chin against his chest. The blow's power buckled his knees, and the passage dimmed in his sight.

"And still you do not listen," Welstiel added, "to your better!"

Pain spread through the back of Chane's skull. He saw only the blurred, dark shape of Welstiel's leg. He strained against his locked arm and sank his teeth through the thick canvas breeches.

No tang of warm blood filled his mouth—no salty sweetness or tingle of life flooded his throat. Only thin, bitter cold seeped from Welstiel's breeches. It flowed quickly through Chane's teeth and a taste like rancid seed oil coated his tongue.

Chane's shoulder cracked again as his jaws tore free and his knees lifted from the floor. He kicked wildly, trying to find footing, and then his whole body spun in the dark and slammed sideways into a stone wall. At the same instant, something struck hard into his chest.

His spine ground into the wall, making his throat clench in reflex. Before his body slid down, he was jerked through the air again.

A second impact, and a third, and he heard but did not feel the fourth. Only half-aware of the grips around his throat and twisted arm, he cried out as both released suddenly.

Chane felt an instant of weightlessness as he tumbled through the dark. He collided roughly with the floor, edges of stone scraping at him as he flopped over and over. When all motion ceased, he weakly rolled his head.

He lay in the entry room near the bottom of the stairwell and firelight flickered off the stone walls. A deeper shadow in blood-soaked boots stood at the top of the stairs.

"Servant beasts should obey," it whispered in Welstiel's voice. "If they want to be fed . . . and have their wishes fulfilled."

Chane's eyelids sagged closed. Something inside him cowered in anguish, like a chained beast with hands instead of paws. It had fed on gristle and joints for too long, while its master had just feasted on fresh meat.

Chane opened his eyes when a cold breeze rolled across his face.

Firelight danced over a stone ceiling above him. When he turned over, he found a congealed puddle of viscous black fluid where his head had rested, and he touched the back of his skull, wincing.

Looking about the entry room, his gaze passed over the withered remains of the young priest.

How long had he lain here unconscious?

The hearth's fire still burned as if recently fueled. A tin kettle rested near it, faint wisps of steam rising from its spout. And the cold breeze . . .

The front door was ajar.

Chane glanced up the dark stairwell. Not a sound came from above. All was silent but for the crackle of the flames and the cold air spilling around the open door. He struggled to his feet.

Twice risen, Welstiel had said, only in his first year of death. Less than a full season past, Chane had been beheaded, and Welstiel had somehow brought him back. The only evidence that it had ever happened was the scar line around Chane's throat—and his forever maimed voice. Some among the dead would say he had been fortunate indeed.

Yet he had just tried to face an experienced undead freshly gorged on life.

Despite festering resentment, Chane acknowledged his own foolishness.

He tottered and bent over to brace his hands against his knees. His left shoulder and elbow burned as if filled with embedded needles. And now he was truly hungry. His dead flesh ached for life with which to repair itself.

But why was the front door open?

Chane stumbled over, pulling it wide. Falling snow swirled in the darkness outside, and he heard a grunt off to the left.

Welstiel knelt in a drift, still naked to the waist. Thin trails of steam rose from bloodstains on his arms and chest. He leaned down, scooping armfuls of snow, and splashed it over himself, scrubbing furiously. He repeated the process over and over.

"Why?" Chane asked.

Welstiel lifted his head. Flakes of snow clung to the locks down his forehead. When his gaze landed on Chane, his expression shifted from numb horror to startled wariness.

"Awake, are you?" he asked quietly, and rose to his feet. "And reason returns once more . . . for the moment . . . but always with one foot perched upon the Feral Path."

"What are you babbling about?" Chane rasped, though that last strange reference seemed familiar.

He tensed as Welstiel approached, but he was in no condition for another fight.

"Perhaps I should not help you reach your sages," Welstiel went on, but he stared into the gorge, as if alone. "Monster with a mind . . ."

Chane hesitated. Welstiel had promised him letters of introduction to gain acceptance at one of the sages' main branches, across the sea—in exchange for Chane's obedient service on this journey.

"A beast," Welstiel whispered mockingly, "sent in among the learned of the *cattle*."

That last word, which Chane had used so often, suggested Welstiel was fully aware of his presence, but the tone made Chane's instincts sharpen in warning. He sidestepped toward the switchback path down the gorge's sheer face, ready to bolt.

"Get back inside!" Welstiel ordered.

Chane halted.

Welstiel stood as still as ice, a pale column of flesh surrounded in a swirling white snowfall.

Chane longed for the denied pleasure of a feast. Sustaining draughts from Welstiel's cup might fuel him more than feeding would, but they left him painfully unsatisfied in other ways. But the existence he most desired still awaited him, where he would spend his nights studying history and languages in a sages' guild. He closed his eyes and saw Wynn's oval face. Could he attain this world on his own and no longer suffer Welstiel's madness?

"Now," Welstiel demanded. "Or stay and burn in the sun!"

Chane raised his eyes to the sky.

In the east, a faint glow exposed the black silhouette of the gorge's distant ridge. Where in this desolate place would he find shelter if he ran? He backed into the entry room as Welstiel followed, slamming the door shut.

"Sit," Welstiel instructed. "I will have need of you soon . . . to guard them until they rise."

Chane looked to the dark stairwell and finally understood.

Once before he had watched an undead feed to bursting and disgorge all it had swallowed. In faraway Bela he had crouched in an alley while his maker, Toret, took his time in choosing and killing two sailors, who rose the next nightfall as undead servants.

"You are making more of our kind?" Chane asked.

Welstiel crossed to the room's front corner and crouched to dig through his pack.

Chane remembered something else of Toret's efforts, and glanced at Welstiel's bare forearms. He saw no slashes there by which Welstiel would have force-fed his own fluids to his creations.

"They will not rise," Chane hissed. "You have not fed them from yourself."

Welstiel clicked his tongue in disgust. "More superstition . . . even among our kind."

Although this was not the first correction Chane had received in his new existence, he knew better than to question it. But if feeding the victim one's own fluid was not necessary, then why did one victim rise from death while another did not?

Chane's thoughts turned to the small cells lining the upper passage. He tried to count off the number of those locked away.

"How many?" he asked.

"We will not know until tomorrow's nightfall," Welstiel answered, making certain the front window shutters were soundly latched against the sun. "I took ten."

Chane stared at him. Toret had taken only two at once, and the act had nearly incapacitated him.

"Ten more?" Chane asked in disbelief. "In these mountains, with nothing to feed upon but those few still alive?"

"No," Welstiel answered. "Ten taken. Not ten undead . . . yet."

Chane noticed the brown glass bottle in his companion's hand.

"Not all rise from death," Welstiel said. "If I am fortunate, perhaps a third of these will." He held out the bottle. "Drink half. You have duties, and I need you whole again."

Chane recoiled. That chained beast inside him struggled against its bonds at being offered more scraps of gristle.

He was trapped not only by the sun but by what little life remained here. Where else in these winter mountains could he hope to feed enough to reach civilization? He was trapped as well by his hope for a future. That was the true manacle around his neck—and Welstiel held its chain.

Chane took the bottle.

Lost in dormancy, the sleeper heard a cry. A second, then a third unintelligible voice joined the first, alternating and growing in volume. The sleeper shifted and began to rouse.

But in the dark, a brief glint vanished. Too quick in its retreat, the flicker seemed like a light upon something huge and black undulating in the dark.

Chane awoke upon the entry room's stone floor and sat up quickly. He had never dreamed in dormancy before.

Muted moans and cries drifted down the stairwell, and Chane took brief relief in realization. The sounds had come from the dead rousing in the cells, not in his dream, and the glint in the dark, as if something moved . . .

Chane turned around.

A dim line of fading light stretched across the floor. The last of dusk's light crept between the window's shutters. The low fire still burned in the hearth, but the young priest's withered corpse was gone, and Welstiel was nowhere in sight. Only then did Chane notice a dim light at the top of the stairs.

The moans and agonized calls pulled at him. He took slow steps up the stairwell and saw a lantern upon the floor. Welstiel sat upon a stool just beyond it in the passage's near corner.

"Six," Welstiel whispered, his voice laced with astonishment. "Can you hear them? Six of ten, all risen. My highest hope had been three."

Chane barely heard him as longing surged at the smell of blood still on the floor. Panicked mewling escaped through the spaces below the cell doors and echoed along the stone walls. Or were they only in Chane's mind?

The second door on the left rattled.

It shuddered twice as something rammed against its inner side, and then lurched as it was pulled hard from within. A sharp grating of metal on stone snapped Chane from his morbid fascination. In place of wood shards, each door handle on the left was jammed with a plain iron shaft.

"*You* will now watch over them," Welstiel said. "I have other preparations to make."

Chane caught the implication. "You have been here watching all day? How . . . how could you keep from falling dormant?"

Welstiel ignored him. More iron bars leaned against the wall beyond his stool.

"You plan to drain more of them . . . and brace them in?" Chane asked.

Welstiel shook his head, still watching the one shuddering door. "The spare bars are for when one is no longer enough."

Chane stared at Welstiel, confused. Had the man abandoned all reason amid a night of gluttony, driven over the edge by his revulsion for feeding? Living priests were still trapped in the right-side cells—to satisfy the appetites of Welstiel's newborns. If he knew his creations would break free, then why wait to reinforce the doors? And why keep his new servants locked up at all?

As if reading Chane's thoughts, Welstiel answered. "To let them hope they might yet break free and feed . . . and as reason fades and desperation grows, to take that hope—and sanity—and leave only the hunger."

Welstiel headed downstairs as Chane stared numbly after him.

"Do not let them out," Welstiel warned softly, pausing at the bottom. "And if by chance you glimpse one through the crack of a straining door . . . do not look in its eyes. You may see too much of yourself reflected there."

Chane backed into the corner, settled upon the stool, and closed a hand tightly upon a spare iron rod.

He couldn't choose the greater madness surrounding him inside this fortress.

Was it the new undeads within those small cells, or was it Welstiel, who had made them?

Welstiel retrieved his pack and headed down the passage off from the front door. He had made it through the day without falling dormant—without a visitation from his patron of dreams. But he would not get through another such day without aid.

He opened the few doors along the way but found only storage rooms, not quite the private place to safely sift through his belongings. The passage's end spilled into a wide room with long rough tables and benches—a communal meal hall—and he wasted no time looking about.

Welstiel threw open the pack's flap to dig inside and withdraw a frosted glass globe. Three dancing sparks of light flickered within it. Their glow brightened at his touch, enough to illuminate the table. Fishing again, he retrieved the iron pedestal with the hoop on top and set the globe upon it. Then he opened the pack wider.

Years had passed since he had needed to drug himself. He pushed aside books, metal rods, a hoop of marked steel, and the box that held the cup with which he fed. At the pack's bottom, his fingertips brushed soft fabric over something more solid. He pulled out this hidden object wrapped in a sheet of indigo felt.

Welstiel unwrapped the covering, exposing a thin box bound in black leather, and tilted the lid up. Inside were six glass vials cushioned in felt padding, each with a silver screw-top stopper. All but one were empty, and that one was filled with murky liquid like watery violet ink.

Two doses per vial, and one dose could stave off dormancy for a few days at best. He needed much more—as much as he could make. Tonight, he planned to search the monastery for the components to create more. Hopefully the hidden enclave of priest healers would have the supplies he required.

He was done being a puppet—done with his dream patron.

From here on, he served only himself, and had no wish to meet those black coils in his dreams ever again. He unscrewed the one full vial and a fishy sweet scent filled his nose as he downed half its bitter contents.

Welstiel grimaced, wishing for tea to wash away the taste. He closed the vial and returned it back to its padded slot. Once the box for his concoctions was sealed and rewrapped, he tucked it in the bottom of his pack.

The orb of his desire, the promised artifact from the world's lost past, was locked away in an ice-bound castle guarded by ancient ones—vampires. When he gained it, he would never feed on mortals again. Or so his dream patron had told him.

Once, he had believed that controlling Magiere, his dhampir half-sister, was the way to acquire this treasure. But her actions grew more and more unpredictable. Still, one phrase whispered by his dream patron rang true.

The sister of the dead will lead you.

Though his patron was often evasive or deceitful, Welstiel believed these few words. In dream visitations to that six-towered castle, he had seen a figure upon its steps, waiting at the great iron doors. He knew he needed Magiere. She was necessary, either to find or to gain entrance to that place, or merely to face its guardians as a hunter of the dead. But if Welstiel could not control her directly nor trust his patron, he would need more than Magiere to assure his success.

He needed minions—mindless, savage, without mortal weaknesses—to serve him in the coming days.

He needed ferals.

Halfway through the third night's vigil, Chane's reason began to fracture. He could barely hold off the false hunger brought on by the wails and hammering within the cells. And though he tried to bury himself in memories of Wynn and fancies of an existence far from this place, it did not work.

At the sound of splitting wood, Chane lurched to awareness and rushed the first door on the left.

The top corner above the latch warped inward. Pale fingers with torn and split nails wedged through the space. They were smeared in fresh and dried black ichor. Chane slammed an iron bar against the wriggling knuckles.

An outraged snarl erupted behind the door, and the stained fingers jerked from sight. The door slapped back into its stone frame, and Chane jammed a second iron bar through the handle.

He covered his ears, trying to shield himself from the yelps and moans and scratching upon wood. Then he retreated down the corridor to the far end—as far as he could get without fleeing the upper floor altogether.

To hunt . . . feed . . . and the blessed release of blood filled up his thoughts.

His gaze drifted to the other side of the passage, and the doors barred only by wood.

How long would Welstiel starve his new children before feeding them? What if there was not enough for them—or nothing left for Chane but Welstiel's little cup? He turned away from the doors, and his gaze fell upon the sixth right-side cell. Its door was still ajar from Welstiel's night of gluttony.

Chane shuffled over to look inside, though his lantern left by the stool provided scant light, even for his keen night vision. A shadowy stain of congealed and dried blood marred an old canvas pillow on a plain bed. Little else in the room promised distraction from torment, from a small discolored chest of tin fixtures to the oval rug woven from faded fabric scraps. The little bedside table . . .

Chane's eyes fixated on the book resting there. He stepped in and seized it.

Its page edges were rippled from long use, and he felt deep creases in the thick leather cover. Old but well crafted, what use would religious recluses have for such a soundly bound volume? Chane stepped out into the passage for better light.

The cover's gilded lettering was half-gone, but he still made out the title written in old Stravinan.

"*The Pastoral Path*," Chane whispered, and flipped pages at random.

It was a book of poetry and verse. He stared into the vacant room, wondering about its previous occupant. Why would anyone living such an austere existence want a poetic work?

A sudden twinge tightened Chane's shoulder and the side of his neck.

He headed back to his stool, skirting the cells of the living but averting his eyes from those of the undead. But as he settled in the passage corner, the book still in hand, he could not stop gazing at those silent doors on the right, their handles barred with only wood. A nagging, unformed thought turned in the back of his mind.

With it came a fear he didn't quite understand.

He flung the book down the passage. It skidded until it caught in the congealing pool of blood.

A loud screech from the first barred cell brought Chane to his feet, and he grabbed another iron rod. He heard wood breaking, followed by growls of fury, but the door did not buck in its frame this time. Something was happening inside the cell.

One voice—female—screamed louder than the first. Her sound was smothered by the hungry wail of a third. A pain-pitched shriek ripped out of her, along with the sounds of tearing cloth and bestial snarls. Her voice broke in panting sobs, then gags. A wet tearing followed.

Chane stood staring at the door, unable to move.

Struggles within the cells faded more each night, but by the fifth, Chane was almost deaf to them.

Welstiel stepped out of the stairwell.

He was dressed in black breeches and faded white shirt, and carried water skins and small sacks that smelled faintly of old bread. He approached the first door on the right, opened it, and tossed in a water skin and a sack. Before anyone within could speak or move, he slammed the door and reinserted its wood brace. He repeated the process twice more.

How often had he done this?

"We must keep them alive," Welstiel said absently and then tilted his chin toward the stairs.

Chane's night watch ended once more, and he slipped down the stairwell.

Each dawn, he'd discovered small oddities about the entry room. Nothing extraordinary, but something different each time. One night, Welstiel's pack had rested by the fireplace. Strange rods of differing dark tones peeked out the side of its top flap, but Chane was too mentally worn to be curious. Later, he had noticed the old tin teapot near the hearth, but no cup in sight and no lingering aroma of brewed tea.

On the fourth night, the room was more orderly but smelled of crushed herbs—and something fishy and sweet that Chane could not identify.

Tonight, Welstiel's pack sat upon the bench, and beside it rested a small bottle and a leather-bound box, longer and narrower than the walnut one which held his brass feeding cup.

Chane had never seen this box before.

A few times in their journey he had wondered what items an artificer of conjury like Welstiel might carry. All he knew of were the brass cup and Welstiel's "ring of nothing," which shielded him and anyone he touched from those who could sense the undead.

Chane crept closer. As he crouched down, a fishy-sweet odor rose around the leather-bound box. When he picked up the bottle, it was strong with the same scent. He returned the bottle to its place and reached for the pack's top flap.

Someone shifted in the upper passage of cells.

He froze, his hand poised above the pack, and glanced toward the stairs as his hearing widened. Welstiel shifted upon the stool in the upper passage. Chane clenched his hand into a fist and lowered it.

If he could hear Welstiel, then the mad undead might just as easily hear him.

And mingling with the fishy odor was the scent of herbs, just as he had smelled in the back workroom.

What had Welstiel been doing down here all through the night?

Chane rose slowly. He paused at each step, listening for movement in the upper passage, until he rounded the second turn into the workroom. The scent of herbs was strong. He ducked and wove his way between the tables and dangling bundles of drying plants, searching for anything odd or out of place.

And on one table, he found a mess.

Among knives and pestles and scraps of wax paper was a tin dish, blackened inside as if a substance had been boiled within it. Then he spotted the dried flowers. He leaned closer and caught the faint residue of color—pale yellow but darkening to plum at the centers—and he lifted a fragile dry petal, taking a careful whiff. The sweet, fishy scent was powerful, and he quickly pulled the blossoms from his face as recognition hit him.

It was Dyvjàka Svonchek, called "boar's bell" in Belaskian, after the shape of its yellow flowers and the superstition that only wild boars and the heartiest beasts could eat it. It had other folk names, with meanings like Flooding Dusk, Nightmare's Breath, and Blackbane.

In other words, poison—toxic and mind altering, if inhaled too deeply by the living.

Chane turned a full circle, looking around.

What use would a Noble Dead have for poison?

What had Welstiel been doing in here?

CHAPTER TWO

"Magiere, look there," Sgäile said, pointing past her. "Your ship comes to harbor."

Magiere stepped to the dock's end beside him and shielded her eyes with one hand against the bright sun.

"That large one?" she asked.

Sgäile nodded, still watching the ship. "Yes."

Even from a distance, the tawny-hulled vessel appeared to glide across the waves as it headed for port at the elven city of Ghoivne Ajhâjhe—Front of the Deep. It rode strangely high, as if moving from one wave top to the next. Iridescent shimmers reflected from its sails like white satin under the late winter sun—or what should have been winter. Here on the Elven Territories' northern shore, the air felt more like early spring.

An ocean breeze whipped a tendril of Magiere's black hair across her eyes. She brushed it aside and peered intently at this strange vessel come to carry her and her companions away. Long and sleek, its prow stretched to a point like a headless spear, and the hull's lip seemed lightly curved like a holly leaf's edge. For an instant, she thought a ripple of dark green flickered across its hull from light reflected off the water, but the color quickly returned to rich golden tan.

Other vessels, both small and large, sailed in and out of the vast bay or were already harbored in its waters and at the long docks. Various barges that had come down inland rivers were tied off at the piers. Elves upon the docks unloaded and reloaded goods to be exchanged with city shops and outbound vessels.

"Ah, seven hells!" someone muttered. "We're actually going to board that thing?"

Magiere glanced back, and Leesil grimaced as he stepped in beside Sgäile. She looked them over.

Sgäile was full elven and an anmaglâhk—a trained assassin and spy, who'd sworn to protect Leesil and his companions, including Magiere herself. She hadn't known him long and could rarely read his subtle expressions.

Leesil was only half-blooded.

With oblong ears less peaked than those of a full-blooded elf, he shared other traits with Sgäile's people, from silky blond hair—white-blond, in his case—to amber eyes and tan skin. Leesil's eyes were smaller than a full-blooded elf's, though still slightly larger than a human's, and his complexion was lighter. Above average height for a human, like Magiere, he was short by elven standards. Beardless—as were all male elves—his wedged chin looked blunt compared to Sgäile's.

"My dinner's coming up just looking at it," Leesil added, glowering at the approaching vessel.

"There's no other way," Magiere said. "Unless you care to cross the mountains on foot again."

She was in no mood for his whining. They'd only been on one short sea voyage, to Bela, and Leesil had been sick the entire journey. With a dramatic sigh, he shouldered around Sgäile to grasp her gloved hand.

After traveling downriver on a barge from Crijheäiche—Origin-Heart—they'd spent only one night and day here, but Magiere was anxious to be off again. Sgäile had brought her to the docks the moment he heard their ship neared harbor.

"When can we leave?" she asked.

Sgäile lowered his eyes to hers. "The ship returns from its run along our eastern coastal settlements. Once cargo is exchanged, it will be ready to depart."

"How long will that take?"

"Several days, perhaps. It depends on the cargo to be acquired."

More delays.

But compared to everything Magiere had been through since entering the Elven Territories, arriving at the city had brought some relief. It was good to see ocean again and breathe sea air, as in Miiska, her faraway home, but it was still elven land. She peered back at Ghoivne Ajhâjhe stretching along the coastline.

Inland elves resided in cultured wild groves of living tree dwellings, but this one and only city was constructed partly of ornately carved wood, partly of stone, and partly of other materials she couldn't name. A wild array of structures spread along the shore above the beach amid sparse but massive trees, not only behind her, but also where the shore continued on the far side of the Hâjh River's wide mouth spilling into the bay.

Various shops, dwellings, tents, and inns bustled with activity. She could just make out the tawny roof of the tall inn where she and Leesil were lodged—along with their companions, Chap and Wynn. It rose three stories high around a giant elm with branches spread like a second roof over the building.

The elves here still treated Magiere like a savage outsider—a human—though more discreetly than their inland brethren. She had long since grown accustomed to thinly veiled loathing, but the greater part of her drive to leave came from something more unsettling.

A dream—and the polite urgency of an old sage in Bela.

The journey's next leg was a search for a long-forgotten artifact. Magiere was determined to keep it out of the hands of a murdering Noble Dead—her half-brother, Welstiel. Wynn's old master sage, "Domin" Tilswith as he was titled, was the one who'd first requested help from Magiere and Leesil. He feared letting an ancient device from the Forgotten History fall into any such hands.

Until recently, Magiere had put aside the master sage's concern. In addition to not knowing where to search for the artifact, she'd had other goals which meant more to her. Then black-scaled coils appeared in her dark dream on the first night within the city.

Taller than a mounted rider, the creature showed her a six-towered castle locked in ice, and a voice whispered . . .

Sister of the dead, lead on.

Magiere had awoken in a cold sweat, crying out for Leesil.

She'd seen the coils once before in far-off Droevinka, but she'd been awake that time, outside the dead village of Apudâlsat. She and her canine companion, Chap, fought to escape from the decrepit necromancer Ubâd. When they gained the upper hand, that madman had called upon something by name.

il'Samar.

Turning black coils materialized ghostlike among the dank trees around the clearing. The voice that came like a whisper throughout the forest ignored Ubâd's plea and left him to Chap's savagery. Earlier that same night, while Magiere had been lost within her dead mother's spirit-memories, she'd witnessed her half-brother, Welstiel, whispering in the night . . . as if to something no one else could see or hear.

Perhaps that something was the same black-scaled thing that had whispered in Magiere's dream—and in the clearing with Ubâd. Perhaps it was the same ancient force behind the old necromancer's scheming of her birth by Welstiel's undead father. In the days following her dream, Magiere remembered a few words Wynn and Domin Tilswith had translated from an old scroll out of the Forgotten. It mentioned an ancient enemy called "the night voice."

And Wynn had translated "il'Samar" as a name or title akin to "conversation in the dark."

In Magiere's time in the Elven Territories, she'd learned that no undead had ever entered elven land, not even in the faraway sanctuary on Wynn's continent, where the last of the living had fled in the war of the Forgotten. But she, daughter of a Noble Dead, had entered here. Her very touch drained life from its trees, and she had taken to wearing gloves, avoiding any direct contact with the elven forest.

Magiere feared all these connections closing in on her. And since the night of her dream, she'd learned to fear sleep as well. As always, fear made her angry—enough to find this forgotten artifact, be done with it, and go home.

And in the dream's wake, she knew where to go, or at least in which direction to start. It pulled at her from within. Magiere hoped the elven ship's crew finished quickly with their cargo.

"We were not in the shop too long! I barely had time to glance about before you pushed me out the door!"

The familiar high-pitched voice drew Magiere from her heavy thoughts to see a silver-gray dog and a tall elf in dark gray-green coming down the dock. Chap led the way, tail high but head low as he glared blankly ahead with an occasional twitch of jowl that exposed sharp teeth. Brot'an walked behind him.

Unlike his people, Brot'an was broad and solid, built almost like a human, but tall even for an elf. His white-blond hair was rather coarse, and its gray streaks turned silvery under the sun. As he neared, four long scars stood out upon his faintly lined face. They ran down his forehead's right side, jumped his eye, and continued across his cheekbone. He was dressed like Sgäile in the monotone cloak, tunic, and breeches of the Anmaglâhk, the caste of elven spies and assassins—though they wouldn't describe themselves as such.

Anmaglâhk feared little, yet Brot'an strode swiftly, as if trying to flee pursuit without being obvious. Even Chap quickened his lope at the berating voice harrying them both.

"We must go back!" the high female voice insisted. "I have not finished my notes. Are you listening to me?"

Brot'an's large stature blocked his pursuer from view—until Wynn Hygeorht scurried around his side, trying to catch up.

"And stop calling me 'girl'! Just because you are longer-lived—and a hulk among your own kind—does not make me a child by comparison."

The little sage took two quick steps for every one of Brot'an's, and her head barely reached his midchest. Somewhere past twenty years of age, Wynn's light-brown hair hung loose and blew wildly about her oval, olive-toned face. Dressed in borrowed yellow breeches and a loose russet tunic made for a youth of Sgäile's clan, her pant legs were rolled up to keep her from tripping. The faded man's cloak she wore, with its poorly hemmed bottom, made her attire even more ridiculous.

"Did you hear me?" she demanded, grasping at Brot'an's cloak.

Anmaglâhk were difficult to read, and more so with the so-called masters among them, such as Brot'an and Urhkar—but not today. Brot'an's stoic expression bore a silent plea for assistance.

Magiere couldn't suppress a smirk. "Wynn, leave Brot'an alone. You've dragged him about enough for one day."

Chap growled with a short bark of agreement and thumped his haunches down on the dock beside Magiere. Wynn glared back in disbelief.

"Elves were using a strangely shaped clay oven to smoke-dry salmon in a fish house. I have never seen the process work so quickly. This is useful information to record . . . and I foresee no opportunity to return here anytime soon. Do you?"

"She was—" Brot'an cut in sharply then regained his polite tone. "She was asking many questions. I felt it best that we leave."

Magiere understood both their frustrations. Neither she nor Wynn nor even Leesil could walk about unescorted. No human had ever been welcome in this part of the world, let alone left it again. Wynn was a scholar and a sage, and thus fluent in the elven dialect from her own continent. But she always had to stick her little nose into everything new and strange that she stumbled upon.

"Look, there's our ship," Magiere said, and pointed, hoping to distract the sage.

Wynn's scowl faded. "The large one?"

Chap pricked up his ears, and Magiere scratched between them. He whined and looked back toward the city. Or was he peering to the forest beyond it? He'd done that a good deal of late, often disappearing for long periods and leaving Magiere to wonder what he'd been up to. Chap swung his long muzzle back toward the approaching ship, and sunlight caught in his blue crystalline eyes and silvery fur.

"Beautiful . . . ," Wynn whispered. "Look at its sails! How does a cargo vessel ride so high and swift?"

More questions, and Brot'an let out a deep sigh.

"Beautiful?" Leesil scoffed. "We'll see how beautiful it is . . . after you've sloshed about in it for a few days."

Wynn arched an eyebrow at him. "I never get seasick. I enjoyed the voyage across the ocean to Belaski."

Leesil's mouth tightened, and Magiere wished Wynn would just stop talking.

"You will adjust, Léshil," Sgäile said, pronouncing Leesil's name in Elvish. "It took days for me as well. But after enough voyages, I no longer succumb to a vessel's rocking at sea."

Brot'an slipped around to Magiere's far side, perhaps using her as a barrier against Wynn. Chap slunk the other way around Leesil and wrinkled his jowls at Brot'an. The dog still didn't care for the master anmaglâhk's presence.

Magiere lifted her chin to meet Brot'an's large amber eyes. Up close, his scars were as light as human skin. He seemed troubled by more than Wynn's pestering.

"What?" she asked.

"The council of elders," he began, "promised a ship to deliver you wherever you wished to go, but so far, you have named no destination. I must give instructions to the ship's master."

Magiere had known this moment would come—and had dreaded it. Brot'an frowned, waiting for an answer.

"I don't exactly know," she said. "Only that we must head south . . . along the eastern coast."

Even to her, the explanation sounded vague.

"There is nothing along that route," Sgäile said. "No settlements beyond our territory, not even for humans, except far south . . . the Ylladon States."

She didn't know the place he mentioned, but Sgäile's voice held a less than subtle malice. Surprising, since he took great effort to remain ever polite. Magiere's frustration increased. She didn't know what to say without revealing that her only guides were a dream and the pull of her instinct.

"Magiere . . . ," Wynn whispered. "There is no other way."

"Wynn, don't—" Leesil began.

"We are not looking for a settlement," Wynn cut in, and pushed him aside, peering around Magiere at Brot'an. "Rather an object, hidden in ice-capped mountains, in a castle on this continent. Long forgotten and guarded by old ones . . . which likely means undead."

Leesil tried to grab her. "Wynn, that's enough!"

The little sage swatted his hand aside and kept on talking, even as Chap growled and grabbed the hem of her cloak.

"My guild believes this artifact is from what we call the Forgotten History. And that Magiere may be the only one who can retrieve it . . . considering she was born a hunter of the dead."

Rising anger choked off Magiere's rebuke, but the small sage only glared back at her.

"They must be told," Wynn said. "How else can Brot'an arrange a voyage without a destination? After all that has happened in Crijheäiche, we have few secrets from him."

"Cork it, Wynn!" Leesil snapped.

"He will know best how much to relate to the captain," Wynn snapped back, and jerked her cloak from Chap's jaws. "Besides, our task is no threat to his people—perhaps just the opposite, if we keep this artifact from the wrong hands."

Magiere's mouth hung partly open, shocked at what Wynn blurted out in front of two anmaglâhk. Brot'an, as well as Sgäile, had risked his life and more to protect Magiere and those she cared for. But still, Magiere had an urge to toss Wynn into the bay.

Yet what was the alternative—to leave Brot'an with no instructions for the captain? Neither she nor Leesil knew the eastern coast, so faking a destination was impossible. Magiere raised a warning finger before Wynn started up again and turned to Brot'an.

"We have to find this thing, whatever it is, and take it to the sages. We promised that much, but we don't know exactly where it is—only what Wynn said, and that we must travel south along the eastern coast."

Brot'an's unblinking amber eyes stared down at Magiere. Sgäile remained silently attentive.

"Who are these sages?" Brot'an suddenly asked.

It wasn't among the first questions Magiere had expected, but Wynn's people had arrived on this continent less than a year past. Even the Anmaglâhk might not know of them as yet. Magiere cocked her head toward Wynn.

"Scholars, like her. Their guild is in Bela."

"One branch of our guild, actually," Wynn corrected. "The Guild of Sagecraft. We build and care for repositories of knowledge. Places of learning where sages like myself live and work. Good people, Brot'an. They preserve what they gather, that which should not be forgotten or lost again. And they can discern what this object is and how to keep it safe."

Magiere wasn't about to let the Anmaglâhk know from whom she'd learned of this artifact—the same person she was trying to keep it from. The sun had slipped down the sky toward the faraway Broken Range, and dusk was settling in.

"I will speak to the ship's hkomas," Brot'an said finally. "I am uncertain how well he will respond to a journey with no destination, especially beyond our own waters. But do not repeat what you have told me to anyone." He nodded to Wynn. "I hold and value your trust."

Another awkward silence followed, until Sgäile spoke. "Brot'ân'duivé, would you see them to their lodging? I have duties to attend."

"Yes, certainly," Brot'an replied, ushering everyone down the docks.

Magiere wondered what duties Sgäile could have here, besides his sworn guardianship. She was still annoyed with Wynn but also a little relieved, though she'd never confess it.

Everyone stepped off the dock onto the sandy shore, and Chap whined, dancing sideways a few steps toward the city. Magiere knew he really wanted to run for the forest beyond it.

"He's been doing that every day," she muttered.

Wynn pulled tangles of loose hair out of her face. "Oh, stop whining and just go."

Chap bolted upslope, disappearing between a tall stone building and a taller elm.

Magiere trudged the shore road until it turned inland across sandy earth, winding toward their temporary home. She glanced over her shoulder at the sea, feeling some ease that they would soon be on their way. But when she turned back, facing south by southeast, the pull within her grew stronger.

Sgäile's thoughts tumbled as he darted through the trees, deeper into the forest beyond Ghoivne Ajhâjhe. From the instant he first intercepted Léshil entering his people's lands, Sgäile had sworn guardianship to protect the half-blood and his companions.

Léshil had somehow managed to pass the Broken Range amid brutal winter and walk straight into the forest, unhindered. He had come to free his mother, Cuirin'nên'a, from imprisonment imposed by her own caste. And in the end, he had succeeded. But so much more had happened during Léshil's time among Sgäile's people, the an'Cróan—Those of the Blood.

Sgäile had guided Léshil to Roise Chârmune, the Seed of Sanctuary, in the sacred burial place of the an'Cróan's most ancient ancestors. There he had watched in awe as Léshil was given—rather than chose—his true name.

Léshiârelaohk—Sorrow-Tear's Champion.

The ancestors accepted a half-blood as an'Cróan and saw fit to call him a champion—but for what reason? Even more, they had *shown* themselves to Léshil—despite Sgäile's improper presence, for name-taking was always done alone.

None of this had ever happened before.

Puzzled, Sgäile could only guard Léshil until the whole truth became clear.

For days, he had wavered over whether or not to accompany Léshil in returning to his home, to make certain he arrived safely. Now it appeared that Magiere was steering Léshil elsewhere toward an uncertain future. Or was this also part of Léshil's destiny?

Sgäile sank to his knees before a wide beech tree. He desperately needed guidance.

Coastal forests differed from the inland and his clan's own lands. Trees grew farther apart, and the earth was gritty rather than soft and loamy. Cool air blew in the branches, and Sgäile drew his cloak close as he took a small oval of word-wood from his pocket. It had been "grown" from the great oak home of Aoishenis-Ahâre, Most Aged Father, the leader of the Anmaglâhk.

Sgäile placed it against the beech tree's trunk and whispered, "Father?"

All anmaglâhk called Aoishenis-Ahâre by this name. The world was silent but for the wind-stirred leaves overhead, until a welcome voice, thin and reedy, filled Sgäile's mind.

Sgäilsheilleache, my son.

"Yes, Father, I am here . . . still at Ghoivne Ajhâjhe."

Has there been a delay?

Sgäile hesitated. "The ship arranged by the council of elders has only just arrived. Cargo must be exchanged before it leaves port, but . . ."

What troubles you?

"Léshil is not traveling home. Magiere has requested that they be taken south along the eastern coast . . . in search of an artifact sought by their human scholar."

Most Aged Father did not respond at first. *What artifact?*

"They know only that it is ancient, possibly as old as the lost days of the enemy you have warned us against . . . from what Wynn calls their Forgotten History. She mentioned a castle in ice-capped mountains to the south . . . somewhere. And they believe Magiere is the one to obtain it. Brot'ân'duivé will ask the ship's hkomas to follow her request."

Sgäile tried to be precise, hoping for wise counsel. But Most Aged Father's silence drew out so long that Sgäile's hand cramped with tension where he held the word-wood to the tree's bark.

Do not worry, my son. I will see to the matter. Once Brot'ân'duivé has instructed the ship's master, have him return to Crijheäiche at once. You will remain to see the humans off.

"See them off?" Sgäile repeated in confusion. He had expected more.

Yes . . . then I believe you wish time in your clan's central enclave, with your grandfather and cousin? It is good to return to family and see firsthand all that we are sworn to protect.

Sgäile stiffened. Was Most Aged Father reminding him of his duty?

Send Brot'ân'duivé to Crijheäiche . . . tonight.

Most Aged Father's voice faded from Sgäile's thoughts, and he knelt there a moment longer in confusion before finally lifting the word-wood from the beech's bark. Sgäile rose to head back to the inn, but froze at a shadow's shift on his left.

"Be at ease," a voice said.

Brot'ân'duivé stepped into sight from beneath an elm's sagging branches. His first movement in the tree's shadow had been but a polite announcement of his arrival.

"You have reported to Most Aged Father?" he asked.

"Yes," Sgäile answered, "and he requested that you return to Crijheäiche, tonight. I am to stay and see Léshil and the others off."

"To see them off?" Brot'ân'duivé asked, his tone hard but quiet.

Sgäile watched his face. Brot'ân'duivé was more than Anmaglâhk. He was Greimasg'äh—Shadow-Gripper—one of the remaining four who had stepped beyond even the most highly trained of Sgäile's caste.

Brot'ân'duivé was a master of silence and shadows.

"Perhaps . . . it is better that you accompany Léshil and his companions," Brot'ân'duivé added, more composed. "Alone among the ship's crew, they will have only young Wynn to translate for them."

At first, the suggestion stunned Sgäile, but relief quickly followed at someone else voicing his own wish. But, not for the first time, Brot'ân'duivé placed him in a difficult position.

"Most Aged Father feels otherwise," Sgäile answered carefully.

"Had he heard Wynn, I am certain he would agree with me. The crew—our people—will never be at ease with humans in their midst. When I return to Crijheäiche, I will explain this . . . face-to-face with Most Aged Father."

Sgäile suspected a polite ruse in those final words, but he had already made his own choice. And perhaps the Greimasg'äh merely wished to give him the excuse to do so.

"I will travel with Léshil," Sgäile said. "I will continue my guardianship."

"Good, then I will stay to see you off"—and before Sgäile raised concern, Brot'ân'duivé shook his head. "Do not worry. Most Aged Father will understand my delay when I speak with him."

With a parting nod and a half-smile, Brot'ân'duivé turned away and melted into the forest's dusky shadows.

Sgäile disliked being caught between Most Aged Father and Brot'ân'duivé—again. But with his decision made, he breathed deeply in relief and turned eastward toward the Hâjh River. Taking the longer way to the shore would give him a few more moments alone in peace.

Soon, he came upon the docks beyond the river's mouth where barges with no seaward cargo tied off. Such a barge was just arriving, though unusual for after dark. About to pass on and turn into the city's near side, Sgäile spotted the green-gray of an anmaglâhk cloak as someone stepped ashore.

Had another of his caste been sent? He veered back through sparse aspens along the river, but even before he cleared the trees, the figure turned and called out.

"Sgäilsheilleache!"

Sgäile halted in surprise as Osha jogged toward him with a youthful grin on his long face. He was taller than Sgäile, and his lanky arms were too long for his torso.

"Why are you here?" Sgäile asked. "Did Most Aged Father send you?"

This hardly seemed possible. Osha had accompanied Sgäile in guardianship of Léshil on their journey through the forest. He was young, still in the early stages of training, and had an open and honest manner that leaned toward naïve.

"No," Osha answered, still grinning, his large teeth exposed. "Gleannéohkân'thva, your grandfather, sent me the day after you left. He said you planned to return home, and that I was invited—so you could continue my training! I came so that we might travel together."

Sgäile's brief peace shattered. For one thing, he was no longer going home, and for the rest . . . Truly, he intended to help Osha, but he had never thought of formally accepting the young man as a student. That was impossible.

As an anmaglâhk, Osha had shown himself to be . . . adequate.

Competent with a bow and sufficient in hand-to-hand, his stealth was poor. His ability with foreign languages was questionable, and he was far too open and trusting.

"I cannot go home," Sgäile said quietly. "I continue guardianship of Léshil and his companions, and leave tomorrow to travel with them by sea."

Osha's grin vanished.

Clearly he had thought that an invitation to winter with Sgäile's family was a prelude to something more. It pained Sgäile to add to Osha's many disappointments, but he had more important matters at hand.

Osha reached up his sleeves and jerked both of his stilettos free.

Sgäile slid back out of reach, apprehension rising.

Osha spun the blades, gripping them with blades pointed earthward. Before Sgäile could protest, Osha fell to his knees and slammed both blades into the forest floor. Sgäile's heart dropped in his chest.

The young anmaglâhk placed both hands flat on the sandy earth and bowed his head.

"Sgäilsheilleache, I beg the honor . . . ," Osha began softly, but his voice shook with desperation. "I beg acceptance into your tutelage. Be my guide to achieve my place among our caste."

Sgäile had no wish to further harm Osha, who acted properly but presumed too much. It was far too soon for Osha to make such a request. But Sgäile faltered before he could utter his denial.

Had that time already passed? Had he somehow given the impression that he would consider such a relationship? Was this his fault? And if he now refused, what would become of Osha?

Sgäile took a step, and each following one grew heavier under the weight Osha had thrown upon him. He reached down, gripped the hilts of Osha's blades, and pulled them from the earth.

Without a seasoned anmaglâhk as teacher to complete Osha's training—and one with exceptional patience—the young man had no future. Initiates fresh from rudimentary training and of lesser years had sought and gained a formal teacher, but Osha had not.

Osha remained still, waiting with head bowed.

Sgäile suppressed a sigh. "Will you follow my teaching, until your need is fulfilled?"

"I swear," Osha answered.

"Will you heed my word and my way, until our bond is fulfilled?"

"I swear."

"And upon that night, when you step into silence and shadow among our caste, what purpose will my effort in you have attained?"

"I will serve the defense of our people and the honor of the Anmaglâhk."

Sgäile flipped both blades, catching their tips. As he held out the stilettos, Osha lifted his head.

Osha's large wide eyes filled with relief, but his hands shook as they closed on the offered hilts.

"It is a great privilege," he whispered, and stood up, unsteady on his feet.

At Sgäile's silence, Osha bowed once, turning toward the city. Sgäile fell in beside his one and only student.

Something struck Chane's leg hard, jerking him awake. He lay by the hearth in the monastery's entryway, and Welstiel stood over him.

"Time to feed them . . . ," Welstiel said. "Just a morsel to fight over."

Chane did not like the sound of this.

"Search the front passage," Welstiel ordered, heading for the stairs. "We need something to bind any resistant candidates."

Still groggy from dormancy, Chane watched Welstiel disappear above. He snatched a burning stick from the hearth for light and walked down the front passage.

Small storage rooms lined the hallway, each containing varied items from barrels of dried goods to stacks of blankets and clothing. He saw little of interest until he passed through a doorless opening at the far end, which led into a larger room.

Long, low tables were bordered by benches instead of chairs—a communal meal hall. Tall, unlit lanterns decorated each table. He picked one up, lifting its glass to light the wick with his smoldering stick.

He spotted another door in the far back corner and approached to crack it open. Beyond it, he found a kitchen and scullery, neither likely to have any rope, so he turned away, intent upon scavenging further among the outer storerooms. Before he got two steps, he paused.

A sheaf of papers bound between plain wood planks lay on a rear table.

Part of Chane did not want to learn any more of this place, but curiosity held him there. He jerked the sheaf's leather lace, slid aside the top wood panel, and stared at more strange writing.

Old Stravinan—but mixed with other languages, each passage apparently written by a different author, and with a date above each entry. He flipped through several sheets, finding headings in Belaskian and contemporary Stravinan.

The entries he could read appeared to be notes regarding treatment of the ill and injured. One set of scribbles explained efforts against a lung ailment spreading through several villages in a Warland province. In places, the notes went beyond accounting, with detailed observations of what had been tried and failed, or had succeeded in caring for the ailing. In some cases, the authors had stated or suggested conclusions concerning future remedies.

Chane was reading the field notes of healers.

He shoved sheets aside, scattering them as he paged toward the stack's bottom. Entry dates below names and places only went back seven years. Yet this place was far older than that. So where had this sheaf come from, and were there more?

He had already been gone too long. Welstiel would grow agitated by the delay. He had no more time to search.

Chane hurried to the storerooms. Finding a stack of blankets, he tore one into strips and sprinted for the stairwell to the second floor.

Welstiel stood scowling with impatience before the first door on the right—the doors of the living. With a sharp jerk, he pulled the wood shard from the handle and opened it. Three monks cowered inside.

"Why are you doing this?" an elderly man asked in Stravinan. "What do you want with us?"

White-peppered stubble shadowed his jaw, though he did not look so old. Welstiel ignored him, turning his eyes on the other two in the cell. Both were male and younger than their vocal companion. Welstiel stepped in and snatched one by the neck of his robe.

The young man tried to pull Welstiel's fingers apart, but his attempt to dislodge the grip was futile.

"Where are you taking him?" demanded the elder, rising up.

Welstiel slammed his free palm into the man's face.

The elderly monk toppled, one leg swinging from under him as he fell against a narrow, disheveled bed. The other young one scrambled away into the room's far corner.

Chane took half a step toward Welstiel's back, then choked down the sudden anger he couldn't understand. He held his ground as Welstiel wheeled and flung the one he was choking into the passage.

The young monk tumbled across the floor, slamming against the stone wall between the first two iron-barred doors. A flurry of screeching and battering rose up beyond both those portals.

"Bind him!" Welstiel snapped, and slammed the door shut on the remaining two monks, returning the wood shard to its handle. "I want no excess difficulty when we take him away from those we feed."

Chane did not understand what this meant, but he fell on the groveling young monk, pinning him facedown and pulling the man's arms back to tie his wrists.

"No, please!" the man shouted. "Whatever you want, I will give you! Violence is not our way!"

Chane hardened himself against the young man's pleas and declaration— as anyone who refused to fight for his own life disgusted him.

"Gag him as well," Welstiel ordered. "I do not want him speaking to his lost companions awaiting him."

Chane wrapped a blanket strip three times around the young man's head and pulled it tight. An iron bar scraped free of a door handle. Chane whirled about in panic as he heard Welstiel shout.

"Get back! Both of you!"

Welstiel stood before the open door, his face twisted in a grimace as he hissed. Chane stepped along the middle of the passage, peering around Welstiel.

The door's inner surface was stained and splintered, as if gouging claws had left dark smeared trails. A pool of viscous black fluid had congealed on the cell's floor. One monk lay in the mess, or what was left of her.

Her throat was a shredded mass, and her robe and undergarments had been ripped into tatters, exposing pale skin slashed and torn down to sinew. Worse still, she tried to move. Her head lolled toward the door, and her colorless crystalline eyes opened wide at Welstiel, not in fright or pain but in hunger.

Her expression filled with bloodlust that echoed in Chane as he stared at her. Her mouth opened, her own black fluids dribbling out its corner.

Two others crouched beyond her, one upon the spattered bed and the other behind a tiny side table, clinging to one of its stout wooden legs. Both shuddered continuously, muscles spasming, as if they wanted to rise but could not.

Chane knew that state well. He had felt the same struggle against the commands of his own maker, Toret.

Their glittering eyes, set deep in pale and spatter-marked faces, were locked on Welstiel. And their black-stained lips quivered with soft animal mewling.

"Take a long look, Chane," Welstiel whispered. "Look upon yourself! This is what you are, deep inside—a beast hiding beneath a masquerade of intellect. Remember this . . . with your one foot always poised upon the Feral Path. It is your choice whether or not to succumb and follow them. Now bring me the food."

Those words cut through Chane's rapt fixation on the cell's inhabitants. He reached down with one hand and jerked up the bound monk.

The young man made one attempt to struggle, but his whole body locked up at what he saw in the cell.

Welstiel ripped the monk from Chane's grip and shoved the man inside. The monk toppled, hitting the floor, and immediately tried to wriggle back toward the door. Welstiel lifted a foot and shoved him back.

"Feed," he commanded.

The two monks still functional leaped upon their living comrade.

Both made for his throat. The larger male slashed the smaller one's face, driving him off, then wrapped straining fingers across the living monk's face and pulled his jaw upward. A high-pitched scream filled the stone cell, muffled by the victim's gag. The sound broke into chokes as the large male's teeth sank into the squirming monk's throat.

The smaller undead let out a pained yowl and hissed in frustration. Bobbing behind his larger companion, he tried to find an opening to get at the victim's throat. He finally scurried in to sink his teeth through the robe into the young monk's thigh. And beyond them, the female's nails scraped on the stone floor as she tried to pull herself to the feast—and failed.

The smell of blood grew.

The two males had barely settled in, their "food" thrashing beneath them, when Welstiel's shout rang through the cell.

"Enough . . . back away!"

Both males flinched as if struck. The smaller squirmed across the floor, clutching at the bed's dangling covers. Blood was smeared all around his mouth.

The larger male pulled his mouth from the monk's throat, swiveling his cowled head and turning maddened eyes upon Welstiel. His jaws widened threateningly, blood spilling out between fangs and elongated teeth.

Welstiel kicked him in the face. "Get back!"

The male's head snapped sideways, and he backed over the mangled female to crouch against the wall. Chane felt an empathetic spasm as the male fought his own body's demand to obey.

Welstiel reached down and seized the ankle of the "food." The young monk's head lolled with eyes rolling up, unaware, as Welstiel jerked him to the door.

Chane's gaze lowered to the young woman still clawing at the floor. Her colorless eyes filled with panic as she watched the monk, once her comrade, slide farther beyond her reach.

"What of her?" Chane rasped.

"She is too far gone," Welstiel answered. "Recovering her is a wasted effort."

Chane fought to remain passive. Something in his mind told him not to speak, but it strained against his instincts.

"You said six risen among ten was fortunate," he argued. "If you need them . . . enough to go through all of this . . . why forgo even one who requires extra effort?"

Welstiel returned him a suspicious side glance.

"Very well," he answered and dropped the monk's leg. "See to it yourself."

Chane looked down at the half-conscious young monk. The memory of a book of poetry and a sheaf of notes nagged at him. He finally pulled his dagger, crouched and flipped the monk facedown, and gripped the man by the back of his bloodstained robe.

As he dragged the monk toward the maimed female, she reached up with clutching fingers, trying to grab hold. The large male beyond her took a step toward Chane.

"Stay back!" Welstiel shouted.

The robed hulk retreated with narrowing eyes.

Chane slashed the dagger deep across the monk's throat and dropped him atop the female. He hurried out the cell door without glancing back.

Hunger roiled inside him, restless at the smell of blood and the warmth of it that had spilled over his hand. Another part of him almost cringed with loathing.

And finally he heard the door shut.

Welstiel slid the iron bars through the handle at the sounds of angry screeching growls and tearing cloth.

"Get more bindings for another of the living," he said. "And be quick this time. I have other tasks to attend."

Chane descended the stairs in slow steps, trying to empty his mind.

When he returned, he bound another living monk. The process repeated for the remaining undead who had not yet fed. And again, Welstiel allowed his new minions only a brief taste before snatching away their meal.

"There are not enough of the living to last," Chane said. "Not enough to truly feed all your minions."

"Yes," Welstiel answered. "Their hunger continues . . . as does your nightly vigil."

He walked away down the stairs.

Chane stood in the hallway, resentment mounting inside him. These newly risen undead were starving, and hunger unhinged their minds. But still Welstiel would not relent in this disquieting exercise. His newborns were becoming little more than beasts driven to feed. Was this the Feral Path that Welstiel had hinted at?

Was this what gnawed at Chane's insides beneath the ecstasy of a true hunt?

He slumped upon the stool beside the stairwell. The passage grew quieter, filled with only discontented rumblings within the cells of the undead.

Chane's gaze wandered to the passage's far end and locked upon the book of poetry he had tossed away. Then his eyes settled upon the cell doors of the living.

CHAPTER THREE

B rot'ân'duivé wove through the coastal trees, troubled by what he had learned this evening. He needed to speak with Sgäilsheilleache's grandfather, Gleannéohkân'thva—and there was only one way. Approaching a twisted maple, he withdrew a smooth oval of word-wood from his cloak and was once again grateful for it.

All the Anmaglâhk past their tutelage years carried a word-wood. With these oval slivers, grown from Most Aged Father's own oak, they spoke with the patriarch through any tree growing in open earth. Such were reserved for the Anmaglâhk or those clan elders needing to communicate with Crijheäiche.

Masters of elven ships also possessed their own word-wood, allowing their clan vessels communication in case of need or emergency, but these were grown from the wood of their own ships.

The smooth oval Brot'ân'duivé held was neither of these.

Few carried or even knew of these special word-woods, for they were secretly fashioned by Gleannéohkân'thva and connected only to his tree dwelling. A revered healer among the an'Cróan, he was thereby also a Shaper—one of those born with the talent to guide and alter the way of living things.

Brot'ân'duivé placed the word-wood against the tree's bark, calling out softly, "Gleannéohkân'thva, are you home?"

Moments passed before a clear voice rose in his thoughts. *Yes . . . but I did not expect to hear from you tonight.*

"It could not be avoided."

Hearing his old friend calmed Brot'ân'duivé as he thought of the eccentric old healer's wry nature, deeply lined face, and steel-gray hair sticking out in all directions.

"Is Cuirin'nên'a with you?" he asked.

Yes . . . but what is wrong?

Brot'ân'duivé closed his eyes and planted his free hand against the maple.

"An unexpected development . . . which means our first step must be taken earlier than planned. Retrieve the first message stone I engraved and the shale plate etched with my drawings. Wrap and seal both so that they remain private. Give this package to the Äruin'nas in the name of the Anmaglâhk. They will pass it to the Séyilf, and one of those 'Wind-Blown' people will deliver it to the mountain of the Chein'âs, as intended."

Why rush this little thing? Léshil returns home with his companions. We know where to find him when the time is better.

"No, Magiere takes them to an unknown destination. Fortunately, they travel south down our eastern seacoast, and I have encouraged Sgäilsheilleache to accompany them. I will instruct him to order the ship anchored at the correct location, so he might take Léshil . . . Léshiârelaohk . . . to the caves of the Chein'âs. Our first small step must be completed before he arrives there."

You send Léshil himself to the Chein'âs . . . with my grandson as guide? Sgäilsheilleache knows nothing of our covert efforts or . . .

Before Brot'ân'duivé answered, a second voice rose in his mind.

We understand . . . and I thank you for my son's welfare.

Cuirin'nên'a's melodic voice filled his head. He remembered the face of Léshil's mother—perfect caramel skin, corn-silk hair, and feathery eyebrows above large, brilliant eyes.

My son must be armed for his future purpose. We shall do as you ask.

Cuirin'nên'a paused too long, so Brot'ân'duivé drew their talk to a close. "I will join you both soon . . . I have much to tell, but I must stay until Léshil departs."

I look forward to your return, Brot'ân'duivé.

He pulled the word-wood from the tree with a breath of relief. So far, he had successfully set events in motion, but he had one more task to complete before Léshil's departure. He strode toward Ghoivne Ajhâjhe's landward side, for this task required two wide strips of leather, loose wool, a needle, and waxed string. He knew where to find such items in the shops by the shore.

. . .

Most Aged Father waited within his massive oak at Crijheäiche—Origin-Heart. As the centermost community of what humans called the Elven Territories, it was also home to the Anmaglâhk caste. He was so old that even the clan elders of the an'Cróan no longer remembered where he had come from or why he had led his people into seclusion in this far corner of the world. And his massive oak was almost as ancient as he was.

One of the eldest trees of the forest, its hollowed heart-root chamber below the earth had been carefully nurtured by long-forgotten Shapers since its earliest days. He rested within a bower shaped from the dark root's living wood, so the oak, with its roots threading out beneath the forest, might sustain him to fulfill his people's future need.

Most Aged Father no longer walked among his people. His withered body clung to life only by the great forest's efforts. But he was still founder and leader of the Anmaglâhk.

"May I bring you tea?"

Most Aged Father peered through milky eyes at his new attendant.

Juan'yâre—Ode of the Hare—stood patiently in the heart-root's entrance, awaiting a response. His expression, as always, was a mask of polite servitude, but Most Aged Father had difficulty adjusting to this recent change.

His last attendant, Fréthfâre—Watcher of the Woods—had been with him for more than two decades. He cherished the daughterly love in her eyes when she looked at him. She never saw him as withered and decayed; she saw only his wisdom and devotion to their people.

Fréthfâre was also his formal Covârleasa—Trusted Adviser—but she had suffered serious injury, a sword thrust through her side by the half-dead abomination, Magiere. Though healers worked to restore her, Most Aged Father was told that a full recovery would be slow in coming—if it came at all.

He missed her, and though he loved all the children of his caste, he could never see Juan'yâre taking Fréthfâre's place as attendant, let alone Covârleasa.

Juan'yâre's eyes held little warmth but shone with abject loyalty in an average and unmemorable face. At present, only his loyalty was required. He had completed his full training with high recommendations from his teacher and had served in the caste for nearly thirty years. His small-boned stature and boyish features made him appear younger.

"No," Most Aged Father finally answered. "We will not require tea. Once this audience concludes, you will prepare to leave for—"

Another voice carried from the outer chamber. "Father, I am here."

Most Aged Father forgot his new attendant. "Come in, Hkuan'duv, you are expected and most welcome."

Juan'yâre's face washed with awe, and he quickly stepped aside for the visitor.

Hkuan'duv entered and threw back his hood, giving no note to the attendant's presence. He inclined his head to Most Aged Father.

"Well met, Father," he said, his voice toneless as always.

Hkuan'duv—the Blackened Sea—was one of the four remaining Greimasg'äh still alive, a self-made master who had stepped beyond the worldly skills of the Anmaglâhk. He so rarely returned to Crijheäiche, preferring solitary tasks abroad, that Most Aged Father had not seen his face in three years. He was a stark sight of medium height, wiry build, and leathery tan skin. Born to a seafaring clan, he still followed their customs and cropped his hair short where other Anmaglâhk let theirs grow long. But it had lost any trace of blond long ago and glowed in shocking white spikes. His eyes were narrow-shaped and a shade of amber so deep they appeared topaz.

"You called for me?" he asked, typically direct.

Most Aged Father gestured Juan'yâre toward a teal cushion on the floor. "Sit quietly and listen. What you hear is never to be repeated . . . unless instructed by me."

Juan'yâre bowed and dropped gracefully, crossed-legged, upon the cushion.

Hkuan'duv stood silently poised, awaiting instructions.

Most Aged Father wasted no more time. "You have heard of what happened here regarding Cuirin'nên'a's son and the intruder named Magiere?"

Hkuan'duv nodded once with no change of expression.

"The council of clan elders arranged a ship to take them down the coast," Most Aged Father continued bitterly. "I wish you to gather a small band and follow them, unseen from a distance. Another ship has been arranged for you."

"You wish to learn their final destination?" Hkuan'duv asked.

"I wish for you to follow them . . . and acquire the object they seek."

Hkuan'duv did not even ask what the object was. He merely waited, and Most Aged Father relayed what little he had learned from Sgäilsheilleache.

"If this artifact is truly as old as the humans' Forgotten History, it cannot remain in their hands. It must come to us. Magiere may be the only one able to obtain it. I have come to accept that she is . . . unique, so you will wait until she has acquired it . . . before you take it."

Most Aged Father hesitated, for the last of Hkuan'duv's task might well seem counter to the will of the elders' council.

"And when you have it, you will kill Magiere. For the safety of our people, no such abomination must ever be allowed to enter our land again. See that it is done."

A flicker of puzzlement crossed Hkuan'duv's lean features, and then it was gone.

Most Aged Father understood. This mission was too deceptively simple for a purpose given to a Greimasg'äh. Others among their caste were certainly capable of taking the artifact and dispatching Magiere, but Most Aged Father wanted one whose abilities—and loyalties—were unquestionable.

"I do not understand," Hkuan'duv said flatly. "You wish me to follow this half-blood and human . . . to a castle somewhere in high mountains?"

"That is all I know, or all they claim to know of the destination. Follow, and do not let them see you until it is too late. I must see this artifact for myself."

Most Aged Father raised a withered hand to halt any further questions.

"I will arrange extra eyes upon their ship. Her name is Avranvärd. She will have a word-wood capable of communication with your ship and report course changes, stops, or anything unexpected to you. Use her to plan your own course."

Hkuan'duv frowned, his first true expression since entering. "I do not recognize her name."

Most Aged Father hesitated. "No, she is not Anmaglâhk, though she has requested entrance to our caste. It would not be wise for one of ours to take this role. Avranvärd is a seafarer, and no one will question her presence aboard the ship carrying the humans."

Using an an'Cróan outside their caste was unheard of, as was placing spies among their own people, but Most Aged Father saw no alternative.

"I would never ask this of you," he said, "unless our people's safety was at stake. Do what is necessary to bring this object to me. The Ancient Enemy is returning, and if this is one of its tools—"

"Of course," Hkuan'duv interjected. "I understand my purpose."

This was the response Most Aged Father expected, but still a relief to hear. Hkuan'duv was loyal beyond question, unlike the treacherous Brot'ân'duivé. Once he accepted a purpose, he fulfilled it, always.

"Be mindful in those you select to share your purpose," Most Aged Father advised. "Choose only seasoned anmaglâhk. A skilled tracker familiar with the human territories south of us along the eastern coast. Perhaps an exceptional archer, and a third as you see fit."

He stared blankly for a moment, trying to remember anyone of note among his caste currently in residence.

"I believe your last student, Dänvârfij, recently returned. Did she not eventually best you with the bow?"

Hkuan'duv's eyes flickered strangely. "She is here?"

"I believe so. She would be a good choice."

Hkuan'duv nodded curtly and turned to leave. "In silence and shadows," he said.

Most Aged Father dropped his head back into the moss lining of his bower. He rolled his gaze toward Juan'yâre, who sat absorbing all that had transpired.

"How quickly can you reach Ghoivne Ajhâjhe?" Most Aged Father asked.

"Quickly? It is eight days by barge."

"But you are a swift runner," Most Aged Father said pointedly. "If you traveled directly on foot, rarely stopping, how soon could you reach the coast?"

Juan'yâre dropped his gaze. "Traveling through the nights as well, I could reach the coast in five days . . . possibly less."

"Good, I thought as much. Leave tonight. Locate Avranvärd and secure her services."

Juan'yâre blinked. "You have not spoken to her already?"

Was he consciously attempting to be dim? He had been recommended on the grounds of being quick and clever—and he spoke five human tongues.

"No, not on this matter," Most Aged Father answered. "Fortunately, she is already the steward on Magiere's ship, which is why we need her now. I refused her entrance to our caste on the grounds that she is past a suitable age to begin training. Speak with her in private. Explain the purpose offered her, and how it might reflect . . . upon my reconsideration of her heart's desire."

"Promise her admittance?" Juan'yâre stood quickly. "Is that within my power?"

"It is within *my* power, and you speak for me!" Most Aged Father snapped. "Hkuan'duv cannot be seen, so he must have her eyes and ears. Promise Avranvärd what she wishes, and do not fail to acquire her service."

Juan'yâre straightened. "I will not fail."

Most Aged Father pointed toward the outer chamber. "In my private stores you will find a cedar box marked with the etching of a mast and sail. Inside is a word-wood from the ship Hkuan'duv will use. Give it to Avranvärd."

Elven ships were older than any who walked upon their decks. Some as old as the forest's great trees, for it took many years to create one. They outlasted any vessel sailing in human waters. Over the years, Most Aged Father had thoughtfully acquired many selected items, and most of his acquisitions eventually proved useful.

"Father," Juan'yâre said with a bow, "I will report from Ghoivne Ajhâjhe as soon as I complete my task."

Most Aged Father closed his weary eyes, hoping his new attendant could live up to his reputation.

By the dim light of a candle on the side table, Leesil lay awake in bed at the inn with Magiere shifting restlessly against him. She mumbled softly in fitful sleep, and he tried to remain still and not wake her.

After supper, he'd had to coax and goad her into returning to their room for rest. Unlike the elven forest's depths, the city didn't feed her with enough life to go without sleep. Still, she had slept little since their first night here, and she'd suffered too much for him in coming to this land.

Leesil relished once more sharing privacy with Magiere, but five nights had passed since Sgäile first pointed out their ship. Its crew still loaded cargo this day, and Magiere was losing patience. Her anxiousness to leave had grown to an obsession to head south. And Leesil's concern for her disturbed him even more than a name that the ancestors—elven ghosts—had tried to force on him.

Léshiârelaohk.

The night he'd freed his mother, and led her back to Crijheäiche, he'd sent Magiere, Wynn, and Chap off to rest. He stood vigil outside Nein'a's private tree dwelling, as she rested in her first night of freedom in long years.

And Brot'an came—that devious, manipulating butcher—leading an elderly elven woman in a maroon robe and matching cloak.

"Do you remember me?" she asked. "From the hearing before the council of clan elders?"

Her elven accent was a bit strong, but her Belaskian was surprisingly precise. Few elves but the Anmaglâhk spoke any human language.

"I am Tosân'leag," she added, "an elder of the Ash River clan."

Leesil nodded his recognition. She had stood among a clan of "scholars" upslope behind him at Magiere's hearing. Taking Brot'an's hand, Tosân'leag carefully kneeled down, studying Leesil's face.

"Tell her what you saw at Roise Chârmune," Brot'an said; ". . . the faces of the ancestors . . . what they said to you."

Leesil had no interest in telling Brot'an anything, but the old woman reached out and touched the top of Leesil's elongated ear. The movement was so startlingly quick for one so old that he didn't pull away until too late. She shook her head with a sigh, as if dissatisfied with his ear, then nodded to him.

"Tell me what you saw and heard. I can help you understand."

Leesil didn't want to understand any of their superstitious nonsense. But she kept staring at him, studying him. Finally, he spoke just to put an end to all this.

"There was a woman . . . with scars down her left upper arm . . . and war daggers on a belt. Human ones, not elven. And she carried a short spear with a shaft of steel. Her hair and eyes were wild, and . . . she smiled at me."

Tosân'leag's brow wrinkled with disapproval, but she smiled as well.

"That was likely Hoil'lhân, whose name means 'Bright Ray.' She is thought to have been a great warrior . . . and possibly the first of the Anmaglâhk, long before the title was even used. Did she speak to you?"

"No," Leesil answered, and his mind conjured images of other spirits he'd seen in a clearing around a naked ash tree. "A man spoke to me first, a tall warrior with a scar near his temple. Said his name was Snaw . . . Snaw-ha . . ."

"Snähacróe . . . 'Threading the Needle's Eye.' " And the old woman nodded as the light in her filmy eyes sharpened.

"There was another woman standing with him," Leesil added, "dressed like you. The two stayed close together . . . and spoke the name they put on me."

"That was Léshiâra," Tosân'leag whispered. "She was a great healer and teacher, and eventually . . . what you would call 'consort' to Snähacróe. I knew you had seen her when I heard your name. She is believed to have been one of the last of the High Council in long-forgotten times. Her name means 'Sorrow-Tear.' "

Even with Leesil's weak comprehension of Elvish, he couldn't miss how close the female ghost's name was to the one she'd put on him.

Tosân'leag leaned slightly toward Leesil. "Your name means 'Sorrow-Tear's Champion' . . . or 'Savior' . . . or close to that in human tongues. Do not forget this. Your name . . . you . . . have meaning to your people."

Leesil shrank away from her.

These weren't his people. He wanted to hear no more. He only wanted to stand vigil for his mother.

Tosân'leag raised a hand, and Brot'an assisted her up. Long after the pair had left Leesil in the dark, that name kept echoing in his head.

Léshiârelaohk—Sorrow-Tear's Champion . . . savior.

If only it meant something else, something other than a half-veiled fate born of spirits and nonsense.

In the dimly lit room of the elven inn, Leesil pushed aside all these thoughts in the only way he knew how. He gazed down at the woman sleeping against his chest.

Magiere lay naked with her white hand upon his arm.

Leesil pushed back her thick black hair to see her beautiful face. She murmured more loudly and frowned in half-slumber. Though he wanted her to sleep when she could, he couldn't help thinking of pleasant ways to wake her.

Magiere heaved a sudden breath, and her fingertips arched, digging into his arm.

"Youch . . . Magiere!"

She thrashed, rolling halfway over the bed's edge before he locked his arms around her torso.

"Magiere, it's all right. Wake up!"

Magiere twisted about, and her fingers dug into the straw mattress. She twitched, arching her back, and her irises flooded black. And when she saw Leesil, she quickly retreated down the bed.

The sight pained him.

She had taken so long to accept that her dhampir nature was no threat to him. When it became too strong for her, he was the only one she recognized, the only one she let near her. But somewhere deep inside, a part of her still feared harming him.

Leesil grabbed her forearms and pulled her back against himself. She was shivering, and her skin felt cold and clammy.

"You're all right," he whispered.

"I saw it again . . . ," she hissed out. "The ice . . . the castle . . . we have to go south."

Magiere's eyes wandered until her gaze locked on the shuttered window across their room. She got up, pulling one blanket around herself, and Leesil didn't try to stop her. She opened the shutters and leaned out, looking left.

Leesil knew she was staring at the harbored ship again, as she'd done a dozen times each day.

"When will we ever get out of here?" Magiere said.

"Soon," Leesil answered, desperate to give her ease. "Sgäile said just a few more days."

"I . . . we need to go," she whispered, and hung her head.

Leesil came up behind her at the window, not knowing what else to say or do. He pressed against her back and slipped his arms around her waist, his hands sliding inside the blanket across the curves of hipbones and stomach.

Magiere straightened, hands tight on the sill. Then she leaned back, and he buried his face in her hair. He finally lifted his face as she rolled her head to the right, and he found her staring into the dark—but not toward the bay. Her lips parted in one soundless word.

South.

Time slipped by like water rippling over stones. Chane woke upon the floor near the entryway's hearth. Welstiel would soon expect him upstairs to begin his nightly vigil.

Chane could not bring himself to go just yet. Pushing up on all fours, he listened to hungry cries rolling down the stairway from above. They always grew louder at dusk.

Longing for a hunt grew inside him at each muffled wail—and false hunger grew as well. He snatched a small twig from the hearth with a clinging bit of flame, climbed to his feet, and stepped through the passage to the back workroom. A lantern rested upon the nearest table beneath hanging branches of drying herbs. He lit it and then snuffed out the smoldering twig.

Several nights earlier, he'd noticed dark archways in the workroom's rear, but he'd felt no desire to pass through any of them to explore the monastery further.

Tonight, he could not bring himself to go upstairs just yet, so he turned toward the workroom's rear left corner and slipped through the dark opening in the wall.

Part of him recoiled from going farther and learning what he already feared . . . that this monastery might be more than some forgotten cloister of deluded priests.

Doorways lined the passage, but before he paused to open even one, his gaze caught on the darkness at the passage's end where his lantern's light did not reach. He saw a doorless opening, and a dark space beyond it.

Chane slowed with each step as his light pierced the portal and illuminated an old corner table. A rack anchored on the wall displayed rows of tiny bottles, vials, and clay containers, all of varied shape and height and sealed with cork stoppers or hinged pot-metal lids. A pile of small leather-bound books sat on the table, along with a scroll on an aged wooden spindle.

He froze at arm's length from the opening, staring at these bits of paraphernalia.

At first, the odor of the place, so faint and overmixed, made it difficult to pick out individual scents. Herbs, floral oils, burned wax, old leather, musty dry paper and parchment . . .

He did not want to enter, but he could not turn away, and finally he forced himself into the room.

Other small tables lined the side walls, each covered in a disorder of implements, metal vessels, and varied texts. Chane's attention fell upon a wide table at the room's left end with a worn, slat-backed chair behind it.

He was in a study, perhaps the chamber of whoever headed this place, and he spotted a grayed wooden door just beyond the bookshelf against the right wall. It stood slightly ajar, as if someone in a hurry had forgotten to close it completely. But Chane turned back to the makeshift desk, circling around beside its chair.

Loose parchments, aged bound sheaves, and even older scrolls lay scattered across the tabletop. He settled in the chair and opened a small text directly in front of him—a thick journal written in an old Stravinan dialect. As he turned page after page, reading entries that had little to do with practices of healing, he found whole chapters in other languages. Each such was written in a singular hand, as if the journal had passed from one person to another over many years.

This forgotten stone enclave housed an order of healers. More monks than actual priests, they followed the teachings of some long-forgotten patron saint, a healer who had wandered this continent long ago. This was the sanctuary of the Sluzhobnék Sútzits—the Servants of Compassion.

Chane stared about the room, and his gaze returned to the gray wood door left ajar. He had come this far and knew he could not turn back until he had seen all that lay here. He lifted the lantern, rounded the table, and pulled the gray door open wide. Dim light spilled into the space beyond.

Bookcases were arranged in rows with their ends against the back wall so that both sides of the shelves could be used, and their tops had been anchored to the stone ceiling.

The library was not large, little more than what he had seen in smaller noble houses during his living days. But he was not looking at handsomely bound volumes, most of which would never be read by the great lord or lady of the manor. No, everything here had an aura of age and sanctity, carefully preserved and arranged, from cylinders protecting scrolls to plain leather overlaps shielding the page edges of books. These were all meant to be used—had been used—treasured and guarded.

Chane's eyes passed over endnotes of sheaves, book spines, and faded labels on scroll cases, picking out what he could read in Belaskian or contemporary Stravinan.

The two easiest to catch were *Process of Distillation and Infusion* and *Spices of the Suman Lands—Properties, Verified & Fallacious*. With effort he deciphered *The Early Works of Master Evar Voskôviskän*, then . . . something *upon the Meadow,* and a thin book called *The Seven Leaves of* . . . its final word wasn't clear. The last thing he spotted was a multivolumed set in a case labeled *The Antithesis Tome, with Commentaries, Volumes 1 through 8.*

Chane backed up until his shoulder thumped the door frame. He spun away into the outer room, sliding down the wall to the floor, and the lantern slipped from his fingers.

It tottered over and rolled away. Melted wax spattered around its glass, spilled over the wick, and snuffed out the light.

How many moments had Chane fancied himself in a faraway place in Wynn's world, filled with intellect and knowledge? Someplace just like this small forgotten monastery—until madness and a monster broke in upon it one night.

Chane pulled up his knees, curling his arms up over his aching skull. Drowning in sorrow, he could not shed a single tear.

The dead could not weep.

Avranvärd, the Meadow's Song, ran through the dark streets of Ghoivne Ajhâjhe, her thick braid bouncing against her back as she hurried for her ship.

Twice since reaching harbor, the hkomas—the ship's master—had chastised her for dawdling while on errands. She had no wish to hear his tiresome rant again. Given any other option, she would tell him to find a new steward and keep his tedious lectures to himself.

Tonight, she had made good time in her tasks, procuring his precious quills, ink, and parchment—and at a reasonable trade of one short rope and six candles. That should keep him quiet this time. With a moment to herself, she stopped and anxiously scanned the streets.

On errands this day, she had seen three clad in forest-gray escorting two humans and a half-blood. Their presence in Ghoivne Ajhâjhe had spread talk through the city faster than she could scurry about, but Avranvärd had no interest in humans. She hoped only for another glimpse of the Anmaglâhk.

The youngest of the three had been only a handful of years older than her, but he looked dull, clumsy, and overall unimpressive. The second was an extreme of another kind—a Greimasg'äh!

Brot'ân'duivé was a towering man who filled Avranvärd with so much awe she almost stared too long and missed the third entirely. Then she recognized the last of that gray-clad trio.

Sgäilsheilleache . . . Sgäilsheilleache á Oshâgäirea gan'Coilehkrotall—Willow Shade, born of Sudden-Breeze's Laugh, from the clan of the Lichen Woods.

When Avranvärd closed her eyes, she still saw his narrow, smooth face, and his gray-green cloak hanging perfectly across his shoulders. She had met and even briefly spoken with him once. Her own clan's ship had taken him to the shores of Bela, one of the humans' reeking cities. Unlike the ship's crew, Sgäilsheilleache had disembarked to explore strange lands and to study other races. Watching the skiff carry him to shore in the dark, Avranvärd knew she would do whatever was necessary to become Anmaglâhk.

Tired of serving aboard ships, either her own clan's or training upon those of another, she wanted to walk foreign lands and see them with her own eyes. Only the Anmaglâhk were so privileged.

She knew she was too old to request admittance. Most started training shortly after their name-taking before the ancestors. Although the calling came late for her, it was no less potent and overwhelming—as was despair at Most Aged Father's denial. But three of the caste had now appeared from nowhere, staying at an inn in Ghoivne Ajhâjhe. Two had even been spotted upon the docks the same evening her ship made harbor.

It was a sign—her fate had to change. If only she could muster the courage to approach the Greimasg'äh, he would see the passion in her eyes and understand. She could not bear any more service aboard ship, and the boredom of inland existence was worse. But if the great Brot'ân'duivé spoke for her before Most Aged Father, the patriarch of the caste could not refuse her again.

The streets were nearly empty. Avranvärd saw no green-gray cloaks.

She trudged the avenues back toward the bayside road, passing a tannery and a smokehouse. The savory scent of fish reminded her that she had not eaten supper yet. She passed a darkened cobbler's shop with a sense of longing. Her own boots were too large. Like her shirt and breeches and tunic, and even her hemmed cloak, they were hand-me-downs from an elder brother. But she had nothing worthy of trade for new ones.

When she was finally accepted as Anmaglâhk, this would change. They wore flat, soft boots for speed and silence, sewn just for them. And they traded for nothing. All their needs were fulfilled just for the asking.

She saw the lanterns hanging over her ship's deck out in the harbor beyond the beach. She wandered down the road and onto the docks, down to her small skiff tied off at the pier's end. She rifled one last time through her packages, checking for everything the hkomas had requested, and then crouched to untie her skiff.

"Please wait," someone called.

Avranvärd jumped in fright and whirled about.

A cloaked figure stood on the shore road to the docks, as if appearing from nowhere. The figure stepped toward the dock and passed beneath a hung lantern, and she saw a man in a gray-green cloak.

"You are Avranvärd?" he asked, and strode down the dock, pointing out into the bay. "The steward from that cargo vessel?"

Avranvärd was struck mute. She had never seen him before, but he was Anmaglâhk. He knew her by name. How? Why? And her thoughts raced to her dearest hope. Had Most Aged Father reconsidered her request?

"Yes . . . I am," she finally stammered.

He was quite small-boned, his young and plain face glistening with sweat. Loose, white-blond hair stuck to his temples and cheeks. Leaves and wild grass clung to his cloak. He glanced around, as if making sure they were alone, and then took a long, tired breath.

"I come with a request from Most Aged Father." He stepped close enough that she could smell his earthy scent. "It is not a difficult task but requires discretion. Are you willing to hear me?"

She nodded, and the motion sent a shudder running up her spine and neck.

"You are aware that two humans and a half-blood will board your ship for the next voyage?"

"What . . . no," she stuttered. "That is not—"

"Yes, as soon as your ship is loaded for departure."

How could a human be allowed on an an'Cróan ship? Would any anmaglâhk join them, or were her crewmates expected to control these savages?

"Some of our caste will follow from a safe distance on another vessel," the weary messenger continued. "A Greimasg'äh and several others chosen by him. He must be kept informed of your stops, changes in course, or anything unusual regarding the humans."

He took a small box from his cloak and held it out.

"This contains a word-wood from the ship that will follow. With it, you will report to the Greimasg'äh. Do you understand?"

Avranvärd hesitated for an instant. Word-wood from ships was only for hkomas—or hkœda, the Shapers who served and cared for a ship's existence. How had such an item come to the hands of an anmaglâhk?

It did not matter. She had been called to do a service for the Anmaglâhk.

"Yes," she breathed. "Does this mean I am accepted as an initiate?"

The young-faced anmaglâhk shook his head.

"I am instructed to tell you that if you accept this task . . . this purpose . . . then Most Aged Father may reconsider you."

Avranvärd snatched the box from him. "When do I begin making reports?"

With pursed lips, he stepped back and turned down the dock.

"At dusk the first day at sea. The Greimasg'äh will expect contact each dawn and dusk, when and if you are able to slip away to privacy. No one must know what you do, not even your hkomas. Simply place the word-wood against your ship and speak. The Greimasg'äh will hear and answer into your thoughts."

The anmaglâhk stopped briefly as he reached the shore road, his soft voice carrying clearly to her.

"Do not fail," he called, and then he was gone.

Avranvärd stood shaking, sweat spreading beneath her tight grip upon the box. By now, her hkomas would surely reprimand her for tardiness, but she did not care. She had a mission—a purpose, as it was called among the caste.

Once completed, and upon her return, she would be Anmaglâhk.

CHAPTER FOUR

Nine days had passed since their ship harbored, and to the best of Wynn's knowledge, no human had ever boarded an an'Cróan vessel. Today they would finally set sail, and it left her emotions tangled as she climbed from the small skiff and up the rope ladder.

Magiere had grown more desperate by the day, and so Wynn did feel glad for her companion's relief at embarking. But for herself, time in the elven city had been far too short and had left her disheartened, as she might never see this place again. Domin Tilswith would be disappointed with her scant journal entries concerning Ghoivne Ajhâjhe.

Wynn reached the ladder's top, stepped through the rail-wall's open gate, and planted her feet firmly on the smooth deck.

Leesil grunted behind her, and she turned.

He climbed with one hand, the other arm wrapped behind to support Chap on his back. Wynn grabbed Leesil's arm and helped him gain the deck. Before he made it all the way, Chap scrambled over his head. The dog nearly knocked Wynn over and flattened Leesil on the deck's edge.

"You're welcome," Leesil grumbled, clambering up.

Magiere, Brot'an, Sgäile, and Osha followed. Only then did Wynn take her first good look about the ship, instantly wishing she had quill and paper in hand.

The strange sidewall—in place of a rail—with its shallow swoop-and-peak edge had caught her eye as she climbed the ladder. But up on the deck, its most striking aspect was a complete absence of planks.

The deck's glistening wood was as smooth as the rainwater barrels she had seen in an'Cróan homes—fashioned from inert wood by elven Makers born with an innate gift for thaumaturgy. Longer but narrower than any three-masted vessel she had seen, the entire hull appeared to have been melded into one solid piece, without a single crack or seam in its smooth, tawny surface.

The masts, rigging, and other fixtures were separate pieces, judging by the way weather had aged them. Wynn wondered even more how the deck remained comparatively smooth and richly colored. Halfway between center mast and forecastle was a meshed grate over a large raised opening.

"What is that?" she asked.

"The deck hatch to the cargo bay," Osha answered in Elvish.

Wynn tilted her head back to see the bulges of furled sails hanging from pale yellow masts. The fabric was almost iridescent white, as if made from *shéot'a* cloth, the elves' equivalent to satin. But this did not seem likely, for where would they find enough cocoons to weave so much material?

"Ah, dead deities!" Leesil moaned.

The ship was still anchored in the bay's calm water, but Leesil already wore a sickly glower.

"Finally," Magiere sighed under her breath.

Wynn knew that nine days was not an unusual length of time for cargo ships to harbor at port—and she and the others lived at the whim and charity of these elves. She could not help note how foreign, though lovely, Magiere appeared on an an'Cróan ship.

Her black hair sparked wildly with red from the bright sun glinting off open water. She seemed even paler than usual, surrounded by the vessel's rich color and the wide blue sky. In black breeches and a white shirt recently tailored within the city, she had donned her studded leather hauberk and strapped on her falchion. And recently, Magiere had taken to constantly wearing gloves.

The crew stared at Magiere as well, but their expressions did not echo Wynn's appreciation. Neither Leesil nor Magiere seemed to notice these angry looks, and Wynn was reminded of one clear fact.

Magiere had to leave elven lands and never return.

Chap had learned why and passed it through Wynn. Magiere, born in a blood rite, had been made for a purpose.

Unlike an undead or just a normal human, she could enter elven land. Its natural safeguards could not stop her. Worse still, she fed upon the forest by her very presence, as her undead father had fed upon the living.

Magiere had been made to breach any place that the undead had not been able to enter during the long-forgotten war. This knowledge left Wynn fearful of what might come in the future. Magiere's very presence and creation suggested that war—like in the time of the Forgotten—would come again.

A tall, thick-armed elf in a brown head scarf dropped from the aftcastle and plodded toward them. Most likely, this was the hkomas—the "able authority" or ship's captain. Brot'an met him halfway, and Wynn tried to edge close to catch their words.

A stab of nausea took her by surprise.

Why do Sgäile and Osha remain with us?

Chap's words flooded Wynn's head, spoken simultaneously in every language she knew. She had grown accustomed to snatching meaning from the tangle of tongues. Glancing behind, she found Chap eying the two elves suspiciously.

More than a dog, Chap was an eternal Fay, born into the body of a majay-hì—a colloquial term, loosely meaning "hound of the Fay." The breed had descended from the long-forgotten times when wolves were inhabited by Fay during the war of the Forgotten History. This made Chap doubly unique, and only Wynn could hear him in her head.

This was not supposed to happen.

Two seasons past, she had meddled with a mantic ritual to help Magiere track an undead. The attempt had gone horribly wrong, and over the passing moons Chap had tried more than once to cleanse her. But the taint remained and kept manifesting in new ways.

"I do not know," she whispered to Chap. "Sgäile said the hkomas would be uncomfortable having humans aboard without an escort."

No—the an'Cróan council of clan elders requested this ship. Sgäile's continued presence is something else . . . and too sudden. Something more has happened since the ship's arrival—and your babbling our plans to Brot'an.

"Oh, drop that already!" Wynn whispered, but her feelings were mixed.

She too wondered why Sgäile chose to continue his guardianship into this voyage, but part of her was glad. A respected member of his caste, when Sgäile spoke, people listened. Osha's presence was another matter, and left Wynn unsettled in ways she did not understand. Their travels and ordeals in an'Cróan lands had brought out the best and worst in him. In the end, she counted him as a friend. But when they said farewell on the river's shore at Crijheäiche, she had never expected to see him again.

Osha caught Wynn watching him and raised thick eyebrows, making his horselike face appear even longer. Wynn turned away, but Chap continued studying the young elf.

He is profoundly relieved . . . concerning something to do with Sgäile.

"You see that in his mind?" she whispered, surprised.

Within his line of sight, Chap could pick out surfacing memories from a sentient being's conscious thoughts, but she was not aware he could sense emotions.

No, it is plain on his face . . . and the way he follows Sgäile about, waiting to fulfill any command in an instant. Osha could not long hide a secret, unless he pulled that cowl over his entire head.

"Stop being so pompous!" Wynn said too loudly.

Slightly raised voices pulled her attention back to Brot'an and the ship's hkomas, and she tried to decipher their rapid Elvish. From what she could follow, the captain's inhospitable manner with Brot'an came from the vague instructions concerning the destination of his "passengers." Wynn had expected this. Moments later, a troubled Brot'an walked past Wynn straight toward Magiere, and Wynn hurried to follow.

"Did he refuse?" Magiere asked.

Brot'an shook his head. "The hkomas will take you south, but the elders did not choose the best ship for you."

Magiere's pale brow wrinkled as she crossed her arms.

"Why?" Leesil asked, already gripping the deck's rail-wall, as if growing more unsteady on his feet by the moment.

"This vessel serves coastal an'Cróan communities," Brot'an answered. "From here, it sails east around the point before it turns south down the coast."

"How long?" Magiere asked.

"Five or six days at a run . . . but this is a main cargo vessel. It will stop at every harbor, especially those of other rivers reaching the coast, where the barge clans bring goods from the inlands."

Leesil's eyes widened as Magiere's mouth fell open. Wynn braced herself for the coming storm.

"What?" Magiere growled. "We were promised a ship to take us any-where we asked to go!"

Osha fidgeted slightly in alarm, glancing about the ship. Several of the crew glared in Magiere's direction. They might not understand her words, but her rising tone was clear.

"Magiere . . . ," Sgäile warned softly.

"You led us onto that barge, and all the way to the coast," she snarled, "promising to get us out of here. But we've been trapped in this city, waiting. Now our ship's stopping at every town along the way? You—you're—"

Magiere turned away toward the rail-wall beside Leesil.

"We need to go south—now." Her voice weakened to a whisper as she closed her eyes. "Please . . . now."

Leesil slid his hand across her back, glancing at Sgäile.

Wynn shared Leesil's concern over whatever had whispered to Magiere in her dream and showed her the six-towered castle coated in ice. But in their travels, they had uncovered no other clues regarding the whereabouts of the artifact. Wynn felt they should do everything possible to help Magiere, and not continue questioning the lead they had.

"This is the only ship," Sgäile said, his voice tight, "unless you wish to linger here even longer. The elders arranged passage once—they would not do so again. It is either this vessel, or we travel back across the Broken Range on foot . . . by whatever way you found to reach us. And then head south. What is your choice?"

Magiere slowly turned her head toward him.

Wynn lost sight of her companion's pale face, but she saw Sgäile's large eyes narrow. He crossed his own arms. Magiere turned away again, staring out over the bay, and Wynn knew Magiere's answer.

"Their belongings have arrived," a crew member called out to Brot'an.

Another skiff pulled in beside the ship, and two elves in the small ves-sel hoisted up baggage. Wynn hurried to help Osha as he began hauling in their belongings, which had increased during their visit in Ghoivne Ajhâjhe.

Magiere's comment about being trapped was not precisely correct. They had used their time in the city to prepare for the coming journey. Magiere was not certain about their path, but she knew their destination lay in a mountain canyon so high up it was locked in snow and ice all year.

"Ah, here are your new coats," Osha said in Elvish, and tapped Leesil's shoulder as he pointed down to the skiff.

"In Belaskian," Wynn chided without thinking. "You need the practice."

Osha gave her a sheepish smile and repeated in broken speech that Leesil and Magiere could understand.

Wynn had not spoken much to Osha since his arrival. It seemed they easily fell back into a pattern in which she insisted he speak an appropriate language that her companions could understand.

One elf in the skiff below climbed halfway up to hand off their new coats. Magiere had specifically requested these garments.

Made of sheepskin with the woolly side inward, they were also lined with a thick layer of rough-spun cotton fabric. The outer hide had been deeply oiled against bad weather, something Brot'an added to their specifications. The new garments would maximize body heat retention in a cold climate.

Meanwhile, Wynn and Leesil had arranged for smoked meats and dried fruits, water flasks, tea, and other goods. They had little to trade, but Sgäile handled the negotiations, ushering them out of any shop to await him. Wynn had an uneasy feeling that most of the items had been donated, since an anmaglâhk had requested them.

The hkomas's harsh voice called out for sails to be set. Wynn watched the crew scramble into the rigging to ready the ship. And it struck her that they were truly leaving. She sighed and returned to her companions. Magiere appeared calmer, but Leesil swallowed hard, looking more uncomfortable.

Wynn heard Brot'an talking in low tones to Sgäile as the master anmaglâhk prepared to descend to the waiting skiff. Then Brot'an handed something to Sgäile. Both his words and gift, if that was what it was, passed too quickly for Wynn to catch.

Sgäile glared at Brot'an with his fists closed tightly on the hidden object.

Osha tensed up, his expression aghast. Sgäile seemed about to argue or question, but Brot'an raised a finger and his lips moved in one brief phrase.

"*Chein'âs?*" Osha whispered too loudly.

"*Tosajij!*" Sgäile hissed at him.

The younger elf cringed in embarrassment. His wide amber eyes flicked toward Leesil, who wavered as he tried to lift baggage from the deck.

Wynn wondered at the word Osha spoke, and why Sgäile ordered him into silence.

Chein'âs—the . . . "burning" ones?

Brot'an started to descend, and Wynn's thoughts rushed to all he had done for her and her companions. She knew how much she irritated him at times, but he had been their protector and adviser—at a cost Wynn could not even estimate.

"Brot'an . . . ," she called, and then lost her nerve.

Brot'an halted, then stepped back up on deck. He came closer, until he towered over Wynn, and grasped her gently by the shoulders.

"Farewell, little one," he said, and lowered his head to whisper, "and do not stop asking questions."

Wynn nodded with a sting in her eyes.

Brot'an turned away, pausing once before Magiere. A shadow of sadness crossed her pale face. She, too, had depended on his wisdom in this strange land. But Leesil . . .

He remained crouched over the baggage and did not rise. Too much had happened between Leesil and the master anmaglâhk for him to ever trust the man. Brot'an climbed over the ship's side and vanished from sight.

Sgäile turned hard eyes on Osha and pulled him away toward the ship's aft.

Wynn desperately wanted to follow and listen, though she knew such action would not be considered appropriate. She was about to go help Magiere and Leesil with the baggage when she noticed that Chap was gone. She spun about, searching the deck.

He stood poised upon a crate near the rail-wall, gazing toward the shore. Wynn came up behind him and stroked his back. She knew what he had been doing all the early mornings and evenings when he had disappeared into the forest.

Out beyond the city, Chap had spent his last days with Lily, the white majay-hì.

He had said his good-bye to her the day they had arrived in Ghoivne Ajhâjhe, but the unexpected delay had weakened his resolve. Lily's entire pack had gone home, but she stayed behind to be with Chap. The white majay-hì feared the populated city, and so he slipped out into the forest whenever possible.

"I am sorry you have to leave her," Wynn said.

She would not come.

"I know."

All around Wynn, the crew bustled with activity as they prepared to leave harbor. All except for one young woman. Wynn caught the girl watching her and Chap. Dressed in too large boots, with a heavy braid hanging forward over one shoulder, she turned quickly away and up the forecastle out of sight.

As the sails caught the wind, the ship turned slowly toward the open sea, and Wynn thought she felt a strange, rhythmic thrum through the deck beneath her feet. Chap whined softly, his gaze still on the coastline, and Wynn felt overwhelmed by loss.

There were so many reasons that they had to leave, but they left so much behind.

Hkuan'duv stood on his vessel's deck and watched the ship carrying the humans as it sailed out of harbor. He waited until darkness came.

Of all the orders Most Aged Father had ever given, this one troubled Hkuan'duv the most. Sgäilsheilleache and Osha, two of Hkuan'duv's own caste, were on the vessel he would track, and they knew nothing of his presence. Such a thing had never happened in his memory.

As he stared toward the open sea beyond the harbor, a slender hand gripped the rail-wall beside him, and a soft voice spoke.

"Your thoughts run in circles tonight."

Dänvârfij—Fated Music—looked him directly in the eyes. Her nose was too long and her cheekbones were a touch wide, but her skin was clean and creamy, like tea stirred with goat's milk. She had been his last student, studying under him for five years, and there was always a quiet honesty in her eyes.

When her skill with a bow clearly exceeded his, it was the final sign that their time together as teacher and student was over. He had spoken for her before Most Aged Father, and she had been given a word-wood in recognition. When she left on her first solo purpose, Hkuan'duv chose to take no more students.

He did not respond to her comment. She knew him too well.

"Have you seen our quarters?" he asked.

"Yes, two small rooms below," she answered. "A'harhk'nis and Kurhkâge can share one, you and I the other."

He nodded, turning from the rail-wall to find the other two members of his team sitting on the cargo hold's grate.

A'harhk'nis—Most Changeable—was unusually silent, even for a member of their caste. He was a skilled tracker, with wild eyes and unruly hair. Though he carried anmaglâhk stilettos, his preferred weapons were more brutal. In his belt at the small of his back he carried a pair of bone knives as large as sickles, their curved blades as wide as a human's sword. He preferred his clothing loose and wore oversized breeches. Even with his cloak corners tied about his waist, it billowed around him.

Hkuan'duv turned his eyes upon the last of his chosen.

Kurhkâge—Sandpiper—was unremarkable but for his missing left eye and his stature. Lack of depth perception did not appear to affect him, and he came from the same clan as Brot'ân'duivé, sharing his oversized build. He had spent years in the human region south of the eastern coast, known as the Ylladon States. Kurhkâge was calculating and tactical, but his experiences among those loosely allied city-states of marauders had left him bitter.

Ylladon ships sometimes grew daring and raided the lower reaches of the an'Cróan coastline. Shortly after Kurhkâge completed his tutelage, he headed south with two others on his first purpose. As the trio stopped over in the most southern an'Cróan coastal community, the village was raided. Kurhkâge lost his eye in that fight, but not one Ylladon marauder escaped.

Hkuan'duv was certain of his choices. Only Dänvârfij troubled him a little. She was the most well-rounded in skills and training, but during their years together, he had grown . . . content in her company.

After they parted, a year passed before Hkuan'duv felt at peace. He had no wish to go through such an adjustment again.

Kurhkâge stalked over. He refused to wear an eye patch, and his left eye socket had healed into rough lumps of flesh.

"The hkomas asks when we will leave," he said. "He seems anxious over the growing distance between our ship and theirs."

Hkuan'duv nodded. He sympathized with the hkomas, who now followed the "requests" of the Anmaglâhk.

"Soon," he answered. "I wish to give our quarry some distance."

Earlier, the crew had prepared the ship. With little to do but wait, several of them cast curious glances at Hkuan'duv and his companions. Another twinge of discomfort passed through him.

All an'Cróan revered the Anmaglâhk, who served to protect them. The ships of seafaring clans sometimes carried one or more into human territories, but the Anmaglâhk were only along for the ride. A team of four, led by a Greimasg'äh who made decisions and gave orders to the crew's hkomas, was unprecedented.

Hkuan'duv looked out into the dark harbor. It was time, and he glanced at Dänvârfij, her loose hair wafting softly around her long angular face.

"I will give the word," she said, knowing his mind as quickly as he did.

"Tell the hkomas to fall off if he sees a hint of sails ahead. We must not be seen."

Dänvârfij headed for the helm at the ship's rear.

Soon, the iridescent sails fell open and filled with the breeze, and the deck began to softly thrum beneath Hkuan'duv's feet. The ship slipped quietly out of harbor and to the east, never far from the coastline.

Dänvârfij finally returned. "Your mind still runs in circles."

Hkuan'duv frowned. So far, he had told his companions little about their purpose. He breathed a troubled sigh as he gestured toward the hatch.

"Get the others and come," he said. "I will tell you all I can."

By the voyage's second dusk, Leesil lay in a bunk below deck, unable to get up.

So far, he'd kept down only small sips of water. Having been through this once before, he knew enough not to eat. Dizziness and nausea rolled in his head and stomach with the ship's relentless teetering. The light of the one dangling lantern shifted upon the cabin walls. He closed his eyes and quickly opened them again. Darkness only made him feel worse.

The cabin was small but well designed. Its walls were smooth, with no sign of individual planks, and pairs of ledges for bunks were shaped on both of the room's sides. High-set porthole openings in the outer wall were sealed with brass-framed glass hatches.

The cabin's short oval door cracked inward, and Magiere ducked her head in. "How are you feeling?"

"I'd rather ride fifty leagues on a half-mad horse," he groaned.

She came in, carrying a bowl of water and a rag for his head.

Magiere's caretaking was the one and only part of this sea voyage preferable to the last. Leesil had to admit that he enjoyed her attention. She sat beside him and dipped the rag without removing her gloves. Her hand was shaking just slightly.

He reached out to touch it. "Are you all right?"

During their time within the elven forest, Magiere had suffered from trembling and anxiety whenever she entered one of the tree dwellings. They hadn't known why, until she'd lost all control in Nein'a's prison clearing. And in that fight with their anmaglâhk escort, her bare hands had touched and marked a birch tree.

Since boarding, Magiere had shown signs of the same manifestations she'd suffered in the elven forest, although they were far from its shore.

"It's not as bad," she answered. "Probably just this nagging instinct to keep going . . . to reach wherever we're headed."

Magiere had finally removed her hauberk and wore only her loose white shirt and breeches, with her hair bound back to keep it from her eyes in the wind.

"Something odd happened a little while ago," she said. "Sgäile politely related that the captain thinks it *best* that we stay on this end of the ship while below deck."

"A suggestion or a threat?" Leesil asked.

"One's as good as the other with these people."

He laid his head back as Magiere applied the damp rag to his forehead and looked up at the smooth seamless ceiling. Such a warning only made him want to go nosing about, but his stomach rolled on another list of the ship.

"Where is everyone else?" he asked, seeking any distraction.

"On deck. Sgäile is just staring out to sea. Osha borrowed some kind of game from a sailor and is teaching Wynn to play. Chap's watching them without much interest, but I'm betting he understands the strategy better than Osha."

Leesil tried to smile. "This is the first time we've been alone since boarding."

Magiere didn't seem to hear him. She gazed at the cabin wall—or perhaps through it to somewhere far away.

"We'll round the corner of the continent soon," he said.

She blinked. "What? Oh, I was thinking about . . . home. The new tables . . . the hearth, even that old burned sword hanging above it. We barely had time to settle in after the rebuild."

Leesil rolled toward her on his side. "Yes, home. A nice thought."

"If we ever reach it, if we are able to stay, if we don't learn any more of ourselves that we don't want to know."

The warm image of home faded from Leesil's mind. Why did she keep bringing up the reason his mother had created and trained him—to use him as a tool against some unknown adversary the elves believed would return?

"We make our own fate," he snapped. "No one changes that."

Magiere dropped her eyes suddenly, and Leesil regretted his angry tone. He should be grateful she shared her worries with him so openly. But he stood by his words.

They did make their own fate. No matter what name a pack of ghosts placed upon him, the only person he would "champion" was Magiere.

She still gripped his fingers in one gloved hand, and he reached out with his other hand to trace the line of her jaw. Her face was so perfect to him. He sat up to kiss her, and his stomach lurched.

"Stop that," she said, and flattened her other hand on his chest. "You're sick."

"Not that sick," he answered.

"Oh, really? You're as green as Wynn's lentil stew, and your breath . . . is terrible."

He stared at her. "How flattering."

"Rest!" She shoved him back down on the bunk. "I'll stay with you."

Leesil's stomach clenched as his back hit the bed, but he still frowned, feeling petulant.

"We're sharing quarters with Wynn and Chap . . . and this could be our last moment alone for a while."

Magiere rolled her dark brown eyes with a huff, as if to respond, but then she spun about and tensed, staring toward the door.

"What—?" Leesil began.

Magiere lunged up, snatching her falchion as she flung open the cabin door.

Somewhere above, Leesil heard Wynn shouting.

. . .

In the scant lantern light, Wynn sat cross-legged upon the deck facing Osha and tried to focus on Dreug'an, an elven draught game borrowed from the hkomas's steward. Osha was determined to teach her to play, but Wynn's thoughts kept wandering.

The ship's strange thrum vibrated under her buttocks, making it impossible to pay attention. And Chap's disgruntled huffs every time she made a move did not help either.

"Do you want to play for me?" she asked.

Chap licked his nose at her, but no reply entered her thoughts.

Sgäile still leaned on the port side, staring out into the darkness. Off the starboard, the tree-lined coast slipped by at a rapid pace.

Wynn sighed and stood up. "I need to stretch my legs."

Even on her feet, she was little taller than Osha on his knees. He started to rise, and she waved him back down.

"No, stay. I will not go far."

Osha frowned, caught between having to watch over her and yet not wanting to impose.

"I will return shortly," she assured him and strolled off toward the aft.

The hkomas had stayed in the aftcastle for much of the voyage so far, and the crew kept busy all over the ship. Wynn had avoided snooping about, knowing her presence was unwelcome. As night came, the hkomas retired and much of the crew went off duty, leaving the deck fairly deserted. Wynn wanted to peek about.

The absence of planks in the deck still astonished her. A crewman sat on a barrel, just as solidly one piece, though it showed far more sign of wear than the deck. He was weaving smooth pieces of cord into a stout rope. As Wynn passed, he spun atop the barrel to face away, and she knew better than to try chatting with him.

She crept idly toward the stern, and the rhythmic thrum beneath her feet seemed to grow. Reaching the aftcastle ladder, she saw its steps worn by years of use—unlike the deck—and she climbed halfway to peer over the top.

Three large lanterns lit up the aftcastle. A male elf loosely gripped the large wheel of the helm. He was stout and solid—or at least wide compared to others of his kind. Many of the crew cropped their hair short, but his sandy locks hung to his shoulders with the bangs cut just above the eyes.

The pilot's large eyes narrowed upon Wynn, and then he returned to silently gazing ahead. Since he had not openly rebuked her, Wynn crept up onto the aftcastle, purposefully ignoring him in turn.

The rhythmic thrum lessened, and she wondered where it came from and if the height of the aftcastle dulled it. She kept to the rail-wall, as far from the pilot as possible. Before she reached the ship's stern, she began to make out its wake under the dangling aft lanterns. Even a fast vessel under a heavy wind would not swirl the water so.

Foam-laced ripples trailed away behind the ship into the dark, and Wynn glanced suspiciously upward. The sails were still billowing but not full, so the wind was not that strong. And yet the vessel's speed was enough to leave a visible wake. Wynn leaned over the aftcastle's rear, peering downward, and sucked in a loud breath. She grabbed the rail-wall and froze.

Water boiled out from beneath the elven ship. Under the sea's roiling surface, she saw twin rudders set wide apart, unlike on human ships—and something moved in the dark water between the twin blades.

A massive ribbon rippled below the ship's wake.

Wynn raised her eyes, tracing it out more than two skiffs' lengths behind the stern. It wormed like the tail of something massive swimming below the hull.

"Osha!" Wynn screamed, and backed up. "Get Sgäile!"

She turned as Chap leaped onto the aftcastle's deck with a snarl. He cast a threatening glance at the pilot before he spotted her. Osha appeared immediately behind Chap.

"What?" he asked in alarm. "Are you injured?"

"A sea beast!" Wynn shouted. "It is pacing us under the ship!"

She had barely drawn a second breath when Sgäile hurried up the aftcastle's steps. Just as Osha reached Wynn, the hkomas, his steward, and two crew members emerged from the stairwells below the aftcastle.

And then Magiere came running along the deck from the forward stairs with Leesil close behind.

Sgäile headed straight for Osha, grunting to the hkomas in quick Elvish that Wynn did not catch. Osha looked over the rail-wall and then turned around. He shook his head, glancing at Wynn in worried confusion.

"Can you not see it?" she insisted. "Look down . . . there . . . in the water!"

The pilot lashed the wheel, then stepped back and leaned over the aft. He straightened, and a glower spread over his face as he looked to his hkomas.

"Weakblood . . . makes for addled wits," he said in Elvish.

Weakblood—*lhâgshuil*—was their scornful word for humans. Wynn curled one hand into a small fist.

"Maybe you should cut your hair higher . . . and further out of your eyes!" She shoved the pilot aside and pushed in at the stern next to Osha and pointed downward. "Osha, look there. You cannot possibly miss it!"

Osha sheathed his blade with a sigh.

"It is all right," Sgäile said in Elvish, with little patience in his voice. "She mistook the ship's root-tail."

"Tail?" Wynn said.

She spun to find him speaking to the hkomas, but the captain stood his ground, gazing expectantly at Sgäile. Magiere and Leesil reached the aftcastle deck, and Magiere came straight to Wynn, falchion in her grip.

"What happened?" Magiere demanded. "Did somebody try to hurt you?"

"Magiere . . . please," Sgäile pleaded, and gestured with an open hand toward her sword.

"I am all right," Wynn said, but she glared at Sgäile. "What tail?"

"It is part of the ship's function," Sgäile said. "What you call . . . propulsion. This is how we move so quickly, despite mild winds."

Chap hooked forepaws over the stern's rail-wall, peering down, and Wynn looked again.

The long and shadowed shape snaked behind the ship in the dark water, but as much as it seemed to swim behind the vessel, it drew no closer. Wynn flushed with embarrassment and cast a dark look at Chap.

"Why did you not tell me?" she whispered.

I did not know. I never saw an elven ship as a pup, nor in the memories of those in the enclave where I was born.

"Ah, seven hells," Leesil grumbled, still pallid and clammy-looking. "Wynn, we thought you were in trouble—instead of poking about again!"

Magiere sheathed her sword and stepped closer, but when she looked down, the same shock Wynn had experienced passed across her pale features. "Leesil, come look at this."

"I don't think so!" he growled, gripping the aftcastle's front rail-wall.

Wynn shook her head. "My apologies. Our ships do not have such propulsion mechanisms."

Osha nodded beside her. "No . . . human ship not alive."

Wynn looked up at his long face, uncertain if she had understood his broken Belaskian correctly.

"What are you saying?" Magiere hissed.

Wynn spun around beside Osha.

Magiere backed away from the stern. Her shoulder brushed the helm-wheel, and she lurched away from it. She cast her wide-eyed gaze about with each hesitant step, as if she were weaponless and surrounded by some unseen threat.

But Wynn was caught up by Osha's words. "How could the ship be alive?" she asked.

"In . . . grow in . . . ," Osha fumbled in frustration and slipped into Elvish. *"Thovarét'nach."*

"Enough!" Sgäile snapped at him.

Their dialect was older than the Elvish Wynn spoke, and she often struggled to comprehend it, particularly names, titles, and other rare noun-declinations from archaic root words.

"Born . . . ," she muttered to herself. "A birth . . ."

The Birth-Water Deep, Chap supplied.

"Alive . . . ," Magiere whispered. "This damned thing is alive!"

"Let's just get below," Leesil urged.

"No," she snarled. "I'm not going down into the belly of this . . . ship."

Leesil half-stumbled as he grabbed for Magiere's arm and pulled her toward the steps.

"Yes, it is best you all retire," Sgäile said, though he watched Magiere with guarded puzzlement. "And remain away from the stern . . . as you were told."

He cast a meaningful glance at Wynn.

"Chap, come on," Wynn said, heading after her companions. "Osha . . . I am sorry for the trouble."

A few of the crew stood about, grumbling as Wynn headed down the steps. The hkomas hissed something sharp at Sgäile, but Wynn's thoughts were elsewhere. She was worried about Magiere's reaction.

If this ship were alive—like the trees of an elven forest—and Magiere touched it with her bare skin . . .

Muted musical tones broke into Wynn's thoughts as her feet hit the main deck. Chap raced by, heading after Magiere and Leesil, but Wynn paused, peering at one aft stairway hatch left open.

Blurred deep notes rose out of it from somewhere below the aftcastle. They did not come from an instrument, though reedy in quality. The sound was more like a baritone voice uttering a wordless refrain. The song's cadence rolled in time to the thrum beneath Wynn's feet—or perhaps it was the song which led the rhythm.

Welstiel felt dusk approach, but his overall sense of passing time had grown hazy. He had lost count of the days and nights. He sat in the upper floor's passage throughout each day with his mind fixed upon the guttural sounds rising within the cells on the left side.

He had taken a great gamble in creating minions without carefully selecting candidates from a large population—and gambled that he might willfully dominate any who rose onto the Feral Path.

His success in both endeavors was a good sign.

He no longer needed the misguidance of the patron of his dreams.

Welcome imaginings filled his thoughts. Once he possessed the orb, something in its ancient nature would relieve him of the need to feed on the living. He could retire to Belaski's remote peninsula and never be soiled again by blood. With Bela and the shipyards of Guèshk just to the south, he would order fine clothes and possessions and spend his time in arcane study. All that remained was to relocate Magiere and drive her onward. Sooner or later, she would lead him to where the orb was hidden.

Welstiel gazed along the three iron-barred doors. His new servants stirred within, restless with aching hunger, but they no longer clawed at the doors or tore at each other. Soon they would be ready for the journey. He looked down at his pack resting between the stool and passage wall.

He had scried for Magiere's location several times since coming to this place. Her position had remained roughly the same, except for once when it had shifted a long distance, north by northeast. By his estimation, she was still within the Elven Territories. But tonight, so close to completion of his tasks here . . .

Sliding from the stool and kneeling, he removed the brass dish from his pack and placed it facedown on the passage floor, domed back upward. Murmuring a low chant, he drew his dagger and sliced a shallow cut in what remained of his left hand's little finger.

Magiere was still unaware of the true purpose of the bone amulet she wore around her neck. That ivory-colored piece set in a tin backing was the missing bone of Welstiel's own little finger. He was not scrying for her as much as for the piece of himself that she carried. He watched his black fluids drip once, twice, three times from the stump of his finger to collect in a tiny bulge at the center of the plate's back. A moment's focus of will would close the slight wound, but he lost that focus before he could finish.

The dark bulge of his fluids quivered upon the brass plate's dome.

It leaned, as if the plate tilted, and ran in a line away from the center, stopping short of the plate's edge.

Welstiel had learned over many years to judge Magiere's position by the length and angle the droplet traveled. She was on the move again, and traveling east too quickly to be on foot. It seemed she might now head beyond the bounds of the Elven Territories. But how? He knew of nothing in that direction and distance but the far ocean on the continent's eastern side.

Welstiel stiffened—Magiere might be traveling by sea.

He could not imagine how. To his own knowledge, no human ship had ever rounded the continent's northeast end into elven waters. He had hoped to hold out a few more nights here to drive his new creations into deeper hunger, until they were mad to feed. That time was lost. An entire range of mountains stood between him and the eastern coastline.

He had preparations to make—and he must feed his ferals one last morsel.

Welstiel cleaned the plate and dagger and tucked both away, but when he stood, he braced a hand against the wall. Lack of rest wore upon him since he had renewed his use of potions to stave off dormancy. He turned his attention upon the cell doors to the right, those of the living.

He'd been too focused on starving the others into a frenzy and driving them further over the edge. How many monks still lived? He would need more life to carry with him for the journey.

When he descended into the entry room, Chane was nowhere in sight.

Welstiel wondered where his unstable companion had slept all day. Or was Chane already awake, skulking about?

Welstiel headed into the back passage, stopping to glance around the archway frame into the workroom.

"Chane?" he called out, but no answer came.

Since the first night in the monastery, when Welstiel had to cow Chane into obedience, the young undead had changed. He grew more sulking, more guarded and resentful. Sooner or later, this behavior would reach a peak.

Welstiel believed a moment would come when Chane's assistance might be more trouble than it was worth. But for now . . .

He had no time to go looking for the young undead, so he kept to the near wall, watching all around as he headed for a large chest. With one backward glance, he flipped it open and rummaged for two more empty bottles with tight stoppers before he returned to the upper passage. He paused long enough at his pack to retrieve the box that held his brass feeding cup and then turned to the first door on the right and pulled the wood shard from its handle.

In the cell, three monks huddled together upon the narrow bed. Welstiel stepped inside, jamming the door shut behind him.

He needed more life to carry on his journey.

CHAPTER FIVE

"What are you doing in here?"

Chane awoke with a flinch. He was curled in a ball against the door frame of the monastery's library; for some reason, he kept coming back to this place.

Welstiel stood inside the entrance with a lantern in his hand.

"Get up!" he ordered. "We leave tonight . . . after the final feeding."

The thought of leaving this place sparked relief in Chane, but that starving beast inside him perked at the mention of "feeding." Gripping the small library's door frame, he climbed to his feet.

Chane numbly stepped past Welstiel, through the work area, and into the monastery's front entry room. All the way, his back muscles clenched at each of Welstiel's heavy footfalls behind him.

"We will feed them one last time—but no more than before," Welstiel admonished. "Then you will gather what supplies this place has to offer. We leave tonight."

Chane crested the stairs and stared down the passage. The blood that Welstiel had disgorged upon the stone floor had dried up. Moans and whimpers of mad undead grew louder now that dusk had come and gone. But the corridor's right side was silent, as if the occupants there did not wish to make a sound.

Only one of the right-side doors was still barred. Welstiel slipped around Chane and opened it.

Two shriveled corpses lay inside. Still garbed in pale blue tabards over dusky robes, it was difficult to tell if either had been male or female, though one was lighter of frame. The sight was nothing more than Chane expected, but knowing how similar the monastery's inhabitants were to the sages, and the world he dreamed of, made him stiffen.

And worse, the cell's last living occupant huddled in a ball on the bed. Its face was half-buried in the corner, with one arm wrapped over its head as if to hide. Then it turned its cowled head just enough to peer toward the door.

Chane's twinge of excitement at the prospect of feeding wavered.

The occupant was a man in his late twenties, haggard with thirst, hunger, and lack of sleep. Welstiel strode in without hesitation and grabbed the shoulder of his robe.

The young monk heaved a sharp breath but didn't have time to release a cry. Welstiel struck him down with a fist, and he flopped across the bed's edge, unconscious.

Chane just stood silent beyond the cell's doorway.

"What is wrong?" Welstiel asked.

Chane lifted his gaze. He saw only cold resolution in Welstiel's face—not bloodlust or even longing.

"I will finish here," Welstiel said, when Chane did not answer. "Search the storerooms. Gather what is of use. And look for clean robes or spare clothing for our new companions. I do not want their present state to attract undue attention if we are seen."

Chane turned away down the stairs, stopping only to light a lantern at the hearth's dwindling fire.

What else could he do? Fight Welstiel for the life of one monk by strength or conjury? Either was pointless. He had already been outmatched in the former, and as for the latter . . .

Conjuring fire and light, or making familiars, was of little advantage. Welstiel preferred artifice rather than the ritual or spellcraft that Chane leaned on for his own conjury. But even Chane resorted to artificing at times, so it stood to reason that Welstiel could resort to the speed of spellcraft in place of the slower but more powerful effect of a ritual. And the older undead had decades of experience.

Also, Welstiel would be guarded by his new children, waiting to feed and then serve their maker.

Chane reached the first storage room in the front passage and pulled on the door latch, and the screaming up above began.

A pathetic sound, it echoed through the monastery. The young monk's cries were little more than a raw voice driven by exhales of terror, as the teeth and cold fingers of Welstiel's children roused him with pain. Every cry made the beast within Chane thrash more wildly—until the voice suddenly stopped.

Chane stepped into the storage room and set down his lantern. He mindlessly rummaged through clothing, blankets, and what canvas he could find for tarps and tents and makeshift packs. When he uncovered a stack of dusky robes, he halted.

Memories of an old barracks in Bela swam in his head. The garments under his fingers felt . . . looked so much like those of young sages in gray robes.

So much like those Wynn had worn.

She had no power or authority, unlike those born to it by chance. No illusory position of influence that set her above the rest of humanity. No, Wynn elevated herself in more meaningful ways.

Chane closed his fingers tightly on one dark wool robe stacked in the storage room. And he tried to crush the longing of false hunger as well. He jerked a pile of robes out and tossed them into the passage.

He gathered whatever supplies might be useful and stacked them in the entry room. Canvas, thick wool blankets to reinforce tents, lanterns, kindling and flint, knives and other weaponlike tools, plus a pot, tea leaves, and several water flasks from the kitchen. He had learned from Welstiel that even undeads needed moisture when they had little or no blood to consume. Finally, he returned to the stairs, and when he crested the last step, he nearly retreated again.

All the left-side cell doors were open. Welstiel stood in the passage with his six minions shifting about him.

Chane had no revulsion to strong scents, but the stench of feces and urine disgusted him. A corpse soon released all its wastes, and these newly risen ones had not bathed since they'd awakened on their first night. Their soiled robes were shredded from assaulting each other in a frenzy of hunger. They were covered in the dried remains of each other's black fluids, but their faces and hands were smeared red with the blood of their last living comrade.

Two were young men not much older than twenty, but they crouched like animals, grunting and sniffing. One drooled heavily, his saliva stained pink.

An older woman straightened up behind Welstiel. She swayed and whispered something as her eyes wandered, but her words made no sense. A tall beardless man with silvery hair hunkered near her like a lost puppy—the same who had torn apart his younger female companion in the first cell.

And that young woman, the one Chane had insisted was worth saving . . .

A mass of snarled brown-black hair hid half her face as she huddled against the wall. Once she might have been pretty, but now Chane couldn't tell. Her face and throat, wrists and exposed chest, were a mass of half-closed wounds set starkly against pallid flesh. She had not fed enough to heal fully. When she looked at him, nearly all color gone from her eyes, her features twitched from either terror or hunger.

The sixth stood with his back against the wall. He was stocky and muscular, and his fingers hooked like claws where his hands pressed against the stone. He had curly dark hair and a square jaw, and he sniffed the air like a wolf—sniffed at Welstiel, intently watching his maker's back.

Chane felt their glittering eyes shift toward him, one by one. Their yearning to feed roused an echo in him, but Welstiel seemed unaffected.

"I made sure they left something for your trouble," he said.

His cloak was brushed free of most of the dried mud stains and other debris of the wilderness. His hair was carefully groomed, exposing the white patches at his temples. Welstiel looked wholly the gentleman Chane had first met outside of Bela, though perhaps a little more traveled. And he stood there like a noble among his fetid servants, fully composed.

But his eyes were cold, devoid of even hunger's passion. He had no concept of what he had done here—what he had forced Chane to do.

Welstiel cocked his head toward the last door on the passage's right.

"Be quick about it, as it is the last chance you will have for a long while to sate your lust."

He snapped his fingers, which made the cowering young female cringe, and then pointed toward the stairs. Chane slipped aside to let them pass.

Only the curly-headed man paused to look him up and down with a sniff, checking to see if he was something to feed upon. When they were gone, Chane crept toward the last door on the passage's right. It had been left ajar. He reached out and pushed it wide with his fingertips.

The boy lying on the cell's floor had red hair and freckled pale skin. He was younger than any of the others Chane remembered locking in these rooms, but his memory of that first night was hazy. The neckline and sleeve ends of his wool robe were torn and smeared with blood, as were his throat and wrists. One slender hand had a slight callus on the index finger from holding a quill or stylus for long hours.

His eyelids flickered. Shallow breaths escaped his diminutive mouth.

Chane crouched over the boy and gripped the back of his skull. Longing—that false hunger—came again.

Left as he was, the boy would bleed to death—a wasted life. But that life had been gone the moment Chane came to this place. He leaned his face close to the boy's own as his canine teeth begin to ache and elongate. He hung there silently, close enough to feel the weak breaths rush over his face.

"What did you study here?" he asked.

No answer came but a brief flutter of the boy's drooping eyelids.

What might he have become? Perhaps something better than another head in the vast herd of human cattle.

Chane closed his other hand across the boy's jaw and pulled it upward. The wounds in that mangled slender throat leaked a fresh trail of blood. He gripped the small head tightly between both hands.

And wrenched it sharply to the side.

With a crack of vertebrae, the boy's rattling breaths ceased.

Chane dropped the body on the stone floor and turned away on his hands and knees.

He clawed up the door frame and lurched out. Halfway down the stairs, he pressed his face into the wall's cold stone, grinding his jaws shut against his elongated teeth.

The boy was lost . . . all here were lost, one way or another. Only what they had accomplished remained, and even that would fade, forgotten by the world in this hidden place.

Chane's fingernails grated down the wall.

An impatient Welstiel was waiting outside, but Chane's mind was elsewhere. He ran down the stairs and raced for the back study and its library. Then he froze in the doorway, panic overwhelming his senses.

His gaze ran along the shelves, over and over, and he shook his head. All the books and scrolls, volumes and sheaves—he could not just leave them.

And he could not carry them all away. How could he choose what to take with so much to leave behind?

Time would not work in his favor.

He snatched one book, and then another. He chose texts he had seen before, their titles vaguely familiar, and some so thick with fine script that they seemed to hold the greatest content. He shoved as many as he could into a canvas sack scavenged from the outer study. Even when the sack was full, he looked wildly about at all that was left. He finally turned to run out of this lifeless place.

Outside, Welstiel stood watchfully over his six children as they scrubbed their naked bodies with snow. He then dressed them in fresh robes and armed them with utility and kitchen knives tucked in their belts. The curly-headed man took up an iron bar as a cudgel.

"Take the baggage," Welstiel ordered them, and like puppets jerked by their strings, the obedient ferals twitched into motion.

Chane winced at this, for he knew what it felt like. His own maker, Toret, had used such a voice on him when he grew reluctant to obey. When a Noble Dead created another of its kind, that newborn was forever doomed to abide by any willfull order from its maker.

Unless—until—that maker was destroyed.

Chane eyed Welstiel as the elderly undead headed for the switchback trail, glancing once at the sack bundled in Chane's arms.

"Soon enough, you will have all the books you could want," Welstiel said, and stepped down the first leg of the narrow path.

Chane waited as the ferals ambled after their master. About to follow, he looked back once more to the monastery carved from the gorge wall. The door was still open.

He grabbed the handle and pulled, making certain the door was soundly closed. If only he could so easily shut away all memories of this place—as if he had never come here.

"In time, you will have your own place among your beloved sages as well," Welstiel called out from below.

The beast inside of Chane lunged excitedly against its chains, as if clutching at some offered and coveted morsel.

"Fulfill your obligation," Welstiel added, his words seeming to rise from the dark, "and then I will fulfill mine."

At those last words, something snapped sharply inside of Chane.

The beast inside him backed warily into a corner. It saw no choice joint of meat in its master's hand. It smelled nothing for its longing hunger. It only heard a spoken promise.

That twinge made Chane whip about and stare at the top of the switchback path.

He had never felt this before. It left him startled, even panicked.

At dawn, half a moon into the voyage, Avranvärd held back near the bow. She watched Sgäilsheilleache standing with the dark-haired human woman.

He leaned on the port-side rail-wall and pointed ahead, speaking some ugly guttural language Avranvärd could not understand. She did not need to in order to know what he was saying. They had reached the peninsula and would now turn south along the eastern coast.

Relief flooded the woman's pale features. Sgäilsheilleache nodded, as if glad to offer her such welcome news.

His reputation among the an'Cróan was so pure. Not as revered as Brot'ân'duivé or the great Eillean, he had still traveled foreign lands and faced humans to protect all the an'Cróan. Now he stood with one of the savages, and Avranvärd swallowed hard in revulsion.

Perhaps his attempt to appease this woman was pretense, for Sgäilsheilleache must have a good reason. When Avranvärd joined the Anmaglâhk, then maybe she would understand.

Predawn's first yellow streaks glowed at the base of the horizon. Avranvärd looked to the hkomas standing behind the helm, busy directing the crew to change sail for the southern run. She slipped quietly into the near stairwell beneath the forecastle, and climbed below to find a private place among the cargo. Her oversized boots caught once on the bottom rung, but she righted herself before stumbling.

Most of the crew was on deck, along with some of the "passengers." She hesitated in the passage, staring at the door where the humans and the half-blood lodged. But it was too risky to nose about in there, so she headed along the starboard passage toward the cargo bay. Once there, Avranvärd crouched behind the barrels of drinking water and pressed her word-wood against the ship's hull.

"Are you there?" she whispered.

Report.

The voice in her head was cold, emotionless. She did not even know his name, only that he was a Greimasg'äh and deserved her obedience. Still, he treated her like a necessity and no more—not like a comrade.

"We have reached the peninsula and turn south. The crew changes sails as we speak."

When is your next stop?

"Four days at most—we exchange cargo at Énwiroilhe."

What have you learned of this artifact the humans seek?

The question surprised her, as he had not asked this before. "I should be listening? I cannot speak their language."

Do not risk suspicion, but anything of use you overhear, report to me.

She hesitated. "Sgäilsheilleache is too protective . . . it seems as if he cares for them."

The Greimasg'äh was silent for too long, and Avranvärd began to wonder whether he was still listening. His voice came again, far colder than before.

You will not speak of him with disrespect. Unless the unexpected occurs, report in four days.

Avranvärd waited, reluctant to answer after this rebuke. Her silence drew out until she knew he was gone.

She had angered him, and it was the last thing she wanted. A Greimasg'äh's discontent would not sit well when it came time to present herself to Most Aged Father. She stood up, taking a deep breath.

Most Aged Father had given his word. If she succeeded, she would be an initiate, and this eased her worry. After all, she had been given a purpose for the Anmaglâhk. She reported directly to a Greimasg'äh, one of their greatest. As far as she knew, no initiate had ever done this before.

Avranvärd hurried out before the hkomas missed her. As she emerged below the forecastle, half the sun peeked above the eastern horizon, dusting the ocean with sparks of light. When she stepped farther out and glanced upward, Sgäilsheilleache stood gazing down at her with unblinking eyes.

For an instant, Avranvärd could not take her eyes from his. Then she scurried off toward the stern, where her hkomas waited beside the helm. But Avranvärd could not shake the sight of Sgäilsheilleache's steady gaze.

.   .   .

Twelve more days past their southward turn, Magiere paced the deck, wearing her new coat and avoiding the rail-walls.

She should've felt grateful to be traveling by sea instead of land. But surrounded by this living ship, her thoughts wandered too often to the dead marks her hands had left upon an elven birch tree. Awareness made the vibration inside her sharpen to a shudder. She laced her fingers together, smoothing the lambskin gloves over her hands.

The season had passed into late winter, but at sea and just beyond the shore of the Elven Territories, it seemed colder.

Wynn sat on the deck talking softly to Chap—something they did more often these days. Leesil and Osha were still below, though Leesil was much improved. He ate almost normally, and as Sgäile had suggested, he was acquiring his "sea legs." Not that Leesil didn't still grumble and whine now and then.

Yes, Magiere should've been grateful. The Blade Range separating Belaski and Droevinka from the continent's eastern coast was impassable. She would've had to trek all the way down through Droevinka amid its civil war, then crossed the Everfen's vast swamplands into the Pock Peaks to reach the eastern coast. The journey would've taken another season, more likely two.

And yet Magiere was helpless to speed up their current pace.

She had suffered two more dreams of the six-towered castle on its snow-blanketed plain, and being blown through the night sky. With each dream, the pull south grew stronger. The only thing missing from those recent night journeys was the black-scaled coils circling about her.

The hkomas called for a stop at each harbor settlement, and Sgäile kept recounting the importance of this vessel. Dockhands unloaded supplies onto large skiffs, which were transferred onto inland-bound barges. The stops always took a day or more.

Several times, Magiere asked to go ashore. Any short reprieve away from the ship would've been welcome, though it meant walking on elven land again. Sgäile refused each time, claiming their presence would cause discord in any an'Cróan settlement. Magiere knew he was right, but it didn't help.

She forgot herself in frustration and almost grabbed the rail-wall. Even with gloves on, she panicked and jerked her hand back at the last instant. The unnerving sensation she felt aboard this strange living vessel was less severe than what she'd suffered inside the elven tree dwellings. But this time she knew what her touch could do. The last thing Magiere wanted was to inadvertently draw life from the ship or injure it in any way.

At times, Magiere had to bite down to keep from shouting at the hkomas to sail more quickly.

"Yes, it is," Wynn said loudly. "Why do you always argue with me? I can clearly see mats starting on your haunches."

Magiere turned her troubled gaze on Chap and Wynn. The sage fished a brush from her pack, but Chap rumbled, swinging his rear out of reach.

"There is plenty of rope about to tie you up," Wynn warned, "like any other dog."

Chap wheeled and made a run for it.

"Get back here!"

Wynn snatched hold of his tail as her brush clattered upon the deck. With a yelp more indignant than pained, Chap swung his head over his shoulder and bared his teeth.

"As if you would dare," Wynn growled back.

With a lick of his nose, Chap dug in with all fours and lunged away.

"No . . . wait!" Wynn squealed.

She flopped forward on her belly, refusing to let go, and Chap's paws scrabbled on the deck as he gained momentum. Wynn's eyes popped wide as she slid along behind him.

Magiere sighed, starting after them. "Stop it—both of you!"

Then Chap rounded the back side of the cargo hold's grate.

Wynn flipped onto her back, still hanging on. Her little body whipped around the corner behind the dog and then rolled, swinging sideways toward the stern. Chap's paws scrabbled wildly as her weight suddenly threw him off balance. He flattened hard on his belly with a grunt, his legs splayed in all directions.

Both sage and dog spun across the deck. With a last yelp from Chap, they tumbled askew toward the aftcastle's wall. Magiere panicked as the two collided into a stack of coiled rigging rope and spare sailcloth.

Wynn sat up quickly, thrashing about as she tried to untangle herself. Chap rose on three legs, attempting to shake the fourth free of a knotted loop of rope.

"You two . . . ," Magiere called out. "Stop acting like a couple of—"

"He started it!" Wynn yelled.

Chap shot a yip and snarl straight into her round face.

"Yes, you did!" Wynn growled back through clenched teeth. "And I have *not* brushed you since we left, you . . . you pig!"

She grabbed Chap's tangled leg and began jerking on the knotted rope to get him free.

An elven crewman leaned over the aftcastle above them.

Magiere caught sight of him just as he vaulted the rail-wall. His booted feet hit the main deck as he dropped directly in front of Wynn. The sage stiffened with a sharp inhale. Before she could move, the man snatched her by one wrist.

His amber eyes filled with anger as he jerked her up, until she almost stood on her toes. He hissed one quick string of Elvish at her. The only word Magiere caught was "majay-hì."

Chap twisted around and snapped at the man's shin, but the rope cinched tight around his leg and pulled him up short.

Magiere vaulted the hold's grate, shouting, "Get off of her!"

The tall crewman's hard and lined face turned toward her as she swung.

The back of Magiere's right knuckles caught his face, and she bored her left fist into his gut. He buckled, and one foot slipped from the deck as he careened back into the ship's rail-wall.

His grip on Wynn tore loose but jerked her against Magiere's shoulder. Magiere tucked her arm around the sage to catch her. Sunlight intensified all around Magiere.

The world turned searingly bright. Her eyes began to tear as her irises expanded to full black.

"Magiere!"

Sgäile appeared beside her with Osha right behind, holding off the angry sailor. The hkomas slid down the handrails from the aftcastle.

"He grabbed Wynn!" Magiere snarled and pointed at the sailor, trying to gain control before her dhampir nature spilled out.

"I saw," Sgäile answered quickly, "but you must stop this!"

The sailor struggled up, flailing off Osha's grip with bitter words. He shook his head, blinking rapidly. Blood trickled from the split skin over his cheekbone.

Wynn grabbed Magiere's arm, her small hands gripping tightly.

Chap appeared, lunging to the cargo grate's edge. He snarled and snapped at the elven crewman. The anger washed from the man's face in sudden shock. Even Osha backed away from Chap in wariness as the hkomas cautiously slowed his approach.

"Enough!" Sgäile said, and followed with a long stream of Elvish.

"What's he saying?" Magiere asked Wynn.

The hkomas answered as rapidly. Other crew members drew closer, putting aside their duties as they listened in.

Wynn stepped around to Magiere's side, whispering, "The sailor thought I disrespected a majay-hì. Sgäile is telling them that this is only a game Chap and I play."

"That's how he explains this?" Magiere snipped, anger rising again.

The number of elven voices increased, but Sgäile stood firmly in front of Wynn and Magiere, and Osha remained rooted before Wynn's assailant. Chap watched in silence, but did not back away.

"He also told them no one is to touch us," Wynn added, "and that he would take such as a sign of disrespect to him and his oath of guardianship. It must never happen again."

Magiere eased a little, and when Sgäile glanced her way, she nodded to him.

The hkomas looked frustrated, but he grabbed the angered crewman and pulled him away, shouting at his crew. All began slowly returning to their duties. In spite of Sgäile's declaration, a few cast puzzled glances at Chap—and Magiere caught more hostile ones tossed her way.

She didn't care. Let them come at her, if they wanted.

Sgäile turned to her. "You will leave such problems to me!"

"There won't be any problems," Magiere spit back, "if they keep their hands to themselves."

"How often must I remind you," Sgäile returned, "all of you, that you do not understand our culture and ways. Your ignorance and continued lack of heed for my—"

"They understand us even less!" Wynn cut in.

The sage's sharp tone startled Magiere.

"For all the time you must have spent," Wynn added, "sneaking about human cultures, perhaps it is time you and your people learned some tolerance . . . before jumping to rash conclusions. Bigotry betrays *your* ignorance."

Sgäile was stunned voiceless, but resentment surfaced quickly through his stoic features, signaling an incensed reply on its way. Wynn gave him no opportunity and pushed past him.

"Come, Chap," she said. "Let us check on Leesil."

Chap hopped down to follow her, his head swinging as he watched the crew with twitching jowls. But as they passed Osha, Wynn brushed a hand lightly across his forearm and spoke softly.

"Alhtahk âma âr tú."

Osha eased with a soft smile and bowed his head.

It wasn't hard for Magiere to understand Wynn's words as thanks.

Sgäile cast one last hard glare at Magiere as he headed up the aftcastle stairs.

Magiere merely snorted and turned toward the ship's side, not satisfied enough to go below and take her eyes off the crew. But her gaze settled on the open sea ahead—south.

Night after night of pushing his ferals through the mountains left Welstiel weary of the constant vigilance required to control them. But they had to reach the eastern seacoast, hopefully well ahead of Magiere.

He longed for a solitary existence. Dawn approached, and he stood watching as Chane set up tents for the day. The cold rocky range was harsh and held little life, and the sky seemed interminably dismal even at night.

Each time Welstiel scried for Magiere's position, she had moved an impossible distance southward, closing on his own trajectory to the coast. Sometimes she seemed not to move for several days. This confirmed his suspicion that she was traveling by ship, making port calls along the way.

Chane proved useful again, finding rock outcrops or solitary stands of thick trees in which to pitch tents and keep their band safely under cover. He made tea every few nights, and eventually succeeded in getting the ferals to drink it—after setting an example a few times. Welstiel could not get them to do anything unless he gave a direct order. But Chane's sullen demeanor had increased until he barely spoke at all.

Welstiel did not care, so long as his companion helped keep the ferals moving. And they were quickly reaching the point of needing a fresh kill.

The two younger males shifted restlessly on hands and feet, sniffing the air in eager, unfulfilled hope. The elderly woman paced among the massive boulders surrounding their camp, and whispered aimlessly to herself. Her emaciated, silver-haired follower stayed right on her heels.

The curly-headed man crouched on his haunches, rocking on the balls of his feet at the camp's edge. Sometimes his eyes rolled in his head over a gaping mouth. Once, when Welstiel looked away and then turned back, he found that one watching him intently.

Only the young dark-haired female, whom Chane had insisted was worth saving, retained any hint of reasoning. She never spoke but often assisted Chane in setting camp or building fires when fuel could be found.

Welstiel was exhausted by perpetual vigilance, and he too was feeling the pressing need for life force. Normally, after feeding using his arcane method, he functioned comfortably for nearly a moon. Perhaps the potions with which he drugged himself, or lack of dormancy, or maintaining control over so many, had taken their toll on him. He felt as if he were starving.

Welstiel dug through his pack, searching for the brown glass bottles filled with life force taken from the living monks. When he found them at the bottom, he tensed, reluctant to even touch them.

Aside from his white ceramic container in the box with the brass cup, he found only two bottles. There should have been three. None of the ferals knew his feeding practices—only Chane.

Welstiel rushed to the nearest tent and ripped aside its flap.

Chane sat inside, beside the young female, with a parchment out, and he was showing it to her.

"You have taken something of mine," Welstiel said.

Chane's own pack and canvas sack rested beside him. He reached into the pack without hesitation and pulled out a brown glass bottle.

"Here," he rasped, and tossed it up at Welstiel.

Welstiel caught it. He did not need to pull the stopper. He could tell by the weight that it was empty.

"Did you drink it?" he asked.

"No," Chane answered.

He turned back to pushing the parchment in front of the woman, but she looked at it and then him, as if unsure what he wanted from her.

Welstiel's confusion increased. The ferals knew nothing of his artifacts or the contents of the bottles. Chane finally dropped the parchment.

He pushed past Welstiel out of the tent and stood up, eyes hard as he pointed to the elderly woman and her silver-haired companion.

"I fed them. They needed it."

Welstiel remained still, absorbing those calm words. Chane's past disobediences had normally been restricted to foolish risks involving Wynn Hygeorht. This was more blatant, and a sign that Chane had forgotten his place.

A lesson was required.

Without a word, Welstiel strode across camp with dawn glowing along the eastern horizon. He headed straight for the elderly female.

She saw him coming and backed against the massive stone outcrop rising from the sloped bank above their camp. Her gaunt companion clutched at her leg in fear.

"Be still!" he commanded. "All of you!"

Tendons in the elderly woman's neck protruded as her body went rigid. Her eyes widened as Welstiel jerked his sword from its sheath. The crouching man began squeaking helplessly.

"What are you doing?" Chane demanded.

Welstiel lashed out with his blade.

Its edge collided with the elderly woman's throat. In predawn's half-light, sparks erupted as metal clanged against the stone behind her. The wall of stone turned dark as her black fluids spattered over it.

Welstiel whirled away before her head thumped upon the ground. Her crouching companion began screeching unintelligibly. And there was Chane, his own blade in hand.

"Another step," Welstiel said, calm and clear, "and I will set them all on you."

Chane stood his ground, not moving. He never looked to the other ferals frozen in place around the camp. One of his eyes twitched in rage and open hatred.

Welstiel did not care. Obedience was restored, and he stepped purposefully toward Chane.

"Remember," he said. "When I have what I seek, you will still be waiting for what you desire. Whether I have reason to compensate you for service is all in your hands. Obey me or leave . . . if you wish."

Rage drained slowly from Chane's eyes, or perhaps it merely crawled into hiding. His gaze shifted above Welstiel as the sky grew lighter.

"Get under cover," Chane rasped.

Not a true answer, but Welstiel was satisfied for the moment. A costly lesson, but one that perhaps even Chane could learn. Welstiel turned his back.

The silver-haired man still howled. Frozen in place by Welstiel's command, his fingers were locked tight about the calf of the elderly woman's corpse.

"Quiet!" Welstiel shouted, and the screeching voice strangled in the man's throat.

Welstiel reached down, snatched the woman's head by its graying hair, and heaved it out into the wilderness. When he turned back, Chane had already ducked into his tent. The young female peeked out, one round eye staring at Welstiel around the tent flap's edge.

With Chane's enraged face still fresh in Welstiel's thoughts, he stared into that one near-colorless pupil and wondered . . .

Did he indeed now have only five ferals? Or were there still six, the last one not chained to his own will?

CHAPTER SIX

Hkuan'duv silently slipped out of his quarters just before dawn so as not to disturb Dänvârfij. He made his way through the ship's passages to its "heart-room" at the stern. Avranvärd would soon try to contact him.

He was disturbed that she possessed a word-wood from this vessel. Such were reserved for a ship's hkomas or its hkœda—"caregiver-journeyer"—the Shaper who lived with each vessel through its life. In order to speak with Avranvärd, he needed to be in the place from which this vessel's hkœda had grown the word-wood.

The passage turned right across the ship's breadth, and the hull's rhythmic thrum sharpened as he stopped before three oval doors at the stern. The doors to either side provided access to the ship's twin rudders; he stepped up to the center one.

After his decades of service and a too-long life, only a few things still entranced Hkuan'duv, like the wonder of these vessels, the Päirvänean—Wave-Wanderers. He tapped two fingers lightly upon the door to the ship's heart-room and waited.

"You may enter . . . Hkuan'duv," said a soft voice from within.

He gently cracked the door open and looked inside the room. His eyes settled on its central feature.

The floor flowed up from the chamber's sides into a hulking mound of tawny wood, like the back of an infant whale arching beneath the belly of the ship. Its smooth, glistening surface rippled faintly like the root of a great tree. This was where the vessel's root-tail trailed out into the waters below. Its constant snaking could drive the vessel at speeds difficult for a human ship to match.

Along both side walls, ledges grew from the hull, but the room contained little else, except for its occupant.

A woman in a plain canvas tunic and breeches, her feet bare, sat on one ledge. Her hair was pleated tightly across her skull in neat curling rows, further exposing skin paler than most an'Cróans'. She sat with her back flush against the hull.

"Easàille . . . you do not sing to your ship?" he asked, and settled beside her.

"It slumbers for a while," she answered, "and its dreams run deep in the ocean."

"I must ask again for a private moment here," he said, "but I will try not to disturb the ship's rest."

A ship's hkœda rarely left anyone alone in a heart-room, and his frequent requests were a severe imposition. But Easàille stretched her arms and rolled her shoulders with a smile.

"More secret talks with some other ship's hkœda," she teased in a soft voice, and leaned her face toward him in mock jealousy. "Or is it some female hkomas you court so covertly?"

"I am too old for such things," Hkuan'duv answered. "And why would I seek such company elsewhere . . . if I come here?"

Easàille rolled her eyes at his faltering attempt to return her flirtation. She patted his leg and left quietly.

Alone, he stood up and lightly placed his bare hands against the great arch of the root-tail's base. He slid his fingers over its smooth, vibrating surface, and wondered what it would be like to be hkœda . . . to slumber in the depths and in the dreams of a Päirvänean.

Avranvärd's voice disrupted his thoughts. *Are you there?*

Resentment, rather than relief or anticipation, welled in Hkuan'duv. "Report."

My hkomas is troubled. Tomorrow, we make an unscheduled stop, and he is angry that he was not previously informed.

Hkuan'duv frowned. "Who requested this?"

Sgäilsheilleache . . . but he will not explain why, only that it is necessary.

Hkuan'duv puzzled over this unexpected change. "Does he plan to go ashore?"

I do not know this either. He will say nothing of his purpose . . . not even to the hkomas.

Avranvärd sounded petulant, and her lack of respect left Hkuan'duv cold toward her difficulties. Why had Most Aged Father entrusted such a juvenile outsider to function as informant?

"Report tomorrow at noon and after the evening meal," Hkuan'duv said.

Without waiting for acknowledgment, he lifted his hands from the root-tail's base.

All these changes meant the hkomas of his ship would need to stop and linger until the other vessel moved on. As he left the heart-room, Easàille came down the aft starboard stairs. He nodded quickly at her coy smile and headed back toward his quarters.

As the ship had slowed and anchored, Chap looked over the starboard rail-wall at a wild shore of gray-tinged sand and beached seaweed with nothing but a thick tree-line behind.

No harbor. Not even a small enclave. And only a rise of high mountains beyond granite foothills broke the skyline.

Chap perched on a storage chest with Wynn behind him and watched the skiff being lowered into the water. He grew more puzzled and unsettled with each passing moment. The day before, Sgäile had announced this un-scheduled stop.

"What is he up to?" Wynn asked.

I do not know.

Sgäile, Osha, Leesil, and Magiere came up the stairwell below the aft-castle, seemingly all talking at once. Osha looked openly confused, but Magiere appeared angry.

"What are you hiding?" she demanded. "Leesil's just supposed to go ashore with you, and you won't tell us why?"

Leesil stood behind her, waiting for an answer. He and Magiere had dressed for cold weather with new coats over their hauberks and weapons strapped to their backs. Sgäile shouldered a canvas pack with a coil of rope lashed down its side and his open distress surprised Chap.

"You were not even to come!" Sgäile said to Magiere.

"That's done with, already," she answered, "and not open to debate."

Leesil, caught between the two of them, let out a deep sigh.

"I have told you all that I am permitted to," Sgäile returned. "This voyage was arranged by Brot'ân'duivé—and Cuirin'nên'a, Léshil's mother. I know little of their intentions, but I swore to Brot'ân'duivé that I would carry out his instructions."

Chap caught the strain in Sgäile's voice, driven by more than Magiere's bullying, and wondered at Sgäile's reluctance for whatever task was at hand. Letting Magiere, or any human, become involved in the affairs of his people was no new burden for Sgäile.

"It is not something I can speak of," Sgäile added. "And not just because of human presence. Before now, this task has only been for the Anmaglâhk. Even Léshil's involvement is unprecedented."

"Yes?" Magiere answered. "All the more reason for me to come along."

"All right," Leesil sighed. "It's settled, so leave it alone."

Sgäile slowly shook his head. "We will travel inland from here."

"How long?" Magiere asked.

"Days."

"Sgäile!" she warned.

He pursed his lips. "Three days in, three days out—considering extra precautions for *your* presence. The hkomas and crew will wait with the ship."

"Six days," Magiere whispered, turning away.

Chap realized he had witnessed the tail end of an extended argument, and he tried to dip into Sgäile's memory. He caught a flash of a dark place where only a glimmer like lantern light reflected off a strange sheer wall of silver. Then came a brief glimpse of a tan elven hand holding a dull black oblong of stone, perhaps ground smooth by the tides over years. For an instant, Chap thought he saw marks scratched into its surface.

The memories sank from Sgäile's thoughts and beyond Chap's awareness.

Chap's companions were not the only ones who had changed during their time among the an'Cróan; Sgäile had been altered as well. The mind of a seasoned anmaglâhk should have been nearly blank of rising memories. These brief glimpses showed that Sgäile's self-control was wavering. It was not a good sign.

Wynn closed on Magiere, and Chap looked them both up and down. No one had asked Wynn to pack for this journey.

The little sage had hardened much in two seasons, but not enough. A time might come when she would be left behind for more than six days. Although Chap's foremost concern was watching over Magiere and Leesil, the thought of Wynn left unguarded worried him more and more.

He had tried now and then to goad Wynn playfully, to make her assert herself. That day on the deck he had not anticipated her grabbing his tail and sending them both spinning into a tangle. In retrospect, he should have considered the crew's reaction to a human tussling with a majay-hì. What came of that was his fault—his foolishness—born of concern for Wynn. Still, it was all he could think of to continue her slow climb to greater internal strength.

"If you are going inland," Wynn said bluntly, "then I am going as well."

Sgäile finally noticed the little sage, and Osha's long face clouded over in silence.

"No," Sgäile answered flatly. "It is enough that I relented to Magiere's . . . request."

Magiere glanced about the ship. "We're not leaving Wynn with this crew."

"Osha will watch over her," Sgäile countered, and turned to his young companion. "Do you accept this purpose?"

Brief shock washed over Osha's face, and he nodded. "Yes, I accept."

"I do not!" Wynn retorted. "Where are you going? And why did you wait until now to tell us any of this?"

Sgäile's jaw muscles tightened as he turned back to Magiere.

"We travel swiftly. Even if I were of a mind for another outsider, the scholar would slow us. She stays . . . but I give my word she will be safe with Osha."

"Wynn . . . ," Magiere began but trailed off.

Wynn's expression drained, losing even indignation. "You want to travel quickly."

"I want to get back as soon as possible," Magiere corrected. "And move on."

Leesil settled a hand on Wynn's shoulder. "I know this sounds insane, but Sgäile wouldn't ask unless it was important, and I—"

"You want to know what Brot'an arranged," Wynn finished.

"Brot'an can rot for all I care!" Leesil snapped, and then calmed himself. "But if my mother's involved in this . . ."

"I understand," Wynn said, looking down at the deck.

Chap sympathized with her, but he had larger issues to worry about—particularly if all this was more of Brot'an's scheming. He tried again to dip into Sgäile's memories.

This time he caught flickering images of Wynn in Crijheäiche and Ghoivne Ajhâjhe, asking questions, nosing about . . . and then perched upon the city's shoreside embankment, scribbling in one of her journals.

Indeed, Sgaile's composure was slipping. He did not want Wynn on this journey, but not for the reason he had given. Once again, Sgäile was caught between his caste's ways and whatever Brot'ân'duivé had pressed him into—something Sgäile did not want Wynn recording.

I will go with them, Chap projected, stepping in beside her, *and tell you everything when we return.*

A bit of mischief at such a notion filled Wynn's eyes as she crouched and cupped his face in her hands. She began to say something, but Chap cut her off.

Stay with Osha.

Wynn looked up at the others. "You should get started."

Magiere frowned, as if wondering at Wynn's sudden compliance, and glared down at Chap. It was clear to Chap that she knew exactly what had passed silently between them.

Magiere turned and headed for the rail-wall. "We'll be back as soon as we can."

The hkomas crossed his arms, and Sgäile would not even look at him. Osha stepped in protectively behind Wynn as Chap trotted off behind Magiere.

A young woman with a thick braid and oversized boots gazed at him with anxious eyes. But Chap ignored her and arched up, hooking his forepaws on the rail-wall's top near the rope ladder. There he waited so he might climb onto Leesil's back.

Leesil raised his feathery eyebrows. "No, you stay here."

Chap wrinkled a jowl. Since when was he to be treated like a dog? He was the guardian of his charges, and neither of them had anything to say about it. He barked twice, loudly, for "no."

Magiere stepped through the rail-wall gate, one foot settling on the ladder. "You can't climb down by yourself, and we're not carrying you."

She swung her other leg over and began climbing down. Chap barked a succession of angry yips.

Leesil followed Magiere, and Chap considered biting the back of his breeches. Sgäile looked uncomfortable as he stepped through the rail-wall gate.

"Apologies," he said to Chap. "We will return soon."

Magiere was right about one thing. Chap could not climb down by himself. But it was time he reminded them of their position as *his* charges. He watched until Magiere settled in the skiff, and then backed a few feet along the deck.

"What are you doing?" Wynn called in alarm.

Chap rushed through the rail-wall gate and leaped out into the air at the last instant. He hit the water just beyond the skiff and sank amid the loud sound of his own splash. The sea was far colder than he had expected.

When he resurfaced, sucking breath through his nose, both Magiere and Leesil were shouting at him. He paddled quickly to the skiff's side. Magiere pursed her lips tight in anger, and reached for him. Leesil just looked worried and both of them hauled him in over the skiff's side.

Chap shook himself hard, spraying seawater everywhere. Both Magiere and Leesil tried to shield their faces, as Sgäile fought to steady the skiff.

"You misbegotten mutt!" Magiere shouted and grabbed for Chap's scruff.

He turned on her, snarling.

Magiere lost her footing and fell back into Leesil, seated in the skiff's prow. The skiff rocked wildly, and both their expressions turned blank with shock.

"What has gotten into you?" Leesil said.

Chap glared back with a low rumble in his throat and then spun to face Sgäile.

"Have you got him?" Wynn called from above.

Chap did not look up, and no one answered Wynn. He remained in place before Sgäile, rumbling a low threat. Elves never interfered with a majay-hì, and Sgäile's behavior had always suggested he knew Chap was much more than even that.

Sgäile slowly raised both hands, palms out. "As you wish," he whispered and reached for the oars.

Chap ceased rumbling and glanced over his shoulder at Leesil and Magiere.

"Fine!" Magiere grumbled, swatting off the droplets of seawater running down her coat.

Chap lifted his muzzle, looking up for Wynn, but instead he spotted the young elven girl with the thick braid. She gripped the rail-wall near the ship's stern, watching as the skiff turned toward the shore. Chap looked past Sgäile, rowing hard, and out over the skiff's prow.

Chattering seagulls circled overhead, and Chap wondered what lay beyond the shore.

Wynn settled on the cabin's floor that night, warming the cold lamp crystal in her hands. Its light increased, glowing brightly between her fingers, and she set it on her bunk ledge. Osha sat cross-legged nearby, arranging their dinner tray of dried apricots, grilled halibut, and elven tea.

The crystal provided their only light. Sea air wafted through the open porthole, and the ship sat steady at anchor. The cabin seemed a cozy and welcome place.

"I am sorry you had to stay behind because of me," she said in Elvish. No one else was present, and Elvish was easier for Osha, even with their differing dialects.

Osha poured two cups of tea. "I am glad to fulfill such a purpose in service to you."

Wynn settled across from Osha, both dressed in their loose elven garments—he in his anmaglâhk tunic and pants, more charcoal gray than green in the low light, and she in the dusty yellow and russet of Sgäile's clan. They had never shared a meal in private, and as they ate, Wynn grew curious. For one, how much did Osha know of where Sgäile had taken Leesil and Magiere—and why?

"Do you know where they are going?" she asked.

Osha rocked backward slightly, trying not to meet her eyes.

"Please do not ask such questions," he said, though it sounded like a plea. "Sgäilsheilleache has put his faith in me. I cannot fail him."

Wynn sighed and leaned against the bunk's edge, feeling a little guilty for tempting Osha to betray a confidence.

"Why are you here, Osha?" she asked. "Why did Sgäile bring you?"

Then she wanted to cringe. That had not come out right. It sounded as if she thought Osha would have been the last of all possible choices. But he appeared oblivious to her slip. He took a breath and exhaled, as if he had achieved something which brought him long-sought relief.

"He is now my *jeóin*."

"Your . . . ," Wynn began, puzzling over the title, and finally had to continue in Belaskian. "Your . . . 'assenter'?"

Osha cocked his head. "It is the word for what he is, my . . ." He, too, had to turn to Belaskian as well. "I find my *teacher*!"

He took another long breath before continuing in Elvish.

"It has been hard to find one who was willing enough for me to even ask. But when Sgäilsheilleache said I should come to stay with his family, I knew my search was over."

Wynn was careful to smile happily at this. Judging by what she had seen and heard, the lanky young elf was not like the rest of his caste, perhaps not even suited to their calling, and yet he would not give up. But inside, she was not happy at all over this news. Osha had found someone to take him in, and Sgäile would apprentice him.

As an assassin, among other things.

"I am glad for you," Wynn said and reached for her tea, contemplating some other topic. "Tell me of . . . your family, where you grew up."

Osha blinked. "My family? You wish to hear about my life?"

Her smile was sincere this time. "Has no one ever asked you this before?"

He shook his head. "No."

"Never?" She sat upright in surprise. "Yes, I wish to know about your life."

Osha seemed to gather his thoughts for a long moment.

"I am of the Âlachben"—he switched briefly to Belaskian—"the Rock-Hills clan . . . a place not like Crijheäiche or Ghoivne Ajhâjhe. My people live simply, raising goats in the foothills to be shorn for their hair."

"And the hides for our new coats?"

"Yes," he answered, then hesitated. "But my father was not well . . . a difficulty with his heart." Osha placed a hand over his chest, and his gaze drifted. "Our healers could not mend it, and he died young, only sixty-three years of age. My mother fell into mourning and could not rise again."

"I am sorry," Wynn said. "You must have felt alone."

He looked at her, amber eyes clearing in the cold lamp crystal's light.

"No, I have three siblings, and my brother and sisters took charge of the herds, but I was the youngest by many years. Even Chionntaj, my sister closest to me in age, saw me as one more duty among others."

He dropped his eyes to the untouched meal between them, and Wynn gleaned a small glimpse of Osha's youth. A lonely childhood at best. And it appeared he had been given little to no responsibility, which might account for his lack of self-confidence or practical abilities. She wanted to take his hand.

"Both my parents passed over," she said, wishing to distract him. "I grew up an orphan in the sages' guild in Malourné."

Osha raised his head. "No clan?"

Wynn smiled again. "Not as you think of it, but I was never alone. The sages became my family, and a good one at that, as I was privileged to grow up among them instead of in the orphanage. I attended one of the public schools they established in the king's city, and something new and interesting was always happening on the guild's grounds. Or I would just listen while my elders sank into one of their perpetual debates, which never seemed to be settled. They taught me history and languages. Later, Domin Tilswith, an elder of the Order of Cathologers, took me as his apprentice. I traveled with him to this continent. I have been most fortunate in my life."

But Wynn felt an ache of longing for her days in the guild, for lentil and tomato stew, for the caring company of scholarly comrades.

"This is why you became a . . . a 'sage' yourself?" Osha asked. "Because you value their way of life?"

She was uncertain how to answer. "Yes, in part. I wanted to learn and explore, to share knowledge and teach others." She tilted her head. "Why did you join the Anmaglâhk?"

Startled by this sudden shift back to him, Osha swallowed.

"Three seasons before I went for name-taking, two of the caste came to my enclave with a message for our clan elders. This had never happened before. And such a pair—two Greimasg'äh at once—Great Eillean, Léshil's grandmother, and Brot'ân'duivé. Everyone was in awe of them, and I had never seen anyone treated with such respect. I could barely bring myself to peer from around the tree of my home, and with all my body, I wished to be like them."

Osha lowered his head, lifting only his eyes at Wynn with a halting whisper, "Not an honorable reason."

Wynn swallowed her reservations and reached for his hand. "To strive to excel . . . especially in service to others . . . is always honorable. Your family should be proud of you."

Through the glow of the cold lamp crystal, Osha stared at her. His hand started to tremble, and he slowly pulled it from hers. Long muscles in his forearm clenched tightly. Wynn realized she had never seen his bare arms before.

"But," she began, "are there not other ways you could have earned the respect you desire . . . other ways to serve your . . ."

She trailed off as puzzlement spread across Osha's long face.

"Never mind," she finished.

"Are you hungry?" he asked.

"No, I do not think so."

He nodded and stood up. "Then you should rest. I will sit vigil."

Was he not going to sleep? Wynn knew it was pointless to argue.

She unrolled one of the mats and a blanket on her bunk ledge, realizing she was tired. When she settled there, Osha had dropped back to a cross-legged position in the middle of her cabin.

Wynn had assumed he would be outside in the hall, or in the next cabin over, with his own door wide to keep an eye on things—but not in the middle of her own room. Suddenly sheepish, she pulled the blanket up and rolled toward the cabin's hull wall.

A few moons past, Wynn would have been shocked at the prospect of sleeping in the belly of a living ship with an anmaglâhk just beyond arm's reach. But she closed her eyes, feeling safe, and quickly drifted off.

Sgäile awoke the following dawn, dreading every step to come. He breathed in the fresh air, trying to center himself, but the name the ancestors had given Léshil was always in his thoughts.

Léshiârelaohk—Sorrow-Tear's Champion.

A half-blood had been recognized as a full an'Cróan. But even such an honor from the ancestors did not justify what Brot'ân'duivé asked—no, insisted upon.

Only Anmaglâhk and clan elders went to the hidden place of the Chein'âs—the Burning Ones.

Sgäile's own grandfather, Gleannéohkân'thva, had once gone to them, but only in the company of Brot'ân'duivé.

Léshil stirred in the bedroll he shared with Magiere and gently gripped her shoulder. Chap remained curled up at their feet.

Sgäile got up and looked about, wandering a short distance from their camp. Years had passed since his last journey through the southern coastal region of his people, but he had always appreciated the terrain. Coarser than the inlands, this place held its own beauty.

Once beyond the shoreline trees, the granite shelves of the foothills climbed like behemoth steps toward the mountains. Their deep shade of blue-gray was dotted with stands of evergreens and patched dusky moss. The occasional firs or aspens grew at subtle angles from sea winds. The forest here was not as thick and varied as in the heart of his homeland. With a vast sky overhead, he could see for leagues, until he looked upslope to those stepped foothills. Thankfully, they would not go as far as the peaks. With his back to the camp, Sgäile fished into his tunic's front and pulled out what Brot'ân'duivé had forced on him.

A lump of basalt, worn smooth by river water.

He turned it in his palm, studying its hand-etched patterns and swirls, and not one mark repeated. Between the tangled lines were dots and independent strokes, but he had no idea what the markings meant, and the Greimasg'äh's instructions for its use did not yet make sense.

"Breakfast?" Léshil called from the dead campfire. "Or should we travel a ways first?"

Magiere was already reaching for her hauberk and sword. Chap stood up, yawned widely, and stretched all his limbs, one by one.

Sgäile sighed, tucked away the stone, and returned to his charges. Another unpleasant task awaited before they could move on.

"What's wrong?" Magiere asked.

Sgäile found her watching him suspiciously. He went to his pack and retrieved two long strips of black cloth and unbound the rope tied to the pack.

"Another requirement . . . one you will not like."

Magiere tensed, and Léshil's eyes fixed on the rope.

A direct approach, clean and quick, was best with Magiere. Sgäile held up the strips of cloth.

"We did not travel far before making camp. Our true journey begins today, but only if you adhere to what I require. The place we seek is a guarded secret, known only to some elders of the Äruin'nas and the an'Cróan . . . and those who have proven themselves among the Anmaglâhk. I cannot allow you to know its location."

"What are you talking about?" Léshil asked.

"You must wear blindfolds," Sgäile answered. "All of the way, both in and out. You will swear on your honor not to remove them . . . or I will not take you another step."

Magiere snorted, black hair loose around her pale face and hard eyes.

"This just keeps getting better," she muttered. "You think we'd ever agree to this?"

Chap crept in without a sound.

As Sgäile looked into the eyes of this strange majay-hì from the outside world, he felt even more uncertain than when the dog had faced him down in the skiff. More than once, Chap had demonstrated ways to communicate his expectations. But would the majay-hì now support him in gaining what he needed from Magiere and Léshil?

Sgäile had no wish to defy one so deeply touched with the element of Spirit.

"You will have a guideline," Sgäile said to Léshil, holding up the rope. "The going will be slow, but it will be your loss if I am forced to turn back. So choose now if you will trust me once more, as you did outside my home enclave, when you relinquished your weapons."

"Yes, and that turned out so well!" Magiere snapped. "We were nearly attacked by your clan."

"I protected you then," Sgäile said calmly. "I will protect you now. This journey is for Léshil, and if he agrees, you will abide by it as well. Or we turn back."

Magiere faltered and glanced at Léshil.

Sgäile knew that on some level, in spite of her volatile fits, Magiere could bring herself to trust him. She had done so before.

Léshil had not donned his hauberk yet, and the wind rippled his over-worn shirt. He stood looking from Magiere to Sgäile in doubt, until Chap circled around behind Sgäile.

The majay-hì released a low rumble ending in a snort. He lifted his muzzle and huffed once at Léshil.

Léshil inhaled. "All right . . . but we'll need walking staves as well."

He reached out and took the blindfolds. Magiere turned away, hands on her hips, but offered no refusal.

Sgäile swallowed hard and glanced down at Chap. The majay-hì wrinkled his nose.

"I must speak to him as well . . . alone," Sgäile added.

"To Chap?" Léshil asked. "What about?"

"I understood his agreement," Sgäile answered. "I have learned that much in our time together, as well as how much he understands . . . and that he has his own reasons in all things."

Magiere looked over her shoulder, though she said nothing concerning this open admission that Sgäile was aware of Chap's unique nature. Léshil simply turned away to gather blankets and bedrolls.

Sgäile stepped off toward a cluster of pines and motioned Chap to follow. He dropped to one knee, his back to the camp, and waited as Chap circled around to face him.

"Hear me," Sgäile whispered. "Your kind . . . or those who at least share your form . . . have guarded my people as far back as any can remember. On their blood, you will swear.

"Reveal nothing of the path we take—or what you learn—to anyone. The place we seek must remain hidden and guarded. I take Léshil this way because I gave my word to do so, but I do not know why we are here. If you would have him continue, as you seem to wish, then do not hinder me in this. Swear to me."

Chap shifted his weight, glancing around Sgäile toward his companions. When his eyes turned back on Sgäile, his jowls quivered slightly—almost a snarl but not quite. Finally, he blinked and huffed once.

Sgäile had witnessed this enough times to know what it meant, and he sighed in relief.

"My thanks."

He stood up, looking upslope through the granite shelf foothills. He focused upon the shortest peak and barely made out its sheared and ragged top—the mouth of an old volcanic vent at its crest. From any farther distance, it looked no different from the others.

Chap had already returned to camp by the time Sgäile walked back.

Chane lost track of the passing nights. They trudged east through the Crown Range, into valleys and gorges, and up through saddles and passes between the high peaks, one after another. They paused only when the sky lightened ahead, quickly setting up camp and crawling into their protective tents to fall dormant. They rose each dusk to move on, over and over again.

The five remaining ferals were weakened with starvation. Chane fed them tea every few nights, and less often, Welstiel rationed out small spoonfuls of life force hoarded in his brown glass bottles. And then the terrain began to change.

The sight of dried, bent trees became more common, as well as open ground between the patches of snow. Clumps of grass and weeds and thickets soon filled the landscape, until the monotony of frozen earth and broken rock was almost forgotten.

"The coast cannot be far," Welstiel said one night, gazing ahead through a rocky saddle between two mountainsides. "Stay with the others and make camp. I will scout ahead a little ways."

Chane did not bother answering and turned about, searching for an optimal place to pitch their tents. The dark-haired young woman hovered behind him, always of more use than the others. He wished she could speak, perhaps tell him of her scholarly pursuits before . . .

Welstiel barked at the others to stay in their places and headed off.

Chane pushed away his wandering thoughts, but hunger for intelligent discussion quickly returned. He closed his eyes, envisioning Wynn's oval face and bright eyes.

A patting sound jerked him from his fantasy, and he opened his eyes. The woman had crawled halfway up a rock-strewn slope and was crouching before a sheer outcrop. She slapped the stone to get his attention. Some semblance of wit still remained within her.

Chane headed upslope. She had found a place where he could tie off their canvas in a lean-to against the stone and make them shelter from the sun. She took one folded canvas from him, and they set to work. He had nearly finished when she reached for a piece of rope in his grasp to lash it around a spike driven into the ground.

He suddenly pointed to himself, his voice more rasping and hollow than usual.

"Chane . . . I am Chane."

He did not expect a response. He was only desperate for some intelligible sound after another night of the ferals' animal noises and Welstiel's long silences. But she stopped struggling with the rope and looked up at him.

Her hair was a disheveled tangle, and in the death-pale skin, he spotted hints of a smattering of freckles. She pointed at herself.

"Sa . . . bel . . ."

Those slow syllables, spoken with such difficulty, startled Chane. He crouched down, and she shifted away from him.

"Sabel . . . ," he said, "that is your name?"

A hundred questions filled Chane's head, but he held them at bay. She sniffed the air around him, head tilted, then flicked a hand toward the eastern sky and went back to struggling with the rope.

Chane did not need to look. Gray light grew behind him over the peaks.

The other ferals were fidgeting. The curly-headed man began trying to crawl across the ground with muffled whimpers of frustration. At first, Chane thought they were agitated by the coming sun, but then he saw what the man was crawling toward—and froze in surprise.

Welstiel's pack sat propped against a spindly gray tree.

The well-traveled undead sometimes set it down within sight, but he never left his belongings in any unsafe place. Even in Venjètz, when they had been locked out of the city and lost nearly everything, Welstiel had held on to his pack.

The stocky feral struggled on the ground, watched closely by the others, but he made no more than an inch or two of headway. Exhaustion and starvation drove him against the power of Welstiel's command, as he knew where the bottled life force was kept.

In their time together, Chane and Welstiel had maintained the courtesies and formalities of two noblemen—now turned Noble Dead. Chane had once respected Welstiel's privacy. But he had begun to see Welstiel's pretense of cold-blooded intellect as nothing more than illusory posturing. And as for Chane . . .

He might be nothing more than a beast beneath his own veneer, but he had never sunk to believing his own pretense. Not as Welstiel did.

Chane had willingly served Welstiel's madness in that monastery, but he could not stop seeing these ferals for who they had once been. Like the ghosts of lost scholars haunting dead flesh now filled with nothing but longing and hunger.

A worthless concern just the same. They were lost.

But Chane still did not care to watch Welstiel butcher another one. He jogged downslope, snatched up Welstiel's pack, and turned away.

A hand latched onto his ankle, closing tight enough to make him buckle in pain.

Chane tried to pull free of the crawling monk, but the man would not let go. The feral lay on his stomach, muscles taut and shaking as he fought against his maker's command, but his colorless eyes were locked on the pack in Chane's arms.

Chane stomped down on the man's wrist with his free foot. The feral squealed, and Chane wrenched free of its grip.

All the crystal-eyed ferals around the clearing watched him. When he headed up toward the lean-to tents, even Sabel's gaze fixed on what he was carrying.

Chane felt the bulge of hard objects in the pack, too many to be just the brown glass bottles. His curiosity turned once more to Welstiel's long-hidden possessions.

The closest Chane had come to uncovering their secrets was the night he first saw Welstiel's extra bottles sitting beside the pack. He had not summoned the nerve to dig into it with Welstiel sitting vigil just up the monastery stairs. And the later night on this journey, when he had stolen one brown bottle, he was in too much hurry. He did not hesitate this time, and threw back the cover flap.

Beneath two remaining bottles, wrapped in Welstiel's spare clothing, Chane saw other items. The first three were already familiar.

The walnut box held Welstiel's feeding cup, along with the looped tripod rods and white ceramic bottle. Beside this rested the domed brass plate, which Welstiel used to scry for Magiere, and his frosted light-orb with its three glowing sparks like incandescent fireflies. Chane set these carefully aside.

For the moment, he ignored the two books and a leather-wrapped journal. But the next item he gripped was cold metal, and he glanced nervously toward the glowing horizon. He pulled out a hoop of steel with etched markings.

Its circumference was slightly smaller than a dinner plate. At a loss, he was about to set it down when he smelled an odor akin to charcoal. He turned the steel hoop and dim light from the sky reflected upon its surface—except for the deeply etched lines and symbols. Their inner groves remained black, and he sniffed the object. The charred odor definitely came from the hoop.

He had little time left, for certainly Welstiel would return before full dawn breached the horizon, but Chane's curiosity nagged him. Holding the hoop to his lips, he licked an etched line running evenly around its outer side. It tasted of bitter ash and char. He set the hoop with the other items and peered into the pack. He caught a glint of copper or brass on one rod, and then movement caught his eye.

Sabel crept in, just out of reach, and pointed east as she sniffed the air. She whined and pointed more forcefully.

Welstiel must be returning.

Chane quickly stuffed all the items into the pack, leaving the clothing-wrapped bottles to place on top. He was about to return the pack to its resting place when Welstiel appeared over the top of the saddle ridge, looking haggard and drained. Chane scrambled to the nearest lean-to with Sabel on his heels. He crouched in front of its open end, setting the pack down.

As Welstiel entered the clearing, he gave no notice to the ferals cringing around him in the half-light, and went straight for the spot where he had left his pack. When he discovered it gone, he spun about.

"I had to move it," Chane rasped. "Even under your command, one of them tried to get to it."

Welstiel looked upslope and spotted his pack beside Chane.

"You took your time," Chane added. "Any longer, and you would be greeting the sunrise."

Welstiel frowned, but seemed satisfied.

"Get inside," he ordered, and waved the ferals up to the tents.

They scrambled for cover like dogs, and he picked his way up the slope to Chane.

"We are not far from the coast," he said. "A few more nights at most."

It was good news, but Chane's mind was elsewhere.

Aside from the three short rods he had not had time to inspect, he had heard a dull knock when he set the pack down. Something else rested in its bottom; something that he had not yet seen.

CHAPTER SEVEN

Three days of being dragged behind Sgäile wore Leesil's patience thin. Blindfolded, with a rough walking stick in one hand and a rope gripped in the other, he trudged onward, with Magiere behind him. Chap ranged somewhere nearby, his claws scrabbling over dirt and stone.

Chap assisted with warning barks whenever they strayed or came upon uncertain footing. Sgäile carefully steered them around anything larger, but the going was painfully slow. From time to time, Magiere settled a hand on Leesil's shoulder.

They exchanged few words on this blind side journey, and Leesil wondered why he had ever agreed to this. Why did he keep giving in to whatever bizarre requests Sgäile made?

Privately, Leesil knew why—to find out what Brot'an—and his mother—had arranged.

Had this been Brot'an's plan alone, Leesil would have rejected Sgäile's requirements. But for his mother . . . no, he'd abandoned her to eight years of imprisonment, and he couldn't refuse her now.

Chap barked, brushed against Leesil's leg, and then dashed away. Leesil heard a small cascade of stones tumble beneath the dog's paws.

"What's wrong?" Leesil asked.

"We have to climb another chute between stone sides," Sgäile replied. "The bottom is littered with debris. I will loop the rope through your belts, so you may use both hands to steady yourselves. Toss aside your staves, as you will no longer need them."

"Then we're close?" Magiere asked.

For a moment, Sgäile didn't answer. "Yes," he replied, as if he didn't care to reveal anything.

Leesil tossed aside his staff as Sgäile looped the rope through his belt. He waited as Sgäile did the same for Magiere and then took the lead once more. Leesil stepped forward, and his left foot shifted on loose stones.

Someone snatched his right wrist and guided his hand to the side, pressing it against a vertical wall of rough stone.

"As I said . . . take care," Sgäile admonished.

Leesil felt his way up the granite chute. Before long, he reached out and felt only empty air. Another step and the ground leveled off. But when he tried to hook the blindfold with one finger, Sgäile pulled his hand down.

"No," he said sharply. "Not yet."

Moving onward again, Leesil grew aware of a slight downward decline. Then he smelled dust, and the sounds around him began to reverberate. He realized they had gone underground.

Sgäile began turning them, this way and that.

Leesil tried to count off the lefts and rights, but he lost track after a while. By the time Sgäile halted their procession, Leesil was slightly dizzy from the winding downward path.

"It's warmer here," Magiere said.

She'd been unusually quiet for the past three days. Leesil reached back until he felt her arm.

"We are far enough," Sgäile said. "You may remove the blindfolds."

Leesil ripped off the cloth, blinking as he rubbed his eyes.

For a moment he wasn't sure the blindfold was gone, as everything around him was so dim. Then the world sharpened slightly.

Magiere's pale face was strangely illuminated by an orange glow— Sgäile had already lit a torch. They stood within a natural rock tunnel wider than Leesil's arm span and half again the height he could reach up on his toes.

"We continue," Sgäile said and walked off down the tunnel.

"We're not there yet?" Magiere asked, but he ignored her.

Leesil sighed and trudged on. When he glanced back past Magiere and Chap, he saw nothing, for the tunnel curved sharply into the dark. He couldn't even guess how far or deep they had come.

They walked down winding passages with craggy walls, but the floors were smooth. Leesil's patience was beginning to wane when suddenly the torch's light reached only open space, and he followed Sgäile into a vast cavern. Before he could look about, his gaze caught on the cavern's most prominent feature.

A large oval of shimmering metal was embedded in the cavern's far wall.

Magiere pushed around him, heading straight for it. Leesil followed with Sgäile and Chap trailing more slowly. When he was within arm's reach, Magiere ran her gloved hand over the metal.

Leesil saw the barely visible, razor-straight seam. The oval split down the center into two doors, but he saw no handle or hinges, or other way to open them. Orange-yellow torchlight glimmered on their perfect polished surfaces, a bleached silver tone too light for steel or precision metals. Leesil recognized the material.

These doors were made of the same metal as anmaglâhk blades.

"They're warm," Magiere whispered.

Leesil put his hand upon the metal. More than warm, they were nearly hot.

"Turn away," Sgäile said wearily.

"Why . . . how do they open?" Leesil asked.

He heard cloth crumple on the cavern floor, and the sound of a blade sliding across leather.

Chap growled.

"I said turn away, now!" Sgäile commanded, and his voice echoed around the cavern.

Leesil turned quickly and dropped one hand to a punching blade.

Sgäile stood before his fallen cloak, his glistening features strained, as if any word or action would cost him. He held a stiletto, its metal gleaming as bright as the doors.

Chap tensed behind Sgäile, ready to take him down if he moved an inch.

The only memory he caught in Sgäile's mind was a brief glimpse of this place—and Sgäile waiting frozen in dread as the silver-white doors began to swing open. The memory faded too quickly, and now it seemed Sgäile would not tolerate either Magiere or Leesil knowing how the portal opened.

"Please . . . step back," Sgäile said more deliberately. "And turn away."

Magiere's hand wrapped around her falchion's hilt, and she didn't move.

Chap was sick of dealing with anmaglâhk and their paranoia. But all that mattered was finding out what waited beyond these doors—what Brot'an had been scheming up this time. Chap circled wide around Sgäile and huffed once at his companions.

"What makes you so obliging to him?" Magiere asked, but she kept her eyes on Sgäile.

"This is ridiculous," Leesil said. "Sgäile, just open the doors!"

"Keep quiet," she said. "You're the one who let him blindfold us."

Chap huffed again. They had come all this way, and he was not about to turn back. He hopped at Magiere and nipped her breeches at the knee.

Magiere jerked her leg back. "You watch it!"

But she finally turned away, and Leesil joined her with a sidelong glance at Chap.

Sgäile's expression remained tense, but he did not ask Chap to turn away. He merely approached the door, stiletto in hand, and then hesitated with the blade point held up.

"Your oath . . . ," he said, "do not forget."

He touched the blade's tip upon the portal so lightly it did not even click. A low grating creak began, and Chap watched as the seam split.

"Move away," Sgäile told him and sheathed the stiletto.

Chap backpedaled toward Magiere and Leesil as Sgäile also retreated.

The doors separated, each swinging outward as they ground across the cavern's level stone. A wall of heated air rushed out to strike Chap's face, and the cavern's temperature rose sharply with a stench like burning coal. He choked on the hot air filling his lungs.

"You will adjust in a moment," Sgäile said, but he had a hand over his own mouth and nose.

The unpleasant burning in Chap's throat slowly became tolerable. Leesil's face was flushed, though he seemed unhurt. Magiere let out a strangled cough and buckled to her knees, fighting for air.

Leesil grabbed her shoulders. "Magiere!"

A few more breaths and she nodded that she was all right.

"You might have warned us," she gasped.

"Apologies," Sgäile offered, but his face was as flushed as Leesil's.

As Sgäile retrieved the torch, Chap circled back to stand between the wide doors. Beyond them stretched a wide passage, and the farther on Chap looked, the darker it became. Sgäile's torch cast only the barest glistening points of light on its craggy walls. The heated air made it difficult for Chap to breathe.

"You must be joking!" Leesil said.

"It will not be comfortable," Sgäile warned. "But we will survive."

With that, he stepped past Chap into the tunnel.

Chap followed, and the hot stone under his pads grew more unpleasant with each step. He heard Leesil behind as Magiere came up on his left. She looked weak and faint. Her dhampir nature worked well for her in the cold, but it did not seem to help in this scorching place.

"You've been down here before?" Magiere rasped.

Sgäile shook his head. "Only as far as the doors, once . . . with my past teacher, before I received his assent to take up full service to my people."

Both Leesil and Sgäile slowly adapted, though their faces began to run with sweat. Magiere panted, trying to bear the heat and keep up. Chap stayed close to her as Sgäile worked his way along the uneven passage. It narrowed suddenly at the top of a carved stone stairway.

A dim red-orange glow from below barely illuminated the close walls. Sgäile set aside his torch. The light increased slightly as they descended, as did the heat in the air. They went down for a long while, stopping once for water. Leesil poured some into a tin cup he always carried for Chap, but the water had grown so warm it offered little relief.

Chap kept a close watch on Magiere, though she stayed on her feet. He reached inside her mind and called up memories of their journey through the Blade Range . . . of snow and freezing wind. She frowned, but this time did not snarl at him to get out of her head. Instead, she put her hand on his back.

"You all right?" Leesil asked her.

"Keep going," she rasped.

Just when Chap thought their descent might never end, Sgäile stepped down onto a landing. Chap peered around the elf's legs through a rough opening in the mountain's rock. Through it, orange-red light brightened slightly, and the opening seemed like the mouth of a dwindling hearth in a dim room.

Chap stepped through and halted at the sight before him.

A wide plateau ran a gradual slant away from the stairway's portal. At its distant edge, red light erupted out of a massive fissure in the mountain's belly, like a gash wider than a river. Smoke drifted up into glowing red air from deep in the earth.

"Wait . . . here . . . ," Sgäile breathed with great effort.

He advanced with slow and heavy steps but went less than halfway to the plateau's edge. He stopped, digging beneath his tunic, and drew something out.

"What's he doing?" Leesil whispered.

Sgäile cocked his arm and heaved. A small dark object arced out and over the plateau's lip to vanish into the fissure. Chap had seen this object in Sgäile's flickering memories—a smooth basalt stone etched with curving lines, sharp strokes, and dots. Sgäile returned but stopped to rest, hunched over with his hands braced upon his knees. He blinked against the sweat running down his forehead.

"Now we wait," he said.

Leesil stumbled closer. "How long? For what?"

Sgäile only shook his head.

They stood there so long that Chap wanted to collapse from the heat. But he feared he might not rise again. Then he heard a soft scraping.

Like metal upon stone, it carried faintly across the half-cavern plateau. Chap looked out beyond Leesil, searching. The plateau's edge was a dark silhouette against the gorge's burning light.

A tiny part of that dark jagged line bulged and moved.

Leesil desperately wanted out of this place, and even more so when he glanced at Magiere.

Eyes half-closed, she gasped for air, and she hardly perspired at all—which was a bad sign. And Chap appeared about to drop with all four legs quaking.

Leesil was furious with himself for ever agreeing to let Sgäile bring them here. Whatever Brot'an and his mother wanted didn't matter anymore. He took a step toward Magiere.

In the stillness, a faint scrape carried along the walls, like a blade scratching stone. Chap lifted his head to stare, and Leesil swung about, hands fumbling for his winged blades.

His gaze lighted first upon Sgäile, who held no weapons but straightened with an effort and looked off toward the glowing fissure's right end.

"Sgäile?" Leesil said.

"Keep . . . your weapons . . . sheathed," Sgäile managed to say.

Magiere stumbled in next to Leesil, hand on her falchion's hilt.

A bulge grew at the precipice's edge, taking form in movement.

At first it was no more than a rippling smudge backlit by red-orange air. Small and blacker than the stone, it crawled up onto the plateau from out of the red depths. Leesil barely made out a pair of thin, spindly arms as it crept forward, dragging something behind.

Its size was difficult to gauge, but by the way the little black shadow hunkered, Leesil guessed it wouldn't be much taller than Chap, if it stood up. And then twin horizontal slits opened in its blotch of a head.

Two eyes, like white-hot coals in the dark, fixed on Leesil.

It crawled a little farther, dragging the bulk of a sack half its size. The charcoal-colored woolly baggage shimmered as if laced with fibers of black metal or glass. Thin smoke rose from the bundle to dissipate in the gorge's heat-rippled air.

"What is—?" Magiere began.

"Chein'âs," Sgäile cut in. "The Burning Ones."

But there was only one, and the little thing fumbled with its sack. It paused, turning searing eyes upslope, and a small maw opened beneath them.

A grinding shriek erupted across the stone plateau.

Leesil cringed as the sound pierced his ears. His skull and bones seemed to vibrate sharply in his flesh.

"Go!" Sgäile ordered, hands pressed over his ears. "Whatever it has . . . is for you, Léshil."

Chap rumbled and took a few shaky steps forward, and Magiere clutched at Leesil's arm.

"It's all right," he whispered, peeling off her fingers.

Magiere trembled but didn't try to grab him again.

Leesil crept down the plateau, closing on the black little thing with lantern eyes. As he drew nearer, its form became clearer.

No larger than a naked child of six or seven years, it squatted there with its scrawny arms and legs folded. The whole of its body was covered in ebony-toned leathery skin. Thin digits sprouting from splayed hands ended in short obsidian claws. Its oversized head was featureless except for the slit mouth, the vertical cuts of small nostrils, and its glowing eyes. Instead of ears, it bore two small depressions on the sides of its skull.

Leesil was still well beyond reach when it began to shiver.

It cringed away from him, clutching itself like a deformed and naked child caught in a frigid winter wind. The closer Leesil tried to get, the more the little thing quivered—as if he were the source of cold. Leesil stopped and crouched, waiting.

With a shudder, it uttered a soft hiss like water thrown on a griddle. Both of its clawed hands reached into the charcoal-colored bag, and Leesil caught a glint of metal inside turning red in the fissure's light. The little one chucked two long pieces of curved metal across the plateau floor.

Leesil quickly scooted back as they clanged across the stone before him. Focusing sharply as the objects settled, he stared in shock.

Twin winged blades lay in the dark before him, so much like the ones he carried strapped to his thighs. A matched set, mirrored opposites but alike in make.

His own blades had been assembled by a master weaponer in Bela, made from sketches he'd drawn himself. But these were not steel. Even in the dark and the chasm's unnatural light, they shimmered too cleanly. They glinted like silver mirrors—like the sheer perfect doors to this cavern—like the stilettos of the Anmaglâhk.

Their wings would stretch down the outside of his forearms, but unlike his, these turned slightly outward at the back end, slender and graceful. The spades extending in front of their grips were thin and fiercely pointed, perhaps slightly longer than his own.

The oval grips hadn't yet been wrapped in leather.

Partway down each wing, half-circles sprouted sideways. Round in shape rather than flat and sharp, they might brace around his forearm and steady the weapons in his grips.

Leesil raised his eyes to the shuddering little creature. His mother had never seen his weapons closely, especially not while in use. The only other who had—who knew that Leesil would come here—was Brot'an.

Leesil's anger began to eat at his insides.

"Take them!" Sgäile hissed from upslope.

Leesil glanced over his shoulder at Sgäile's shocked and lost expression. It was plain the man had expected something else—perhaps stilettos like his own. Then Leesil saw Magiere watching him as she knelt beside Chap.

He had to get her out of here.

He snatched up both blades with one hand, nearly dropping them from the heat in their metal, and then tucked them under his arm as he stumbled upslope. He grabbed Magiere's arm.

Sgäile held out both hands toward the small being down the plateau. He began speaking softly in Elvish, his words filled with strange reverence.

Chap was already limping toward the stairway as Leesil hauled Magiere up. Sgäile backed slowly and turned to follow.

Another metallic screech tore at Leesil's ears.

Chap went deaf for an instant.

He wheeled about, nearly toppling beside Sgäile, and looked down the plateau. The small creature's sound still rang in his head, and he could not help barking at it to stop.

"What now?" Leesil shouted.

Sgäile just stared toward the fissure's edge in silence.

The black visitor seemed somehow familiar to Chap, but heat made his mind hazy. Perhaps the memory of this small being was something else the Fay had taken from him at his birth—or was it something he had seen since walking this mortal world? He could recall nothing regarding these "burning" beings—these Chein'âs.

The creature hunched again over its bag, becoming a lumped silhouette, and then its forelimb lashed up and out.

A metallic object flickered with red light as it tumbled from the creature's pointed digits. It fell to clatter and clang across stone. Before Chap could try to make out what it was, the creature's hand shot out again.

This time the sound was thicker—heavy and dull—and the second object did not glint like the first.

"What now?" Leesil repeated, releasing Magiere to head downslope.

Sgäile shook his head, his expression anxious, even wary. "I do not understand."

The creature threw its head back, eyes closing as its maw opened. Another shriek echoed off the half-cavern walls and through Chap's bones. His ears still rang as the creature raised a clawed hand, hissing like fire consuming water.

It reached out and gouged downward, seeming to claw the air toward itself. The gesture was aimed at Chap's charges.

Leesil had tried to return, but the dark little one responded in denial. Its call was not for him.

Chap looked fearfully at Magiere. What did it want with her?

Sgäile had only been ordered to bring Leesil. Whatever Brot'an's scheme, he could not have known Magiere would bully her way into this side journey. What had the black visitor thrown out upon the plateau?

The creature clutched the air again, its gesture aimed at Magiere.

Magiere felt chilled inside, though the air was hot in her lungs. The clash of sensations left her dizzy and weak.

Sgäile stumbled a few steps downslope, shaking his head. But when he looked back at her, his sweat-glistened face twisted in a grimace.

Magiere had seen that look before, the first time Sgäile had watched her crawl under a blanket next to Leesil, and the day he'd looked into her eyes when she'd lost all self-control in Nein'a's clearing.

The small, dark being from the fissure's depths called to her . . . waited for her.

This turn of events sickened Sgäile as much as it stunned him. Suddenly, he waved her on.

"Go . . . now!" he snapped.

"I'll take you," Leesil whispered to her.

"No!" Sgäile commanded and swallowed dryly. "She must go on her own."

Chap pushed in against Magiere's legs. She settled a hand on his back and felt him quivering. As he advanced, she followed his lead. Sgäile took two unstable steps, but as always, he balked at interfering with a majay-hì.

Magiere burrowed her fingers in the scruff of Chap's neck. As he led her onward, she fixed upon a shimmer of red light on the plateau's stone. In one final step, her boot toe planted before it. She collapsed to her knees and felt along the stone.

When her fingers touched the bright spot, she snatched them back from its uncomfortable heat. Then she saw the object more clearly through her blurry sight.

The dagger was as long as her forearm, its base above the guard wider than a clenched fist. The tang sprouting below the guard, where a hilt would be affixed, was bare of wood or wrapped leather. That piece of narrow metal ran straight to the round pommel. The blade was two-thirds the length of a shortsword—a war blade. From its fine tapering edges to its point, its pure finished metal gleamed silver-white and perfect . . . like the doors Sgäile had opened in the upper cavern . . . like his stiletto.

Chap hacked and swallowed, and Magiere looked up, her eyes itching as they dried in the heat. The dog padded slowly to the second object, and lowered his muzzle. Magiere crawled forward on her hands and knees.

Beside Chap lay a circlet of ruddy golden metal, too red for brass and too dark for gold. Thick and heavy looking, the circumference was larger than a helmet, and it had strange markings upon it that Magiere couldn't see clearly. About a fourth of its circle appeared to be missing, and Magiere willed her sight to clear.

The circlet wasn't broken. That gap was part of its making. Small knobs protruded inward from its open ends, pointing straight across the break from one to the other.

Magiere wobbled on all fours and tried to lift her head.

The black leathery being watched her, and then suddenly raised a clawed hand to the side of its earless head. Long fingers traced down its skull, as if combing through hair it didn't have. The gesture pulled a memory into Magiere's thoughts.

One winged, frail female—a silf—not much larger than this thing, had appeared at her trial before the council of the an'Cróan. And that feathered being had run delicate taloned fingers through Magiere's hair.

A crackling hiss leaked from the black creature's lipless mouth, and its phosphorescent eyes rolled closed. It threw back its head, covering its flat face with both hands. The hands slipped downward, exposing its mouth gaping in a face stretched by anguish.

A mournful bellow rose from its convulsing chest, like a horn blown rough and weak.

The sound vibrated in the stone beneath Magiere's hands and knees, making her nauseated. As her arms buckled, the last thing she saw was its gaping mouth.

In place of teeth were opposing dark ridges, the shade of dull iron.

Somewhere, she'd seen such before, and the familiarity made her shrivel inside.

Chap watched the tiny visitor lift its face upward, away from Magiere, and bellow in grief.

This creature recognized Magiere, or knew of her.

Why else would it have brought her tokens—a weapon and a broken hoop of mysterious metal? Neither Brot'an nor Nein'a could have known Magiere would come here. These gifts had come directly from the Chein'âs.

But the sight of Magiere seemed to wound this one from within, and then she collapsed.

"Magiere!" Leesil called out.

Before Chap could scramble to her side, the visitor wailed again. As the echo faded and Chap shook off the pain in his head, it dashed toward the plateau's edge.

Chap froze as it leaped out over the massive fissure.

The small being did not plummet; it appeared to float upon the air. Red light engulfed the spindly black form as it swirled upon the rising heat, like an insect in a desert whirlwind. It began to tumble downward.

Chap lunged to the plateau's edge before it vanished, reaching for any memories he might catch.

Fire erupted in his mind.

It burned through Chap until he felt only stinging pain, and the cavern vanished before his eyes in a flash of searing white.

Leesil scrambled toward Magiere as Chap's piercing yelp struck his ears.

The dog fell twitching upon the stone. Chap's prone form shuddered and writhed as if he were trying to thrash free of something.

Leesil closed on Magiere and grabbed the back of her hauberk, but when he reached out for Chap, the dog lay too far off. He flipped Magiere over, put his ear close to her mouth, and heard her low breaths. She was alive, but Chap's piercing whimpers continued. Leesil went for the dog, and a hand snatched his shoulder, jerking him back.

"I will get him," Sgäile shouted. "Gather Magiere's gifts and take her out!"

"What's wrong with Chap?" Magiere whispered.

Leesil swung around to find her eyes barely open.

He didn't mind that Sgäile told him what to do. He wasn't even interested in the strange objects lying beside Magiere. All that mattered was getting her and Chap out of this place, before he collapsed from the heat as well.

"I don't know," he answered, and snatched up the earthy golden loop and the hiltless blade. "Sgäile will bring him."

Leesil hooked the loop over one shoulder, holding the dagger along with his new blades under the same arm. He hoisted Magiere, slipping her arm around his neck, and wrapped his free hand around her waist. Neither of them looked back as they hobbled toward the passage and the stone steps.

Sgäile dropped beside Chap's whimpering form, and his knees ground harshly on the stone. He grabbed hold of the dog, whispering over and over, "Ancestors, protect him . . . I beg you!"

Chap squirmed wildly, and he was heavier than anticipated. Twice Sgäile shifted his grip until he finally gathered the dog in his arms. The intense heat had no power against the pain of Sgäile's guilt.

He had brought outsiders before the Chein'âs. He had brought a pale-skinned predator to this place, and watched as she was "gifted" along with Léshil. And now Chap—who was touched with the ancient Spirit—had fallen in agony. And Sgäile could not fathom any of this.

All because he could not refuse Brot'ân'duivé.

Each day brought more confusion and cast him into impossible circumstances, until he could do little more than cling blindly to his faith. But he could not bear it if this ancient spirit died in his arms.

"Please, be still," Sgäile whispered in Chap's ear, heaving the dog up and running for the passage.

Chap's bones became coals searing his flesh from within. All around, fire and glowing hot stone half-blinded him. Agony in his heart and mind rose from this stolen memory of the small black visitor from the chasm.

He saw others of its kind who crawled and scampered among mounds of smoking stone surrounding a molten river. Some swam within the orange fluid, small blackened creatures in a wide sluggish stream almost too bright to look upon.

Lost in the memory, Chap saw his own dark and leathery hands. Spindly fingers ended in glossy black claws that caressed the hot ledge on which he crouched.

Please, be still.

The words came like a whisper from somewhere inside of Chap, and his pain began to dwindle, until he felt only the pleasant heat under his black hands and feet.

Then fear rose at the creatures' metallic wails.

Small ebony bodies raced and leaped about the chasm like rodents scattering along an alley to hide. The fissure's charred and smoking walls undulated faintly, becoming roiling black. Soft points of light emerged and flowed across them. Chap lost focus as something new caught his eyes.

It—he—floated in the heat-rippled air above the molten river. The air churned in whirling white-gray about the figure drifting forward.

The surface of his long, hooded robe swirled like oil, and the molten river's red light shimmered on the faint symbols scripted upon its folds. The upper half of the face within the hood was covered by a mask of aged leather that ended above a withered mouth and emaciated chin.

The mask had no eye slits, but the decrepit figure twitched its head about, watching the small black ones flee in terror.

Chap's own memory overlaid the stolen one, and he tasted flesh and blood in his teeth.

Ubâd, mad necromancer and engineer of Magiere's birth, floated in an airy vessel made from his enslaved spirits. Pieces of that wispy gray-white globe peeled away in ribbons that dove and harried the fleeing figures. And one struck true.

A small black body screeched in torment as one of Ubâd's spirits passed through its gaunt chest. Ubâd descended and snatched it by the neck.

Chap leaped forward upon black hands and feet.

He bounded from one stone to the next along the river's shore, trying to close on Ubâd. The dark-robed madman began to rise upward in his spirit cocoon, lifting into hot air. Chap clawed his way up the fissure wall and leaped outward.

No, the visitor leaped for its captured kin.

Chap relived the black visitor's memory, as it had tried to reach the one Ubâd seized—the one who had been butchered in the keep of Magiere's father to make her birth possible. His black hands caught in the necromancer's robe.

Ubâd's face turned downward as he squeezed his captive in his bony grip. His vaporous shell began to turn in a vortex around Chap's narrow black arms.

Intense cold ate away all the heat in Chap's body.

Chap's grip broke from the robe as a metallic scream tore from his throat. And he was falling.

Awaken . . . please do not die . . . come back to me!

Another whisper echoed inside of him. He heard it an instant before his spindly black body hit the scorching molten river.

Chap opened his eyes with a convulsive shudder.

He stared into amber eyes sunk deep in a dark-skinned face coated with sweat.

Sgäile sighed raggedly. His head drooped for an instant before he turned on his knees to look the other way.

"He is awake!" Sgäile called.

Chap saw the world tilted sideways where he lay with his head resting on a smooth stone floor. His vision was blurred, but he made out a silver metal oval. The doors were closed, sealing off the passage to the burning chasm below. They were back in the entrance cavern far above.

"How fares Magiere?" Sgäile asked.

Leesil half-sat, half-lay behind her, his arm wrapped around her waist. She breathed in long slow gasps, but her eyes opened now and again.

"She'll make it," Leesil said. "But we need more water for both of them. And we should head further up, out of this heat."

Sgäile nodded agreement. He dug into his pack and pulled out a water bottle. At his shift of position, Chap spotted the pile of metal items on the floor halfway to Magiere and Leesil. His gaze slowly cleared, until he made out the twin winged blades, the hiltless dagger, and the strange arc of earthy golden metal. The last item troubled him most, but he focused on the dagger.

He and his companions had stumbled upon another of the lost races—

the Úirishg—one of five nonhuman species that were thought to be but a myth.

Like the séyilf at Magiere's trial, that one chein'âs upon the plateau had known Magiere and perhaps mistook her for some strangely formed kin. It had brought her tokens—or was there more to those gifts?

The visitor had seen one of its own taken long ago, and knew its lost companion would never return. Was that dagger a token of recognition for the shared blood that had been spilled at Magiere's conception?

Or was it a plea for vengeance?

One that the little visitor, or all the Chein'âs, could never gain for themselves, locked away in the searing depths of the earth.

Chap closed his eyes. There was no way he could have offered solace. No way to tell the visitor that he had already torn out Ubâd's throat.

The dreamer fell through vast darkness, and then suddenly stood upon a black desert. Dunes began to roll on all sides, becoming immense writhing coils covered in glinting black scales.

"Show me the castle," the dreamer demanded.

Flight through a night sky resumed once more.

Here . . . it is here.

The voice rose as the dreamer tumbled downward. High mountain peaks of perpetual ice loomed all around like a jagged-toothed maw. In its gullet was an immense sunken plateau crusted by snow. A speck within gained size, and for an instant the dreamer saw it become the six-towered castle bordered by stone walls.

The white plateau rushed up in the dreamer's sight and winked out.

But no impact followed in crashing down.

The dreamer suddenly stood before high arched gates. Mirrored twins of ornate iron curls joined together at their high tops in an arched point. Mottled with rust, they were still sound and had not yielded to time. Beyond them, the castle's iron doors rose atop a wide cascade of stone steps.

At a caw, the dreamer looked up. A raven sat upon the high gates.

The dreamer turned from the distraction, looking back to the steps and doors. Something white moved past a low window in one front tower.

It was a woman. Before she vanished beyond the window's far side, the dreamer saw a face like snow and coal black hair.

South . . . you must travel south.

"I am," the dreamer answered.

No . . . you do not even try!

"How . . . when will I find it? When will you leave me alone?"

Succeed . . . and there will be no more need for dreams. Lead on, my child . . . great sister of the dead.

Magiere opened her eyes wide and lurched from under the blanket, sucking air as she looked wildly about the night.

She still lay beside Leesil where they were camped for the night on their journey back toward the shore. Chap was curled upon Leesil's cloak near the dwindling campfire, and even Sgäile appeared sound asleep. Just beyond him lay the pack containing the "gifts" from the scorching cavern.

The blindfolded trek down the granite foothills should have been quicker than the ascent, but they'd stopped often to rest. None of them had the same strength with which they'd begun this side journey.

Tomorrow they would reach the ship and return to their voyage, guided only by Magiere's instinct. She stared southward into the dark. All she wanted was to run until she found . . . whatever she had to find . . . and got free of this driving urge.

Magiere lay down and rested her head on Leesil's outstretched arm. She scooted in until she felt his chest against her back. But when she closed her eyes, she saw the castle of her dream—and a pale-faced woman passing behind an ice-glazed window.

Chane had caught strengthening whiffs of sea air for the past four nights. Tonight, the salt breeze grew stronger. The ferals smelled it, too, and became restless, shuffling about each other.

Welstiel suddenly halted and pointed ahead. "There . . . look over the slope of trees!"

Chane craned his neck, eyes wide as his sight expanded.

At first he saw only a flat plain in the distance, impossibly flat. Then he caught the faint ripples upon its surfaces. Tiny shapes of waves rippled upon open water stretching to the night's horizon.

Then another scent filled his head.

Life—human life.

The curly-headed feral began hissing and spitting, and the two younger males wailed and darted forward. Chane knew the smell would be even more intoxicating for them; it was all they desired. The silver-headed man and Sabel whimpered in excitement.

"Stop!" Welstiel ordered. "All of you hold!"

Like puppets jerked by their strings, the scampering monks halted. One young male fell to his face, unable to keep his feet as his rush ended. Sabel buckled to the ground, rocking back and forth on her haunches as her whimpers of joy became panting moans.

Their desperation wormed into Chane. He had gone longer without feeding than any of them, and he wanted blood.

"Follow me," Welstiel said to Chane, and then looked briefly at his minions. "Do not move from this place until I tell you." He pointed toward Chane. "Or he does."

Chane followed Welstiel through the sparse trees. Every step along the forested ridge intensified the scent of life on the salted breeze—and the smoky odor of a campfire.

Welstiel finally dropped and flattened on his stomach. He crawled forward as Chane did likewise, and they peered over a cliff above the shore.

Chane was not surprised to see the men below, gathered around a campfire in a sandy beach cove, but the ship in the waters beyond was another matter. A three-masted schooner was harbored not far into the water, and two long skiffs had been dragged up the beach. Each was half-filled with barrels.

"Who are they?" Chane whispered.

Welstiel continued to watch the men below, so Chane returned to studying them more closely—six sailors in varied worn clothes. He could smell sweat along with their life force. Two returned to the skiffs, loading a barrel. Judging by the way they hefted it, the barrel was full of something. He could just barely hear others speaking around the fire, but he did not recognize their language.

"Why have they come here?" he whispered.

"Seeking fresh water, I believe," Welstiel answered. "The tall one in the leather jerkin said something about their supply being contaminated."

"You speak their language?"

"Not well. I have not heard it in many years, not since my father was . . ."

Welstiel fell silent.

Chane's curiosity was piqued. He knew little of Welstiel's living days; only that the man was not a native of this continent. And that Welstiel's father had worked his way up through the ranks of Droevinkan nobility.

"I can pick out a few words," Welstiel finally added. "There must be fresh water near here. Seafarers keep careful track of such things, though I wonder about any human this far north, so near the Elven Territories."

"They will have more to contend with than water shortage," Chane said, true hunger mounting upon his longing. "We should bring the others."

"No, this is better than I hoped for," Welstiel answered, and lifted his chin toward the anchored ship. "Magiere travels this coast too swiftly to be on land. That schooner will be useful to us."

Chane couldn't believe what he was hearing and looked more closely at the rough seamen below. Some carried curved daggers tucked into their belts, and a few had squat cutlasses sheathed at their sides. Most were plainly dressed, though some had vests and tunics of leather, a lightweight armor for seafarers.

"I doubt they are interested in passengers," Chane said dryly. "We could feed on them, revitalize your followers, and take the ship. But I have little knowledge of sailing, and likely your monks would know even less. Do you?"

Welstiel shook his head, eying the cove floor. "No, we will need the crew . . . and count on their greed to favor us."

He drew a pouch from his cloak, jingling the coins inside, and Chane stared at it blankly.

They had lost most of their money back in Venjètz, or so he thought, and used what was left to purchase horses and supplies. But then Chane had never inquired, as they had never needed coins in the mountains.

"Where did you get that?" he asked.

Welstiel loosened the pouch's string. "From a chest at the monastery."

"You intend to bargain our way onto the schooner?" Chane said in surprise. "I doubt the monks had enough with which to tempt those sailors."

"And I doubt," Welstiel replied, "they will pay attention to anything but the clink of coins . . . and the possibility that we might have more."

Chane scooted back from the ridge and sat up.

Getting out of this forsaken range was an attractive prospect, but he saw holes in Welstiel's plan. Unless Welstiel knew these seafarers' language better than he suggested, they could end up embroiled in a fight before a bargain was struck. The sailors below looked more likely to rob wayfarers out of the wilderness than to offer rescuing passage to the nearest port. And even so, how did Welstiel think they would react when his monks emerged from the dark, full of witless gibbering and hungry stares?

"We will circle around and search for a path down the ridge," Welstiel said.

Chane shook his head but followed. In the end, he believed they would still have the ship—with no one left who could sail it.

CHAPTER EIGHT

Welstiel poured most of the monastery's coins into his own pouch, but he kept out a small sum of silver pennies.

Chane watched in puzzlement. "How did monks obtain that much?"

"A wealthy patron, perhaps," Welstiel suggested, but he did not care.

He filled the emptied pouch with small stones, adding the pennies on top so the pouch would clink when jostled.

"What are you doing?" Chane asked.

"Just follow me."

Welstiel led the way around the cliff until they found gradual sod shelves leading down to the beach. During their descent, he contemplated the best way to approach these marauders.

Though he could pick out a few words of the mishmash Ylladon tongue, he could not truly speak it. Perhaps they'd once had a central language, or several, from whatever long-forgotten descendants had first come to this continent's shores. Now they spoke a conglomeration of differing dialects fostered among their individual city-states. Some factions spoke old Droevinkan as well.

In his living youth, Welstiel had only had brief contact with the Ylladon, when his father came to seek his fortune on this continent. They stayed in one city-state, but his father had quickly realized that the lack of a stable hierarchy offered little opportunity for him. The Ylladon raided each other's territories as often as they raided any outsiders' they could reach.

They were parasites. Slavers, pirates, and thieves by the very make of their fragmented culture, but to call them unintelligent was rash. Their way of life had survived as long as the continent's western nations, and perhaps longer.

Still, he could think of only one reason these sailors might travel so far north. And trying to hit the lower settlements of the Elven Territories marked them as foolhardy, from Welstiel's perspective.

"Keep your sword sheathed unless I say otherwise," he advised.

Chane followed in silence as they stepped onto the beach above the cove, and Welstiel rounded the point until he spotted the campfire. He called out a greeting in old Droevinkan.

Men scurried around the beached skiffs, then poised, waiting as he entered the firelight's reach. All six drew cutlasses and thick knives, except the one with the horn bow aimed at him. In their mismatched attire and oiled-down hair, each was nonetheless dressed for efficiency in duty. Most wore leather vestments or tunics and either hide or heavy canvas breeches. Half had studded or steel-ribbed bracers on their forearms.

They were surprisingly robust; none appeared malnourished or inebriated. They quickly shifted positions, two flanking Welstiel on the shoreward side to back him and Chane into the water if needed.

"Be at ease," Welstiel called, and held up both gloved hands.

The pebble-filled pouch dangled by its string hooked around his fingers, but the Ylladon did not lower their weapons. One sailor between the skiffs glanced toward the campfire as another man stepped forward from beyond the flames.

Somewhere in his late twenties, he wore a close-trimmed beard and was rather short of stature. He barked at the others, but his gaze never left Welstiel. This man had not drawn a weapon. The sheath on his hip was too narrow for a sailor's cutlass, perhaps made for a saber instead. The sleeves of his azure shirt beneath the quilted and padded leather vest were a cleaner cut than the rest.

"Stop there," he said in the old Droevinkan, his words strangely sharpened by the accent of his native tongue.

Welstiel halted, as did Chane.

"You are the captain?" Welstiel asked, and jingled the pouch. "We seek passage on your vessel."

"Passage?" the man repeated.

He looked Welstiel up and down, snorted, and then cocked his head toward one of the two who had flanked Welstiel at the beach top.

"He captain," the young man said in his broken speech. "But he not speak your words. I am helm."

"Helmsman?" Welstiel corrected politely.

The short helmsman said nothing as the captain took a few steps down the sloping sand.

He was the tallest and bulkiest, and shirtless beneath his cloak and tunic. His thick leather vestment was adorned with spaced steel studs shaped like diamonds. Heavy armor for a seafarer.

His hair and face were hidden beneath a helm of hardened, shaped leather, with three evenly spaced flat iron strips across its skull top. The long nose guard and wide cheek and jaw wings were reinforced as well. This left only two eye loops connected to the narrow opening exposing the middle of his mouth and the front his chin. Welstiel found it difficult to gauge the man's expression.

The captain never looked at the pouch—only at Welstiel—and inched forward with a thick short sword poised in his grip. Clearly these men thought it easier to take Welstiel's money, and his attempt at barter was not even worth amusement.

Welstiel flipped the pouch up with his fingers and caught its falling bulk in his palm.

The captain paused, but still his gaze did not shift. Welstiel opened the pouch, pinching out silver coins into plain sight.

"We need passage for seven."

"Seven?" the helmsman repeated, and rattled off something to his captain.

The captain growled a few words to the man behind him. That sailor scurried off the way Welstiel had come. Another bolted along the cove's southern curve.

"Welstiel!" Chane hissed. "What are you doing?"

He stepped in, pushing back his cloak to expose his longsword, and kept shifting his head, watching all the sailors still in sight.

Again the captain appeared unimpressed, but he took a few quick glances. Not at the pouch and coins but toward the cove's far reaches, where his two men had run off.

Welstiel slowly pushed back his cloak to expose his own sword.

The captain did not seem foolish, and the mention of seven in Welstiel's party had made him wary. A piercing whistle carried from the north, and then another from the south. The captain clenched the shortsword's hilt hesitantly.

Welstiel took another step forward. The helmsman closed quickly on him, but Chane moved in to block his path.

"Let him come," Welstiel instructed.

Chane backed up one step and held his ground with a soft hiss.

"I offer more as well," Welstiel said, waiting as the helmsman translated for his captain. "Something rarer than coin."

He slowly swung his pack off his shoulder and dug inside it. At the glimmer rising from the opened pack, the captain raised his sword, its point reaching out.

Welstiel lifted his globe of three flittering lights.

"Tell him the lights never go out," he said, and waited while the helmsman explained.

The captain reached out and wrapped thick fingers around the globe. He lifted it before his face.

Its light flooded the shadowed openings of his helm. He did not appear remotely awed, but his interest was clear. A good light source requiring no fire was useful to a seafarer.

Welstiel held up both pouches and shook the one from the monastery, so that its few silver pennies made noise.

"A third now . . . the rest when we reach the first port on your route."

The helmsman repeated, and the captain returned a question.

"Why is you out here, where is nothing?" the helmsman asked.

"Not your concern," Welstiel returned. "My people will stay below deck, and we are not to be disturbed. We have our own food and water, so we will be no more burden than the rest of your . . . cargo. Passage is all we require."

The captain and helmsman broke into a quick and sharp exchange, and then the captain looked at Welstiel and nodded once. The helmsman held out his hand, and Welstiel rendered up his smaller pouch containing nearly all his true coin. When he reached for the globe, not offered as down payment, the captain curled it back in his grip and turned away.

The helmsman merely smirked.

Welstiel understood this game. The captain accepted the bargain, but now he would wait. Once his passengers were aboard in the hold, it would be far easier to take all of their possessions. No one would even find the bodies, sunk to the sea bottom.

"My name Klâtäs. You get people," the helmsman encouraged. "We leave soon."

Welstiel decided to stay and keep his eyes on these men. He also knew how Chane longed for real blood.

"Bring the others," he told Chane, "but only as far as the turn into the cove. Keep them away from the camp until it is time to board."

Welstiel found it puzzling that his ferals obeyed Chane in most things, especially the young female. As Chane disappeared down the beach, passing a returning Ylladon scout, Welstiel backed toward the water and away from the skiffs to consider his options.

Magiere traveled south, but she had not come this far, judging by her position in his last scrying. Whatever might come, he could not allow her to get away from him. If she stopped short and headed inland, he would have to force the Ylladon ship to turn back north. But that was not likely, since the impassable Blade Range separated the eastern from the western coast. Magiere was far more likely to sail onward beyond the range's southern end, where it broke into the scattered rugged terrain of the Pock Peaks. It was the only place he could think of that she might enter the high mountains on foot. If that was her plan, her ship might eventually catch up to Welstiel's, and then he would have harder decisions to make.

Sgäile pulled in the oars and stood up as the skiff floated in beside the ship. No one had spoken since they pushed off the beach, and both Magiere and Léshil had been unusually quiet during their three-day return. Chap was fully recovered, much to Sgäile's relief, but he dwelled on the gifts that the "burning" one had brought—and for whom the last two were intended.

Léshil had not taken his new blades from their canvas wrap. Those weapons, so like his own, were disturbing enough to Sgäile, but they were nothing compared to the items presented to Magiere: a war blade made of Chein'âs metal and a strange heavy circlet.

Sgäile had thought long and hard on this as he led Léshil and Magiere out of the granite foothills. Brot'ân'duivé could not have known Magiere would force her way into this journey, for the Greimasg'äh's instructions only concerned Léshil. Yet somehow the Chein'âs had known she would come.

What was the hidden meaning behind these strange gifts, and the way that dark little one had looked at her with such pain? Its expression had reflected that of the séyilf who had appeared at Magiere's hearing before the clan elders and claimed an impossible shared heritage with her.

One night in the granite foothills, Sgäile had heard Magiere mutter fitfully in her sleep and then sit up, breathing hard. He remained silent, watching her through the slits of his eyelids, until she finally curled up under the blanket with Léshil.

They were all traveling south to find an object for these human "sages," but Magiere was much more involved than she admitted. Sgäile now felt as though he were the one being dragged along blindfolded.

"They are back!" a glad voice shouted from above. "Osha, quickly—come help!"

Sgäile glanced up to see Wynn's smiling face hanging over the ship's rail-wall. Osha appeared beside her an instant later.

"Hold on," Osha called, and a crewman tossed down lines.

Sgäile stepped around Chap to secure the skiff's prow. When he turned back, Magiere had done the same at the stern. About to reach down for his pack and the canvas bundle of gifts, he saw Léshil had already picked up the latter.

It was the first time he had touched them since leaving the tunnels. Sgäile could not comprehend Léshil's reluctance.

Léshil handed off the bundle to Magiere and crouched as Chap approached him.

"I will carry him," Sgäile said quickly.

Léshil's face clouded, but he nodded. "I'll head up and help haul him over. Magiere, go ahead."

Magiere climbed up, and then Léshil, and Sgäile crouched to offer his back to Chap.

"Please allow me to assist you," he whispered.

With a soft rumble, Chap hooked his forelegs over Sgäile's shoulders, bracing his rear paws on Sgäile's belt. The dog was heavy and made climbing the rope ladder precarious. When they reached the top, Wynn scrambled into Sgäile's way.

"I will get him," she said cheerfully, reaching out.

At the sight of her, Chap lunged.

The dog's push-off flattened Sgäile onto the deck's edge. When Chap's weight lifted from Sgäile's back, he climbed through the rail-wall's opening and paused at the sight before him.

Wynn sat with legs splayed where she had toppled, and clutched the majay-hì's neck. Chap lapped at her face as she laughed.

"I missed you!" Wynn said, grabbing his face by the jowls.

Sgäile shook his head. At least it was heartening to see this ancient one's hidden burdens lifted for a moment.

"Greetings, Sgäilsheilleache," Osha said. "It is welcome to see you."

"Osha!" Wynn grumbled at him.

He groaned with a roll of his eyes and repeated his welcome in Belaskian.

The hkomas strode over, displeased as ever, and Sgäile steeled himself to remain polite. The ship and its keeper had remained idle for six unexpected days on this well-kept route between the coastal communities.

"We pull anchor," the hkomas said. "We are far behind schedule for our next stop."

"Of course," Sgäile answered. "If I can assist in—"

The hkomas turned on his heel and began shouting to his crew.

A cold gust rolled across the deck, and Wynn crossed her arms with a shiver as she stood up. Osha immediately opened his cloak, stepping closer, and Wynn slipped in against his side as he pulled the cloak's edge about her.

Sgäile stared silently, as did Magiere and Léshil, but the two young ones did not notice everyone's attention fixed upon them.

"Hungry?" Wynn asked, peering from beneath Osha's gray-green cloak. "Have you had supper?"

In the lingering silence, both Wynn and Osha finally noticed the tension around them.

"We need to get below," Magiere said, still holding the bundle of gifts. "Now, Wynn."

Some of the crew paused amid their duties, casting displeased and troubled glances at the returned foreigners. One stopped altogether to watch them. The continued interest of this young woman, the hkomas's steward, did not escape Sgäile's awareness.

Osha swept back his cloak as Wynn hurried after Magiere. Léshil and Chap followed. Sgäile watched with mixed feelings as they headed for the aft hatch. He prayed that Chap would keep his oath.

Uncertainty was a foreign state of mind for Sgäile, and lately he had been perpetually lost in it. He believed in his self-chosen purpose to protect Léshil. But Magiere's presence nagged at him. Between the séyilf's claims at Magiere's hearing and the gifts and actions of the emissary at the fissure's edge, Sgäile wondered what role Magiere played in Léshil's future.

She was a monster. She could be irrational and consistently ill-mannered. But she also possessed attributes Sgäile found admirable—fortitude, courage, and an unshakable loyalty to those she cared for. He had once asked her to watch over young Leanâlhâm, and she agreed without hesitation. And two of the ancient races expressed mysterious interest in her.

Sgäile grew weary of thinking.

"What happened," Osha asked, "when you took them before the Chein'âs?"

Perhaps Osha had spent too much time with these outsiders. He had many shortcomings that made Sgäile doubt his suitability to be Anmaglâhk. It would not serve the young man to sympathize with humans.

"Wynn is safe," Sgäile said. "You served your purpose well."

"Purpose?" Osha blinked, and his gaze wandered toward the aft hatch. "Yes, Sgäilsheilleache . . . a pleasant duty."

Sgäile stiffened.

"There is no pleasant or unpleasant for Anmaglâhk," he said coldly. "There is only your purpose to fulfill for your people. If you cannot hold this above all else, you have no place among us."

Osha's jaw dropped slightly, like an ignorant boy regretting an error he did not understand. "Forgive me," he stammered. "I meant no . . . I live in silence and in shadows. I am Anmaglâhk."

Sgäile offered no reassurance. Putting Osha at ease would be no kindness.

"See to our charges," he said. "Bring them supper."

"Yes, Sgäilsheilleache."

As Osha walked to the hatch, Sgäile turned to the rail, watching the coastline and dwelling on Magiere. Perhaps he should chastise himself as well.

· · ·

Most Aged Father rested within the root chamber of his great oak. Alone for a moment, he tried to quiet his restless mind.

Father?

He opened his eyes at Hkuan'duv's voice and placed a hand on the living wood of his bower.

"I am here," he replied, concerned, for Hkuan'duv would need a tree for his word-wood to function. "Where are you?"

I halted the ship to go ashore so we could speak. Hkuan'duv hesitated. *I have been in contact with the informant you arranged. Sgäilsheilleache's ship anchored for six days, and he took Léshil and the human called Magiere ashore. By the location described, I believe Sgäilsheilleache took them to the haven of the Chein'âs.*

"What?" Most Aged Father tried to sit up.

When they returned, Magiere bore a canvas bundle, which the informant had not seen when they departed. It was of sizeable bulk.

Most Aged Father had been shocked when he first learned that Sgäilsheilleache had continued to accompany Léshil. But guardianship was a difficult burden to put aside, especially for one such as Sgäilsheilleache, who clearly felt his oath was not yet fulfilled, misplaced as it was.

Father? Hkuan'duv asked. *Is there more concerning this purpose . . . that I should know?*

Most Aged Father was troubled. Since leaving Ghoivne Ajhâjhe, Sgäilsheilleache had made no reports. Now he had made an unscheduled stop near a place no human should ever know. Had Sgäilsheilleache taken Léshil and that undead woman into sacred fire?

Father, are you still with me?

Most Aged Father's frail body flushed with indignant heat. Oh, the answer was obvious.

Brot'ân'duivé—the Dog in the Dark—betrayer of his people. But why would the deviant Greimasg'äh want Sgäilsheilleache to do this? Why, when he knew what it would cost once the truth came out?

This breach was all Most Aged Father needed to begin planning the swift end of Brot'ân'duivé.

Father?

"Yes, I hear you!" Most Aged Father hissed, and then calmed, weighing his next words. "Sgäilsheilleache's loyalty is unquestionable, but his purpose has been twisted by one among our caste who works against us . . . like that traitor, Cuirin'nên'a. If he now serves a purpose that neither he nor we know fully, then this object the humans seek has greater import than I first thought. Upon your return, speak of it to no one, even among our caste. You will bring it only to me."

Another pause and Hkuan'duv replied, *You have no reason to doubt.*

Most Aged Father leaned back shakily in his bower. "In silence and in shadows," he whispered.

Was there no limit to Brot'ân'duivé's treachery?

"What is wrong?" Wynn asked, closing the cabin door. "What has happened?"

Chap dropped his haunches to the floor, but he sent no words into her head.

Magiere roughly tossed her coat onto a bunk. She dropped on the bunk's edge, looking tired and drawn, as Leesil sank to the floor beside Chap.

Daylight had faded, and Wynn took out her cold lamp crystal, rubbing it briskly until a glow filled the small room. Her curiosity—and worry—sharpened with the light, and she glanced over at the strange bundle in the corner by the door.

"What is in there?" she asked.

Magiere leaned back, her jaw working beneath tightly pressed lips, as if uncertain how to answer.

"Talk to me!" Wynn demanded.

"Ooeer-ish-ga," Leesil whispered.

Wynn spun toward him. "What?"

Úirishg, Chap corrected for Leesil's badly spoken Elvish.

Leesil sighed. "I think we met another one of your forgotten mythical people."

Wynn stared at him, but she flooded with excitement.

Úirishg was an ancient Elvish name she had learned from recorded myths gathered by her guild—a legend of five races matched to the five elements of existence. Of these, Elves and Dwarves were known. Wynn had considered the other three no more than fancy, until . . .

She had followed Leesil and Magiere into Droevinka, and they had uncovered the hidden crypt below the keep of Magiere's undead father. And one of the Séyilf—the Wind-Blown—had appeared at Magiere's trial before the an'Cróan's council of clan elders.

Spirit, Earth, Air, Fire, and Water.

Essence, Solid, Gas, Energy, and Liquid.

Tree, Mountain, Wind, Flame, and Wave.

Elf, Dwarf, Séyilf . . . and . . .

"Which race?" Wynn asked.

"The one left in the iron crate," Magiere said.

In the hidden crypt, Leesil had discovered one set of remains near an age-crusted iron crate. Beneath the grime and dried rust, Wynn had found gouges in the metal. Whatever it had held had tried to claw its way out. The skeletal remains near the crate were as dark as its iron, and the bones of its toes and fingers ended in curved obsidian points. Its skull was small, with sharpened charcoal gray ridges in place of teeth.

"Just listen," Leesil said, but he faltered, looking to Magiere. "I don't even know how to start."

"Show her," Magiere said.

Wynn did not wait. She rushed for the bundled canvas and tumbled it open upon the floor.

"Sgäile took us down . . . somewhere under a mountain," Magiere began. "A small, black-skinned creature came out of a deep fissure, carrying those things. The winged blades were for Leesil, but it tossed the other two at me."

Wynn was spellbound by the four objects. A pair of winged blades, not unlike Leesil's, yet made of unmistakable metal. The other two left for Magiere—a long and heavy hiltless dagger of the same material, and . . . a *thôrhk*?

But the engraved characters upon it were not Dwarvish, although it was shaped like one of the collar adornments worn by some of their warriors. Wynn turned her frustration on Chap.

"Well, say something! You were supposed to be my eyes and ears."

Chap dropped his head upon his paws. *Chein'âs—the Burning Ones.*

But then Magiere began recounting all she remembered, and Wynn listened intently.

"Before we could leave with Leesil's blades," Magiere said softly, "it shrieked at me, and left those things."

"Sgäile wasn't happy about it," Leesil added. "He had no idea, and I don't think Brot'an and my mother had anything to do with those."

"It knew me . . . ," Magiere whispered. "The gift-bearer was hurting . . . or in mourning."

Wynn glared at Chap, but he remained silent. What was wrong with him? He had made her a promise. She turned back to Leesil.

"We have already learned that you and Magiere were created by opposing sides," Wynn said, "for a conflict yet to come, though the sides of that conflict are somewhat ignorant of each other. And the Fay seem to want neither of you involved. The an'Cróan ancestors saw Leesil as a future savior, and Chap believes Magiere is to lead an army for the long-forgotten enemy that Most Aged Father fears. Both of you have rejected these paths, but now . . . with these things . . ."

Wynn looked down at the items and lingered upon the ruddy-colored circlet.

"Perhaps these old peoples, Chein'âs and Séyilf, do not care how or why either of you were made. They either offer their help . . . or are asking you for help."

"Help with what?" Leesil snapped. "Enough already! We'll find this orb thing, keep it from Welstiel . . . and then we're done!"

Magiere stretched out a hand to Leesil, and he rose to join her on the bunk.

Wynn shook her head in resignation. She had no wish to upset them nor to make them think she wished either to succumb to a purpose others thought they should serve. She only wished she had been in that cavern to understand more of what happened.

"You had better start explaining," she growled at Chap.

No.

Wynn's stomach rolled, more at his denial than at his voice in her head.

I can only clarify what Magiere and Leesil can tell you. That is my word to Sgäile.

His rebuke stung, for Chap had made a promise to her. And now, that meant nothing compared to his word to an anmaglâhk?

Wynn could not even spit out a retort, so she snatched up the circlet—or tried to. She nearly toppled off her knees at its weight, and then slammed it down before Chap's nose. He flinched.

"What is this *thôrhk* for?" Wynn demanded.

Leesil wrinkled his brow at the strange term.

I do not know, Chap answered. *Sgäile did not recognize it either.*

"What about the chein'âs?" Wynn pressed. "And do not tell me that you did not delve its memories . . . I know you!"

"Enough!" Magiere warned. "And where did you get the name for the hoop? A torc?"

Wynn ignored her.

Chap fidgeted on the floor, reluctant to look at the object. Wynn's ire waned at the suffering in his eyes. He shuddered.

I saw the gift-bearer's memory of a loss, when one of its own . . . one that meant something to it . . . was taken by Ubâd.

Wynn repeated Chap's words for the others, and Magiere sat upright with widened eyes.

"That . . . fiend came to the chasm?" she whispered sharply. "How? We barely survived a short time on the plateau."

Leesil tried to pull her back but she resisted. Chap recounted all that he had seen in the forlorn being's memory as Wynn reiterated for the others.

I could not tell the gift-bearer that Ubâd is already dead.

Chap's blue crystalline eyes strayed to the hiltless dagger—as did Magiere's—then he laid his head down, gazing at the *thôrhk.*

It seemed the blade given to Magiere had been some plea for justice, but the *thôrhk* brought Wynn only doubts and questions.

"Let me know," she grumbled at Chap, "if there is anything more you *can* tell . . . that might help."

Chap lifted his head, and his doggish brows wrinkled in an echo of Magiere's perpetual scowl.

Wynn put a hand on his head. He bucked it sharply off with his snout, but then lapped his long tongue between her small fingers.

"Wynn," Magiere said, "how do you know what to call that thing?"

"*Thôrhk?*" she answered hesitantly. "It is an old Dwarvish term for a circlet shaped somewhat like your open-ended loop. They are made of semi-flexible braided metal, and often worn by a Thänæ—an elite dwarven warrior, sometimes in service to one of their high lords."

A knock sounded. Wynn climbed to her feet, stepping over Leesil's shimmering new blades, and opened the cabin door.

Osha stood outside with a tray of food, and the aroma of roasted fish and herb-garnished potatoes surrounded Wynn.

"Thank you, Osha. Will you join us?"

He would not meet her eyes and merely handed over the tray.

"Whatever is wrong?" she asked.

Osha turned away, heading back for the hatch stairs. Wynn stared after him.

Six days alone with him and she had finally begun to think they were friends. Now he would not eat or speak with her? It seemed that no matter how much they learned of each other, as elf, an'Cróan, or anmaglâhk, Osha might always be a stranger.

Wynn closed the door with her elbow and turned as Magiere slid to the floor, leaning her head against Leesil's leg. Sadness welled inside Wynn—or was it loneliness?

She reached back in her memory, seeking a moment of intimate comfort. All she recalled were evenings sitting close to Chane over a parchment, drinking mint tea, his strong hands tight around his cup. During the battle in Toret's house, he had abandoned the fight and thrown her over his shoulder to flee. She had fought and kicked him, until she realized his true intention was to remove her from harm's way.

Chap was watching her sternly.

Wynn flinched, hoping he had not been wandering in her memories. But when she settled beside him, handing out small wooden plates, her stomach rolled once more.

And I think of Lily.

She reached out to softly stroke his back.

Magiere took the plate Wynn offered, and another knock sounded at the cabin door. She waved Wynn back down as the sage started to rise and went to the door herself.

The last face she wanted to see outside was Sgäile's.

He averted his eyes and clutched at a long and narrow paper-wrapped bundle. He also held a seamless wooden tube about the length of his forearm. The narrow container looked much like the wood of the rain barrels in elven homes—one perfect piece, except for the unadorned pewter cap.

"May I enter?" he asked.

Magiere almost slammed the door in his face. Six days with Sgäile, most of it blindfolded, left her with little patience, but she stepped back. He entered with a respectful nod and crouched near the pile of gifts.

"Before our ship left Ghoivne Ajhâjhe," he said, "Brot'ân'duivé gave me things for you, Léshil."

Both Leesil and Chap narrowed their eyes at the master anmaglâhk's name.

"I did not understand their purpose," Sgäile went on, setting down the wooden tube, "until I saw what the Chein'âs gave to you."

He tore open the paper bundle, exposing a matched set of long padded bars of leather.

Magiere was mildly curious. Before she could ask, Sgäile picked up one silvery winged punching blade in the pile and then rolled one bar of padding over. Its backside was split cleanly down the center between its edge stitching.

Sgäile spread the slit with his thumb and carefully slid the back of the blade's wing into it. There was a narrow ledge of metal along the wing's back that Magiere hadn't noticed before, and it slid smoothly into the leather. The padded bar settled perfectly along the back of the wing.

Magiere remembered the day Leesil had bolted across the border at Soladran.

He'd viciously assaulted Darmouth's forces hunting down peasants who fled for safety. When he returned to the city, a blow from a sword had smashed one of his blade's wings into his forearm, leaving him black and blue for days.

But with the padding, and those half-hoop braces sprouting midpoint from the wings, these new blades would be far more stable and sure on Leesil's forearms. Still, she knew he wouldn't touch them.

Magiere had no doubt who'd designed and requested those blades from the Chein'âs. And who better to improve on Leesil's original blades than someone who'd been killing all his long life?

Brot'an was up to something—again.

Before Leesil spit out his rejection, Chap snarled and rose on all fours. Head low, he growled at Sgäile, and clacked his jaws sharply as he barked twice for "no."

"Stop it!" Wynn said.

Chap ignored her, closing on Sgäile, who froze at the dog's rage.

"Don't bother," Leesil added. "I prefer my own weapons."

Sgäile stared at Leesil in bewilderment, as if he'd been insulted for no reason. He turned his eyes back on Chap and asked, "Why?"

"Because those are Brot'an's doing," Wynn said tiredly.

"Shut up, Wynn!" Leesil growled.

Magiere grabbed his arm, and Leesil turned his angry gaze on her.

"Brot'an's the one who tricked Leesil," Magiere explained, "into finishing his mission to kill Darmouth. And Leesil . . . doesn't want anything to do with him. Neither does Chap."

"Do you not understand?" Sgäile said and held up one silvery winged blade, turning it slowly in the air. "No such thing has ever been made by the Burning Ones . . . only anmaglâhk blades and rare items for elders and other honored ones. Brot'ân'duivé may have requested Léshil's new blades—but that is all! No one *tells* the Chein'âs what to make."

Magiere wasn't sure she believed that, no matter that Sgäile did. But weapons were only tools, and these new blades looked better than Leesil's own.

"They're just weapons," she said to him. "You choose how to use them . . . nobody is going to make you do anything."

"Ah, so you're perfectly comfortable with your 'gifts,' are you?" he returned.

Magiere clenched her teeth. She wanted to smack him for turning things back on her—and because she couldn't think of a way around his counter.

She twisted about, looking to the hiltless dagger and that thing Wynn called a torc.

"The dagger needs a hilt," she said suddenly.

Sgäile looked down at the blade and then to Chap, waiting.

Chap shook himself all over. With one last snarl, he circled away around Wynn.

Sgäile let out a deep breath as he set down Leesil's new blade. He picked up the long dagger and, with a nod to Magiere, turned and left.

"Happy now?" Magiere asked Leesil.

He glared back at her. "Oh, I'm overjoyed."

"But what about this?" Wynn said. "Sgäile brought something more for Leesil."

Magiere glanced back to find Wynn had retrieved the wooden cylinder that Sgäile had left with the other items. The sage popped the pewter cap and peered into the narrow tube, then she frowned, glancing nervously at Leesil.

"Well?" Magiere asked.

With a sigh, Wynn tilted the tube, and out slid a narrow shaft of wood—a bare length of branch. And Magiere recognized it immediately—the branch of Roise Chârmune.

When Leesil had gone with Sgäile to the burial place of the an'Cróan ancestors, he'd been given more than a new name. Leafless and barkless—yet somehow alive—the slick, fine-grained slip of branch had been needed to prove Magiere's innocence in the face of Most Aged Father's claims against her. And here it was again.

Magiere heard Leesil's groan even before she looked back to find him with his face buried in his hands.

Sgäile closed the cabin door and paused in the hallway. Between Léshil and Chap's deep hatred of Brot'ân'duivé and the rejection of gifts he himself could not fathom, he felt at a loss. Magiere's contentious nature had broken the stalemate, but the whole exchange had left him exhausted.

He stepped down the passage to the hatch stairs, and when he reached the deck, he headed for the aftcastle stairwell. As he passed under the lanterns hanging there, his gaze caught on the dagger glinting in the light. He noticed a crack down the blade's center.

No, a seam.

It ran perfectly straight, ending well short of the tip and the cross-guard. Sgäile studied it more closely.

The black-filled seam was so thin he could barely run a fingernail along it, and the char-colored material that filled it was as hard as the blade itself. He lifted it closer to his face and caught a whiff of cinders—or perhaps it was just the lingering smell of the heated cavern.

Sgäile headed onward for the one place a proper hilt could be made. When he reached the center of three doors in the ship's aft, he knocked gently upon it.

"Enter . . . Sgäilsheilleache," a deep voice answered from within.

Sgäile had not met the ship's hkœda, yet the man called him by name. He grasped the latch, peering around the door's edge.

Inside the ship's heart-room chamber was a tall elf dressed in plain canvas tunic and breeches. His feet were bare, and he stood beside the large bulge in the floor that was the root-tail of the vessel, this living Päirvänean.

By the lantern's light, he appeared gaunt but young. With his own hands, he massaged the root-tail's base with fresh seawater. Sgäile smelled the strong aroma of herbal oil permeating the chamber.

"What do you need?" the hkœda asked.

But Sgäile was looking beyond him.

Below the side walls' higher ledges, two long tanks stretched the full length of the heart-room. From forewall to the stern, their shorter walls flowed out of the floor, and each was filled with seawater. Within those two containers, something moved beneath the water's surface.

Like the ship's own tawny root, yet ending in roundly pointed heads, their tails undulated and flexed, making the tanks' waters ripple gently.

"You have 'swimmers'?" Sgäile asked, distracted from his purpose.

"Yes." The hkœda's soft smile faded. "I once served on a military Päirvänean and grew accustomed to their company."

Sgäile hesitated. Hkœda lived out their lives on the Päirvänean with which they bonded. If this one had once served another vessel, then he had suffered a great loss—no less than one suffered in the loss of a life-mate, and not all survived such a loss. But Sgäile had never seen "swimmers" except on vessels guarding the open waters of his people.

Perhaps they were an added blessing, but he hoped there would be no need of such on this journey.

"I would ask you to grow wood for a hilt," he said, and held up the long dagger.

The hkœda's melancholy faded. He stepped closer, bare feet slapping wetly across the floor, and took the blade, raising one eyebrow slyly at Sgäile.

"Well . . . this is unusual." His smirk only rankled Sgäile more. "Not a typical blade for an anmaglâhk."

Sgäile had never cared for the inappropriate joviality of hkœda.

"Just the same," he said shortly, "please treat it as such in preparation. And when the wood is fitted, wrap it thoroughly in gut-hide, so the wood is not exposed."

The hkœda nodded and turned away. He placed a hand on the bulge in the floor, still shimmering wet with seawater, and laid the blade atop the root-tail's center.

"We have something new to do," he whispered to it, and then, seeing Sgäile still in the doorway, he flipped a hand in dismissal. "Off with you. We will let you know when your new toy is ready."

Sgäile shook his head as he left. And perhaps he closed the door a little too hard.

This had been a very, very long day.

CHAPTER NINE

Magiere stood on deck with her companions as the crew loaded boxes and barrels into two skiffs. After three days, their ship had reached its next layover.

The cargo grate was still open, and she looked down to see the hold was nearly empty. She turned back to the wild coastline where one dock served a small settlement upon the rocky shore. Leesil stepped up beside her, and everything seemed peaceful.

But it wasn't. She could feel it.

The crew stole furtive glances at them. They were far too quiet, even considering the presence of humans on their ship.

Sgäile, Osha, Chap, and Wynn joined Magiere at the rail-wall.

"What's wrong?" she asked quietly.

Wynn kept her eyes down.

"Last stop," she whispered. "We have reached the end of an'Cróan waters. If not for us, the ship and crew would turn back north for Ghoivne Ajhâjhe. Because of us, they cannot go home."

Magiere didn't doubt Wynn—as her explanation made sense—but sometimes the sage's interpretations weren't completely on the mark.

"Is that true?" she asked Sgäile.

His thick hair hung loose today, blowing around his face in coarse, white-blond strands. The effect made him look less proper and civilized. Before he answered, the hkomas closed on all of them, speaking short, clipped Elvish. His leathery skin looked rough next to Sgäile's, and the two conversed in careful tones.

Chap stood near Wynn, watching them.

"What's this about?" Leesil asked.

Sgäile glanced at him and then Magiere. "It is true—we have completed the last stop. The hkomas agreed to take you wherever you asked, but now he . . . requests a more specific destination. He has sailed out of our waters a few times, but the southern coastline is perilous for his ship and crew."

"Is the weather more severe beyond your waters?" Wynn asked.

"No," Sgaile answered slowly. "It is a matter of protecting this vessel, as it is not military."

"So you have other ships guarding your people?" Leesil suggested.

"We have vessels which patrol," Sgaile confirmed and returned his attention to Magiere. "I must tell the hkomas something. Willing or not, he expects to know how far he is to go and where he leads his crew and this ship."

Helplessness made Magiere almost as angry as did fear. She studied the hkomas, who stared back with hard eyes. He looked about fifty in human years—which meant he was much older for an elf. He crossed his sinewy arms in stiff challenge, and for all Magiere's frustration, she couldn't blame him. She'd have felt the same in his place.

"I don't know," she finally answered. "I wish I did. We need to keep heading south, until I get a sense of when to stop."

"That is not specific enough," Sgäile countered.

"What about a time frame?" Leesil suggested. "Ask the captain to carry us south for seven more days. If Magiere hasn't found the right place by then, he can let us off, and we'll go on foot. Either way, we'll get there in the end."

He touched Magiere's arm with a knowing nod. "And well before anyone else."

Magiere only cared that they kept going but shouldn't have felt so urgent. Her half-brother, Welstiel, couldn't know where she was or that she had a lead on what he was after. But sometimes she forgot Leesil's way of cutting cleanly to the quickest solution.

"Yes, tell the captain," she said to Sgäile. "See if he'll agree to that."

Sgäile conversed with the hkomas, but the man shook his head and snapped something back. They fell into another sharp debate, and all Magiere picked out was "Aoishenis-Ahâre."

At those words, the hkomas wavered. He nodded curtly and walked off.

Magiere winced. "You asked him in the name of Most Aged Father?"

"You have your seven days," Sgäile answered coldly.

Magiere was even more unsettled by this. Most Aged Father's influence could be dangerous.

Well before midday, the skiffs returned from their last trip ashore, and the ship set sail, heading south.

Chane walked out of one hell to sit and rot in another.

A few nights had passed since they'd boarded, and the Ylladon ship ran south at full sail. The vessel was barely as large as a schooner, and its hull was made of double-thick planks overlapped upon each other. It was reasonably swift, but he had learned little since the night they had boarded—when he was ushered below deck with Welstiel and the ferals to their "accommodations."

Chane stood in the rocking ship's dank, dark, half-filled hold.

Sabel crouched nearby, rocking on her haunches as she hummed a tune Chane did not recognize. Her eyes had turned glassy and lost again. All the monks were starving.

So far, the crew had been staying clear of the hold, although upon boarding, both the captain and the helmsman, Klâtäs, had studied Sabel the same way the captain had first eyed Welstiel's globe of lights.

Chane expected the crew to attack at any time. Each dawn he fought off dormancy as long as possible, still gripping his sword when he finally succumbed.

Upon rising tonight, Welstiel had gone off on his own, leaving Chane to watch over their tattered and pathetic group. The two younger males and the silver-haired one curled unmoving upon the hold's floor. Sabel and the fierce curly-headed man crouched in place as if vaguely aware of their surroundings.

If Welstiel intended to use these monks in acquiring his treasure, they needed to be fed tonight or risk incapacitation—and Chane wasn't far behind. Should the crew move against them, even these mad undead might not all survive the fight.

Chane held up a hand to Sabel as he headed for the door. "Wait here. I will return."

The hold was in the stern, but crew quarters were located near the bow.

Leaving the hold and finding himself alone, Chane crossed over to a port-side stairwell up to the deck. At its top, he cracked the squat door and waited.

He smelled life on deck. Each time he saw someone moving, he restrained himself from lunging out. He waited for the right sailor to come near, ignoring a thin, middle-aged man and one less than twenty years old. He could only risk taking one and needed someone large and healthy.

A portly sailor in a rust-colored shirt and open vest turned around the mid mast, and as he strolled within reach, Chane lashed out with one hand.

His fingers clamped across padded jowls and thick lips. He jerked the sailor into the stairwell. The sailor bucked and thrashed.

Chane slammed his fist into the back of the man's skull, stunning him limp. He dragged his prey halfway down the stairs. A pulse still pounded just below the man's stubbled jawline, and Chane could not hold back any longer. He bit hard into the sailor's throat, drinking in gulps.

He hardly even tasted the blood, and sagged in relief at life's heat filling him. Then he snapped his head up as if someone had jerked a chain around his neck. He had taken enough to sustain himself, but oh how he wanted more.

The man began to rouse, struggling weakly, and grunted beneath Chane's hand.

If anyone heard and came to check, Chane might find himself quickly outnumbered.

He dragged the sailor along the cross hall and down the passage to the hold's lower door. He kept fierce pressure on the man's mouth and throat, only letting go long enough to flip the latch and shoulder the door open. He did not notice the change in the hold until he had the sailor halfway inside.

All the ferals were on their feet or crouched in waiting. Wide eyes fixed on Chane's prey, as if they knew he was coming and what he brought.

Sabel began shaking. Between her parted lips, her canines had already elongated. The curly-headed monk sniffed through both his nose and open mouth as if he could taste the blood in the air.

"Quietly," Chane warned. "If you wish to survive."

The curly-headed one rushed in.

Chane shoved the sailor forward, shut the door, and backed against it.

The sailor sprawled across the hold floor as the two younger monks rounded to both sides. The man tried to shout but only managed a gurgling gag. He backhanded one feral and reached for his cutlass. The curly-headed one slammed his iron cudgel down on the sailor's head.

The sailor flopped limply, and the monks fell upon him, ripping into his skin and suckling his spilled blood like dogs. Sabel was the last to join in.

She bit into the man's thigh, shredding canvas breeches to get at his flesh. Her head lifted with a squeal, and the gray-haired male slammed his palm into her face, knocking her back. He dove for the wound she had opened. Chane almost stepped in, but Sabel snarled at the elder monk and slashed his face with her fingernails.

Her attack launched a frenzy, and all of them began fighting each other as they tore the sailor apart.

Chane began to panic.

A loud ripping of heavy cloth came from somewhere above on deck.

Chane heard men shouting wildly to each other, and then running feet as voices calmed. Whatever had happened above, it did not sound critical, and he was thankful for anything that might mask the raucous sounds filling the hold.

He turned his head away, pressing an ear to the door to listen and hoping the feeding frenzy would not last long. But inside him, the beast pulled on its chains and howled to join in the slaughter.

The sailor had fallen silent beneath the grunts and gibbering, the wet sucking, and the tearing of flesh. When the noise finally waned, Chane was panting—another succulent meal denied the beast inside of him.

He looked back and stared at . . . it.

One arm and an opposite leg were torn off at the sockets. The head was nearly severed, and only the vertebrae held it in place. A younger male still sucked upon the raw half of a hand he'd bitten off. The curly-haired one licked at the red-drenched floor.

Chane could barely believe the mess on the floor had been a man only moments ago.

Sabel lifted her smeared face from the thigh stump of the severed leg. Below colorless eyes, her smile broadened, exposing crimson-coated teeth.

"Thank . . . ," she stammered at Chane. "Thank."

Chane clenched his jaws against his churning hunger. He did not want their gratitude—only their continued survival, until Welstiel needed them.

All that Sabel had once been was lost. He had to accept that and try not to think of anything beyond this moment.

"Clean this up," he hissed at Sabel, and gestured toward the dismembered body.

He circled round the feast's remains, searching for spare canvas to soak up the gore, and then spotted a hatch high up in the hull wall. Climbing onto a crate, he pulled the iron slide bolt and pushed it open. Sea wind hit his face and cleared the aroma of blood from his head. When he looked back, Sabel was the only one on her feet, watching him as the rest gnawed at the remains.

"Bring the pieces," he told her.

Chane dealt with what followed in cold fashion, from severing the head and remaining limbs to gutting and dividing the torso with his sword so the pieces would fit through the small opening. Sabel hauled these up to him as he returned to the high hatch. But when he reached down to her once more, she just stood there and cowered under his gaze, as if he, like Welstiel, had issued a command she could not fulfill. Then she glanced back at the others.

The other monks were still sucking on their scavenged bits and pieces, like beggars at a noble's back door when the meal's remains were tossed out. The older man's face was slashed from temple to chin from Sabel's fingernails.

Chane climbed down, closing on them.

"Drop it!" he ordered.

The old man merely wrinkled his nose.

Chane whipped his sword around and blade's flat side thudded hard against the old one's back. The elderly monk dropped his morsel and spun away, locking his eyes on Chane. All the ferals froze in place.

"Stay down!" he hissed. "And drop the pieces."

As much as Chane had no wish for Welstiel to walk in on this mess, his presence would have made this far easier. The curly-headed monk inched forward a step. Chane swung the sword tip directly in line with his face.

One by one, the ferals relinquished their morsels. Chane kept his eyes on them as he kicked the pieces across the floor toward the hatch. He backed away, gathering the bits and throwing them out the hatch. But the floor was hopelessly soaked in blood.

Even if he had a way to drain water off after rinsing it, the stain had already soaked into the wood. In the end, he could only goad the ferals into wiping it down with a spare tarp, and then he tried to cover it up. The ordeal was over, and the monks looked more alert.

Chane longed to be away from here and from these mad creatures. Sabel peered at the older man's face and the scratches she had made, and then looked to Chane.

"He will heal," Chane said. "The life he has consumed will do the work."

Sabel tilted her head with a frown, and Chane did not know if she understood. A few strands of her wavy dark hair were glued to the drying blood on her cheeks. She pointed to the older man.

"Jakeb."

Chane paused, for it sounded like she recalled some part of the man's name.

"Jakeb," she repeated, and then pointed toward the curly-haired one. "Sethè."

She squinted at the younger pair of men, and twisted her head like an owl, huffing in frustration.

Chane found the sight tragic.

He backed into the hold's far corner and slouched upon a canvas-covered bulk.

Welstiel walked the deck, pretending to take the night air while carefully examining the lay of the ship.

Even the sailors not on duty were still up on deck and sat playing cards as they passed around a clay jug. Clearly, they were unaccustomed to having passengers walking among them, and they stared at him openly. Klâtäs and his captain watched from the ship's stern.

Welstiel felt relatively safe, though he knew it was temporary. And then this crew would get its own final shock. He counted a total of only fourteen men, but they handled the ship with the relaxed efficiency of a long-term crew.

He strolled casually toward the bow and, with a rapid flick of his hand, peeked under a tarp covering something large up on the rail. Underneath, he found a ballista—a large mounted crossbow that fired quarrels heavier than a footman's lance. He had already spotted three other such covered bulks positioned around the deck. The ship was armed for fighting.

A voice called out above, and Welstiel looked up. One sailor was watching him from a crow's nest. He barely had time to lower his gaze before Klâtäs was halfway to him.

"What you do?" he demanded. "You say stay below!"

"And we have," Welstiel responded. "I did not count on the smell. I need air."

"Deck not for passenger in night. Go below!"

Welstiel thought he heard a muffled cry beneath the deck's planks. Then a loud ripping sound pulled his attention, and Klâtäs whirled about. A forward sail had torn loose above.

Its outer half cracked forward in the night wind, pulling on the rigging. The captain shouted, and Klâtäs ran to the bow, calling out to the men scrambling upward.

Welstiel quickly retreated toward the aft hatch. Judging by the stench in the hold and other signs of wear, this ship had been abroad for a long while. And with so little cargo in the hold, he found this surprising.

Perhaps the captain and crew had not fared well in their scavenging, and they had too long stretched their time away from safe port. Welstiel turned down the steps, but he halted halfway.

He smelled fresh blood—until a gust of wind twisting down the open hatch swept it away. The odor had been thin but unmistakable, more than a lingering whiff from a sailor's injury.

Welstiel's anger flushed. What had that fool Chane done now? He descended, but stopped short and looked toward the ship's bow.

The crew was too busy with the loose sail to notice him, and he might not get this chance again. He needed to know what resources were available in case he was forced to take the ship. Locating something to help him navigate these southern lands and waters would be most helpful—such as the captain's charts.

Welstiel climbed back up on deck. One sailor was nearly slapped from the rigging by the whipping sail, and the rest redoubled their efforts. Welstiel slipped along the rail toward the nearest forward hatch.

Twice he ducked aside for a hurrying deckhand, but all the others were too preoccupied in getting the ship under control.

He inched along until he fingered the hatch open and then dropped down the short, steep steps to find the captain's small, cramped quarters—just a bunk, a table, two chests, and a porthole in a room below the ship's prow.

His globe of flickering lights rested on the table, and Welstiel began searching through papers for a navigation rudder or a map. He found nothing, but was not surprised. The favored hunting grounds of Ylladon crews never remained secret but were guarded as such for as long as possible. It was not uncommon for a crew member to buy favor and advancement on another ship with such information.

Welstiel found a small drawer under the table's edge. Inside it, a cracked leather journal lay atop parchment scraps and worn-out quills. He could not read the entries, but he scanned for any place-names of common stops to reference against those he might find on a map. It was the only way to know how far abroad this ship was traveling, in case Magiere headed for a habitable port. He guessed she would journey far south before searching the heights, for the Blade Range separating the western nations from the eastern coast was impassable. Welstiel briefly scanned the parchment scraps but found nothing useful.

Where would the captain hide his maps and charts?

Welstiel paused, sharpening his hearing. The crew still called to each other above deck, so he had time left to look further for niches or cubbies—any hiding hole known only to the captain and helmsman. But the walls sported no closets or shelves. He picked up the globe and crouched to peer beneath the bunk. There was nothing of note, so he flipped open the unlocked chest and rifled its contents without success. The second chest was locked, and he could not break it without leaving evidence of his passing. In frustration, he returned the globe to the table and grabbed the door to pull it closed behind him.

He caught an odd shadow on the wall beyond the table, and swiveled about.

The shadow looked like a faint warp in the wood. He stepped quietly around the table, but not so far as to block the globe's flickering light. The shadow intensified, as if the aged planking flexed inward.

Such a weakness in the hull would never be left unmended. When he ran a hand over it, he found no seams but those where the plank ends met squarely. He went all the way down before spotting a small square of wood in the floor, flush against the wall's edge. When pressed, it gave slightly. Welstiel stood up and stepped on the square with his boot heel.

The square's outside edge sank down into the floor.

A piece of the faintly warped wall tilted inward and lifted from the floor seam. Welstiel shoved the panel with his palm.

The panel tilted farther inward, but not all the way, and Welstiel inspected its lower edge. The panel rested in some cradle beyond the wall, for he saw heavy iron strips extending from under the foot plate to under and beyond the wall. He pushed one side of the panel, sliding it away and behind the surrounding wall, and then grabbed the globe of lights. Crouched to step into opening, he straightened up as the globe filled the hidden space with soft light.

To the opening's right, iron bars partitioned half the space and broke the globe's light. Black shadow stripes obscured what lay beyond them. But between them and the bars, light sparked in two pairs of amber irises too large for any human.

Two elven women were locked inside the hidden cell—one fully grown and the other no more than an adolescent. They stared at him in silence. In spite of tangled hair and torn clothing, both were lovely and slender, with their smooth tan skin, lithe bodies, and large amber eyes. Both were tied and gagged with knotted cord.

This was why the Ylladon had been so far north. Perhaps the captain indeed desperately needed to make up losses. These two women, offered up in a Ylladon market, would each be worth far more than his globe of lights. Such exotic "items" would create a frenzy of bidding.

He remembered mention among the men in the cove of need to replace their water. Had one of these women managed to get loose and contaminate the ship's supply?

And the prisoners had seen him here, nosing about.

How much would they think such information was worth in bargaining with their captors? It would do them no good, but that would not stop them from trying.

Welstiel gritted his teeth. Killing these women would not serve him either, for their bodies would be discovered within a day.

Both women continued staring at him, examining his clothes, for he dressed distinctly different from the Ylladon. Could he use this to his advantage? But he could not speak Elvish.

"Do you . . . understand me?" he whispered in Belaskian.

Neither responded, and he repeated himself in Droevinkan.

The adult female perked up.

Welstiel focused his will, calling upon the latent talent that had grown in his years as a Noble Dead. Staring into her eyes, he raised his voice above a whisper, and its low thrum reinforced his words as clear and true in the hearer's mind.

"Not yet . . . when we near a place close to shore . . . I will come for you."

She blinked twice.

Had she understood? Did she comprehend enough Droevinkan for his suggestion to take root deep in her mind? He repeated more slowly, word by word.

The young one craned her head, turning frightened eyes upon her companion. The adult frowned and blinked, and glared suspiciously at him.

He looked different from her captors, but was human nonetheless and not to be trusted. Then slowly, she nodded.

Welstiel returned her nod with a soft smile and placed one finger to his lips. He slipped out, sliding the wall panel back into its floor bracket. It took a moment to figure out how to close the portal fully, until he realized stepping on the floor's wood square lifted the panel back into place. He placed the globe back on the desk and stepped out of the captain's quarters.

He was not clear of danger as yet.

Hopefully the adult female would keep her young companion quiet. He had heard tales of human ships trying to round the northern peninsula into elven waters, but in these stories, not one had ever returned. The elves were savage in protecting their own. More than likely, he was not the only one who knew of the two stolen women. Magiere came south at a fast pace, and her vessel had its own purpose.

As Welstiel crept back along the ship's rail toward the aft, and slipped down its steps, the smell of blood rose around him again. His patience was already taxed to its limit.

What had Chane been up to now?

CHAPTER TEN

The moon rose as Chap paced the deck amid the sounds of wind and wave, but his thoughts drifted. He had forsaken so much to protect Leesil and Magiere, yet now felt uncertain of the correct path—again.

How had the Chein'âs known of Magiere? What did they want from her in exchange for their gifts of a dagger and what Wynn called a *thôrhk*? Something beyond vengeance, most certainly. And in the great scheme of things, what was the purpose for the artifact which Magiere sought?

She and Leesil only wished to finish this last task and go home. With all Chap's mortal heart, he wished this might be. But amid worry for them, something more nagged him tonight as he paced near the ship's rail-wall. He felt a strong sense of something out there, coming closer—like a hole in the world he could not pinpoint.

Chap hopped upon a storage chest near the rail-wall and stared ahead into the dark.

Several elven crew members watched him curiously. They found it unnatural for a majay-hì to willingly leave its homeland. The young woman with the thick braid and oversized boots studied him like a mystery to be unlocked. But the crew's discomfort did not matter, and he watched only the sea.

"Chap, where are you?" Wynn called out.

He glanced back as she emerged from the hatch below the forecastle, dressed only in her white shift, boots, and Chane's old cloak. Chap sighed, concerned for her as well.

His kin, the Fay, might still want Wynn dead. Not only for her ability to hear and perceive their presence, but also because she knew they were up to more than just sending Chap as a guardian to Magiere. And why did Wynn keep wearing that old cloak instead of her new coat?

Her preoccupation with Chane worried him—no, it was outright disturbing. He looked out across the rolling water rushing around the ship's prow and tensed, looking for . . . something.

"There you are." She scurried to his side. "It is getting late."

Being treated as her charge—instead of the other way around—was annoying, but it still warmed him at times. Normally, Wynn did not come on deck without Osha or Sgäile. He was surprised to find her alone and knew he should take her back downstairs. But that hollow in the world that he could not quite find began to make him ache. To make him want to . . . hunt?

Chap inched to the storage chest's far end, but his sharp eyes saw nothing upon the ocean ahead.

"What is wrong?" Wynn asked.

Chap hesitated. *Something is out there.*

Wynn put a hand on his head and slid it down his neck. "I do not see anything."

You are only human.

"Only?" she answered indignantly.

A wink of light rose ahead in the dark.

Chap reared up with his forepaws perched on the rail-wall.

"Vessel ahead!" someone shouted from up in the rigging.

Chap already saw it. The distant wink came again, catching upon sails, and the hackles on his neck stiffened.

Chane sat upon an old canvas tarp spread over the stained floor. He had propped open the hatch, but the hold still reeked of blood. All was quiet above on deck.

Welstiel stepped in, glaring at him.

Chane climbed to his feet, half-hoping Welstiel would make some self-righteous demand for an explanation. He was sick of this existence and spoiling for confrontation.

Welstiel turned his eyes on each monk, one by one.

The ferals were markedly better off than when Welstiel had left—more aware and curious about their surroundings. The one Sabel had called

"Jakeb" was especially improved. His face had nearly healed of her scratches, and he studied Welstiel calmly. Sethè was also less agitated.

Yet all the monks were smeared or splattered with blood.

But Welstiel said nothing.

He crossed to a bare space below the open hatch, dropped to the floor, and immediately pulled out the brass dish to scry for Magiere. Perhaps he was relieved that Chane had taken care of feeding the ferals. Or he was just lost in his own obsession yet again.

Either way, Chane did not care.

A loud call from above vibrated through the hold's ceiling. Welstiel looked up, having barely nicked his stubbed finger, and only one drop of black fluid had fallen onto the plate.

"What is it?" Chane asked.

"Something about a ship . . . ," Welstiel began, but his gaze dropped to the brass plate.

Welstiel spun up to his feet and rushed back out of the hold. As his pounding footfalls filled the outer passage, Chane glanced down at the brass plate.

The one droplet of Welstiel's black fluids bulged at the center of its domed back, and the droplet had not moved at all.

Chane bolted after Welstiel.

Magiere's ship was nearly on top of theirs.

Welstiel burst onto deck and looked up to see the loose sail secured. Chane came out behind him, searching about in confusion.

"Where is it?" Chane rasped. "Do you see the other ship?"

Welstiel spun toward the ship's aft.

Both the captain and Klâtäs stood beyond the helm, exchanging quick, sharp words. He looked past them, senses widening, and caught sight of distant sails shimmering in the moonlight. Chane had followed, and Welstiel grabbed him roughly by his shirt.

"We must drive Magiere to ground!"

Chane scowled, but his gaze fixed into the distance behind their vessel.

"How?" he hissed.

"We sink her ship."

"No!" Chane spit back, swatting off Welstiel's grip. "Wynn is on board!"

"We must get them back on land," Welstiel insisted. "It is the only way we can follow them now. They will have time to abandon ship . . . including your little sage!"

He strode for the stern before Chane could argue.

Klâtäs saw him coming and shouted, "Go down in hold!"

The captain began calling to his men, and the tall, helmed man's voice was tinged with fear. He walked past Klâtäs toward the bow. Welstiel ignored the helmsman's order and followed the captain from a short distance with Chane close behind.

Ylladon sailors rushed about at the captain's orders. Two raced aft and uncovered the stern ballista. One by one, all the deck lamps were doused. Darkness enveloped the ship as Klâtäs suddenly threw his weight into turning the wheel.

Welstiel grabbed the rail as the vessel listed sharply, turning from the shore for the open sea. Men in the rigging worked madly to raise more sails.

"He's running," Chane said, watching the captain clinging to a rigging line at the ship's side.

"Obviously!" Welstiel returned, and then thought of what the captain had locked in his quarters. "We will change his mind!"

He ignored the captain standing midship and headed back to the helm.

"Get below!" Klâtäs yelled, still clinging to the wheel.

"You cannot outrun that ship," Welstiel said in a low voice.

The helmsman spit at his feet, eyes on the ship's arcing course. "What you know of it?"

"I know it is elven," Welstiel answered, inching closer. "And I saw what your captain has locked in his quarters. That ship will never stop coming for you—and the two women you have taken. It is faster than your vessel, and your only chance is to turn and fight."

Klâtäs shook his head but did not respond. It was clear the captain feared pursuit, as did the helmsman. Klâtäs spit out a stream of words that Welstiel could not follow, but he spun about at the sound of running footsteps.

The captain closed on him, his heavy shortsword in hand. Chane drew his longsword at the sight.

"Tell him that he must turn and fight!" Welstiel shouted at the helmsman.

Another sailor grabbed the wheel as Klâtäs let go, still speaking loudly to his superior. The captain slowed, listening, then eyed Welstiel as he barked a short phrase.

"If is battle vessel, we not can fight," Klâtäs said to Welstiel. "Their ship keep going fast . . . even crippled and sails down. Something under waves can break our hull, sink us."

An elven battle vessel? Welstiel had never heard of such, and the idea of something beneath the water that could sink its enemies sounded like nonsense.

"Load your ballistae with burning quarrels," he said. "Set fire to the sails, and its crew will abandon ship. But you must come about. If we charge, we have the element of surprise."

Klâtäs shifted anxious eyes toward his captain. The fact that he was even trying to convince his superior—on the word of a foreigner—meant he feared they could not escape. The captain snarled back, grabbed Klâtäs by the hair, and shoved him away.

"He say we run," Klâtäs answered. "Even under full moon, we maybe lose them in dark."

Persuasion was not working. Welstiel spoke calmly to Chane in Belaskian but kept his eyes on the helmsman.

"Kill the captain . . . and show them what you are."

The captain barked a question at Klâtäs, stepping toward the smaller man.

In the same instant, Chane thrust out with his longsword.

The startled captain tried to raise his shortsword in defense, but Chane's sword was already embedded through the side of his leather armor. The shortsword clanged against Chane's steel anyway. The impact jarred the longsword, twisting it in the captain's ribs. He buckled to his knees.

The fight should have been over, but Klâtäs reached for his saber. Welstiel pulled his sword before the helmsman could draw his and grabbed Klâtäs by the throat. He heard Chane's hiss grating like some enraged reptile.

The captain wrapped his thick hand around Chane's embedded blade.

The crewman at the helm abandoned his post to rush in.

"Move and you die," Welstiel growled in Klâtäs's ear, and lashed out his sword.

The tip clipped the rushing crewman and tore through the side of his face. The man twisted away, screaming as he tumbled to the deck.

Chane opened his mouth, exposing jagged, elongated teeth.

The captain tried to raise his shortsword again. Blood ran along Chane's blade in his side, either from the wound or from his free hand gripping the sharp steel. Chane lifted one booted foot.

He stomped down on the captain's forearm, just above the man's grip.

The captain's fingers sheared off on the longsword's edge. He dropped his shortsword with a guttural cry.

Klâtäs bucked in Welstiel's grip.

"Tell your men to stay back or they die!" Welstiel shouted. He dropped his sword to grip Klâtäs's hair. "Tell them now . . . or I save you for last."

Chane slammed his jaws closed on the captain's throat. He thrashed his head like a wild dog ripping prey in its teeth. Dark blood splattered across the deck, and flecks of it struck Klâtäs's face and chest.

Cries of hunger and desperation rose from somewhere in the belly of the ship.

Chane dropped the captain's limp body in the red pool spreading on the deck. He spit out torn flesh and turned glittering eyes upon the closing crew.

Welstiel focused his mind on his ferals below.

"Come!" he shouted. "Come to me now!"

Screams of release filled the ship's hull as Klâtäs cried out to his men.

Wynn spotted a point of light on the sea as the elven steersman called for his hkomas. But she could not see a ship. The light vanished as the hkomas came at a jog. He glanced at Wynn standing on deck in her shift—without Osha or Sgäile—and stopped below the aftcastle.

"I have lost sight of it," the steersman called, releasing the wheel to a crew member beside him. He came down to the deck and pointed. "It was there, ahead of us."

Chap began to growl.

"What is it?" Wynn asked.

He only huffed and rumbled.

"Go below!" the hkomas shouted at her.

"I will not! Look at him." She gestured to Chap. "Something is very wrong."

"Wynn—where are you?" Osha emerged below the forecastle, holding his gray-green cloak closed against the wind.

"Here," she answered, then turned quickly back to Chap. "Tell me what you see!"

Chap's growl deepened, but he would not look away from the ocean.

The steersman grabbed the back of Wynn's cloak. "Do as you're ordered!"

Osha reached Wynn's side and snatched the man's wrist. He shook his head slowly until the steersman released his grip.

"What is wrong?" Osha asked.

"An unknown ship ahead," Wynn answered, "and it is making Chap uneasy."

Osha leaned over the rail-wall, following Chap's gaze. "I see nothing."

"It vanished in the dark, but it must be there."

"Ship ahead!" someone called from up the front mast. "Human sails in moonlight, turning seaward."

"Human?" the hkomas repeated.

"Could it be the one?" the steersman asked.

"Ylladon!" the voice above cried out. "It is Ylladon!"

Osha glanced upward once, his expression confused. "You are seeking a ship?" he demanded.

"At our last stop, we heard of a raid on a lower coastal enclave," the hkomas answered, and the steersman rushed for the aftcastle as the hkomas called out, "All crew on deck! Full sail—and tell Âlhkasge to rouse the ship!"

Wynn turned to Osha at this new name. "Who is . . . Closing-Stone . . . and why must he wake up the ship?"

"He is our vessel's hkœda," Osha said quickly. "Even asleep the ship keeps swimming, but the hkomas now wishes for more haste. You should go below."

"Chap, come on," Wynn said.

The dog remained poised. Wynn grasped Chap's shoulders, and he growled at her without turning.

The stairwell's hatch shattered outward, and feral monks poured onto the deck.

Chane knew he was trapped.

Somewhere behind them, Wynn was on that other ship.

He had followed Welstiel's every demand. If not, Welstiel would have been overrun by the crew, leaving Chane alone amid marauders and a pack of ferals with no master. And killing the Ylladon captain had made his head swim with euphoria.

He tried to clear his mind as scattered sailors grabbed for weapons to fend off the monks. Welstiel still gripped the helmsman, but his face . . .

His colorless eyes glowed in his pale white features. His lips pushed apart around elongating teeth.

Chane had never seen Welstiel in full vampiric state. Perhaps the man had fallen so far over sanity's edge that his aristocratic veneer had cracked completely. The sight ate at Chane, until all he wanted was another warm body to tear apart. And someone kept squealing behind him.

He snapped his head to the side, glaring over his shoulder.

The sailor Welstiel had slashed rolled on the deck, clutching his face with blood dripping between his fingers. Chane jerked his sword from the captain's corpse and skewered the crewman through the heart. The man fell silent and limp.

Half of the crew had recovered from their initial horror and were now facing down the monks. Ferals worked their way around the sailors to cluster near Welstiel.

Sabel looked to Chane, sniffing the air, and then her gaze found the pool of blood around the captain's corpse. Chane backed against the starboard rail.

Could Welstiel control his children cut loose among the living?

"Tell your men to get back into the rigging!" Welstiel hissed into Klâtäs's ear. "You turn this ship back . . . or you'll be bloodless before your body hits the deck."

"They not do this," the helmsman choked, "not charge elven ship!"

"Look around! Who do they fear more . . . the elves or us?"

Welstiel felt the helmsman's pulse under his hand and heard its pounding rhythm in his own ears. The hunger it brought made him sick inside—because he wanted to feed.

The crew stayed beyond the reach of the hissing, sniffing ferals, but their faces were tense as they clenched their weapons. Klâtäs finally shouted at them.

Two shook their heads, and one lost all color in his face.

Welstiel shoved the helmsman into the wheel.

Klâtäs caught himself on a spindled handle, but he glanced down in horror at his captain's body. He began shouting again at the crew, but not one of them moved.

Welstiel needed at least six of them, more likely ten, enough to man the ballistae and at least keep the ship on course once it turned.

"Feed!" he snarled.

All five ferals rushed the crew with wild cries of release. Only two crewmen stood their ground as the others scattered.

Welstiel retrieved his sword. "Turn north, along the coast . . . while some of your men are still alive."

Klâtäs threw his weight into the wheel, cranking it hard. "Stop your beasts!"

Welstiel grabbed the side rail as the ship listed sharply and looked out across the deck.

The two sailors who had stood their ground were already dead, hidden beneath growling and tearing ferals. Their feast was broken as their bodies slid along the deck's tilt. Stumbling monks turned frenzied as each tried to close on the bodies first.

Welstiel counted off crewmen within sight. Four or five more were not to be seen—likely in hiding—and the rest had fled into the rigging.

"Halt!" Welstiel shouted in Stravinan.

As the deck leveled and the ship's prow swung north, he stepped out among his cowering minions. Again, the curly-haired man was last to back away from the torn bodies, his neck and forearms ridged with straining muscle. He still clutched at the deck, reaching for the nearest slaughtered crewman.

Welstiel raised his face to the ship's heights and the crewmen clinging to the rigging. Klâtäs shouted at them, and they scrambled to their duties.

Only moments had passed, and Welstiel remembered his companion. He turned to find Chane standing at the rail.

"Go forward and below," Welstiel said, "to the captain's quarters. But first check his body for keys. Behind the table in there, you will find a loose panel in the wall. Break it in and bring me the prisoners you find inside the wall."

Chane's eyes narrowed, but he silently searched the captain's corpse. He stood up with a soft chitter of keys and slipped away toward the bow.

Someone shouted from the rigging, and Klâtäs craned his head to search the night ahead.

"What is it?" Welstiel asked.

"The elf ship . . . come fast . . . we are seen!"

Welstiel looked out past the prow. "Put men on the ballistae. Now!"

Leesil roused from half-sleep as Magiere thrashed against him. She rolled toward the narrow bunk's edge, and he tried to grab for her, but she slipped over to the floor.

"Magiere?"

He pushed up onto one elbow, trying to come fully awake in the dim light.

Magiere crouched on all fours. Both of them were fully clothed, since they had to share a cabin with Wynn and Chap. Amber light glinted in her black hair hanging around her face—and she was panting.

Had she been dreaming again? Perhaps another nightmare?

"What's wrong?" he asked.

He clutched blindly for the lantern or whatever light Wynn had forgotten to put out, but he couldn't get a grip on it.

"Leesil . . . ?" Magiere whispered, and started to lift her head.

With a frustrated grunt, Leesil sat up and reached out. The light didn't come from a lantern.

At the head of the long bunk ledge, he saw the topaz amulet Magiere had given him. It glowed softly.

Leesil sucked in a harsh breath and looked at Magiere.

Yellow light exposed her pale features through the tendrils of her hair. Her irises were blacker than the room's shadows.

An eerie wail rang out from somewhere in the ship.

"Chap?" Leesil said, but Chap wasn't in the room—and neither was Wynn. "Oh, dead deities!"

Magiere scrambled up, snatched her falchion, and jerked open the cabin door.

"Where are they?" Leesil growled. "And how could an undead get on board?"

She didn't answer and ran out as he snatched up the amulet and pulled its loop over his head. He grabbed one of his winged blades, but with no time to strap it on, he threw aside the sheath and raced out.

Running, he caught up to Magiere as she slammed the hatch door with her palm. Its latch shattered, and they both burst onto the deck at the ship's seaward side.

The crew raced about purposefully. Several of them strung longbows and shouldered quivers. But Leesil saw no sign of a conflict or fight.

"Wynn?" he shouted, and then spotted her before his call faded.

She ran toward him with Osha close behind as they rounded the cargo grate. She skidded to a stop before the shore-side forward hatch.

"Leesil . . . Magiere? I was coming for you." Wynn whirled, pointing ahead. "Undead . . . another ship ahead . . . Chap sensed undead and ran up the forecastle!"

Magiere leaped to the cargo grate's edge, running past Wynn, and Leesil heard Chap cut loose another shuddering howl. Several elven crew members cast frightened glances toward the bow as the sound spread over the deck.

Leesil started to follow but stopped short when Sgäile appeared from the other forward hatch. He was struggling to pull on his tunic. All around, crew scrambled as the hkomas shouted over Chap's howls. Sgäile twisted about in the commotion, pausing to listen to elven voices. He grabbed for Leesil as he stepped in beside Osha.

"The ship will need a wide berth," he said. "The hkomas will head seaward to bypass the other vessel. Be ready to assist as needed."

"No," Wynn said quickly. "The other ship turned out to sea. We are closing for a look."

"What?" Sgäile asked in open surprise. "If it is Ylladon, that is folly! This is not a fighting vessel."

Chap's howls waned, and Leesil stepped back to peer up into the forecastle. The dog hung upon the forward rail-wall with Magiere.

"Show me!" she growled, her voice nearly lost in the noise on deck.

Chap stretched his head out as far as he could. Magiere leaned over the dog to follow his sightline.

"What is that?" Sgäile whispered.

Leesil glanced at him in confusion and found both Osha and Sgäile staring at him. No, rather, at his chest. He looked down once to the soft yellow glow of the amulet.

"Magiere gave it to me," he said, frustrated by the distraction. "It glows when we're near an undead."

"That is why Chap is howling," Wynn added urgently. "He wants to hunt . . . because he senses an undead. And it is on that other ship!"

Sgäile exhaled sharply, as if overwhelmed.

Two pairs of elven sailors thumped up the aft hatchway. One set carried a tall, stout wooden stand, while the other hauled a long heavier bulk wrapped in canvas. They trotted along the seaward rail-wall and up onto the aftcastle.

One pair set the stand on the aftcastle's seaward side, and the second pair mounted the canvas bulk on top. When they ripped off the covering, the first two lifted a broad steel bow, and then locked it down across the mounted stock of a ballista.

Two more crewmen ran past Leesil for the forecastle and its shoreward side.

"It appears the hkomas made extra preparations for this journey," Sgäile said and glanced to Osha. "There are also swimmers in the heart-room."

Osha's long face went slack as he looked toward the stern.

Before Leesil asked what this meant, both anmaglâhk headed up the forecastle stairs. Leesil grabbed Wynn's small hand to follow.

Magiere and Chap still hung upon the bow, peering intently out to sea. Chap ceased howling but fidgeted anxiously, and Magiere's irises were so fully black it was hard to tell if they were focused on anything in the dark. But when Leesil looked ahead, his own gaze locked on the ship.

He'd assumed the other ship was still a good distance off, but its square sails clearly caught the moonlight. The vessel aimed a course to pass on the elven ship's seaward side—then it veered.

Wynn's hand tightened on Leesil's fingers. "They are coming straight at us!"

Chane hauled the two bound elven women onto the deck by their hand shackles. The adult one was as tall as himself, though her slender build seemed as fragile as her younger companion. Neither had struggled when he pulled them from the hidden cell, but both jerked back as they emerged on the dark deck.

Even without light, they saw the feral monks hovering about. The bodies of the two slaughtered sailors were gone, but the curly-haired feral licked at the blood running upon the deck. The younger elf's voice filled with breathy panic as she said something to the elder.

Chane's anxiety for Wynn began to grow.

Sailors prepared ballistae under the watchful eyes of the hungry ferals. Men pulled off tarps and cocked back cable strings with cranks on the heavy weapons' stocks. Each ballista swiveled upon a tall stand mounted to the deck and all pointed forward along the ship's course. Quarrels the length of Chane's body were slid into place, their long steel heads wrapped in oil-soaked cloth.

Two more sailors came from below, carrying buckets of glowing coals.

"Keep those covered until we are ready to fire," Welstiel called, and Klâtäs echoed his command to the crew.

Welstiel trotted along the deck, weaving between the crew and his crouching ferals. He grabbed the shackles of the adult female out of Chane's grip.

"Bring the other," he ordered and passed by.

"This is too risky!" Chane hissed, holding his ground with his own captive. "What if Wynn—or your precious Magiere—is hit by a burning sail as it falls?"

Welstiel ignored him and shoved his captive toward the prow. He turned and called out to the helmsman, "How soon can we fire?"

Chane turned as well.

The captain's body was gone, likely thrown overboard, and Klâtäs held the wheel tightly in both hands. His face was as rigid and white as his knuckles.

"When closer," the helmsman shouted back. "We first fire at deck side. Cause fear and running. Keep elves busy and slowed."

"No!" Chane shouted. "You might kill anyone on that side of the ship."

Again, both Welstiel and the helmsman ignored him, and Chane charged after Welstiel, dragging his young captive.

Welstiel removed his captive's lower shackles and tied a rope end around her ankles. She struggled only at the last, until he grabbed her by the throat. Welstiel shoved, and the woman toppled over the side. The younger one in Chane's grip cried out in horror.

"What are you doing?" he snarled.

Welstiel held the rope pulled taut in his hands, and Chane peered over the ship's side. The elven woman dangled upside down, halfway above the dark water rushing past the hull.

"Take the rope," Welstiel ordered. "Now!"

Chane grabbed it with his free hand, and Welstiel whirled and slapped the smaller female across her temple.

She fell, and Chane released her manacles to keep control of the rope. The young one hit the deck in a half-conscious flop, eyes rolling. Chane was more concerned with whatever Welstiel had planned and tied the rope off on the bow's rail. Welstiel grabbed a dangling lantern from its hook and handed it to him.

"When I tell you, open its shutter and hang it over the side, so all can see the woman dangling there. We need an instant of shock on that elven ship to give us an advantage. When I give the order, cut the rope."

Chane suddenly understood, but it gave him no ease regarding Wynn's safety.

"Watch the helm," Welstiel ordered, and then closed his eyes.

He sank cross-legged in the bow and wrapped his left hand over his right, closing it tightly upon the ring on his right middle finger. He began thrumming a soft chant.

Chane crouched behind the rail, feeling lost as he clutched the lantern and rope.

Welstiel focused his will upon the ring.

Klâtäs had implied that they would need to be close for the ballistae's quarrels to succeed. This meant bringing himself and his followers very near Magiere and Chap. With so many undead aboard, their collective presence would not escape either of those two's heightened awareness.

The ring's power hid Welstiel and those he "touched" from anything but mundane senses, but now he required more from it. Once before, he had expanded its influence to smother Ubâd's spirit-sight, as the old one held Magiere captive. Now he had to hide any undead's presence on this vessel from Chap and Magiere's unnatural awareness for as long as possible.

He chanted quietly and felt the ring's sphere of influence twinge through his flesh—spreading, growing, and enveloping the whole ship.

. . .

Chane felt a strange tingle pass over him, as if his skin had gone numb for an instant.

He had no idea what Welstiel was doing. His thoughts wrestled for a way out of this situation before Wynn was placed in danger again. If the helmsman ordered a shot at the deck, Wynn might be killed—unless the elven captain had ordered all passengers below. And then she might be trapped once the ship began to burn.

Welstiel sat with eyes closed, hands clenched together, and a hum in his throat—and a cold notion entered Chane's panicked thoughts.

All he need do was draw his sword and cleave off Welstiel's head. The unleashed ferals would ravage the ship, and Chane might jump overboard amid the chaos.

But what if some of the sailors managed to survive? What if the elves attacked, seeing one of their own dangling from the ship's rail? What if the ferals panicked and fled amid the fire and quarrels, as the Ylladon crew responded in defense?

And no matter what, Wynn was still trapped in the middle.

Welstiel's interest in keeping Magiere alive, forcing her aground, meant giving the elven crew time to abandon ship—and Wynn along with them.

The half-conscious young elf lying on the deck moaned softly.

Chane held his place, ready to open the lantern.

Magiere locked her eyes on the approaching vessel, its moonlit sails bright in her night sight. It came straight at her, but not quickly enough, and the hunger burning in her belly began to rise into her throat.

Someone shouted, and amid that string of Elvish, Magiere heard Sgäile's longer elven name.

"The hkomas orders us below," he said. "I do not think that wise, but we should leave the forecastle, so the crew may function freely."

Magiere glanced back and saw the hkomas standing near the aftcastle's steps. When her gaze locked with his, he went still as he studied her. His head cocked suspiciously.

"Magiere . . . ," Leesil began, and then stopped as Sgäile sighed in resignation.

Magiere's awareness of them was smothered beneath hunger and the memories of a falchion in her hand and headless corpses at her feet, their black fluids running from her blade.

She had felt this before—but never so strongly. Whatever was coming on that ship, it overwhelmed her and nearly severed her self-control. But the need to hunt was a welcome relief against the pull to go south that plagued her.

She could slaughter what was on that vessel without holding back. She wanted—needed—that release. Her fingernails began to harden, and her teeth ached as they pressed her clenched jaws apart. She tried to force it down, keep it suppressed and hidden until she needed it.

And her hunger suddenly vanished.

Magiere teetered, suddenly faint at its loss.

Chap shifted frantically with a pained yelp.

"What?" Leesil snapped.

The soft light around Magiere vanished, and she looked to the topaz amulet hanging upon Leesil's chest.

The stone was dead and lifeless.

Magiere's stomach turned and shriveled at the loss of promised release as she stared back at the oncoming vessel.

Chap's foreclaws ground upon the rail-wall as he strained to peer more closely at the ship. He had felt the undead—as certain of their presence as of his own breath.

Where had they gone?

Though the ship still came at them, he sensed nothing upon it. This was not possible. He had not been wrong.

But the same thing had happened to him once before, in the streets of Venjètz. He had been running down an undead with Magiere and Leesil, and then his prey suddenly vanished—just like now.

Chap snarled in frustration, and Magiere slammed both her hands on the rail.

"No," she whispered, her voice pained. "No . . . no . . . no!"

Chap slipped into her thoughts and saw her rising memories of hunting . . . memories with far too much longing, close to lust. Someone shouted in Elvish from the rigging.

"It veers again!"

Light flashed on the waters ahead.

Chap slipped from Magiere's mind as he saw the oncoming ship. Its prow aimed to pass close on the elven vessel's seaward side. The light came from one bright spot near its bow.

"What is that?" asked Leesil, pointing out over the rail.

Chap's eyes adjusted and he saw . . . her.

An open lantern illuminated a tall elven woman dangling inverted over the other ship's near side. A rope cinched around her ankles suspended her with long hanging hair trailing in the rushing water. Half the elven crew ran to the seaward side as the other vessel began to pass.

"Hard to starboard!" the hkomas shouted. "Do not let them round our stern!"

Chap bolted around the seaward ballista and its crew to stand at the forecastle's stairs. Below on the deck, several elves began uncoiling rope with grappling hooks. Magiere passed him by, leaping down to the deck as she tried to keep the passing ship in her sightline. Sgäile moved to follow, but Leesil grabbed his arm.

"No, they're baiting you! They want you to rush in!"

The ships drew so close that Chap heard a voice shouting upon the other vessel. Sgäile jerked free of Leesil's grip.

"They have one of our people!" Sgäile shouted. "We do not abandon our own."

Chap's awareness suddenly sharpened—as if he were surrounded by undead.

All the voices around him muted in his ears. He shook inside with the need to hunt. Before he could search for the source of his returned drive, the rope on the other vessel's prow went slack.

The elven woman fell into the sea and vanished beneath the water.

Chap barely heard Sgäile's anguished cry.

Fire arced into the night from the Ylladon ship, rising in trajectories toward the elven vessel's sails. Magiere lunged for the deck's rail, shoving elves out of her way.

As the first burning shaft hit, panic flooded Chap's mind.

All he could do was howl, as he searched frantically for his charges—and some means to get them out of harm's way.

CHAPTER ELEVEN

Magiere rushed the rail-wall, bile rising from her stomach and burning her throat. She barely saw the elven woman strike the water; all her senses were focused upon the presence of undead. Someone behind her cried out in anguish, and Sgäile appeared beside her.

She had to jump, swim, do whatever it took to reach that other ship. She had to hunt.

Chap's howl rose above the commotion, and a volley of fire arced in the night sky from the other ship.

Magiere's rage burned hotter at the sight, and she lifted one leg over the rail-wall.

Something snagged her breeches leg and heaved. Her grounded foot slid, and her back slammed flat on the deck. She rolled over wildly, and there was Chap with his ears laid back, blocking her way to the rail-wall. Sgäile looked down at her, his expression unreadable. Someone shouted in Elvish, and he lifted his gaze up and past her.

The voice was vaguely familiar. Was it Osha?

Sgäile locked eyes with Magiere for a breath, and then he dove over the side, vanishing from sight. Magiere lunged up to follow him, to reach that ship . . .

Chap charged straight at her, snapping and snarling. He was one with her, alike in the hunt, yet he turned on her? Magiere snarled back at him.

The sky above ignited with fire and light.

Magiere flinched, shielding her tearing eyes as she raised them. A long metal spear with a flaming head slid down the mainsail, leaving a burning trail in its wake. It slammed point first into the deck.

A cracking impact shuddered through the deck, and Magiere lost her footing, buckling to one knee. Yellow light burned her eyes as fire scattered from the spear's head. She threw herself toward the aft, rolling away, but when she came up, her rage vanished.

Chap bolted the other way, toward the forecastle. He dodged droplets of flaming oil falling like burning rain.

Magiere tried to scream his name, but it didn't come clearly through her elongated teeth.

He arced around to the ship's shoreward side, but with the fire spreading on the deck between them, Magiere wasn't certain if he'd been burned. She took a breath and coughed as smoke filled her lungs.

What was happening? Where were Leesil and Wynn?

The hkomas shouted loudly over the din. Magiere snapped her head up at the crack of the forward elven ballista. A thrum of bowstrings sounded all around her as a flight of arrows arced toward the other vessel.

Welstiel pulled himself up the rail of the Ylladon ship, worn and drained from widening the influence of his ring. He had barely spread its reach long enough to get close to the elven vessel. When the first volley of burning ballista spears launched, his concentration had snapped, but now it did not matter.

Magiere had more to concentrate on than the presence of undeads.

Two burning lances cut along the shimmering elven sails, instantly spreading fire. The third went long, and its light snuffed in the sea. A fourth hit the hull at the waterline and fizzled out, but it remained embedded.

Welstiel faltered.

Had he gone too far? Had he put Magiere in too much danger, or could she still get clear and make it to shore?

A loud double crack rang out from the other ship.

Welstiel saw two heavy spears with long heads arcing straight toward his vessel. He dashed along the deck but only made midship before one hit—and Klâtäs screamed.

The ballista spear slammed through the wheel, and the helmsman vanished amid shattering wood. Welstiel skidded to halt and looked back to the prow.

The younger elven female tried to push herself up, staring dumbly about. Sailors at the ballistae abandoned their stations, running for cover.

Two leaped over the seaward rail and disappeared. And then Chane raced past Welstiel toward the stern.

What was that fool doing now?

Chane was almost to the aft when another ballista spear struck. It shattered the rail two steps behind him. He stumbled and fell, sliding along the deck amid scattering wood shards. The ferals went mad, screaming as they raced wildly about.

One pair of Ylladon crewmen kept their wits and fired the shoreward ballistae again. Another blaze of fire arced toward the elven ship. Then the pair crouched and took up oil-filled glass balls on long leather cords.

Welstiel had not noticed these before. The crewmen lit rags tied to the globes and began whirling them to sling toward their enemies. Welstiel charged them, panicked over Magiere's safety.

The engagement was not playing out how he had envisioned. But he was not quick enough, and the crewmen released their whirling glass balls.

Welstiel watched their small flames rise and then fall through the night air. The deck shuddered hard beneath his feet as another elven quarrel struck the hull somewhere below the rail. He ducked in against the rail as a rain of arrows fell around him, and he never saw the oil globes strike.

Running and shouting and screaming surrounded him as everything fell into chaos.

Sabel rushed by toward the bow, almost scrambling on all fours, and Welstiel snatched her by the arm.

"Get the others," he commanded. "Go below for our gear. Hurry!"

The terror did not leave her eyes, but she scrambled for the aft hatch.

They had to abandon ship, and Welstiel hoped Magiere would do the same.

Salt water closed over Sgäile's head, and icy cold spread through his muscles. He kicked for the surface, still doubting his actions.

He had sworn guardianship to Léshil and his companions. His first duty was to protect them, and the ship was on fire. But when he saw the elven woman vanish into the sea, his heart seemed to stop.

He was Anmaglâhk, sworn to protect his people. He could not let her die.

Sgäile broke the sea's rolling surface and gasped for air, but in his mind, he kept seeing Magiere's face up on the deck.

Eyes black, lost in vicious madness—the same monster that had attacked his caste in Cuirin'nên'a's glade. Even though he had sworn guardianship, his first instinct had been to kill her. Then he saw Wynn and Léshil on the deck's far side, dodging falling pieces of the burning sails.

Osha ran for them, shouting. "Go! I will protect them!"

And Sgäile had jumped.

The sea swells made it hard to search. Everything was beyond his control but the woman who had been dropped to her death. He only hoped she had stayed calm enough to flatten herself and float until he could find her.

Wynn gasped for air and coughed amid the growing smoke. Terrifying sights and sounds drove away reason, and all she could see was the horror of the burning ship.

A living ship.

Some of the crew tried to douse the fire with buckets of seawater, but spattered oil and falling sails kept feeding the flames.

And then Sgäile jumped overboard.

Wynn looked frantically about. Magiere knelt on the deck's far side beyond the cargo grate, but she couldn't see Chap anywhere. Elven crew ran about amid the flames, and a sizzling crackle sounded from up in the rigging.

And Leesil's shout carried to Wynn over the noise. "Magiere! Get out of there!"

He bolted toward Magiere, and Wynn saw the burning foremast crack midway up. It began to topple.

"Leesil, stop!" she screamed out.

He leaped the cargo gate. Rigging and shredded sails tore away under the falling mast as it slammed down on the deck's center—and Leesil vanished from sight.

"Leesil!" Wynn cried out.

Two sudden impacts, like shattering glass, struck somewhere on the deck, and a wall of flame erupted around the fallen mast. Droplets of ignited oil splashed up like fiery fountains and scattered everywhere.

Wynn twisted away, swatting at burning oil spots on her cloak. In one flailing spin, she saw Osha.

He ran along the shoreside rail-wall, the glint of a stiletto in his hand.

Before Wynn knew what was happening, he ducked and drove his shoulder into her chest. His arm coiled around her as the breath was crushed from her lungs.

Wynn gasped for air as her feet left the deck. Over Osha's back, she saw a long pillar of fire rolling from the deck's center toward the rail-wall—toward her.

The whole ship swirled away as she slammed down hard, sliding across the deck beneath Osha. She felt him roll, curling himself around her, until they slid to a stop.

And that rolling column of fire—the fallen foremast—crashed against the rail-wall where she and Osha had been an instant before.

Osha lurched up on his knees and slashed down at her with his stiletto. She barely flinched before the blade split the side of her cloak's collar. He ripped it off of her, nearly flipping her over on her face, and grabbed her by the arm. As he pulled her up, they both looked frantically about.

The crew had abandoned any attempt to control the flames. A visceral scream, like a great cat in anger, broke over the fire's crackle. Before it had even faded, Osha shouted.

"Léshil!"

Wynn saw Leesil half-crouched on the cargo grate's far side, surrounded by fire. Magiere clawed at the flames, trying to reach him. Her eyes were black disks as tears ran down her snarling face. The grate burned too wildly around Leesil, as did the forecastle and deck between him and the aft. Even the far rail-wall was ablaze. He ducked low, shielding his face and eyes as he twisted about.

Wynn rushed for Magiere, looking for any way to get to Leesil. Then her feet left the deck again.

Osha swung her back with his arm around her waist.

"Put me down!" Wynn shouted. "Leesil cannot see. He needs help!"

"Bith-na!" Osha shouted in her face, then shoved her into the corner between the aftcastle and rail-wall.

"No" to what? Wynn struggled against him. What did he mean?

Another bright red-yellow light grew in the air. Gasping, she saw the burning mainsail sagging toward the deck.

"Magiere, look up! Get back!" Wynn called, choking on her words.

Cargo hold. Now!

Chap's voice erupted in Wynn's head.

She saw him racing along the far rail-wall from the forecastle . . . running on top of the rail. His shimmering fur glinted with red and yellow firelight.

Wynn writhed in Osha's grip. "Come on! Below . . . we meet Chap below!"

Osha released her, shaking his head, and she grabbed his wrist, pulling him. She stopped at the hatch stairwell and shouted as loudly as she could.

"Magiere, come on! Chap says to go to the cargo hold!"

But Magiere either did not hear her or would not leave. The burning mainsail writhed in the wind, like a living thing of fire that coiled down to snatch her in its grip.

Magiere cried out like an animal, reaching through the flames for Leesil. Her gloved hand began to smoke, and she snatched it back. She let hunger fill her and shut her eyes against the fire's brightness. She tried stepping into it.

Heat instantly seared her face and hands, and she leaped back.

Wynn shouted over the roar—something about a cargo hold—but Magiere couldn't take her eyes from Leesil's blurred shape amid the blaze.

Another flickering blur raced toward him from the ship's far end. It loped along the burning rail-wall, and then brightened by firelight into a silvery canine form.

Chap leaped high through the flames.

His forepaws struck Leesil's shoulder. Both toppled upon the burning cargo grate, and it shattered beneath their sudden weight.

Firelight surged around Magiere as she screamed.

Leesil was gone. And Chap with him.

More light descended from above her.

She saw the first whipping corner of the burning sail coil around the mid mast. She threw herself backward, rolling away as the descending inferno swallowed the midship.

Wynn had shouted something about the cargo hold.

Magiere turned on all fours, knocking aside a deckhand as she lunged toward the hatchway. A blur of gray-green cloak disappeared down the stairs, and she rushed in behind it, nearly falling over the first step.

Osha turned with wide eyes, and Wynn stood below the last step.

"Chap said we must get to the cargo hold!" she shouted.

Magiere understood now.

"No!" she growled back. "You . . . get off the ship! I'll . . . get to Leesil and Chap."

Wynn opened her mouth to argue.

"Take her!" Magiere shouted into Osha's face.

She shoved him against the stairwell wall, grabbed Wynn by her shift's shoulder, and nearly threw her at the young elf. Without waiting to see if they obeyed, Magiere ran down through the ship's passages. At the bottom, she followed the only narrow corridor that headed toward midship. There was a door at the end.

Magiere didn't even slow. She hit it with her shoulder at full speed, and the door crashed open, dangling in pieces from its hinges.

"Leesil!"

Water sloshed knee-deep around her legs as she slogged in. The hold was filling with seawater through a hole torn in the hull's far side. And then she heard splashing that didn't come from her own steps.

Leesil broke the water's surface, rising up, and Chap half-waded and half-paddled toward him.

Magiere struggled forward, her boots already heavy with water. She was breathing too fast and couldn't say anything as she pawed frantically at Leesil, searching for injuries.

Runnels of water left soot-smudged streaks on his face, but his expression melted in equal relief at the sight of her. His was still holding on to his one winged blade, and he grabbed her wrist with his other hand.

"I'm all right," he said and then looked down. "Your hands!"

Her gloves were charred and blackened. She hadn't even noticed the sting in her hands.

Fire around the grateless cargo hatch above filled the hold with flickering light, and seams of flame began spreading along the ceiling.

"We have to get out of here," she said.

"We won't survive onshore without our gear," Leesil argued, and headed for the shattered door.

Magiere almost grabbed him from behind, ready to throw him over her shoulder and flee—but she knew he was right. He led the way with Chap right behind as they all trudged through the water in the outer passage.

They hurried to their quarters, grabbing what they could—weapons first. Leesil found their coats, and then hesitated for breath. He took up his new winged blades, but Magiere's dagger was still missing. Sgäile had not brought it back yet.

"Forget it!" Magiere snapped, and jerked him toward the door.

They slogged back for the stairs, and then an elf they'd never seen before came through the passage's other end. He was dressed in a plain canvas tunic and breeches, and his feet were bare. He carried a large barkless root almost too heavy to hoist, smooth and round and dully pointed.

Magiere froze. The root's long tail trailing behind the man moved on its own—like the ship's tail that Wynn had spotted so many days past.

The elf stopped at the sight of Magiere, and then crouched to set down the strange squirming bulk. He glared up sternly at Magiere and then Leesil, and spoke quickly in Elvish. It sounded like a question.

Magiere could only shake her head and point toward the hatch stairs.

"We have to get off," she said. "So should you."

She had no idea if he understood.

He lowered his head, muttering in Elvish, and reached around his back to fling something toward her. The long white-metal dagger fell in the shallow water near Magiere's boot.

She reached down and picked it up. Its hilt was now thick and wrapped tightly with leather. By the time she looked up, the elf was gone, then she spotted the tail of his wooden burden whip as it slid up the hatchway stairs.

"Put it away and let's move!" Leesil growled.

Magiere shoved the blade in the back of her belt. They emerged to find the deck engulfed in flames feeding upon remnants of sails, rigging, and crumpled masts. Magiere looked about for the tall, barefooted elf.

He stood at the seaward rail-wall just below the aftcastle, the only place on that side not blocked by fire. Magiere saw no sign of the moving root he'd been carrying.

"Come on!" she shouted. "Get to a skiff!"

He never even turned around. The tall, barefoot elf just stood there. Beneath the crackle of fire and splitting wood, Magiere heard a low rolling hum, like a song without words. He slowly lifted his head, as if watching something moving in the open water.

The deck creaked beneath Magiere's feet.

Chap barked sharply as he scrambled toward the shoreward rail-wall.

Magiere had no choice but to follow him.

Sgäile's arms grew heavy in the cold water, and despair began to mount.

Where was the woman?

He swam back along the Ylladon ship's course, but through one swell after another he found nothing. And both ships had drifted onward behind him. Then he saw something swirling upon the surface.

It was too light to be kelp or debris. Then it sank again, gone from sight.

Sgäile thrashed forward. When he reached the spot where it had gone down, he dove under.

Beneath the surface, the water was so dark that all he could do was hold his breath and grasp about. His hand struck something rough and thin—a rope. He grabbed hold, winding it around his hand and wrist, and kicked for the surface.

Sgäile's head broke through. Before he even sucked in a breath, he pulled. Twice he sank under, reaching down, hand over hand along the rope. Until his grip closed on soft, cold fingers. He grabbed hold and kicked back up to the surface.

She came up, gasped for air over and over, panic-stricken.

"Float," he managed to say. "Relax yourself."

He kept an arm under the middle of her back as they both rolled over the crest of another swell. The woman tried to turn her head, blinking water from her eyes so she could see him.

"Sister," she choked. "My sister . . . is on the ship."

Sgäile grew even colder.

Another of his people was on that human vessel? Still holding her atop the waves, he looked back. The elven ship—the Päirvänean—was burning in the night.

By now, the hkomas would have ordered the crew into the skiffs. The Ylladon vessel had been damaged as well, and listed deeply to one side. It was so far away, how could he do anything to save this woman's sister?

A thundering crack rolled across the night swells.

The Ylladon ship rocked, and its stern shifted suddenly toward the open sea.

"No . . . ," Sgäile moaned.

Another thundering impact filled the night. The marauder ship's prow dipped sharply into the sea and did not come up again. It was sinking.

The hkœda had released his *shävâlean*—the "swimmers." They would not stop pounding and ramming at the Ylladon vessel until either it sank beyond reach in the depths or they became too damaged or worn themselves.

Sgäile looked away as the woman tried to lift her head to see.

"Do not," he said.

He pulled a stiletto to sever the rope, then grasped the back of her tunic and towed her as he swam. Another crack sounded in the distance from the hull of the Ylladon ship.

All Sgäile could do now was try to reach the shore.

Chane watched helplessly as oil globes struck the elven ship and flames erupted across its deck.

"Wynn," he whispered.

He lunged across the ship, searching to slaughter whoever had flung those globes.

"Stop!" Welstiel shouted.

Chane turned, sword in hand.

Sabel came behind Welstiel, along with the other ferals, all laden with canvas and ropes and packs.

"You said they would have time to escape!" Chane rasped, and his throat turned raw.

Welstiel's lips curled angrily. He opened his mouth to spit a response, but Chane never heard it. The sound of wood smashing filled his ears.

The Ylladon ship lurched sharply, and seawater sprayed over the rail, driving debris across the deck. Welstiel clutched the mast, glancing about as half the ferals were thrown from their feet.

"Take the packs and gear from her," Welstiel said, pointing to Sabel. "Tie the canvas to your back."

Chane glared at him and did not move.

"We have to swim," Welstiel snapped, "as far north as possible before going ashore. We cannot risk Magiere or the dog sensing us."

"Swim?"

"We will be too visible if we take a skiff," Welstiel answered. He turned to Sabel and the others. "Leave no one here alive, and then follow us."

Another thundering crack sent the ship spinning sideways, and the bow dipped sharply.

Chane grabbed the rail to keep from sliding. The ferals snatched at anything they could hold on to. For once they showed little eagerness for feast or slaughter. And Chane's own hate faltered under his instinct to survive.

"We all go now!" he hissed. "Any crew left would never let themselves be caught by the elves. We are hardly in danger of them revealing you!"

He pulled himself up the slanting deck and took Sabel's bundled canvas. He tried to wrap it tightly about his own pack, to protect the precious texts from the monastery, before tying the bulk across his shoulders.

Welstiel never answered him, just threw his own pack full of arcane objects over his shoulder. Without hesitation, he shouted, "Come!" to his monks and vaulted the ship's rail.

Another loud crack exploded into the hull. Chane clutched the rail, waiting for the ship to settle, and then jumped overboard.

In a brief glimpse of the burning elven ship, his thoughts filled with the image of Wynn's oval, olive-toned face. Then he sank beneath the cold, dark water.

"Sgäile!" Leesil shouted from the skiff's front, one hand gripping its upturned prow.

He searched the ocean swells with Osha crouched beside him.

Magiere and Chap sat in the back with Wynn, now wrapped in her coat, as two elven sailors pulled on the oars. At least two other skiffs headed for shore, but not this one. Leesil had turned their small vessel southward, parallel to the coast and back along the marauder vessel's course.

"He's got to be out here," Leesil said tightly. "He's too much of a pain in the ass to end up dead."

"Yes," Osha answered. "We find him."

But the young elf looked no more certain of his claim than Leesil. And Sgäile was indeed a pain in the ass.

Leesil was sick of the way the man looked at him, as if he was supposed to do something that Sgäile wouldn't actually say. All the man's superstitious nonsense about ancestors and his people's old ways did little more than complicate Leesil's life—or hint at a life he wanted no part of. Now that self-righteous, long-boned, sour-faced throat-cutter—that idiot—had thrown himself overboard to save someone he didn't even know.

But . . . Leesil couldn't let him die out here.

Chap barked, and Leesil's grip tightened on the prow as the skiff crested another swell.

"There!" Wynn cried.

She pointed beyond where Chap clung to the skiff's edge with one fore-paw. Out in the water, Leesil caught a flash of white.

"Sgäile!" he shouted again, and looked down to Osha. "Tell the crew-men to turn us that way!"

Before Osha finished rattling off instructions to the elves, that light spot in the water rose again.

Sgäile swam on his side as he towed the elven woman floating on her back. He looked exhausted and pale, with his wet hair flattened around his head and face.

"Here!" Leesil cried out. "Osha, get us alongside of him."

Sgäile paused, lifting his head. When he spotted the skiff, he redoubled his efforts.

Osha pressed in beside Leesil, speaking Elvish to the two oarsmen.

"We'll take the woman back here," Magiere called out, and pulled Wynn and Chap from the side. "You take Sgäile up front."

The elven crewmen turned the skiff sharply as it rolled down a swell, and then shipped their oars. Sgäile closed with two final strokes and reached for the skiff.

Magiere leaned over the side, but the woman hardly moved, unable to help herself. One elven crewman knelt to assist, and they pulled her over the edge.

Leesil grabbed Sgäile's arm as Osha took hold of his belt, and they dragged him in. He collapsed on the skiff's bottom, soaked and shivering.

"Blankets, coats!" Leesil shouted. "Get me something to cover him!"

Osha stripped off his cloak and threw it over Sgäile as Magiere dug among their belongings. She tossed Leesil his coat then spread her own over the woman. Wynn started to remove her coat.

"No," Magiere said. "All you've got is your shift under that."

The crewmen took up the oars and began rowing hard for the shore.

Leesil struggled to pull off Sgäile's soaked tunic and wrap him in the coat. He spread Osha's cloak over the top as Sgäile leaned back into the prow's cubby, still shaking uncontrollably. Sgäile snapped a long string of Elvish through chattering teeth.

Osha stared back at him, stunned motionless. Leesil couldn't follow Sgäile's words, but he understood the tone.

"It is not Osha's fault!" Wynn cried out. "And he *was* protecting us!"

"Yes," Osha added sharply. "We find you . . . *jeóin.*"

"Don't blame him!" Leesil snapped at Sgäile. "You're the fool who jumped overboard in the middle of an assault. And he wasn't the only one who chose to come searching for your waterlogged carcass."

Sgäile struggled to sit up. His gaze slipped from the rowing crewmen to Magiere. He seemed to look her over, or look for something in her face; then he settled back, exhausted.

Leesil plopped down beside Osha, shaking his head. For an instant, he entertained the notion of tossing Sgäile back overboard.

The notion passed.

Wynn huddled with Magiere and Chap in the skiff's rear. The thundering cracks behind them had ceased as the other ship sank below the surface. But the elven vessel drifted slowly, still burning alive.

She pressed her hands over her face, trying not to cry.

When she dropped them down, the others were repeatedly glancing behind the skiff with somber eyes. She heard the hissing crackle of water meeting fire but could not look.

The elven woman lying at her feet coughed and sputtered but looked as if she would survive. She curled on her side, closed her eyes, and began to sob softly. Her tears were lost in the seawater clinging to her long triangular face.

No one spoke the rest of the way to shore.

When the crewmen shipped the oars and jumped into the surf, Wynn spotted three other skiffs on the beach. Torches had been lit and planted nearby. Leesil and Osha jumped out as well. Other elven crew came out, and they all pulled together until the skiff came to rest upon the gravelly shore.

Chap hopped out, and Wynn climbed after him.

She saw familiar faces among those present, though she knew none of the crew's names. She was relieved to see that the hkomas had survived. His left arm and one side of his face were seared, but he appeared not to notice. Two of the crew hurried in to help the rescued woman from the skiff.

One bowed his head slightly as Sgäile staggered out and Osha helped him to a dry spot on the beach.

Wynn tried to count those who had survived. Just beyond the hkomas stood the girl with the thick braid and oversized boots, whom Wynn had learned was his steward.

"Sgäilsheilleache . . . ," the hkomas said and faltered.

He gave no thanks for Sgäile's actions, nor did he commend him for his courage. Anmaglâhk did not expect thanks—that much Wynn had learned from her time in Sgäile's company.

Out in the distance, lingering flames from the elven ship flickered upon the water. And then they were gone. Wynn felt the mood around her change as relief sank into mourning.

"May your ancestors take you and watch over you," the hkomas whispered, looking out over the surf and into the empty darkness.

Feeling helpless, Wynn mouthed this same Elvish epitaph for the living ship.

The hkomas's face darkened as he turned upon Magiere.

"Who were they?" he demanded. "Even Ylladon do not charge us in a reckless assault . . . just to kill our Päirvänean at such cost to themselves."

Magiere could not follow his Elvish, but she stood her ground, returning his glare. Sgäile climbed to his feet, wobbling as he stepped between them.

"She knows nothing more than we do," he said.

"I saw her on deck!" the hkomas growled back. "She sensed something coming . . . as did the majay-hì."

"Such debate will not help us now," Sgäile countered. "Were you able to send a distress call?"

The hkomas's suspicious gaze stayed on Magiere. "Yes. I reached a sister vessel of my clan. She is a scant two days out of Ghoivne Ajhâjhe . . . a long distance north."

Sgäile nodded with little relief. "She will send word at the next harbor and locate a closer ship. Our people will come."

At this, the young steward fidgeted behind her hkomas and glanced northward.

Osha stepped in, turning to the hkomas. "We must hide the skiffs and get our people off this beach . . . and see to our wounded. Anything else should wait until morning."

Everyone fell silent at this calm but solid counsel, and finally the hkomas nodded. Both Magiere and Leesil silently watched this exchange, and Wynn felt sudden shame in forgetting to translate for them.

"I will tell you later," she said. "Osha wants to get the boats off the beach and find shelter further inland."

Leesil scanned the waters. "He's right. Especially if any of the other crew survived . . . and made it to shore."

The skill of swimming came back to Chane. As a boy, his father had taught him—if "teaching" was the right word for being tossed into a cold lake, with rope around his waist to keep him from drowning.

He swam a northward course behind Welstiel several lengths ahead. Hopefully far enough not to be seen when they came ashore—and not to be sensed by Magiere or Chap. His cloak and gear made the process difficult, but neither the cold nor the lack of air concerned him. At first he held his breath, as in his living days. When he finally gasped reflexively, opening his mouth, water surged into his lungs. He choked in panic, but it was only an unpleasant sensation, no longer harmful to a dead man.

Finally, the sea floor rose into sight.

Chane followed Welstiel's lead, clawing along the bottom until there was not enough depth to bother staying submerged. They broke the surface amid the surf, and Chane's soaked cloak became a massive weight. He was halfway up the rocky beach before he stopped, bent over, and vomited salt water from his dead lungs. As he finished stripping off his pack and cloak, the ferals emerged from the water.

One by one, pale faces rose from the dark surf as they shambled from the sea to the shore. Sabel had gone over the side just before Chane, but she was last to emerge, just behind Jakeb.

Chane shook his head and hands, trying to clear some of the seawater, and he turned his gaze south.

"Are we far enough?" he asked. "Will she sense us?"

Welstiel stared off along the shore. "Yes, we are safe from detection . . . if Magiere survived."

He sounded less than certain, which brought Chane pleasure at first. If Magiere were dead, Welstiel would suffer, perhaps never finding his coveted treasure. Anything that wounded Welstiel was now sweet to Chane, but he quickly lost the taste of it.

If Magiere had not survived, what chance could Wynn have?

"Check now!" Chane hissed. "Get out that damned dish of yours!"

Welstiel turned with a sharp glance. "My exact intention."

He crouched, opening his waterlogged pack, and drew out the domed brass plate, shaking it several times to scatter clinging droplets of water. With his back turned, he drew his dagger. Chane could not see anything as Welstiel chanted softly.

Welstiel lifted his head, facing south and away for Chane.

"She lives . . . and she is a short distance away."

These words only made Chane burn silently.

"But that says nothing," Welstiel added, "concerning your little sage."

Chane could not go see for himself—not without being detected and hunted. Not without Welstiel's protection, or rather that of his ring of nothing. And the situation could grow even worse if the ferals came after him or were discovered. He wanted those creatures nowhere near Wynn—if she lived.

Dawn was half a night off, but they would travel no farther. The mortals would sleep, and tomorrow at dusk, Welstiel would verify which direction Magiere had taken.

"I will find us a camp," Chane hissed and stalked off into the trees.

CHAPTER TWELVE

Sgäile awoke groggy and weak at the first streaks of dawn, but he remained silent until the others began to stir. To his surprise, the fire was still burning—someone had fed it regularly during the night. He sat up and found Osha squatting beyond the circle of bedrolls, keeping vigil.

Sgäile said nothing, though he wondered if he had been too harsh on his young student the night before.

His breeches were still damp, but his tunic and boots were reasonably dry by the fire. As the crew roused, daylight brought a sense of greater safety, and some wandered closer to the beach. Soon they had cookfires burning while others searched for wild berries or sea life along the beach's rock jetties. He watched their quiet attendance to necessities, until the hkomas approached.

The man's burns looked worse in the morning light. He made no mention of pain, but Sgäile knew better.

"We will travel the coastline," the hkomas said. "The forest here is dense, and we are too near human lands. We will be safer the farther north we go, though we must keep to the shore for our ships to find us."

Sgäile agreed but hesitated. "I travel south with my charges, as required by guardianship."

The hkomas's amber eyes flickered in surprise. All an'Cróan respected the tradition of guardianship, but perhaps the hkomas thought Sgäile's protection of his own people should take precedence. With a frown, he turned away toward the beach.

Sgäile sighed and looked about to check on his charges. Wynn was again dressed in her loose elven clothing with the pant legs rolled up. She and Osha foraged for berries with the crew, while Magiere and Léshil inventoried the belongings they had salvaged before abandoning ship. Thankfully they had also retrieved the gifts of the Chein'âs.

Strangest of all, Magiere had the dagger tucked into her belt at the small of her back. Its hilt was complete with leather strapping over the living wood that Sgäile had requested from the ship's hkœda. He wondered how and when she had retrieved it.

Chap scrambled among the crew who were digging for clams. He sniffed about the beach, barking loudly now and then. At his call, crewmen came to dig where he stood. This morning, Sgäile's people did not seem to mind humans, half-bloods, or a wayward majay-hì in their midst. He was about to join in the foraging when the hkomas's young steward cautiously approached him.

"I am called Avranvärd," she said.

"I know who you are," Sgäile replied and finished pulling on his boots.

The girl's eyes widened briefly. "May I speak with you ... Sgäilsheilleache?"

He stopped, suddenly uncomfortable. Something in this young woman's tense manner troubled him.

"Of course," he answered.

She gestured toward the clearing's edge, away from the camp. "In private."

He had little strength left for intrigue, but he followed her beyond earshot. At first she would not look him in the eye.

"I must come with you on your journey."

Sgäile's discomfort increased. "Your place is with your crew and hkomas. But do not fear. One of our ships will come for all of you."

Avranvärd shook her head. "I am not concerned for my safety. I ... I was sent by Most Aged Father to watch the humans and report."

"That is impossible," he stated flatly. "You are not Anmaglâhk."

"I will be," she answered and finally raised her eyes to his. "Most Aged Father sent me—gave me this *purpose*. I must come with you."

She was so plainspoken and steadfast that Sgäile almost believed her. He felt the blood drain from his face. How could Most Aged Father place an untrained girl in this position? And why send someone to report on those under Sgäile's guardianship ... as if he could not be trusted?

Avranvärd's young face grew troubled. "Sgäilsheilleache?"

He glared down at her until she began to fidget.

"Listen carefully," he said, exerting calm into his voice. "You will remain with your crew and make your way with them back to our lands. Do otherwise, and I will expose you to your hkomas. Do you understand?"

"But . . . I have a purpose . . . from Most Aged Father! There is another—"

"You will serve no purpose at all," Sgäile cut in sharply, "should your hkomas and all the seafaring clans learn of your subterfuge among them. Your duty is to your hkomas and crew!"

He grabbed her by the wrist, prepared to haul her back to camp, but she broke free before he took three steps. She shifted toward the beach, watching him with a pained shake of her head as if her world had turned over and was not as it should be.

Sgäile remained silent and stern. Avranvärd turned and ran.

He had no patience left for hero worship or shattered illusions. Perhaps now he understood why Brot'ân'duivé and other caste elders so often shied from the people. An'Cróan saw their protectors in the garb of the Anmaglâhk, but they knew little of what that life required.

And now he, too, was left in ignorance.

Sgäile had tried to ignore the growing animosity between Most Aged Father and Brot'ân'duivé. It seemed both had expectations for his current purpose—and neither had fully related these to him. He did not know who to trust, and this left him reeling.

All Anmaglâhk must trust in each other, or their people would suffer from the discord.

He scanned the beach, spotting the hkomas near the hidden skiffs. The man must still be wondering why two anmaglâhk would abandon a stranded crew for humans and a half-blood. But Sgäile had no time for guilt-driven explanations, as he headed over.

"Your steward is more traumatized by the death of your ship than the rest of your crew," he began. "Keep her close, and be certain she remains under watch for a few days."

The hkomas studied him and then slowly turned sad eyes to the empty sea.

"I never thought to see any Päirvänean, who blessed my clan, murdered by humans. Yes, Avranvärd is young, and such a loss might be worse for her . . . I will watch over her."

Sgäile nodded with gratitude and walked back toward the campfire, but the exchange did nothing to ease his mind.

Magiere and Léshil had finished repacking and stood talking quietly. Léshil had suffered only minor scorches on his face and hands. In all other respects, he was well enough, but Sgäile remembered the state of Magiere's gloves. She no longer wore them.

Her bare hands were pale and unblemished—with no sign of burns.

Sgäile looked up quickly at her face, but she did not seem to notice. Dressed in breeches, hauberk, and coat, she hefted one pack.

"Can we get started?" she asked.

"Yes," he said, still staring at her.

Magiere returned her habitual scowl. "What?"

"Nothing."

A tall elven sailor hurried upslope, stopping in front of Sgäile.

"The hkomas says you go south . . . with the humans." And before Sgäile could respond, the sailor pulled off his thick cloak and held it out. "Take this and my gloves. I will not need them, as our people will come for us."

The cloak was deep brown, not dark shifting green-gray. Sgäile's exhaustion mounted at this sacrifice. The sailor did not know him; the man saw only a revered member of the Anmaglâhk.

"I cannot."

"Please," the man said. "Do me this honor."

Sgäile almost flinched. His thoughts slipped once to a strange lesson his own *jeóin*, his teacher, had once told him.

What are we beyond how our people see us?

Young and ignorant, and still full of awe for his teacher, Sgäile had been unable to think of an answer. Years later, he overheard Brot'ân'duivé reiterate this lesson to a handful of new caste initiates, all still years away from seeking out their own *jeóin*.

We are more, we are less, Brot'ân'duivé admonished, *and we are nothing but silence and shadow. All we can do is accept their hope in us with the humility it deserves.*

This was the truth behind the litany of Anmaglâhk—in silence and in shadows.

To serve, and not to place oneself above or below that service, no matter what shape or form it took. To be the silence of peace that surrounds duty, and the one who guards it from within the shadows.

Sgäile slowly reached out and grasped the cloak and gloves. "Thank you."

The sailor smiled with great relief and headed back for the beach. But the man's reverent act of kindness left Sgäile more burdened—more uncertain.

He wanted to slip away with his word-wood and speak to Most Aged Father, to somehow understand the patriarch's sudden lack of faith in him. Then he thought on Brot'ân'duivé's silent scheming and the Chein'âs's gifts given to Léshil—Léshiârelaohk, so named by the ancestors. And a majay-hì, like those of ancient times, had thrown itself into the lives of a half-blood and a pale monster of a woman.

Stretched between too many paths, Sgäile had to choose one to follow.

"Are we going or not?" Magiere demanded.

Sgäile turned toward the beach. "Chap, it is time!"

Not long ago, the thought of calling a sacred majay-hì by a personal name would have shocked him.

Chap loped upslope, looking over Magiere and Léshil as Wynn and Osha joined them as well. The majay-hì glanced at the cookfires burning along the beach, where the crew prepared a good catch of clams. He released a groaning whine.

"We will find breakfast along the way," Sgäile assured him.

Chap grumbled and trotted off, and Magiere followed. As Léshil stepped in behind her, Sgäile noticed the tips of the Chein'âs's winged blades peeking from his pack. Léshil's continued discomfort regarding the weapons was clear.

"May I wear your old blades?" Sgäile asked cautiously. "The new ones should take their place, and you will walk more easily with less weight."

Léshil cast a narrow-eyed glance over one shoulder. "Why don't *you* wear the new ones?"

It was more of a challenge than a question.

"I could not." Sgäile shook his head. "They were given to you."

"Oh, just do it, already!" Magiere snapped at Léshil. "You're the one who insisted I accept the dagger."

"They don't fit my sheaths," Léshil argued.

"I can make alterations," Sgäile countered, "while we walk."

For all the bitter ire in Magiere's voice, none showed on her face as she looked intently at Léshil.

"They're only weapons—nothing more," she said. "You choose what to do with them."

"Fine!" Léshil growled and dropped his pack. He jerked the tie straps of his old blades, pulled the gifted ones from his pack, and thrust both sets at Sgäile.

Sgäile took them, and Léshil hoisted his pack and pushed past Magiere after Chap.

Sgäile slipped Léshil's old blades from their sheaths. He handed both sets of blades to Osha, and, as they walked along the shore, he drew a stiletto and began altering the sheaths.

As he worked, he pondered this next leg of their journey—born not from hope but determination. He was tired of Magiere's and Léshil's ill-mannered petulance. Their mood proved infectious, and Sgäile grumbled under his breath as he cut leather.

By midday, Hkuan'duv was pacing the deck.

Avranvärd had not contacted him at dawn, and he had called for anchor, not knowing how far ahead the other ship might be. Soon his concern gave way to open worry.

Dänvârfij leaned with one hip against the rail-wall, watching him. "Can you not contact her instead?"

"No . . . I cannot risk revealing her presence, even to that ship's hkœda and hkomas."

"Then cease stomping on the Päirvänean's back," she said. "You will disturb it."

He glared at her calm face, her skin like tea tinted with goat's milk. "Something is wrong."

"I know we cannot be seen," she returned, "but neither can we lose track of their ship."

"Inform the hkomas," he said. "But make certain our pace is cautious."

Dänvârfij pushed off the rail-wall and headed for the aftcastle.

Hkuan'duv turned his gaze down the coast, feeling trapped by the constraints of his purpose. He was not accustomed to hiding from his people or those of his own caste.

Kurhkâge emerged from the hatch below the forecastle, followed by A'harhk'nis. As always, the latter appeared deceptively spindly in his over-sized cloak. Kurhkâge fixed his one eye upon Hkuan'duv.

"We are moving," he said. "Have you received communication?"

Hkuan'duv shook his head. "We must attempt to locate the ship ourselves."

Dänvârfij rejoined them, and all four headed up to the bow, scanning the waters ahead. Several crew members glanced at them, but no one spoke. The hkomas's strained voice rose in orders to his crew.

A'harhk'nis looked up into the rigging. "I should relieve the lookout and watch for myself."

His voice was so quiet that it was difficult to hear, but Hkuan'duv agreed. "Yes. Good."

A'harhk'nis stepped upon the rail-wall, snatched the rope ladder to the mainmast, and clambered upward.

His sharp eyes might be no better than those of a seasoned crewman, but should they close too quickly upon the other ship, Hkuan'duv felt more secure in A'harhk'nis's judgment. But as the day wore on, no word came from above.

"What if the girl was discovered?" Kurhkâge asked. "What would Sgäilsheilleache do?"

Hkuan'duv turned away from the prow, not wanting to answer. Indeed, what would he himself do if one of his own caste were sent to spy on him? He did not wish to even think about it. He must focus on his purpose, for the sake of his people.

"Greimasg'äh!" A'harhk'nis called from high above. "Look to the beach!"

Hkuan'duv turned to lean upon the shoreward rail-wall.

Even at this distance, their hair glowed in the afternoon sun. Tall figures moved up the coastline and became distinct as they approached. He realized he was looking at an an'Cróan ship's crew, but why were they ashore, and where was their Päirvänean?

"Are there outsiders with them?" Hkuan'duv called up.

"No . . . I see only an'Cróan."

Amid the captain's call and the crew's shouts, they began preparing a skiff. Several people onshore saw the oncoming ship. They waved their arms and cloaks in the air.

Hkuan'duv leaped down the forecastle stairs, closing on the skiff being lowered over the side.

"A'harhk'nis, come down," he shouted.

He scanned the sea, but saw no sign of the other Päirvänean. What had become of Sgäilsheilleache, Osha . . . and the humans?

As the ship came to anchor, Hkuan'duv stepped to the rail-wall gate, taking up the skiff's anchoring line. The hkomas rushed in and jerked it from his hand.

"This is no longer your concern," he said. "Our people are stranded. They take precedence over this pursuit of yours."

Hkuan'duv almost let anger get the better of him. But the hkomas was correct, his harsh tone justified, and who could blame him? Anmaglâhk had taken polite control of his vessel, and they trailed their own people like a pack of skulking Ylladon.

"I must know what happened," Hkuan'duv explained, "and as quickly as possible."

"Then you are welcome to accompany my crew, Greimasg'äh."

The hkomas's hard words clearly implied who was now in charge.

"You may ask your questions," the hkomas added, "so long as you do not impinge upon the well-being of those left stranded."

Hkuan'duv nodded slowly. He gestured to his team to wait on board and descended quickly into the skiff.

As the small boat closed upon the shore, two of the exhausted land-bound crew waded out to guide it in. Hkuan'duv saw burns and other injuries among those stranded, and the knot in his stomach tightened. He counted heads, and by a quick estimate, a fourth of a standard cargo vessel crew was missing. A middle-aged man in a brown head scarf came closer. His face and arm were badly burned.

"Anmaglâhk?" he breathed in surprise. "How did you reach us so quickly? Did Sgäilsheilleache send word?"

"You are the hkomas?" Hkuan'duv asked. "Where is your ship? Where is Sgäilsheilleache?"

The questions sounded cold even to Hkuan'duv.

"We came upon and pursued a Ylladon ship, after hearing of a settlement raid." His voice faltered. "They turned on us with no regard for their own vessel . . . and burned the Päirvänean."

Hkuan'duv blinked in chilled disbelief.

"Our hkœda sent a swimmer," the hkomas added. "Which sent the Ylladon to bottom."

"You had swimmers on a cargo vessel?" Hkuan'duv asked, and then waved off the question before the hkomas answered. "What of Sgäilsheilleache?"

The hkomas scowled, not expecting this exchange. "He left with the humans and a majay-hì, traveling south along the coast."

"On foot?"

"Yes, on foot," the man snapped. "How else?"

Shame flooded Hkuan'duv as he looked at the pinched, burned faces and frightened eyes of his people. Their ship had been murdered and a fourth of them with it, while he had sat waiting beyond the horizon for Avranvärd. She must have died in the battle, or she would have called him.

"You have my sorrow," he whispered and meant it. "We will take every-one aboard and get them home."

The hkomas closed his eyes and nodded.

The skiff was loaded first with those with the worst injuries. Hkuan'duv waded into the surf as two more skiffs arrived. He pulled one ashore and began helping his people climb in. As the last boarded, Hkuan'duv reached out and touched the hkomas's hand.

"I have others of my caste on board. Please tell them I wait here, and to bring all of our gear. Tell them to ask the ship's crew for as much white canvas or cloth as they can spare. Safe journey and peace to you."

The hkomas nodded. "And to you . . . wherever you walk now."

Hkuan'duv stood alone upon the shore, watching the skiffs rock through the surf toward the ship. Or was he alone?

He cocked his head at footsteps coming along the beach behind him.

The sound faltered several times in a fumbling attempt at silence. He did not turn until he knew this amateur skulker was within reach, and then he found himself facing a girl with a thick braid and oversized boots.

"I am Avranvärd," she said quietly.

Hkuan'duv suppressed his surprise.

"Why did you not board with your crew?" he demanded.

After an instant of her own shock, she replied, "I belong with you—"

"Why did you not contact me?"

"It all happened too quickly," she rushed on, her voice pained. "I was on deck amid the fire and could not abandon my duties to send word. I . . . I tried to help . . . but everything was burning."

Hkuan'duv breathed out through his mouth. This child was not to blame. She was not Anmaglâhk and never should have been placed in this role.

"It is all right," he said. "You followed your duty. No one would expect otherwise."

He waited as Avranvärd regained her composure.

"Can you tell me more of what happened?" he asked.

She sniffed and began recalling bits and pieces of the marauder vessel's first sighting—and the strange behavior of Magiere and the majay-hì. She told of the an'Cróan woman dangled over the side of the Ylladon ship, cut loose to drown, and how Sgäilsheilleache had jumped overboard to go after her. Beyond these details, events had become too chaotic for the girl to follow as she recounted trying to put out the flames consuming the ship.

Hkuan'duv listened silently with patience.

"But on the beach," Avranvärd added in the end, "Sgäilsheilleache abandoned us! I told him who I was . . . that Most Aged Father sent me . . . but he refused me and left with those humans."

Hkuan'duv's lips parted in brief hesitation. "You did not tell him of my presence?"

She straightened. "Of course not. My *purpose* was to watch and report to you, and nothing more. But now I am cut off."

"Do not be concerned. Join your crew, and you will be home again soon."

Avranvärd stared at him, and her young features went slack. "But . . . I am with you. I did just as Most Aged Father asked me."

Hkuan'duv was uncertain how to respond. What had this girl been promised?

"I must travel quickly," he explained. "My team and I go south. You must return with the ship."

"No!" she nearly shouted. "I am to be Anmaglâhk! Most Aged Father promised. I will help you track Léshil and the humans."

Hkuan'duv had no intention of explaining the skills required, ones Avranvärd did not possess. Yet, for all she had done and all she had been through, he pitied her.

This selfish, defiant young woman would never be accepted as an initiate. Her spirit was entirely unsuitable. How could Most Aged Father promise such to someone who did not possess the necessary potential? But that lie was all Hkuan'duv had left to save Avranvärd from herself.

"If you are Anmaglâhk," he said sternly, "you will follow the request of your caste elder. Join your crew and return to Ghoivne Ajhâjhe."

"No!" she cried angrily. Then she cringed, looking at him—not unlike an obstinate child second-guessing her outburst.

"Should I escort you to the ship?" he asked.

Avranvärd's lips rolled inward, clenched tightly, but her eyes began to glisten. Before one tear could fall, she turned away and dropped to her haunches upon the rocky beach.

Hkuan'duv remained silent, even as the skiff turned from the distant ship and headed back for shore with his comrades. In part, he regretted any ill feelings toward this girl, who had fed him information in the pursuit of his purpose. But kindness was not always a kindness. In the end, any solace he offered would only sting Avranvärd more.

A'harhk'nis, Kurhkâge, and Dänvârfij jumped into the surf and pulled the skiff ashore.

Avranvärd remained as still and quiet as a small stone on the beach. As Hkuan'duv's companions joined him with their gear, the girl finally climbed into the skiff. The two crewmen pushed the boat back into the surf.

Hkuan'duv faltered, calling out before he thought better of it. "In silence and in shadows . . . Avranvärd."

She did not turn to acknowledge him.

"What was that about?" Dänvârfij asked, gazing after the girl.

"Nothing," he answered.

This was the first lie he had ever told Dänvârfij. He had been asked to track—and perhaps betray—members of his own caste, including the honorable Sgäilsheilleache. Now Most Aged Father had made false promises to an immature girl. It was obvious that Avranvärd had been denied admittance to the caste once before. Why else would she have been offered this odd purpose, and cling to it in frantic desperation?

Hkuan'duv steeled himself against doubt.

Most Aged Father had always placed the people's welfare above all things. If he had done this, then he had a purpose.

"Sgäilsheilleache will keep to the coast for as long as possible," A'harhk'nis said. "If he and his charges seek a destination in any mountains, they must round the far end of the Blade Range. They have over a half day's lead on us."

A sensible assessment. "Then let us begin," Hkuan'duv said and turned south at a jog.

But he glanced once at the ship, the living Päirvänean, still floating upon the sea. That tawny vessel, flickering with green in the sunlight, carried the girl with a twice-crushed dream.

Wynn tried to hide her relief when Sgäile called a halt to the day's trek.

Walking all day after so much time aboard ship was an unexpected effort. By noon, her knees were trembling, and near dusk she was struggling to keep up. Even worse, no one else was having the same trouble.

Leesil was only too glad to have his feet on dry land, and Magiere's obsession gripped her even harder. Sgäile told her to slow down several times during the day. Even Chap had difficulty keeping ahead of Magiere.

Trudging along behind everyone, Wynn had studied her companions. At times her sorrowful memories of the night before seemed echoed in their expressions. No matter how hard she tried, she could not put aside the fire and screams and smoke—and the sight of the ship's tawny deck blackened and splitting beneath the flames.

"Stop," Sgäile called out. "We must make camp."

Magiere whirled around at the lead. "There's plenty of daylight left!"

"Preparations must be made before entering the mountains," he said. "We will need this daylight, and more each day, to gather necessities."

Thankfully, Leesil dropped his pack. "He's right. Help me start a fire."

He reached out for Magiere's hand. She breathed through her mouth a few times, and finally let him pull her along.

Osha gathered their gear by a fallen tree at the beach top, and Wynn crouched with him behind that barrier against the wind.

"This will do nicely," she said.

Osha nodded, but he peered over the tree's weather-bleached trunk, watching where Leesil had taken Magiere. Wynn hoped Leesil could keep Magiere pacified in their slow progress, and she set to inspecting their supplies and gear.

So far, she'd had no chance to see what Leesil had salvaged from the ship. He had assured her that the elven quill, ink, and parchments Gleann had given to her were in one of the packs. Chap came to sit beside her.

Wynn studied the sleeves of her coat. She had worn it a few times to satisfy Magiere, but the garment felt constricting and heavy—and she had lost Chane's cloak in the fire.

What of the cold lamp crystal?

She blinked at Chap's sudden question, and reached inside her coat to the pocket of her elven tunic.

"It is safe," she answered.

Osha turned a puzzled glance her way, obviously thinking she spoke to him.

"Never mind," she told him. "Just . . . it is nothing."

He wrinkled his brow and went off to scavenge firewood.

To Wynn's surprise, Sgäile knelt down to examine the packs, and his tan, handsome face leaned close to hers. His manner had changed since their first meeting, though he remained reserved in her company.

"Do we have a cooking pot?" he asked.

Together, they pulled objects from the packs. Wynn found a large pouch of herbal tea, also several flints, coils of thin rope made from silken fibers, three water flasks—but only two wooden mugs. They would have to share.

"Ah, here," she said, pulling out a tin pot. "We can make tea, but we will need more fresh water soon."

"We will find streams along the way. But in the mountains, higher up, we must melt snow to fill our flasks."

Wynn looked at their few other belongings.

"Leesil grabbed some tarp and two small blankets." She sighed. "But no food . . . after all Magiere's careful preparations. We never anticipated being shipwrecked."

Sgäile reached behind himself, beneath his cloak, and pulled out a folded square of green-gray. When he shook it out, it became a drawstring bag of reasonable size.

"Come," he said. "Fire will be more of a concern in the heights than water."

Wynn was uncertain of his meaning, but she followed him into the trees above the beach. Chap trotted after her.

The landscape was appealing in a harsh way. White-edged waves tumbled against the beach below, driving foaming arches up the gravelly shore and sending soft spray into the air over craggy jetties. The rough foothills were covered with dense pockets of spruce and aspen, and Wynn spotted thick redwoods higher up. To the west and above, the snow-capped peaks of the Blade Range cut the sky. More directly south, she thought she could make out where they ended far away. Somewhere in that direction was their way into the higher mountains, the Pock Peaks.

"Look here," Sgäile said and crouched down.

Wynn clambered along the sharp slant between the trees. Where he pointed she saw animal droppings at the base of an aspen.

"From a deer?" she asked. "Are you going hunting?"

"No, I will find sea life near the jetties. You can gather droppings and put them in this bag."

"Excuse me?" Wynn said.

"If Osha or I have time, we will help," Sgäile added. "This must be done every evening so long as we have opportunity. We will dry what we find by the fire."

Wynn wrinkled her nose. "You want me to collect . . . animal dung?"

"Yes," he answered, as if the reason were obvious. "From what little Magiere described, we will go far above any tree line, where there is little or no fuel for a fire. Herbivore droppings can be burned, and this may be our only source of heat."

"Oh . . . clever," Wynn said, but it was still a disgusting task. She knelt at the aspen's base, calling out, "Chap, time to put your nose to work."

Chap let out a rumbling whine and licked his nose at her, but he began poking about the rough slope. When Wynn looked up, Sgäile was gone. She picked up her first chunk of dung with only forefinger and thumb and dropped it quickly into the sack.

She kept at this until daylight waned, following Chap's huffs and barks to find fuel more quickly than she could by sight. In the end, they barely filled the bottom of the sack. Wynn decided to clean her hands in the sea and headed down for the beach.

When she emerged on the rocky shore, she did not see their camp. Rather than stop to wash just yet, she stepped farther out and looked both ways. She spotted the old downed tree to the north and headed off with

Chap following. Before she was a stone's throw from camp, she slowed, and all thoughts of cleanliness emptied from her head.

Sgäile and Osha stood bent over in hip-deep water where the surf was calmer behind a rocky outcrop. They were bare to the waist, their cloaks and tunics lying high on the beach. A pile of silvery fish wriggled on the rocks near their clothing.

The two elves kept as still as trees with their hands sunk just below the water's surface. Their blond hair hung loose across their tan shoulders.

Osha dropped sharply, his arms spearing deep into the water.

He straightened, droplets spraying off his wet arms, and a flat gray form thrashed in his hands. He waded quickly toward the beach, and when the foaming surf receded to his shins, he flung the captured flounder onto the gravel.

"How many?" he asked in Elvish.

Wynn started and then hurried over to the pile. "Um . . . eight."

But Osha had already waded back out to Sgäile, and they spoke too low for her to hear over the surf.

Wynn kept staring. Osha seemed different—less awkward, almost graceful in the undulating water, catching fish with his bare hands. He turned back with Sgäile and they waded toward her and stepped smoothly out of the surf.

Wynn fidgeted with a strange nervous energy, as if Osha were a stranger. Half-dressed, with the ends of wet silken hair clinging to his shoulders, he looked so . . .

"What is wrong?" he asked.

Wynn swallowed. "Nothing . . . um . . . we will never eat all these tonight."

"There are ways to make it last longer," Osha answered with a smile.

He and Sgäile began pulling on their tunics. Wynn looked away until they finished.

"Can you carry our cloaks?" Osha asked and, without waiting, he snatched up the remaining catch and headed off after Sgäile.

"Of course," Wynn answered, but as she crouched to pick them up, she spotted Chap.

He was squatting on the gravel, watching her intently, and then glanced once after Osha before wrinkling his brows at her. A heated blush spread over Wynn's face.

"Just keep your muzzle shut!" she said and quickly bundled up the cloaks to stalk off.

Back at camp, Leesil had started the fire and already boiled water for tea. Magiere leaned against the fallen tree. She faced toward the south.

Sgäile and Osha set to cleaning fish over a hole they had dug in the gravel. Once done, they buried the waste and spitted several fish to roast over the flames. They hung the rest of their catch higher above the fire's rising smoke. Osha produced a small pouch and pinched out a green powder. He rubbed this all over the hanging fish.

Chap whined and licked his muzzle.

"Not long now," Sgäile said.

"Why so much?" Leesil asked. "The extra won't smoke or even dry fully by morning."

"Yes—they will," Sgäile answered. "Osha is using powdered *cl'leichiojh*."

"Woodridge?" Wynn asked. "The tree growths Osha showed me on our journey through your land?"

Sgäile nodded.

"Hold on," Leesil cut in. "He's rubbing fungus all over our food?"

Sgäile shook his head. "It is edible and has astringent properties. We must build food stores before reaching the high range Magiere seeks."

Magiere continued staring south, her features intently drawn. Her fingers kept clutching and scraping absently upon the dead tree's gray wood. Wynn exchanged a glance of mutual concern with Sgäile. Fortunately the water reached boiling, and they set to making tea.

For the first time, Wynn was genuinely glad Sgäile had chosen to come with them.

And Osha as well.

CHAPTER THIRTEEN

Welstiel had rested through the day in the makeshift tent Chane had rigged among the beach-top trees, but he had not fallen dormant. He still possessed enough elixir to keep him conscious for many days, so he'd merely remained quiet until Chane and the ferals roused. Now the monks crawled to their hands and knees around him. Despite their long swim, their tabards were still bloodstained.

"She has a long lead," Chane said. "Likely traveling all day."

Welstiel knew Chane's true thoughts were not fixed on Magiere but rather on his little scholar, Wynn. Such a trivial matter did not deserve attention. He left the tent and walked through the growing darkness down to the gravel beach, to crouch and pull out his domed brass plate.

"Straight south," Chane said, standing over him. "Between the Blade Range and the ocean, she can only follow the shore."

"For now," Welstiel responded.

He stood up, not liking having Chane at his back, and decided not to scry for Magiere. It would be pointless so early in her journey. His main concern was to follow her closely enough not to miss any major course change—and yet keep his group beyond her or Chap's range of awareness. A fine line to walk.

The monks clambered downslope, sniffing the shore air.

"Have them pack up," Welstiel said. "We will start as soon as they finish."

Despite recent events, he believed himself in a good position. Still unaware of his presence, Magiere was moving onward.

The sister of the dead will lead you.

Of his former patron's taunts, this one phrase held true. He would allow her to lead, without needing to rein her in under his control.

Two ferals mewled softly in agitation. Jakeb began slapping a tree with his hand and then motioning southward. Sabel grabbed Chane's arm.

"Chhhhhaaan," she slurred, and dragged Chane a short distance past Jakeb's tree.

"What is it?" Welstiel asked.

"I do not know," Chane answered. "Their senses are stronger than mine, even when . . ."

He fell silent, his nostrils flaring wide as he looked off through the trees.

"Life?" Chane whispered. "They could not be so close and . . . wait . . . it is gone."

Welstiel hurried over. Chane's sense of smell was more developed than his own, but Welstiel doubted Magiere could be this close—or could she? His concern turned to anxiety.

Had she or one of her companions been injured? Or had something else delayed her? He could not allow Magiere to learn of his group's presence; she must not have warning.

"Wait here," he said. "Keep the monks quiet. Get them back in the tents if I do not return by dawn."

"By dawn?" Chane asked in surprise. "Where are you going?"

"Do as I instruct!"

He pushed past along the rough forested slope, staying clear of the beach. If Magiere was ahead, his ring would hide him from her. He caught only glimpses of the ocean as he worked his way south. Then he began sniffing about for himself, until he finally picked up a scent.

He crept on, and the odor sharpened more frequently on the unpredictable ocean breeze twisting through the foliage. Then it seemed to surround him from within the trees, and he halted, peering about with his senses fully opened.

Life-blood filled his nostrils, but it was different and faintly familiar—earthy and rich, yet less musky than a human's. He closed his eyes, with the scent filling his head, waiting for a triggered memory . . .

Of the lower levels of Darmouth's keep.

A tall figure clad in a green-gray cloak carrying another over his shoulder.

Welstiel opened his eyes.

He smelled elves.

He stepped onward, and the scent broke and faded in the breeze. So he reversed until it strengthened once more. And yet he saw nothing. He turned all the way around.

They were here—he had to be right on top of them.

Hkuan'duv heard footfalls on fallen leaves as something approached from the north. It was still a ways off when he tapped his companions awake. He swiftly motioned them into the dense heights of the nearby pines and evergreens, and they climbed and vanished from sight.

He stood watching north, and when he saw as well as heard movement, he backed into the depths of a thick fir, melding against its bark. He pushed up his face wrap until its edge slipped over his nose, and then tilted his head down so his cowl shadowed his eyes.

The stillness of thought is a silence, unheard and unnoticed.

The silence of flesh leaves only shadow, impenetrable and intangible.

This was how Eillean, Léshil's grandmother, had once tried to describe it, as she sat with him one long night in Crijheäiche. So seldom had they crossed paths. And that night, two Greimasg'äh attempted to describe the mysteries of silence and shadow. In the end, they merely chuckled at each other—for who could truly put such into words?

Hkuan'duv loosened his cloak and pulled its folds around himself. He let his mind clear, becoming nothing but an empty vessel filled by what his senses perceived. Sinking into a quiescence of mind, body, and spirit, he let the shadows embrace him.

A stranger walked straight through the spot where his comrades had rested moments ago.

Pale-skinned, even for a human, the man's dark hair was marred by white patches at his temples. His well-tailored cloak was shabby and his boots scuffed, as if he had walked countless leagues. The man stopped and sniffed the air.

He turned a complete circle, wandered the sharply sloped little clearing, and then returned to its center, scenting the air once more. He came so close that his shoulder brushed the branch tips of the fir Hkuan'duv stood within.

The man's eyes glittered softly, his irises nearly colorless.

Without moving, without thought, Hkuan'duv drew air through his nostrils. A stale scent, devoid of human sweat, lingered beneath the odor of the fir.

Welstiel smelled more than one elf—three, maybe four. The scent hung in the small clearing, waxing and waning in the shifting breeze. Yet no matter where he turned, no matter where he looked, he saw no one.

Magiere's venture among the elves might explain their presence. But why would they trail her—or were they following Leesil? Either way, he worried how this might affect his plans. He wanted no one to get between himself and Magiere.

The scent of life waned, diminishing, until he smelled only moss and needles and the salted breeze. He peered about but still saw nothing, and finally turned back north to where Chane and his monks waited.

Welstiel could not hunt something he could not find.

When Hkuan'duv lost sight of the stranger, he clicked his tongue three times, telling his companions to wait. Slipping from the shadows, he followed the stranger's trail. At a glimpse of movement ahead, he slowed, pausing until it disappeared. He followed again in silence, tracking the pale human by sound.

Then he heard grunting and snorting.

Hkuan'duv closed in, one silent step at a time. As the sounds grew closer, he spotted more movement in a clearing just above the beach. He sidled into an aspen, barely making its leaves shiver. Once again, he let shadow take him.

The dark-haired stranger approached another human, tall and younger with red-brown hair. All around them, others moved like half-crouched beasts, snuffling in agitation. They showed some fearful obeisance to the dark-haired man. Their faces were twisted, and their eyes glittered like his. Their tabards and robes were splattered with dark stains.

The tall young one spoke. "Was it Magiere?"

Hkuan'duv closed his eyes, letting their words fill his emptied mind. The strangers spoke Belaskian in low tones, and the younger man's voice never rose above a hoarse rasp.

"No . . . I do not think so," answered the man with white temples.

"Then what? Who else could possibly be out here? Some Ylladon survivor?"

"Not them," the elder answered. "They would not . . ."

Someone began savagely sniffing the air, and Hkuan'duv parted his eyelids.

Several of the crouching figures snarled and inched along the slanted forest floor.

"What now?" the dark-haired man asked.

"I do not scent anything," his companion answered. "They grew agitated when you left. It may be nothing more than wildlife."

Hkuan'duv had been detected somehow. What were these robed humans who acted like beasts? He dropped low, bunching his cloak and pulling its folds snugly close. He slipped into the forest as silently as a prowling majay-hì. It took only a few breaths before he was certain no one was pursuing him.

Once clear, he sped up and slipped swiftly through the trees. He whistled softly before entering the clearing, and his comrades dropped from above.

"Who was he?" A'harhk'nis asked. "He did not breathe as we do."

"And so pale . . . ," Kurhkâge added, "like the one Most Aged Father accused before the council of elders. This can be no coincidence."

"What did you find?" Dänvârfij asked softly.

Hkuan'duv was unsure how much to discuss—as he was uncertain himself. Magiere had been accused of being an undead. Though the council of clan elders had dismissed Most Aged Father's charges, the patriarch's firm belief had never wavered.

Magiere, the monster and undead, had walked freely in the protected realm of the an'Cróan. Now others, so similar in coloring and attributes, trailed her.

"An entire group camps some distance behind us," Hkuan'duv finally said. "I counted seven. I believe they are following Magiere as well, but I do not know why."

"How did they come to be here, so close upon her heels?" A'harhk'nis asked, his voice hard. "Did they make any mention of the Ylladon?"

Hkuan'duv shook his head. "The hkomas said their ship was destroyed."

"A Päirvänean was also burned," Dänvârfij pointed out, "and yet most of our people reached shore."

Hkuan'duv had considered this.

"Should we capture one of them?" Kurhkâge suggested. "Perhaps glean more information?"

Hkuan'duv saw hazards in such a pursuit. When finished, they would have to kill the prisoner . . . thing . . . to maintain secrecy. He looked at Dänvârfij.

She shook her head.

"They know little to nothing of our presence," she said, "and pose no immediate threat to us or to Sgäilsheilleache and Osha. But if these pale ones have a claim concerning Magiere, they could be useful later. We cannot leave Sgäilsheilleache at odds between our purpose and his guardianship."

"If they posses useful knowledge," A'harhk'nis countered, "we must have it. And if they murdered our ship, they should die."

Hkuan'duv glanced at Kurhkâge, who looked silently troubled. It was clear he saw merit in both his companions' arguments. Duty and sense required that Hkuan'duv listen to all worthwhile input, but the final choice was his.

"We will watch and wait," he said. "But now we are monitoring two separate quarry at once . . . one of which appears to travel by night. We must move farther up into the foothills, ranging lower only as needed to track them. We will need all your skills, A'harhk'nis."

"Of course, Greimasg'äh," he answered.

Hkuan'duv's decision ended all discussion.

Just past dawn, Chap watched Sgäile, Osha, and Wynn pack up the dried fish. Leesil broke camp and then joined Magiere, who was once more peering southward over the fallen tree.

Chap had heard her murmuring in the night. Though Leesil tried to comfort and quiet her, Chap had slipped into her sleep-muddled mind. He tried to bury her dark dreams beneath recollections of hearth and home, of warm nights in the crowded Sea Lion Tavern, where familiar townsfolk filled the common room with chatter and clanking tankards.

His efforts were fruitless. Each memory he called up was quickly obliterated by the one of perpetual ice clinging to a six-towered castle. And for an instant, he glimpsed a pale-faced figure flicker past the frost-glazed pane of a window.

Now Magiere stood by the fallen tree, dressed in breeches and hauberk, with her black hair unbound and her falchion on her hip. The Chein'âs's long dagger was tucked slantwise into the back of her thick belt. Her dark eyes shone in the morning light with a hard intensity.

Sister of the dead . . . my child . . . lead on!

Chap recoiled at those words rising from Magiere's memories, back-stepping once as he pulled from her mind.

That voice hissing in the darkness of her thoughts . . . like something on the edge of his own memories that he could not place. He shivered, and when he looked up, Magiere was watching him.

Chap's earthly instincts screamed that they should turn back. And in that faltering instant, he considered committing a sin. He remembered a law of the Fay:

Whatever they might do otherwise, no one of them would ever enslave the will of any being.

In part, this was why he had chosen to be "born" rather than invade the spirit of one already living. But if he wished, he could take Magiere, possess her even for a moment, and turn her from this journey. In his time with her and Leesil, he had come to respect their need for free will. So how could he take that from her now?

For that matter . . . why did he think of enslavement as the first "sin" of the Fay?

And how did these sudden fragments of his memories—and the voice of Magiere's dreams—connect to this artifact she sought?

More missing pieces that his kin had torn from him at his "birth."

Magiere reached down to stroke his head.

"When we get there, I'll know what to do," she whispered.

The others were packed up and ready to leave. Leesil stood with Sgäile, and Wynn walked with Osha, chatting away in Elvish, forgetting to enforce his practice of Belaskian.

Chap turned his eyes up to the west, and the high wall of the Blade Range, seemingly distant beyond the forested foothills. He traced the jagged silhouette far southward to where the range broke against the even higher snow-capped mountains.

"We'll travel the coast as long as possible," she said. "I'll know when we need to turn inland."

Leesil took her hand.

As the others headed down the open beach, Chap remained a little longer. He had forsaken everything to protect his charges from death and from their fates. But a chill ran beneath his thick coat, as if the worst was yet to come, and he dropped his head, feeling helpless.

He tried to focus on Wynn's light chatter to Osha about screeching seabirds wheeling high above the shore. And he loped after them across the gravelly beach.

CHAPTER FOURTEEN

Chane was still young in his undead existence and, at times, felt he knew too little of his new nature.

Almost a full moon had passed, and now he and Welstiel climbed into the high, snow-choked Pock Peaks south of the Blade Range. He gave little thought to the temperature dropping lower each night, as he never truly felt the cold.

As dawn approached, his fingers would not close.

Chane stared at his hands, paler than ever before.

"Welstiel?" he rasped.

Jakeb whimpered and began biting at his fingers.

Chane tried to fold his fingers against his thigh. His legs had stiffened and barely moved.

Welstiel cursed under his breath and dropped heavily to his knees, digging furiously in the snow with stiffened fingers.

"Set up shelter, quickly," he ordered, but his words were half-mumbled.

"What is happening to us?" Chane demanded.

Sabel and Sethè wrestled with the tent's cold-stiffened canvas as Welstiel uncovered a flat rock beneath the snow. He fumbled with his pack, but his hands were too stiff to open it. In the end, he simply bit through the flap's tie and dug clumsily inside before drawing out what he sought. The steel hoop with dark etchings was hooked over his wrist, and he dropped it in the hollow.

At the clang of steel upon stone, Chane remembered the hoop's scent and taste of char. He no longer felt his legs, but he kept silent, waiting to see what Welstiel would do.

Humming softly, Welstiel swept stiff fingers around the steel hoop, and its hair-thin lines and symbols began to change. Red sparks appeared, quickly spread, and those dark etchings brightened until all the hoop's markings were as fiery as a smith's forge. Heat began to emanate from the steel.

"Thaw your hands," Welstiel ordered, "but keep them still until they loosen . . . or you could lose a finger. We do not have enough stored life to repair severed digits."

Chane dropped hard to his knees, relieved he could bend at all, and glared at Welstiel.

"Why did you not warn me!" he hissed.

"I thought if we kept moving," Welstiel began, "we would not succumb to—"

"Answer me!" Chane spit back.

"We have bodies, dead or not," Welstiel returned in a low voice, "susceptible to freezing . . . but unlike the living, we do not succumb to pain . . . so we had no warning."

More secrets of Chane's new existence—fire and beheading were not the only things for a Noble Dead to fear. And again, he'd narrowly escaped a harsh lesson before Welstiel finally revealed the truth in little pieces.

"Put out your hands!" Chane whispered at the ferals.

He held his own above the arcane source of heat. Monks scrambled in around him to do likewise. Within moments, Chane's fingers began to flex, though his legs and arms were still stiff.

They raised the tent over the snow hollow and the glowing hoop, and then huddled together once more around the source of warmth. Welstiel shed his gloves, warming his fingers more directly, and Chane noticed his ring of nothing was now on his left hand. Perhaps the change meant nothing, and he never asked. He would not get an answer anyhow, and he passed the crawling time in seething over Welstiel's continued secrecy.

The only thing keeping him steady as he felt the sun rise outside the tent was the knowledge that Wynn had survived the shipwreck.

During one predawn pause in the foothills of the Broken Range, Welstiel had slipped down to the shore to check Magiere's trail. Chane could stand it no longer. He had followed at a distance, watching from hiding.

Welstiel had crouched low just beyond the reach of the noisy surf surging up the beach, and then he went a little farther, turning toward the tree line. He stopped to study the ground there. When he finally turned away, he headed back toward camp at a slow and steady pace. Whatever Welstiel sought, he looked no further.

Chane knew what Welstiel had found.

Magiere had finally turned into the foothills, headed for the mountains.

The moment Welstiel was out of sight, Chane had rushed south through the trees rather than heading for the beach. He came upon a stream weaving down the rocky slope. At a lip of sod overhanging the trickling water, he found three distinct footprints among others in the mucky earth. Small and narrow, they could only be Wynn's.

As Chane hunched in the tent over the glowing steel hoop, he clung to that memory. He tried to shut out the presence of Welstiel and the ferals as he curled up on the ground. Soon dormancy took him, and he sank in the brief respite of dreamless nothingness for the day.

More nights passed.

Welstiel led them on, always following after Magiere. Each night, the temperature dropped lower as they climbed higher. Chane learned to keep moving.

As long as he did so, his body resisted freezing. Friction was also useful, for though his dead flesh generated no heat, rubbing his joints harshly and often kept them limber. He taught the ferals to do the same.

The steel hoop became a common sight, always present at dawn when they crawled into the tent. Sometime during the day's dormancy, its burning lines always faded to charcoal black. When they rose at dusk, Welstiel briefly reinitialized the hoop while they broke camp.

Chane tried to study it, to learn more.

One night, Welstiel shut down the hoop but was distracted by another disturbance from Sethè. He left the hoop lying in the snow hollow, and Chane surreptitiously crouched and reached for it.

He snatched his hand back at the sizzle of his fingertips and stepped away before Welstiel saw him.

When Welstiel returned from giving another beating to Sethè, he absently reached down for the hoop to return it to his pack. Chane heard nothing as Welstiel gripped it, and he suppressed his awe—and his frustration. Welstiel did not even flinch.

Chane appreciated secrecy. No mage revealed more than he had to. But he was tired of Welstiel doling out tidbits concerning undead existence only when necessary. Now it appeared that Welstiel's arcane knowledge was greater than Chane had estimated.

To create an object that conjured fire within itself was one thing. But Welstiel's steel hoop included something more that made only him immune to its damaging effects. But a few nights later, a more immediate problem reared up. The last of Welstiel's stored life elixir was gone, and the monks grew difficult to control—especially Sethè.

Chane awoke one dusk to find Welstiel gone. He stepped quickly from the tent to find his half-mad companion sitting in the snow, scrying for Magiere.

"I feel she draws close to her destination," Welstiel said, as if sensing Chane's presence.

Chane did not care. The monotony of hunger, cold, and suffering continued each night. And for what—the promise of a better existence?

"Then we are not long from completing our bargain," Chane whispered.

"Yes," Welstiel answered. "You will have your letter of introduction to the sages' guild."

A twinge whipped through Chane. The beast inside of him scurried into a corner, hiding from an unseen threat. Chane stared at Welstiel's back.

This had happened once before, as he had left the monastery behind Welstiel. Twice was too much to ignore.

What was this abrupt panic springing from mere words that only his instinct seemed to know? Not just suspicion or wariness, but an ache in his head, like atrophied muscles used too harshly before they could be strengthened.

But the sensation left Chane with one unexplained certainty.

Welstiel was lying to him.

A full moon after the shipwreck, Magiere tightened her coat's collar and resecured her face wrap beneath her hood. Fortunately, Osha had carried a spare pair of gloves. The fingers were too long, but she did not care. She forced one foot after another through the deep snow.

After finally reaching the high mountain altitudes of the Pock Peaks, south of the Blade Range, she had not seen a tree in the last six days. Only crusted snow choked the paths between jagged outcrops and canyon walls, and charcoal black peaks speared into the dingy white sky.

The icy winds were harsher than those of the Broken Range, when Leesil had dragged her through to the Elven Territories. And worse, breathing took effort. They halted often in the thin, frigid air and buckled where they stood to catch their breath.

Daylight waned, and Magiere could barely make out anyone's face beneath their cowls, hoods, and the cloth wraps Leesil had made by shredding spare clothing.

Chap pushed on ahead. Wind-driven snow coated the blanket lashed around his body and neck. Leesil and Sgäile trudged directly behind Magiere. Wynn and Osha staggered along at the rear.

Wynn was too fragile for this terrain, and her small body lost heat quickly. Her short legs took more steps to cover the same distance as the others. Osha had never been outside the elven forest and its constant climate. The cold heights were proving a shock to his body, and he had the most trouble breathing.

But these worries remained faint in Magiere's obsessed thoughts. Only the pull upward and the dreams mattered. Only finding the orb before anyone else could.

Chap barked from ahead, and Sgäile struggled past Magiere.

"Here," he called, voice muffled beneath his face wrap.

Magiere almost shouted at him to keep moving. They still had daylight, and she was still on her feet. She had to go on.

Chap struggled halfway back through the deep snow. He stood in her path and would not move. Magiere looked beyond him.

He'd found a depression at a granite wall's base. The vertical face curved away from the wind, and the pocket was large enough for them to take shelter.

So far, Sgäile and Chap had managed to find a suitable place to camp each night. In the worst cases, Sgäile and Osha piled and packed snow walls, which they would then roof and enclose with a canvas tarp. Everyone huddled together, sharing coats and cloaks as blankets, having long abandoned all sense of modesty.

Magiere heaved a breath, and its vapor tore away in the wind. She knew they couldn't pass up shelter so close to dusk.

Leesil trudged over and looked inside the depression's mouth, only the slits of his eyes visible within his cowl.

"This is good," he said. "We can curtain the opening with canvas . . . and trap some heat from the fire."

Osha's hands shook as he tried to dig in his pack, and Sgäile took the pack from him.

"You and Wynn go inside," he ordered.

Without a word, Osha crawled to the depression's back with Wynn close behind. He leaned against the stone wall, opening his cloak, and she collapsed against him. He drew the cloak closed, and she became nothing but a gray-green lump on his chest.

Sgäile pulled his face wrap down, exposing cracked lips as he glanced at Leesil. They were both freezing and exhausted.

Magiere finally rolled her pack off her shoulders.

Without a word, they set to staking the canvas tarp to block the depression's entrance. When they finished, Magiere took the small pot from Sgäile's pack.

"Start the fire," she said, her voice cracking. "I'll get snow to melt."

She slipped out through the canvas's edge as Sgäile arranged a small pile of deer droppings and Leesil retrieved their nightly rations.

They were all sick of berries, which turned mushy once thawed, and flaking fish made bitter with powdered fungus. Most of them couldn't even take food until they'd downed tea or hot water to warm up. For the past three nights, Wynn only wanted sleep when she stopped, and someone always had to force her to eat.

Magiere scraped the pot against the snow, filling it, and ducked back into their enclosure. The stench of smoldering dung filled the space. The barely recognizable lump of Osha and Wynn heaped together hadn't changed, except that Chap now lay curled up against Wynn. The shelter began to grow warmer, at least above freezing.

Leesil unwrapped his hands and pulled the tattered cloth from his face. His lips and the skin around his eyes were badly chapped. He leaned against the depression's side, rubbing his hands together as he held them out to the tiny fire. Magiere settled beside him as Sgäile took the pot from her.

"We should let Osha and Wynn rest a while," Leesil said. "Even into midday tomorrow."

"Midday?" Magiere hissed. It was hard enough to sit through the night, waiting for another dawn.

"They need it," Leesil said and grasped her hand. "We all do . . . including you. We'll travel better after, and I doubt we'll find shelter like this again."

Magiere tried to relax beside him, shoulder to shoulder, but inside, she quaked with the urge to move on.

Hkuan'duv halted when he saw A'harhk'nis hopping back across the deep snow. The scout's early return meant he had tracked their quarry more quickly than expected.

"Sgäilsheilleache found a shallow cave and called for early camp," he said.

Hkuan'duv nodded and pointed to a small outcrop. "We can set up behind those rocks."

Neither Dänvârfij nor Kurhkâge spoke as they pulled off their makeshift overcloaks of white sailcloth. During the days, the garments made it harder for them to be spotted in the snow. At night they draped them over the tent, camouflaging it.

They had remained behind and to the north of Sgäilsheilleache's group, but A'harhk'nis often scouted closer, slipping unnoticed through the frozen slopes and crags. He also tracked the pale pair of men and their crouching companions, who steadfastly remained farther behind. At first the distance they kept had confused Hkuan'duv, as nights here were as long as the days, providing these nocturnal travelers ample time to catch up.

"They travel slowly on purpose," A'harhk'nis had told him. "They seem even more hesitant than we to draw close."

A'harhk'nis suffered least from cold and altitude. He had ranged for many years in all forms of wild climate and terrain. Kurhkâge and Dänvârfij were more accustomed to covert purposes in urban areas, the former in the southern coastal regions and the latter in the wetlands of Droevinka. A whole moon on light rations in this frigid range took its toll on the two.

Hkuan'duv removed linked pieces of wooden rods from his pack and assisted A'harhk'nis in erecting the tent.

"We are hidden enough for a small fire," he said. "Can you take first watch?"

It was unfair to ask this of A'harhk'nis after he had scouted for most of the afternoon, but the others needed to rest.

"I am usually still awake," A'harhk'nis answered, "when Kurhkâge starts snoring."

A weak but welcome jest, and Hkuan'duv began building a small fire with elk droppings they had gathered in the foothills. Soon small, stinking flames danced before the tent's opening, and he ushered Dänvârfij and Kurhkâge inside.

Crawling in after them, Hkuan'duv pulled down his face wrap. The quarters were cramped but thereby better for sharing heat.

"Are you well?" he asked.

Dänvârfij uncovered her face, and only half-smiled with chapped lips. "Of course—and I need no nursemaid. We have all spent nights in the cold."

"Not like this," Kurhkâge said.

Hkuan'duv agreed, but if Kurhkâge or Dänvârfij were in trouble, he needed to know.

"No," she agreed softly. "Not like this."

Hkuan'duv pulled out his bedroll, and Dänvârfij untied her own.

"Do you think we are near the destination?" she asked.

This was as close as she would ever come to telling him she could not last much longer.

"A'harhk'nis says we now climb the highest of the Pock Peaks," he answered, "so they could not go much farther."

He did not add that each day they went on meant another day for the journey back.

"Rest, both of you," he commanded. "I will see how A'harhk'nis fares with the tea."

"Will you bring me shortbread, too?" Dänvârfij asked with a slight scowl. "Oh, and if you spot a wandering snow hare, you could shoot it for me as well."

He looked into her face, her words a reminder that this was not the time nor the place for lost sentiment to muddle their purpose.

"There are no rabbits up this high," he answered and crawled out.

But as Hkuan'duv stood in the cold darkness beside their small fire, he knew a small part of him would regret this mission's end. In Dänvârfij's company, he did not feel alone.

. . .

The dreamer flew closer to the castle with a hissing voice whispering all around.

Here . . . it is here . . . only steps away and your journey nears an end.

Six towers loomed, their ice fringes and the rocky peaks more familiar. She was so close.

Then she stood upon the stone steps before the high iron doors.

Only steps away . . . and the castle vanished.

Magiere slipped sideways off the depression's wall, flopping to the frozen ground before the hanging canvas. Through the crack along that curtain's edge, she saw a world of snow and ice, waiting so close.

She crawled into the open and trudged off into the night.

Wynn lay half-conscious against Osha, both of them reclined on a pile of packs against the wall. She could feel Chap curled up against her back.

Too exhausted for true sleep, she loathed the thought of opening her eyes to a world of endless snow and ice. Outside the cramped shelter, a hard wind whistled through the peaks.

The cave and Osha's body offered warmth, and beneath the wind's noise, she heard their small fire sputter. Sgäile must have kept it burning and, even better, Leesil promised they would rest late into the morning.

Osha's chest rose and fell beneath Wynn's head, and Chap was snoring again. Even if she could not fall asleep, these sounds and small movements brought her comfort. She had never suffered so much as in the past moon.

A numbing pain in her right foot grew every day, creeping up her calf. Today it had spread to her left foot, as if her body were warning her that it would soon quit altogether. Her eyes burned from so many days of blinding white.

She rolled off Osha's chest and wrapped her arm around Chap. The dog's snoring ceased when she tried to pull him against her, but he was too heavy.

"Scoot closer," Wynn whispered. "Move your rump!"

Chap grumbled and sidled in, and Wynn pressed her face into the fur between his shoulders.

"Only steps . . . away . . . ," someone murmured. ". . . Journey nears an end."

Wynn tried to lift her head, barely cracking her eyes open.

Sgäile slept on Osha's other side, and beyond Chap, Leesil leaned against the wall in deep sleep. Wynn laid her head back on Chap's shoulders, closing her eyes.

A cold breeze gusted into the shelter under the rustle of canvas. Chap shifted, and Wynn's head rolled off his shoulder.

"No," she groaned, "it cannot be morning. Just lie still. Sgäile will tell us when it is time to get up."

But Chap did not settle. Maybe he needed to go outside and relieve himself. Wynn's arm slid off his back as he rose, and she tried pulling part of Osha's cloak over herself.

Another cold gust reached her as she heard Chap slip out.

Gone! She has gone on without us!

Chap's multitongued words shouted in Wynn's half-awake mind. She flinched and lifted her head.

Who was gone?

Wynn looked blearily about. Everyone slept deeply and the sight only made her more weary. Leesil's chest barely even moved, and just beyond him . . .

Magiere was not there.

Wynn blinked to clear her sight. She scrambled over Leesil's legs for the canvas, and he barely stirred. When she stuck her head out into the harsh wind, snow stung her face, and she shielded her eyes with a hand.

The world was barren darkness above the dim gray of night-shrouded snow. Then a silver shadow bounded toward her.

Wake the others—Magiere is gone!

Chap's words filled Wynn's head an instant before he took full shape in the blizzard, ears flattened as he struggled across the snow.

"Magiere?" Wynn shouted. "Where are you?"

Get them up!

Wynn ripped aside the hanging canvas. "Leesil, come quickly!"

CHAPTER FIFTEEN

Leesil burst from the shelter but tripped on the tarp's corner. He stumbled to one knee outside. Flakes pelted him at a slant in the hard wind, and snow began collecting on his coat and hair. A blizzard had built while he slept.

Sgäile flew out behind him, looking about with his face twisted in wary fright. Wynn and Osha came last, gripping Magiere's coat. Leesil turned even colder inside at the sight of it.

Magiere was out in the storm wearing nothing but her hauberk and wool pullover.

Sgäile dashed farther out and peered toward the peaks.

"Can you see her?" Leesil shouted.

"No!"

Leesil turned to Wynn. "What did you see? Why would she run off?"

"Chap noticed first," she answered, looking toward the dog. Her expression went blank as if she were listening. "He says he lost her trail across a rocky slope above and came back to get us."

Leesil fastened his coat and took Magiere's from Osha. He ran upslope along the rock face of their cave, following Chap's tracks. He stopped where these faded to mere depressions in the deepening snow and looked down to the camp.

Leesil snarled under his breath. He should've had a grip on Magiere before he fell asleep. Her dreams had been worsening, coming more often the higher they climbed. He should've heard her or noticed when she stirred.

Sgäile came across the lower slope, back toward camp, and Leesil scrambled down as well. Wynn hastily relashed the blanket around Chap's torso.

"Did you see anything?" Sgäile demanded.

"The tracks fade," Leesil answered, knowing Sgäile would count this as another failure of his guardianship. "I don't know if she has a path in mind or if she's wandering half-asleep, but either way, it's not the easiest path."

"We must find her quickly," Sgäile said and spun around, looking in every direction.

Leesil didn't see many choices. Trudging blindly about in the dark was dangerous enough, but doing so in a blizzard was madness.

"Upward," Wynn said, fastening her hood. "I know that is not much, but it is the way she would head."

Leesil stepped farther out, surveying all upward paths, as Chap bounded upslope around stone outcrops rising through the snow. The dog came in and out of sight several times, and Leesil felt a small hand close on his arm.

Wynn clutched him, watching for Chap, and then pointed high above their camp.

"The path above our shelter leads to a rocky passage farther on," she said, "where Chap lost her trail. But the way beyond it splits in several directions. He cannot tell which way she went."

Osha peered curiously at Wynn and then at Chap.

Leesil had no time to explain how the sage knew what the dog had found. He studied the rock-face slope above, still uncertain if Magiere would take such a difficult route. He scanned the open slope for an easier way to scale to the same heights. Too many choices, and no sign of Magiere's passage.

The terrain broke and twisted everywhere in white paths between jagged stone crags and ridges rising in the dark. Chap came hopping back downslope, chunks of snow tumbling along in his path. He whined once, as if he, too, had no answer.

Leesil turned to Sgäile. "Take Osha up above our camp. Chap and I will try the open slope. Hopefully he can track her. We can cover more ground if we split up."

"I am coming with you," Wynn said.

"No!" Leesil snapped too harshly, and then calmed himself. "Someone has to stay in camp . . . in case Magiere comes to her senses and makes it back on her own."

This mountainside's maze of small ravines and gullies would slow him enough, and he had to move fast. Without waiting for Wynn's agreement,

Leesil clambered upslope through shin-deep snow. Chap passed him, lunging up the white hillside.

"Chap!" Wynn called. "Leesil!"

She stood where they left her, watching them fade in the thickening snowfall. When she looked back toward the cave, Osha and Sgäile had already headed up along the rock face above it.

"Go back inside the shelter," Sgäile called.

His voice barely reached her above the blizzard, but she squinted into the storm after Leesil and Chap.

"No!" she shouted back, and headed upslope. "I am going with Leesil."

"Wynn!" Osha called out.

She ignored him, pushing on, though she sank knee-deep with each step. She finally glanced over her shoulder.

Osha was bounding toward her. Sgäile passed him with a growl.

"*Valhachkasej'â!*"

Wynn stepped away. "Go on—both of you—and stop wasting time! I am more use helping Leesil than sitting about."

She turned, trying to run as Osha shouted after her.

Wynn knew she could not outdistance them, but Sgäile's anger at her would be quickly outweighed by his fear of losing Magiere. Soon their angry voices fell behind, and Wynn knew she was right. Leesil and Chap needed her, and she followed the muted depressions of their tracks.

The slope sharpened, and the pain in Wynn's right foot forced her to slow. She looked up, trying to spot where they had gone. But she had to turn away as snow peppered her face and caught in her eyelashes. Digging into her coat pocket, she pulled out the cold lamp crystal and tried to warm it with her hands.

"Chap!" she shouted. "Wait!"

The crystal glowed dully in her cold fingers, so she put it in her mouth as she trudged on. The incline decreased over a knoll's crest, and she parted her lips. A glimmer of light leaked out through her teeth. Wynn spit the crystal into her gloved hand and held it up.

It glowed at half-strength, and its light turned the falling snow into a white gauze curtain shifting all around her. But it was enough to navigate by, and she thought she glimpsed movement higher up to her right.

"Leesil?"

No answer, and the ache in Wynn's right foot seemed to spread to her left calf as well. She took a step, but when she looked down at the snow, Leesil and Chap's tracks had faded altogether.

Wynn turned about, looking down the long slope for the way back to camp.

Between black crags and snow turned pale gray in the dark, she saw at least three separate ways. But which one was correct? Even her own tracks were quickly filling with snowfall. Anger crept in, pushing back Wynn's fear.

She was always the one to fall behind. But it was safer to go on than get lost on the way back to camp. Leesil and Chap could not be far ahead, and she was more likely to meet someone if she pressed on.

"Leesil!" she called out, but the wind drowned his name.

Wynn stumbled on over another crest, into the next chute between high stone, and then around three bends as the broken mountainside forced her to weave in the dark. But still she found no tracks for Leesil or Chap.

She clambered through a saddle between two massive outcrops, jutting high like miniature peaks. When she looked back, only her last six steps showed clearly through the blizzard.

"Chap!" she shouted,

Only the moans and half-whistles of wind over stone answered her. Fear crept back in, eating away resolute anger.

She was alone—as lost as Magiere.

But if Magiere indeed wandered in some half-conscious state, she would travel upward, as she had done for so long. Leesil would continue his climb until he found her. And everyone else would be searching the heights.

The ache in Wynn's legs and feet dwindled. This was no relief—it was a bad sign. Cold seeped deeper through her clothing, and she pulled the coat closer, tugging the hood forward. At least she had her gloves, but she had forgotten her face wrap. If only she had eyes like Leesil or Osha, or even Magiere—some way to see clearly in the dark.

Or did she?

One night in the elven forest, Chap had bolted off after a pack of majay-hì. Wynn had tried to follow, but the forest toyed with her mind and left her lost. In desperation, she had willfully raised her sickening mantic sight, left

228 · BARB & J. C. HENDEE

from the taint of wild magic in her flesh. Chap became her beacon, glowing more brightly than any other life in the forest.

These frigid mountains were barren—and lifeless. If she raised her mantic sight once more, and saw the world's elemental Spirit layer, she could not miss him in this place.

But the notion was easier than the act.

She had only succeeded in the forest by sinking into memories of Chap. As if he were some mage's familiar who lived in her mind. And she had not been able to end the nauseating sight until she found him, a Fay in hound's flesh who could drive down the taint within her.

If she succeeded but could not find Chap . . .

Wynn dropped, her knees sinking into the snow, and closed her eyes.

She forced calm and quiet within herself, shutting out the cold and wind. She recalled all the sensations she had ever experienced in Chap's presence, from the feel of his musky fur to his breath on her face and the sound of his multitongued voice in her head. She conjured his presence in her mind's eye with images of him in her mantic sight . . .

Glistening as if he alone were the only "whole" thing she saw . . .

Or wrapped in white vaporous fire as he assaulted his own kin to save her. . . .

Wynn sank into inner visions, until they blocked all else from her senses. Then her mind slipped into one past moment.

Chap sat before her in a room at Byrd's Inn, staring into her eyes. At the feel of his thick fur in her fingers, with her thoughts working upon what he was, her mantic sight overwhelmed her. The room had turned shadowy beneath an off-white mist just shy of blue.

It permeated everything, like ghosts overlaying her normal sight. These showed where the element of Spirit was strong or weak. Only Chap remained whole.

In her mantic sight, his fur glistened like a million threads of bristling white silk. And his eyes scintillated like crystals held before the sun.

Wynn clung to that memory as she opened her eyes.

Cold, wind, and snow assaulted her, and the world looked exactly as it had when she had closed them.

Perhaps she was too exhausted, too cold, too weak. As much as Wynn feared what the sight did to her, its absence toppled her into despair. And still, she struggled to her feet.

Leesil and Chap were out here, somewhere, and she had to find them.

Chap fought through the drifts, trying to track Magiere, but no odor lingered on the snow. His nose was useless unless Magiere stumbled directly into his path, upwind and close. He searched by sight between the crags, but the blizzard had covered any trace of her footsteps—if she had come this way at all.

"Magiere!" Leesil shouted.

Chap slowed, reaching out with his awareness to pick up Magiere by any rising memories. It was a worthless act of desperation, for he knew he needed a direct line of sight.

"Magiere!" Leesil shouted again.

Under the blanket across Chap's torso, his body heat was fading. Leesil would be suffering the same, but they had to keep trying.

Chap lunged onward—and a whiff of sweat stung his nose.

He halted, looking about, but the swirling wind twisted so much that the scent vanished before he could draw it deeper.

"What?" Leesil asked, his voice faint beneath the wind even from a few steps behind.

Shallow gullies led upward through varied breaks in the mountainside. If they took the wrong path, they might bypass Magiere, not even seeing her. Chap had to be certain.

He stood his ground and raised his face into the wind. Every time the wind shifted, so did he, turning into it as he paced in half-circles.

"Damn it, Chap!" Leesil shouted. "What are you doing?"

Chap snarled back. He could express nothing more without Wynn to speak for him. He paced into a rise between two outcrops.

Magiere's clear scent filled his nose.

Chap bolted into the wind with a howl, charging between the spires. Leesil pounded through the snow behind him. Chap's thoughts raced as well.

How could Magiere be sweating in this cold?

They struggled on, weaving through more outcrops and past stone spires. Then ahead in the darkness, the flat face of a gully's wall sprang up before them. Wind whipped around in the wide boxed space, making snowflakes twist like a slow-turning cyclone.

Chap pulled up short in anguish. They had reached a dead end.

But something was moving at the far wall's base.

It was barely more than a shadow against the dark stone beyond the whirling snow.

Chap threw up his head and howled. The wind drowned his voice, and the shadow in the dark space did not turn. Leesil came up beside him, looking ahead, and Chap bounded into the dead end. Only one person wandered these barren heights.

Leesil's shout chased Chap across the box gully's floor. "Magiere!"

And it was her, but Chap slowed to a stop as he closed in.

With her back turned, she was clawing so hard at the gully's sheer face that her fingers were marred with her own blood. Even in the turning air, Chap smelled a thick stench of sweat at close range. Thin traces of steam flowed around her head, as if she were breathing too hard and fast.

She did not even seem aware of him.

Leesil caught up, dropped Magiere's coat, and reached out to her.

"Magiere, we have to go back!" he called, and his grip settled on her shoulder.

Magiere lashed back with one hand.

Her arm struck his, knocking it away. She let out a snarl, more panicked than angry. Chap caught a glimpse of her profile.

She shuddered in the cold, yet beads of sweat had crystallized on her pale skin. Her black irises had expanded so much they nearly blocked out the whites of her eyes. She turned back to the sheer rock and tried to reach up.

"Magiere!" Leesil shouted. "Look at me! Wake up!"

Leesil tried to reach her again, and Chap shifted into his way.

Magiere was enwrapped in some delusion, and Chap worried she might not recognize even Leesil. He tried delving for her thoughts, hoping to catch any rising memory that might reveal what she saw inside her head.

He could not touch dreams any more than conscious thoughts. He only saw or experienced rising memories, triggered by whatever entered a person's awareness or where their conscious thoughts turned. But as Chap looked into Magiere's deluded mind, a barrage of flickering images flooded through him.

The castle from a distance, just for a moment . . .

The same dim and desolate winter wasteland he had seen in Magiere before, but no blizzard raged. The ancient fortress sat in pristine stillness, deceptively peaceful upon a white plain surrounded by distant peaks like black teeth.

Then, approaching massive iron gates, Chap felt the overwhelming urge to pass through, to press his hands against the gates' scrollwork, push them wide, and rush for the steps to the doors. . . .

Hands? No, this was Magiere's memory—not his.

Chap struggled free before her obsession swallowed him.

He called up her past memories, one after another, of Miiska and warm nights in the Sea Lion Tavern. He dug in her mind for anything he could use to break this waking dream or make her stop and question where she was . . . and what she was doing.

Magiere kept trying to climb, her boots scraping for footholds.

Chap pulled from her mind and lunged. He clamped his teeth on the leg of her breeches and jerked back.

Magiere snapped her leg out, kicking him squarely in the chest, and he tumbled away in the snow.

Chap righted himself as Leesil shouted, "Magiere, stop it!"

Large flakes of snow powdered her black hair. Her half-closed eyelids fluttered as the pupils rolled up in her head. Magiere's slack lips trembled as if she were whispering, but Chap heard no words. And before Chap could move, Leesil charged.

He wrapped his arms around Magiere, locking his hands across her upper torso to pin down her arms.

Magiere screeched like an animal and shoved off the wall with her foot. They both stumbled back, and Leesil's grip broke. Magiere instantly turned on him, drawing back one hand with fingers hooked like talons.

Chap snarled and lunged in.

Magiere faltered, staring at Leesil in sudden silence. Her hand began to drop, fingers shaking, as fear spread across her pale features.

Chap halted, watching her closely. More than once, Leesil's presence had cut through her fury and brought her back to reason.

Magiere's eyelids fluttered again.

Her black pupils rolled up, leaving nothing but white. She swung as Leesil's amber eyes widened.

Leesil sidestepped, catching her forearm in both hands, but his legs buckled under her force, driving him to his knees.

Chap rushed in and clamped his teeth around her boot top. He ground his jaws closed on her shin. Magiere cried out as he dug in with his paws and yanked, pulling the leg from under her.

Magiere twisted on one foot and toppled, and Chap released his grip. He wheeled away, but she fell straight into Leesil. They both slammed down in freshly fallen snow. Leesil threw his arms around Magiere lying faceup against his chest.

Chap scrambled to get at Magiere before she turned on Leesil. The instant his paw ground upon her chest, he snarled into her face.

Magiere's black eyes opened wide. Instead of answering him in kind, she shrank from his bared teeth.

She began shaking with true cold. She rolled her head, looking about as if not knowing where she was.

Chap backed up, pulling his paw from Magiere's chest. The dhampir had receded, leaving only Magiere. Leesil pinned her tightly against himself, not allowing her to move.

"Shhhhhhh," he murmured in her ear. "It's me."

Magiere's eyes finally cleared, and Chap watched her black pupils shrink and fade to dark brown. She looked directly at him.

"Where . . . ?" she whispered but never finished, and then heaved a panicked breath.

She curled to one side, covering her face with bloodied fingers.

Chap sagged in exhausted relief. They had found her, and she was herself again—for the moment. He barked twice to gain Leesil's attention, then rushed toward the gully's opening to stand and wait. They must get back to camp, and fast.

Leesil struggled to his feet, pulling Magiere up. He managed to get her into her coat and then stumbled out of the gully, half-dragging her. Chap paused, gazing up the sheer wall at the back of the gully.

There was no way Magiere could have climbed it. But in half-consciousness, driven by instinct, she had chosen a precise direction to reach that castle in her mind.

"Can you find our way back?" Leesil called.

Chap turned out of the gully and struggled into the lead. Their tracks in the snow were all but gone. He quickly traced any remnants, but soon there were none left.

Leesil followed him, half-dragging and half-carrying Magiere. Chap plowed through the unblemished drifts, searching for a way to their camp.

Leesil was merely cold at first, but even in his coat, he began having trouble breathing. His leg muscles burned as his skin chilled, but he kept hauling Magiere through the snow and wind, trying to shield her with his body.

"Not far," he whispered to her over and over. "Almost there."

In truth, he didn't know where he was and only put one foot before the other, blindly following Chap—then the dog halted and barked. Leesil lifted his head.

In the dark, a narrow slope ran along a sheer rock face. He almost groaned but didn't want Magiere to hear. They had wandered in a circle, returning to the narrow alley into the boxed gully.

Chap lunged straight for the rock wall and turned down the slope.

Leesil thought the dog had lost his wits. He managed a last burst of strength to follow, but when he neared the slope's bottom, he didn't see the gully's far wall. The corner of a cold-hardened canvas tapped against the stone in the wind. He stepped around the rock face's gradual turn.

The canvas was staked across the opening of the depression. Leesil's last few steps into the shelter were the hardest of all.

He crouched to drag Magiere inside and settle her against the side wall. For a moment, all he could do was catch his breath as Chap wriggled by to the shelter's rear. The dog came to him, dragging the bag of droppings in his teeth.

"Yes," Leesil breathed.

He took the bag and turned back to the fire's smoldering remains. He wished he could get word to Sgäile, but he could barely walk, and he wouldn't ask Chap to go. They were both spent.

Magiere slid along the wall and slumped on the floor, watching him as he blew on the embers, trying to coax a flame.

"What happened?" she whispered, barely loud enough to hear.

"I don't know," he answered.

Chap pricked his ears. He ducked around behind Leesil and out through the canvas.

Leesil heard the dog bark loudly, and Chap returned before he could peek out.

Sgäile followed an instant later. Panting, he held aside the canvas for Osha, who immediately crawled to the depression's back and collapsed. All of Leesil's exhaustion was mirrored in Sgäile's relief as the elf dropped to his knees at the sight of Magiere. Leesil glanced at the closed canvas and then looked at Osha.

"Where's Wynn?"

Sgäile stiffened and lifted his head. "With you . . . she insisted on going with you."

"When I didn't find her here, I thought she'd gone with you." Leesil shook his head in disbelief. "I told her to stay. . . . You were standing right above her, Sgäile!"

Chap snarled at both of them and bolted out of the shelter.

Leesil started to follow, but his legs were so cold he couldn't get to his feet.

"You not see her come for you?" Osha demanded. "She run behind you!"

"No!" Leesil growled back.

Magiere weakly pushed up on one elbow. "What's going on?"

Frozen canvas crackled sharply as Chap burst in. He raised one silver paw and hit the floor over and over. He barked twice, paused, and barked twice again.

Leesil didn't like what he heard. Chap had found no tracks but still intended to search. The dog was the only one still on his feet.

"You can't . . . not alone," Leesil whispered.

Chap wheeled about, and before Leesil could grab him, the dog rushed out.

Leesil jerked the canvas aside, peering into the empty night. Then he felt Magiere's hand close on his arm.

"Where's Wynn?"

Her pale face was windburned, and worse, she wasn't demanding or angry, as in any other crisis. She just sounded lost.

Leesil didn't know how to answer her. He stared out into the blizzard. Snowfall was already burying Chap's tracks.

Hkuan'duv took second watch, but A'harhk'nis did not retire.

"I will check upon the other camp," he said, "and make certain they remained at the cave. It is doubtful they pressed on in this blizzard, but I would have difficulty tracking them if they did."

"Yes," Hkuan'duv agreed. "Be quick, and then return to rest."

A'harhk'nis vanished, and Hkuan'duv settled against the tent, trying to stay out of the wind's worst force. After a while, he looked in on the others.

Dänvârfij seemed fast asleep, and Kurhkâge breathed easily, wrapped in his cloak and blanket. Hkuan'duv returned to scanning the mountainside.

Snowfall thickened as the wind picked up. Fortunately they had found rock formations to shield their tent, but he hoped they neared the end of their purpose. The prospect of facing Sgäilsheilleache, when the time came to seize the artifact and eliminate Magiere, was still discomforting.

Hkuan'duv would do it, regardless of the costs—he would protect his people, as always. But he had never before been placed in conflict of purpose with a member of his own caste. Until the recent gathering of the clan elders, he had never even heard of such an occurrence.

Hkuan'duv was startled from his pondering as A'harhk'nis hopped over the rocks and landed before him—with a wild glitter in his eyes.

"Wake the others!" A'harhk'nis urged. "Something is happening in Sgäilsheilleache's camp."

CHAPTER SIXTEEN

Wynn bent over and stumbled in the wind, too numb to even call out. She still hoped to find Leesil and Chap, or happen upon Sgäile and Osha. But as night dragged on, hope faded with the heat in her body. Odd fleeting notions kept popping into her head.

How long until dawn? Could she keep moving until then? Would the storm break and let in a little sun? What would Sgäile say if he were here?

He would give her another lecture about her foolishness. No doubt followed by the threat of more stringent methods in his guardianship.

Wynn wished he were here to do just that.

She lost track of the rise and fall, the twists and turns of her path. Then the blizzard's white blur before her turned black in the crystal's light—as though a large, looming shadow had suddenly appeared.

Wynn did not even flinch.

She raised her head and blinked frost-laced eyelashes. A rock face blocked her way—another dead end. Before she dropped her head, weakly resolute to turn about, she spotted a blacker space along the wall's surface.

She forced her legs to move. As she neared the black space, it became a hollow in the ridge wall. Peering around its edge, she looked up a steep chute where the ridge wall had cracked through. Its rock-strewn bottom was clear of most snow, for heavy wind could not drive the snowfall inside the narrow space.

Perhaps she had been wrong about Chap going back. What if he and Leesil had found this passage as well? And if not, at least she might hide from the wind.

Wynn stepped in and took some mild relief as the wind cut off. Loose stones turned under her numb feet, and she slapped a hand against the chute wall to catch herself.

She wanted to slump down—just for a while, to get out of the wind—as she could not stop shivering. Maybe sleep a little before going on. A small voice whispered in the back of her mind.

"If you stop, you will freeze to death."

Oh, yes, that was such a good sign—now she was talking to herself in her own head.

Wynn took another step upward, pawing along the chute's left wall. She had to keep her blood circulating, but that thought just brought despair. She needed to rest—not sleep, just a rest—but she forced herself a little farther.

A rock shard shifted beneath her foot, and her ankle rolled.

She barely winced, for the pain was dulled by cold. But as she fell, her gloved hand struck the chute's floor and broken rocks ground through her glove against her palm. She lifted her head, looking up the chute with tears freezing on her face. The top opening lay just above, and she started crawling. But when she looked out the chute's top, only more ice and a snow-coated landscape awaited.

Nothing else—no one else.

Wynn rolled away, curling up on her haunches against the chute's wall. Better to just close her eyes and hide from this world.

A tinge of nausea rose in her stomach. The two small bites of dried fish she'd had for dinner threatened to rise.

Wynn squirmed in resentment—even her own body could not leave her in peace!

Nausea sharpened as the sound of a leaf-wing buzzed in her head.

Wynn?

Chap struggled through trackless snow with no scent to follow.

At first he simply retraced the path he and Leesil had taken. If Wynn had tried to follow them, perhaps she was within reach. But he second-guessed himself as small gullies broke off in ever dividing directions—all leading up.

Wynn was unique among Chap's chosen companions. Only she heard his words and felt the part of him that was Fay. But not in the way of Sgäile's blind worship or Osha's perplexed elven awe for all majay-hì. Wynn did not treat him like some otherworldly being.

And Chap cherished her for this.

He halted beneath an outcrop and closed his eyes. Even slightly shielded from the wind, he could not stop shaking. He and Leesil had taken a left fork into a boxed gully, where they had found Magiere, but Chap had seen no other tracks. The blizzard had erased them.

When Wynn was close, all Chap need do was *think* to her through his own spirit, as he would when he "communed" with his kin. Or at least that was how Wynn described it. But without knowing where she was, or how far, could he call to her? Could he do so from a distance without drawing the attention of the Fay?

His kin were of all elements, and not just Spirit, the one that collected strongest in living things. Fay were of Water and Earth, Air and Fire, as well, and as they wished, so there was no place in this world they could not come to at will.

If they felt him try to call to Wynn from a distance, they might find her before he could.

And they had tried to kill her in the elven forest.

Chap could not take such a risk. He veered from the outcrop, continuing up until he passed through a saddle between two rock spires. It looked too much like the path into the boxed gully, and doubt pressed him down.

Wynn had been near exhaustion when they made camp. How could she have come this far, if she had come this way at all?

He circled back, loping across the rocky saddle, and turned up another cut in the mountain. He barely finished three strides before he slowed to another halt.

Even if Wynn heard him call, as in communion with his kin, she could not answer him back the same way. But he had to try something other than wandering in the night blizzard.

Chap ground his numbed paws, digging down through the snow until his claws scraped frozen ground. He rooted in this for Earth and snow for Water. Hard wind in his face brought Air, and lingering body heat gave him Fire. With the Spirit in his own living flesh, he bound himself to these elements of existence and sank into what Wynn had once called his "communion."

But not with his kin—he focused only upon his memories of her as he called out through his spirit.

Wynn?

No response came.

Wynn . . . call out to me.

Chap heard nothing but the wind tearing at the mountainside.

Please, if you hear me . . . feel me . . . even a twinge in your stomach . . .

He stood poised and listening until panic made him rush blindly upslope.

Wynn . . . answer me!

"Chap? . . . Here . . . I am here!"

He froze with ears pricked at the weak shout, faint in the storm's noise.

Again! Do not stop until you see me!

"Here . . . in the chute."

Chap spun about, cutting along a slant below an overhang.

Her voice could only reach him by traveling upon the harsh wind. So he turned into its currents racing between the crags. Pattering snow stung his eyes and filled his ears, but he pushed on—and then stopped short, staring into a dead-end gully of sheer walls.

"Chap . . . in the chute . . . look for a crack!"

He paced along one high wall where the snow was shallower. In the dark path, he did not notice it until a break appeared suddenly beside him. A rocky-floored chute blocked out the wind-driven snow. Chap scrambled up over loose stones. His heart beat faster when he caught a familiar whiff.

I am coming!

And he saw Wynn curled against the chute's wall near the top.

Snowfall had dusted the back of her cloak with white. Chap struggled upward as she reached out for him.

You must try to move. Put your hands under my blanket and against my fur.

Chap shoved his head into Wynn's cloak. He pressed against her to lend her what little body heat he could. Wynn sagged atop his shoulders, her face buried in his neck, and her weight grew as if she sank in exhaustion.

He had to keep her awake and so began babbling mindlessly.

We found Magiere . . . she is safe . . . the others are with her at camp. You and I must live until morning and find them again . . . everything will be as it was. Wynn?

She did not move.

Put your hands into my fur—now!

Chap tugged her coat's ties with his teeth and burrowed through its open front. All the while, he prattled into her head, trying to bring her fully awake.

Wynn's fingers clutched weakly at his fur.

"You . . . stink," she mumbled through chattering teeth. "Need . . . a bath."

Chap took a deep breath. *You are no spring flower right now.*

The quick moment of relief passed, and Chap lifted his head and looked warily about—at stone for Earth, snow for Water, and the wind of Air. He and she would always be surrounded by the elements.

Chap hoped that only Wynn had heard him.

Hkuan'duv had left Dänvârfij to stand watch at camp and now crouched with A'harhk'nis and Kurhkâge behind ice-encrusted rocks. Wind and snow churned in a full blizzard. Across the slanted slope, he watched the canvas-covered depression as Sgäilsheilleache and Osha returned and slipped from sight.

"What did you see earlier?" Hkuan'duv asked.

A'harhk'nis never took his eyes off the shelter. "The human, Magiere, came running out and headed up the mountain. Not long after, the others followed, but they hesitated and then broke into two groups. I do not believe they knew where she went. Later, the half-blood and the majay-hì brought her back, and I returned to report to you."

"Where is the small one?" Kurhkâge asked.

A'harhk'nis shook his head. "She had not returned when I left."

Loud barking carried from the shelter. The silver-gray majay-hì boiled out through the canvas, heading upward through the crags. Hkuan'duv frowned, rising slightly to watch.

"What has happened that they continually risk this terrain in a night storm?"

Neither of his companions ventured a comment.

Hkuan'duv waited, but no one else exited the shelter.

"Should we follow the majay-hì?" Kurhkâge asked.

Hkuan'duv was uncertain, and the dog was already out of sight.

"Stay back, and downwind," he ordered. "We cannot allow the majay-hì to scent us."

They slipped silently over rocks and snow as A'harhk'nis led the way.

Fortunately the majay-hì could not move at full speed in the drifts. A'harhk'nis occasionally signaled them to slow or change course. They stayed well behind the majay-hì, no closer than needed to keep its shadowy form within sight through the blizzard.

Snow fell so thick that A'harhk'nis stopped more than once in tracking through the mountainside's twisting paths. As they passed through a saddle, Hkuan'duv heard someone cry out.

"Chap . . . here . . . I am here!"

A'harhk'nis signaled them into hiding as the majay-hì wheeled and headed back their way. All three of them sank into the snow at an outcrop's base and spread out their white makeshift cloaks. They became no more than snow-blanketed boulders.

The majay-hì ran straight past them into a high-walled gully.

All three rose and crept onward as Hkuan'duv took the lead.

Had that fatigued cry come from the young human? Why had the majay-hì gone alone to search for her?

Hkuan'duv realized he was higher than he had thought, perhaps close to the top peaks. Could this little female have found Magiere's destination? And if so, why had she gone out alone?

Too many questions with no answers, and then he saw the majay-hì veer in against the gully wall—through the gully wall.

Hkuan'duv dropped and inched forward on his belly. Pulling his white hood low, he peered into the break.

A chute ran upward through the stone, and near its top someone hunkered against the left side. He made out the shape of the small woman, and her cloak bulged as if something shifted beneath it, halfway into her lap. She mumbled too low for him to hear, and then the majay-hì's head popped out of her cloak.

Hkuan'duv ducked back along the snow and rolled up to lean against the gully's rough wall. A majay-hì risked itself for a human, but no such guardian of his people had ever shown affinity for an interloping weakblood.

Sgäilsheilleache kept strange and deviant company, and Hkuan'duv wondered if his caste brother was wholly self-possessed. Or had Sgäilsheilleache fallen under some undetected influence? Hkuan'duv glanced at Kurh-kâge and A'harhk'nis, crouched and waiting.

If anyone had located Magiere's final destination, Hkuan'duv needed to know. The most expedient option was to take this little woman and question her. Lost as she was, her companions would never know what had become of her. But the majay-hì was a more difficult concern.

No one ever interfered with its kind's comings and goings.

Hkuan'duv signaled Kurhkâge to follow, leaving A'harhk'nis to guard the chute's entrance. He rose and turned into the stony passage, but he had barely taken three silent steps when the majay-hì's head reared again.

Its crystal blue eyes glinted in the dark space, and a low growl rolled down the stone chute.

Hkuan'duv froze, but the majay-hì tilted its head upward, and he followed its gaze.

A flicker, darker than the night sky, dropped down between the chute's high walls.

Somewhere out the chute's bottom, Chap heard the hiss of fallen snow driven by the wind. Then it stopped, too suddenly. Chap raised his head from Wynn's coat.

Above him, a bird's caw trailed out like a scream.

Chap lifted his eyes skyward in surprise. No bird could survive up here.

A black shadow dropped out of the night, darker than sky or stone. It passed high through the chute's stone walls.

Chap felt a heat spread within him . . . on an urge to hunt. His heart pounded as his awareness filled with the presence of an undead. But as he traced the shadow's passing, it took the shape of a large bird—perhaps a raven.

Wynn, get up!

She stirred, lifting her head to look about.

Another flicker dashed between the chute's high walls in the shadow bird's wake.

This one was not black. Muted in the blizzard, it was as white as the snow, and leaped between the chute's sheer walls.

Chap's hunting heat turned suddenly cold. He shook free of Wynn's grasp, lunging out with his head high. He tried to spot that fleeting patch of white, and then he saw two tall figures at the chute's bottom.

Their cloaks were covered by white cloth, but the corners were tied around their waists—across the gray-green tunics of the Anmaglâhk.

Hkuan'duv thought he saw a raven's black silhouette. Its wings were so wide that one tip brushed the high stone wall. As it descended through the chute, he glimpsed the wall beyond it.

No, he saw through it—as if the mere shadow of the large bird had lifted from the stone and moved in the air. It dove straight for his face.

Hkuan'duv ducked at the last instant. As he turned, he never got out a word of warning.

The shadow shot straight through Kurhkâge's upper chest.

Kurhkâge's one wide eye did not blink as the black form flashed out of his back and arced up to vanish in the dark. His gaping mouth quivered as he stopped breathing and collapsed against the chute's side.

Hkuan'duv snatched Kurhkâge's cloak front and lunged for the chute's lower opening.

What was this shadow of a raven?

Kurhkâge's cloak tore in Hkuan'duv's grip.

His arm snapped straight behind him, jarring his shoulder. Loose stones made his foot slide, and he quickly shifted his balance. He glanced back to see what had snagged his companion, expecting a crack or the edge of a rock.

Hkuan'duv stared into a woman's face, nearly as pallid as snow.

Not the one he tracked, the one called Magiere. All his senses sharpened in alarm.

Colorless crystalline irises stared at him from within eyes shaped like slanted teardrops—and they closed to menacing slits. Her oval face narrowed smoothly to the chin, like a hint of elven heritage. But those eyes were far too small below thin-swept black eyebrows that were not those of his people, not even those of a half-blood. She was human, but not of any race that Hkuan'duv had ever seen.

Wild obsidian hair dangled around her head and throat, hanging nearly to the chute floor, for she crouched sideways upon the sheer wall, anchored by one hand as if her nails could carve into the stone. Her narrow-limbed body was completely naked, yet she did not shiver in the freezing air. Her other delicate hand was wrapped tightly over Kurhkâge's face, pinning his head to the chute's wall.

Hkuan'duv released Kurhkâge and grabbed for a stiletto on his wrist. But his hand never reached the hilt.

The woman's face wrinkled in a silent snarl as she spun down from the wall, and her small hand lashed out into his chest. His feet lifted from the chute's floor as he hurtled back through the air.

Snowy ground and black sky spun before his eyes. Both stopped suddenly as he slammed down amid a spray of fallen snow. He penetrated through to frozen earth, and his shoulder and arm crushed against his side. He lay at the gully's far side, a good distance from the chute's opening.

Hkuan'duv's chest ached as he rolled over, gasping.

The woman stepped into the open, her narrow feet sinking through the snow.

Wind whipped her long hair about in writhing black tendrils, exposing her throat. Hkuan'duv caught the metallic glint, thick and golden, of something hooked about her neck, and then his gaze caught on something else.

Her left forearm and hand were coated with dark red. She clutched a bloodied mass that dripped a spattered trail behind her.

A'harhk'nis circled out with both oversized curved blades in hand.

He was not tall for an'Cróan, but this feminine apparition would barely reach his collarbone. She crouched so deep and quickly that A'harhk'nis stalled in his first attack.

Desperate to help, Hkuan'duv struggled to all fours. His left arm gave way and he crumpled.

The white woman shot up from the snow directly before A'harhk'nis.

A'harhk'nis had barely reversed his blade's swing when her free hand shot straight for his throat. His feet left the snow at that impact, and the white woman rose with him, falling upon him as he toppled.

Hkuan'duv saw her tiny mouth widen around fangs and jagged teeth. He tried to rise again as she drove her face into A'harhk'nis's throat.

Fresh powder splashed around them. Hkuan'duv took only one step before the wind cleared the air. A head of whipping black hair snapped up amid settling snowy mist—and a wet tearing sound filled the gully.

Blood spattered from her mouth as she threw back her head.

With a crack of bone, her narrow arm whipped out, tossing a bulk too large for the red mass she had held. Cold sank through Hkuan'duv as he watched the object hit the gully wall.

It bounced with a mute thud. A shredded hood came loose from it, exposing locks of blond hair. Hkuan'duv watched A'harhk'nis's head fall.

Runnels of blood flowed from the ragged neck stump to mar the snow.

The white woman still straddled A'harhk'nis's torso. Blood ran from her jaws down across her small breasts. She ignored Hkuan'duv, simply staring at the red mass in her other hand. Thin steam rose from it in the cold air.

Somewhere in the dark space of the chute lay Kurhkâge's body. Hkuan'duv steeled himself as the small woman stood and cast aside Kurhkâge's heart.

What was this creature who felt no cold and slaughtered two of his own with so little effort? He tensed when she turned icy eyes on him—and a snarl sounded on the wind.

But not from her. She whirled the other way.

The majay-hì burst from the chute's opening.

Hkuan'duv caught movement above, and a shadow dropped through the blizzard.

He threw himself over a mound of snow, and his injured shoulder grazed a boulder beneath the white covering. The shadow raven passed through the mound a hand's length behind him, and he heard the majay-hì's snarling snaps.

He did not wish to abandon the dog, but two of his companions had been slaughtered before either could strike once. He could not throw his life away. He had to live to fulfill his purpose and serve his people.

He had to run.

Wynn's sight had barely cleared when Chap bounded down the chute. She braced against the cold wall and struggled up. By the time she hobbled down the loose stones, Chap had leaped out into the gully, but Wynn stalled at the chute's bottom.

Something lay slumped against the wall.

She heard Chap's snarls, but she hung there in the dark, staring at the body.

The tall elf's one eye was locked open in perpetual shock, and his mouth gaped. There was only a mass of old scars where the other eye should have been. The front of his cloak was so stained, at first it was hard to see the hole surrounded with severed shards of his ribs amid his tunic's shredded remains. He was covered in his own blood.

Wynn could not even cry out.

Run! I will find you.

Chap's words echoed in her head. She lifted her gaze from the corpse and saw his forepaws strike a white figure from behind.

Chap's adversary seemed like a white-cloaked companion of the corpse lying near Wynn. But then she saw that this person was much smaller.

The pale figure barely flinched as Chap collided with its back and pushed off, landing aside. The black-haired figure whirled, and a choked squeak escaped Wynn's throat.

Naked and frail, the woman was no taller than Wynn, but her pallid face and torso were covered in blood. Chap darted at the woman, and her tiny mouth mirrored his snarl.

The woman had teeth as canine as Magiere's whenever she sank too far into her dhampir nature. But this woman's strange narrow-slitted eyes were colorless.

How could an undead exist here in these desolate peaks with no life to sustain it?

Wynn spotted another body at the woman's feet. She barely made out the gray-green breeches and tunic, obscured in snow and more blood. And its head was gone.

Chap danced around the white woman, as if simply trying to keep her attention. She lunged at him again and again. Her narrow fingers were so quick that twice Wynn thought the woman had caught him.

Wynn could not leave Chap like this, but she could think of no way to help him.

The woman flashed forward, clawing at the dog. When he spun away behind her swing, she lashed in reverse and caught him with the back of her hand.

Chap's silver-gray body shot across the gully with a yelp that ended when he slammed against the gully wall.

He slid down, his body pressing a hollow in the snow. He lay there coated in white powder and did not move.

Wynn opened her mouth to call to him.

Something flashed in front of her—and she stared directly into crystalline irises.

The white woman was so close that Wynn's quick breaths shot vapor across her red-stained features. A narrow, blood-smeared hand latched around Wynn's throat, slamming her shoulders against the chute's wall.

Wynn sucked a breath and screamed, "No, do not!"

The tight grip vanished.

Wynn slumped down the wall, her feet slipping on loose stones as she cowered.

The white woman stood backed against the chute's far wall, seeming to cower like Wynn, but not in fear.

Instead, she stared back at Wynn in pain and fury, with bloodied hands clamped over the sides of her head.

Chap drifted back to consciousness. His first breath made him whimper at the sharp twinge in his ribs.

This undead was like none he had hunted; she left him cold and terrorized inside. Her deceptively fragile form moved so quickly and with such power. Yet she had not fed on her prey—only slaughtered them, as if incensed that they dared cross her path.

Chap struggled to rise, and the pain sharpened in his chest. Then he heard Wynn scream.

"No, do not!"

He lunged for the chute's opening and movement brought agony. When he rounded into the darker space, he pulled up short.

Wynn cowered alone at the chute's left wall. And to the right stood the white woman, clutching her head.

No—covering her ears.

Chap's instinct urged him to attack before this thing came back to its wits. But even uninjured, he had barely kept out of her reach and then failed. She had killed two anmaglâhk, and yet now she was backing away from Wynn.

Why?

The woman slowly dragged one hand down her cheek, fingertips smearing bloody lines below one oddly shaped eye. Her narrow fingertips came to rest on her small stained mouth.

Wynn tried to shift closer to Chap.

The white undead stepped forward so quickly she seemed to blur. He snarled at her as he shouted into Wynn's thoughts.

Do not move!

Wynn froze, but she began shaking uncontrollably. The white woman held her place as her fingertips traced her own lips.

She did not even look at Chap but watched only Wynn's face. Chap's eyes flicked between the two of them.

Not Wynn's face—but her mouth.

Had Wynn's cry somehow hurt this thing? Or was there something else . . . the words Wynn spoke?

The white woman kept fingering her mouth as she stared at Wynn's. The sound of the sage speaking had somehow stopped this undead.

Speak, he told Wynn, but she glanced toward him in confusion. *Talk . . . it distracts her.*

Wynn's voice shook as she spoke. "We . . . are lost. We only want to find our way back."

The woman flinched at every phrase. Her features wrinkled once, and then her expression shifted to startled fascination.

Chap lifted one paw to step closer to Wynn.

The white woman lunged before his paw settled. She slammed Wynn against the chute wall with a bloodied hand.

Chap went rigid. If he attacked now, Wynn would die. Then he heard another moaning caw from overhead.

Two shadow birds drifted high in the air above the chute—above this undead—hovering on their translucent wings. The woman's thin black brows furrowed as she cocked her head like a crow. She studied him with sharpening suspicion in her delicate features—or was it recognition?

Chap tried to think amid the fear. He needed some way to hold the woman's attention long enough to get Wynn free.

The woman whirled, gripped Wynn's coat, and leaped up the chute as if the sage weighed nothing.

Chap lunged upward over the shifting stones.

Wynn!

When he reached the chute's top, a harsh wind struck his face. Both Wynn and the white woman were gone.

CHAPTER SEVENTEEN

Welstiel scried for Magiere two or three times a night. Keeping his group close to hers yet remaining undetected proved a tedious balance. He glanced east, away from the peaks.

Dawn was still a way off, but throughout the night, the snowfall had increased to a blizzard. Welstiel tired of fighting the weather.

"We stop," he called out.

Chane said nothing as he searched for a place to set up their shelter. Since entering these mountains, he had almost ceased speaking at all. Welstiel did not care—conversation was wasted effort. He waited for Chane to finish setting the tent around a hollow dug in the snow, then stepped in and pulled out the heavy steel circlet.

With a brief trace of his fingertips and a thrumming chant, Welstiel evoked the circlet's power to conjure fire, but only at the lowest level. Its marks glowed and slowly filled the tent with warmth. The monks huddled close, their mad faces dull with relief. Chane crawled in last and reached his hands toward the circlet as Welstiel turned to leave.

"I will scout," he said, his voice nearly as raspy as Chane's. "And see how far ahead she is."

Without waiting for a reply, Welstiel slipped out and trudged upslope through the wind.

When the time came, he hoped his ferals would be as useful as expected, but a part of him missed the simplicity of traveling with only one companion. As long as Chane stayed close enough to touch, Welstiel's ring of nothing could hide them both—a much more convenient arrangement. But lately Chane's seething glances raised other concerns for Welstiel.

Hopefully all this would soon be finished, including the growing problem of Chane.

Welstiel tried to gauge how much night remained. His last effort to scry had given him a clear direction for Magiere's location, but he caught no whiff of life until he heard voices in the night. Slowing with his senses opened wide, he spotted a dim glow at the bottom of a sheer rock face. He crouched behind an outcrop.

Light filtered dimly through a snow-crusted canvas strung over the rock's surface. Why were Magiere and her companions still awake? Or had they risen for an early start?

Magiere stepped out around the canvas's edge, and Leesil followed, grabbing her arm before she headed off.

"Not yet," he said, voice strained. "The moment we have light."

A tall male elf in a brown cloak stepped out as well. "Back inside," he said. "We leave soon, so do not waste body heat by standing in the cold."

Another younger elf peered around the canvas behind the first.

Welstiel focused his senses and all his awareness. It was difficult, with so many close together, but he sensed no other life within the shelter. Nor did he catch the scent of a canine. Where were Wynn and Chap?

Leesil did not acknowledge the first elf, and Magiere crouched, staring across the snow, as if searching for something. Welstiel realized why they were up before dawn and yet had not broken camp. Two of their group had gone missing.

The sky began to lighten, and Welstiel scowled, unable to remain and learn more. The last thing he wanted was for Magiere to be diverted by another distraction. He turned away, slow and quiet until he was beyond earshot, and then hurried for his own camp.

Chap ran as fast as the snow and his injuries allowed. He tried to follow the tracks before the blizzard buried them. But as the sky lightened and the snowfall died, he spotted the white woman and Wynn far ahead.

He did nothing to hide his approach, but the undead never looked back. She slowed at a rocky split between two peaks rising into the clouded sky.

The incline was so steep that she used her free hand to climb—her other remained clamped around Wynn's wrist. The sage stumbled in exhaustion, and when she fell, the undead dragged her without breaking pace. They crested the narrow space between the peaks and vanished over the far side.

Chap scrambled upward and emerged at the top. He looked out over a pristine white plateau resting between high mountains all around in the distance. The snow appeared untouched by any footfall in centuries, except for one vague trail leading into the distance—to a six-towered castle, as in Magiere's dreams.

Down the broken slope, the undead had already reached the plateau. She ran effortlessly across the snow, carrying Wynn over one shoulder.

Chap stumbled down and out onto the plain. Fresh snow and older undercrust shattered beneath his paws. He sank and floundered with each step as the white woman and Wynn grew smaller in the distance.

He kept going, and the closer he came, the larger the castle loomed, until it was greater in size than any fortification he had ever seen. Its towers dwarfed those of Darmouth's war keep, or even the spires of Bela's royal castle. Curtains of ice hung from each conical cap. But as Chap neared the outer wall and the peaked iron gates, he saw that it was not the perfection it appeared to be within Magiere's dream.

The gates' curling scrollwork was deeply rusted. One side hung a-kilter, its bottom hinge decayed beyond use. At the top where their curved points joined into a peaked arch, the two ravens gazed down at him, now whole and no longer translucent. The trail of the undead's light footfalls passed between the gates, straight to the high steps leading to the iron doors.

There she stood upon the top landing.

She threw her lithe body against one massive door. It seemed impossible that she could open it alone, especially while still gripping the crumpled sage.

The hinges of the great door squealed.

Chap slipped through the space between the gates and plowed across the inner courtyard's snow. He had to reach the doors before she could shut him out, and he caught only glimpses of the castle in his rush.

Half the stones of the arch framing the great doors were cracked. Here and there, corners of the blocks had broken off and fallen away. The wide staircase was just as deeply aged and worn, and its first step sagged midway along the seam between two of its stones. Glass panes in the high tower windows, which had been clearer in Magiere's dream, were opaque with age and frost.

The iron door's hinges screeched again.

Chap's forepaws hit the sunken bottom step. He tried to howl, but his voice failed in his dry throat.

The door's noise ceased.

He slowed, panting hard, to find the woman watching him with intense fascination from around the door's edge.

Long black tresses fell back over her perfect white shoulders, and for the first time, Chap saw the burnished metal hoop hanging around her naked throat. He looked more closely at its open ends resting below her collarbone. Each had a knob—exactly like those of the *thôrhk* that Magiere carried.

Chap slunk to the top landing and paused before the white undead.

Wynn . . . are you all right?

"Chap?" she called out. Her frightened voice echoed out of the narrow space between the iron doors.

The woman flinched at the sage's words.

"I am . . . all right . . . I think. Only bruised and cold."

The white undead cocked her head.

"Who is she?" Wynn called. "Why did she kill those elves . . . and not me?"

Chap had no certain answer, and no time to ponder this creature's reaction to the sage's spoken words—nor what anmaglâhk were doing out here in the middle of nowhere.

This undead was hardly predictable or stable. There was no telling what might cause her to turn lethal again, and little Chap might do to stop her.

She just stared at him and then pressed her porcelain face against the door's edge.

Chap saw only one crystalline eye as the visible half of her expression wrinkled in a snarl.

She shoved the door, and it lurched with a moan of rusted metal.

Chap stopped breathing, but the door moved only an inch.

Her one eye watched him, daring him to enter, and only waited so long to see if he would.

Even if this undead allowed Wynn to live, let alone leave, the small sage would never survive the trip back. Neither might he.

Chap slunk forward. When his nose breached the narrow entrance, he darted in.

Wynn felt only a flicker of relief as Chap rushed in. Then the naked woman slammed the door shut, and they were all enveloped by darkness. Wynn fumbled quickly for her crystal.

When its light erupted between her rubbing hands, the white woman still stood before the iron doors. Wynn cowered under her cold gaze and scooted in retreat until her back collided with stone.

She turned to see two rows of massive columns along a wide corridor leading into the castle's dark interior. The darkness behind the pillars began to move.

Pieces curled out into the edges of her crystal's light and undulated like black smoke. Instead of rising into the heights, the wisps turned and twisted, almost willfully. One trailed out behind the pillar Wynn leaned upon, then snaked down to splash upon the stone floor.

Some of the smoke coalesced to form a wide paw of shadow. From around the pillar, the lanky silhouette of a wolf stepped out into the crystal's light.

Chap snarled and bit into the bottom of Wynn's coat. He dragged her to the wide corridor's center, still growling, as more shadows shifted beyond the pillars.

More forms appeared in the dark. Another black translucent wolf stepped out across the corridor, and its rumble rolled around the stone walls. It lunged and snapped before Chap could dart into its way.

Sooty jaws passed straight through Wynn's ankle.

She screamed as frigid cold knifed deep into her bones.

Get up! Chap ordered.

He charged the shadow wolf, snapping his jaws over its muzzle—through its muzzle.

Chap's yelp echoed down the corridor as he lunged away with a shudder.

Wynn scrambled up, limping from the cold ache in her ankle. Smaller indistinct forms slithered in the dark around the white woman's leg—and she advanced.

Keep away from her!

Wynn retreated as Chap's warning filled her head.

The shadows came no closer. They only shifted behind the pillars as the white woman stepped slowly forward. Wynn and Chap backed along the corridor as she herded them.

Wynn barely noticed when the row of pillars ended and lost track of the twists and turns along the way. As they turned into a passage no wider than a common cottage, a shadow wolf appeared in their way.

The only path left was a doorless opening on the right, leading into a room. No one—and nothing—followed them inside. Chap whirled to block the entrance as Wynn slumped to the floor in chilled exhaustion.

The rest of the night was horrible for Magiere, listening to Leesil's tale of how she'd run off in her sleep and the others had gone looking for her.

"I told Wynn to stay!" he finished, and Sgäile's amber eyes echoed Leesil's frustration.

Neither of them blamed Magiere for Wynn getting lost. Indeed, they were both concerned for her state of mind. But it wasn't hard to see that each wrestled with heavy guilt.

Osha sat near the canvas, often peering out into the night. Once, Sgäile had to stop him from leaving on his own.

"Chap will find her!" Leesil said harshly. "But we won't find either of them in the dark. Chap will hole up with Wynn somewhere until morning and wait for us."

Osha just kept peering around the canvas' edge.

Magiere couldn't bear the sight and lowered her eyes. No matter what Leesil or Sgäile said, this *was* her fault.

Something had taken her in sleep, in dream, until she couldn't tell what was real anymore. She'd put everyone at further risk after dragging them into this world of snow and ice. For all Leesil's assurances, Wynn might not survive long enough for Chap to find her. The thought of continuing without Wynn made Magiere want to weep, but she couldn't.

"Don't let me sleep," she whispered.

Leesil glanced over with a puzzled expression. Sgäile lifted his head and then sighed—he knew what she meant.

"I can't . . . ," Magiere whispered, biting down anger. "I can't take any more dreams. Not if I can't tell what's real anymore."

Her sheathed falchion was still leaning against the depression's back wall. She snatched it up and tossed it to Sgäile. He caught the blade with a look of puzzlement on his dark face.

"Don't give it back . . . unless I need it," she warned.

Before Leesil could explode, Magiere put her fingers over his lips.

"I remember . . . barely seeing Chap standing on me," she said. "The way he looked . . . he wouldn't have come at me, if I hadn't done something that scared him . . . unless you were in danger."

Leesil sighed sharply in anger. "I should keep your—"

"No," she cut in, and looked to Sgäile. "If I lose myself again, I might only recognize Leesil or Chap. Either way, I don't want them near me and carrying anything I might see as my own weapon, or I might try to take it and . . ."

Sgäile understood, and closed both hands tightly around the falchion's sheath. He nodded. Not his usual curt bob, but slow and slight and all too resolute.

Even Osha had turned to listen. The worried look on his long face suggested he understood most of her words.

"Magiere . . . the dagger?" Sgäile said softly.

She went cold, remembering she still carried it tucked in the back of her belt. If she'd thought of it out there in the dark, when Leesil and Chap came for her . . .

Magiere reached quickly around her back, but the blade wasn't there.

"It's under your pack," Leesil said.

Sgäile pivoted over on one knee, retrieving the white-metal blade. He held it out to Osha, and Magiere sat upright in alarm. Osha could not stop her if she wanted it.

"Better to divide your arms," Sgäile explained, "in case you try to come for them. I will keep your sword upon my back . . . for when you truly need it."

Osha took the long war dagger with a nod to Magiere, but his assurance didn't squelch her doubt. He slipped it into the back of his belt beneath his cloak.

Magiere slumped against the depression's wall, resting her head upon Leesil's shoulder. No one spoke, and morning was a long time coming.

Finally, Osha glanced back at everyone. His jaw clenched and his brow lined determinedly. He jerked the canvas aside.

The sky was tinted light gray, and the storm had died down.

"Yes," Sgäile said, rising.

Osha was out before the word finished.

Sgäile strapped the falchion over his back, its hilt rising above his left shoulder. Then he pointed to the depression's back.

"Take your new blades," he told Leesil.

Magiere clenched up, anticipating Leesil's angry denial, but she glanced where Sgäile pointed.

He had cut away the sheaths' bottom ends to make room for the gifted blades' longer tips. Halfway up each sheath's side, where the wings settled, were now small hollows to accommodate the half-circle bars that would brace outside of Leesil's forearms. Not the safest way to carry them, with those long points sticking out, but they were better than no sheaths at all.

To Magiere's relief, Leesil gathered them without a word.

She began to pack up and saw the metal circlet among her scant belongings. She hesitated and then slowly picked it up. She didn't want or need it but didn't care to leave it unattended. So she hung it around her neck over her wool pullover and hauberk, as this seemed the easiest way to carry it without a pack. Leesil watched her in puzzlement but didn't ask.

With everyone geared for speed, they stepped out to find Osha waiting anxiously.

"We together," Osha said in broken Belaskian. "No parting."

Leesil pointed up and left. "If Wynn tried to follow me and Chap, she'd have gone that way."

Osha took off in the lead.

The going was slow in the blizzard's fresh snowfall. Osha did his best to plow a path for everyone else to follow. After a while, Sgäile took his place, and Osha fell back to the rear of their line. Later, when Sgäile paused, bending to catch his breath, Leesil moved up to take over, but then he stood there a while, just looking about.

"Chap and I came this way," he said, pointing. "But I don't know how long or far Wynn followed before getting lost."

"Then head toward where you found me," Magiere suggested. "We'll call out from there. If Chap is anywhere nearby, he'll hear us."

Sgäile moved to the rear as Leesil pressed on. But when Magiere stepped forward, the first clear impression of what she'd felt the night before surfaced in her mind.

Running . . . the need to go higher . . . to climb straight up through the cragged mountainside.

She pushed that returning urge aside. Only the search for Wynn mattered.

When they reached the boxed gully where she'd been found, they turned aside onto other paths. Sunlight broke through the clouds now and then, making the white snow too bright. They searched until the sun crested the sky and began its downward path west, toward the peaks upslope.

Osha walked back along the base of an overhanging ridge.

"Wynn!" he called.

They kept in sight of each other as they spread out and began calling, but no one answered. Magiere returned to their central starting point as Leesil came jogging back, hopping across exposed rocks to avoid wading in the drifts.

"This is no good," he said. "We need to backtrack and look for a different path up. I don't think she made it this far."

Once the sun passed beyond the peaks above them, the slopes would be swallowed in false twilight by midafternoon. And they were no closer to finding Wynn and Chap.

Sgäile returned as well, but when Leesil repeated his suggestion, Osha spit an angry string of Elvish. Instead of a sharp rebuke, this time Sgäile only frowned and shook his head at the young elf. They all headed downward, still searching for side paths. Osha often ranged too far, forcing them to wait on him before they could move on.

A strange sensation flowed through Magiere, and she stopped.

"Here?" she said to herself, turning around.

Osha came running back to them from that same direction, his face flushed as he pointed back the way he'd come.

"Look!" he panted, waving them to follow.

They all trudged along through the broken snow of his path.

"Fork here," he said. "This way go your path"—and he tipped his chin at Leesil. "Wynn may follow other!"

Sgäile looked both ways separating around the point of a high-rising cliff. Even Leesil seemed doubtful and uncertain. Magiere studied the separate paths, but the one Osha chose made her feel warm inside.

Was it just the pull within her, playing on her again . . . or was it hunger?

No—there couldn't be an undead out here in broad daylight. And then the heat in Magiere turned sharply cold. Her stomach knotted as the chill spread.

"Yes," she whispered.

Magiere only realized she'd spoken aloud when Leesil stepped before her, watching her in wary concern. Osha's intense eyes were locked on her as well, and when she nodded slowly toward the path he'd chosen, he took off down the fork. Magiere lunged after him.

Leesil and Sgäile followed in silence. Magiere looked back once at Leesil's chest, but the amulet hanging over his coat wasn't glowing.

"What's wrong?" he demanded.

She didn't answer—didn't know how—and tugged him forward by the sleeve as she hurried to catch up with Osha. She was right on top of the young anmaglâhk when they crested a snow-choked saddle and clambered down into yet another dead end.

"Magiere!" Leesil shouted, panting as he came up behind her. "Slow down!"

She hadn't slept or eaten since the night before. None of them had. Perhaps she just wasn't thinking right, and the spreading chill was nothing more than fatigue.

The world brightened sharply in her eyes.

Tears slid instantly down her cheeks. Her mouth began to ache as she spotted a tall, wide crack farther along the gully wall.

Leesil came around her side, and his eyes widened. She knew her irises had expanded and blackened.

"What is it?" he whispered, following her gaze along the gully wall.

Osha had already jogged ahead, but he came to a sudden halt. He stood there just short of the chute's opening, staring into it, and Sgäile appeared at Magiere's other side.

Nothing marred the snow, but Magiere knew the blizzard had covered what had happened in this place. Osha turned, looking back at them in anguish.

"It's blood," Magiere whispered to Leesil. "Just barely . . . I can smell it."

· · ·

Hkuan'duv sat in the tent as dawn broke.

"Greimasg'äh?" Dänvârfij said hesitantly.

She crouched before the tent's opening, but he did not look up. He kept trying to understand what had happened in the night and the sudden deaths of Kurhkâge and A'harhk'nis. This was no time to grieve or face his shame for leaving their bodies.

"Hkuan'duv!" Dänvârfij insisted. "Sgäilsheilleache's group is on the move, but they did not break camp. They may still search for the small human, but we must know for certain."

He breathed deeply, and she backed away as he crawled from the tent.

After his return and the tale of what had happened, she had acted as both night watch and scout while he rested. But like Hkuan'duv, she was keeping grief locked away until their purpose was fulfilled.

In truth, he had needed time alone, though it brought him no revelations. The white woman had taken two of his caste and disabled him—all before she could be struck even once. Her frail form was a deception, hiding startling speed and strength.

Hkuan'duv stood up, facing the white, rocky world around him. Wind and snowfall had ceased by dawn. He ran a hand through his short, spiky hair, secured his face wrap, and pulled up his hood. Without a word, he and Dänvârfij slipped along the white landscape and crouched to peer at Sgäilsheilleache's abandoned camp.

"When did they leave?" he finally asked.

"At first light."

He could not decide whether to wait or to follow their clear trail. "They must be searching for the small human and the majay-hì."

"Both were alive when you escaped?" she asked.

"Yes, but the majay-hì charged the . . . white woman. He could not have survived long, and the human would have died quickly after. We have only to wait until Sgäilsheilleache discovers their bodies and returns to camp."

"And the bodies of our fallen," Dänvârfij added. "Sgäilsheilleache will know his caste is following him."

She was not blaming him for leaving their companions behind, but shame slipped past Hkuan'duv's guard just the same. It sickened him that he had left Kurhkâge and A'harhk'nis where they lay, without even a hurried ceremonial call to the ancestors to come for their spirits.

"They were lost," Dänvârfij said, "and you were not. I would have done the same."

"Your sympathy does not serve our purpose," he replied.

Greater concerns plagued him. Two more members of his caste now searched the land where this savage white woman ranged. Sgäilsheilleache and Osha had no idea what was waiting up there. His first instinct was to warn them, but he could not do so without exposing his presence.

"Fulfilling our purpose will be more difficult," Dänvârfij said. "A'harhk'nis was wilderness-wise, but so are you. Perhaps we should monitor the search?"

"Not yet," he said. "We wait. Whether they find the bodies or not, they have to return. There is no point in risking ourselves."

Dänvârfij shifted closer beside Hkuan'duv to share warmth.

Wynn stirred, memories of the past night flooding back—the slaughtered anmaglâhk, Chap falling as if dead, and the white woman with black hair. She sat up in panic, opening her eyes.

A dull orange glimmer dimly lit marred stone walls, but Wynn could not remember where she was.

I am here.

She spotted Chap across the room, staring out the entrance. Only remnants of hinges showed that there had once been a door.

The orange light came from a wide and shallow tripod brazier sitting on the stone floor to one side. It had not been there when she collapsed to the floor, but the brazier did not hold fire.

Instead, a pile of fist-sized crystals glowed like coals in its black iron depression. These filled the small room with more heat than light, raising the temperature above freezing.

"How long have I been asleep?" she asked.

Chap kept his gaze fixed outside of the opening. *Day has come . . . I have seen traces of sunlight down the corridor outside.*

Wynn's stomach rolled slightly at his words. Her right leg throbbed painfully, but she could feel her toes again. She crawled over to where Chap sat vigil, remembering translucent wolves, ravens, and swirling dark forms.

"Are they still out there?" she asked.

They appear and vanish . . . but they are there, always.

"What are they?" she whispered.

Chap remained silent for a long moment. *Undead ... though I have never heard of animals as such ... let alone ones like shadow and yet not.*

She rose up on her knees to peer over Chap. Nothing distinct met her gaze—but something like shifting soot moved in the dark spaces across the corridor outside.

"We are prisoners," she whispered. "But why does she keep us alive?"

Chap did not answer, and Wynn wondered where the white undead might be. She dug out the cold lamp crystal and rubbed it quickly.

The room was perhaps twelve by fourteen paces with no other openings. Its old stone walls seemed deeply marred in places by wild swirls of tangled scratches. A decayed desk near the back wall had collapsed on one side, and its slanted top had long ago spilled its contents on the floor. Iron brackets supporting shelves were mounted on the right wall, but the lowest wooden board lay in pieces on the floor amid scattered papers and books grown brittle and tattered with age.

"Where are we?"

Chap growled at the doorless opening but did not answer.

"Last night . . . ," she said, "you kept looking, until you found me."

He turned his head and quickly licked her hand.

Wynn was thirsty, but she saw no sign of food or water. Then she spotted two small bottles among items near the broken desk. She crawled over and picked one up. Remnants of dried black stains flaked off its open mouth, and she realized it once had held ink. Quills lying in the mess were nothing but stems, the feathers rotted completely away.

"We're in an abandoned study," she said, and went to inspect the shelves.

A few books were so old that their covers were damaged with mold. They looked so weak and brittle she was afraid to pick one up.

Another shelf held rolls of rough wood-pulp paper and animal skins stripped clean of fur. She knew enough about old archives not to touch them just yet, lest they crumble and break in her hands. Down another shelf she found stacks of old bark with markings on their inner sides.

Other works were bound in sheaves between hardened slats of leather or roughly finished wood panels. One was sandwiched between what looked like scavenged squares of iron the size of a draught board.

"Chap . . . come and look at these."

Look to the walls first.

Wynn glanced at him, but he had not turned around. What would she want with decaying walls? She stepped closer, holding the crystal high.

The marks on the walls were not the etchings of age.

The crystal's light spilled over a mass of faded black writing. Patches of words, sentences, and strange symbols covered the stones. They ran in wild courses, sometimes overlapping and tangling in each other. Wynn tried to trace one long phrase.

It might have been a sentence, if she could have read it—but it seemed to go on without end. And the words were not all in the same language. Even the symbol sets differed, and some had faded, becoming illegible.

One word was composed of Heiltak letters, a forerunner of Wynn's native Numanese, but the letters were used to spell out words in a different tongue, one that she did not recognize. A piece of old Sumanese was followed by an unknown ideogram, and then a set of odd strokes tangled with short marks. She found one possible Dwarvish rune, but it was so worn she could not be certain.

The passages were in scattered patches, as if the author had run out of paper or hide, or anything else to write upon. Over time, driven by some desperation, this disjointed and manic record had been made on any surface available. But what had the author used for ink that would adhere to stone for so long?

Wynn shifted back, until all the lines and marks became tangled chaos.

Like reading madness itself recorded on forgotten walls.

Now . . . look next to the archway.

Chap's words startled her. Obviously he had been nosing about before she awoke. Stepping toward the doorless opening, she found a column of single . . . words? It seemed so, though again the languages and symbol sets varied.

The highest lines were too faded, as if the words had been rewritten in a downward progression over many years or decades. Midway to the floor, Wynn recognized what seemed to be ancient Elvish by its accent marks, written in the rare Êdän script. Further on was more roughly scripted old Sumanese. Near the bottom, almost to the floor was . . . was it some form of Belaskian?

And each line was only one word.

The symbols differed, yet they always recorded two syllables or sounds.

"Li . . . kun . . . ," she sounded out, and glanced at Chap. "Do you know this term?"

More than a word, I think. . . .

Wynn studied the repeating column of the word. "A name?"

Chap slowly turned his head. He scanned the column once before looking back out into the dim corridor.

I think it is her.

Wynn gazed out the archway, suddenly fearful that the white woman might appear as if called.

"If those shadow animals have not entered by now, perhaps they will not."

No, they only keep us in. Chap stood up and padded across the room, studying the walls. *Can you read any of it?*

"Not truly. I know some of the languages, and some of the symbol sets are familiar. But many do not match the language they are used for."

She rubbed the crystal harder, and held it close to the patch beside the shelves.

"Old pre-Numanese tongues . . . and Êdän, an older Elvish system," she whispered.

Can you read it? Chap repeated, his tone impatient in her head.

"I told you no!" Wynn answered, but her brief anger was born of fright. "All I can make out is gibberish . . . between words that have already faded."

Try another wall.

She looked about and spotted smaller writings above the desk's remains. As she crossed, she tried not to step on the old parchments stuck to the floor by years of dried humidity. Holding the crystal close, she traced lines of marks, careful not to touch them.

"This word . . . looks like tribal Iyindu—old Sumanese—and part of it is in the correct letters."

What does it say?

"Give me a moment!" Wynn snapped. "It is nearly a dead dialect."

She struggled to sound it out in her head. The middle characters were too faint. She sighed in frustration. But the beginning and end caught in her mind, and the sound was familiar somehow. She thought she remembered it written somewhere else in other letters.

Wynn hurried back to rescan the tangled passage beside the shelves. She came to one word written in Êdän-Elvish, but it spelled out the same beginning and ending as the Iyindu-Sumanese—and its middle was clear to read.

"Il'Samar!" Wynn whispered.

What? Chap shoved in beside her. *Where do you see this?*

Wynn pointed.

"Samar" was obscure, meaning something like "conversation in the dark." And "il" was a common prefix for a proper noun, sometimes used for titles as well as predecessors in a person's lineage. The old necromancer Ubâd had cried out this name as Magiere and Chap closed in upon him in Droevinka.

Wynn hurried back to the wall above the desk, forgetting to watch her footing, and brittle parchment shredded beneath her feet.

Now she understood the word with the faded middle, and she went over and over that sentence, trying to pick out more, but it was so badly worn.

" 'Guardian' . . . no, 'guardians for' . . . something that is 'unmaking' . . . and then *il'Samar.*"

Wynn slumped in exasperation.

"That is all I can follow. Is she . . . this woman, one of these? Welstiel spoke of ancient ones guarding whatever treasure he sought. By the look of her, she is undead, but that would mean . . ."

All the wall writings appeared to be in the same hand, though Wynn was not certain, considering the rough surface. But she had read mention of more than one "guardian."

She scanned among the shelves' contents, finally reaching for the bottom iron-bound sheaf, which looked relatively sound. It weighed more than she expected, and she knelt awkwardly, trying to set it down. The old leather binding strap had turned as hard as wood.

"Bite this open for me."

Chap began gnawing the hardened hide strip. *What are you looking for?*

"Other writing . . . in other hands."

The leather tie cracked in Chap's teeth, and Wynn lifted the top iron plate with effort.

The inner sheets were made from squared hide stretched thin and had withstood time better than parchment or paper. They were now as hard as bone, and their inked lettering was difficult to read on the dark squares. Wynn lifted multiple sheets at once, watching for changes in handwriting.

And she saw them.

At least three different people had recorded entire pages in this volume. Unlike the wall writings, these passages were coherently scripted in one matching language and letter system at a time. How old was this sheaf?

"There are other guardians," she whispered, growing frightened again. "Perhaps two or three. How long have they been here?"

No . . . she is now the only one.

Wynn raised her eyes. "We have seen no more than the corridor and this room. But at least three different hands have written these pages."

I sense only her . . . I cannot even sense her shadow servants . . . only her.

Wynn glanced toward the archway, and then to the mad writing surrounding this old, decayed room.

She has been alone . . . for longer than we can measure. And even before the others were gone . . . I would guess she has been here since . . .

"Since the war," Wynn finished in a whisper. "Since the Forgotten History and the war that erased it."

Wynn shivered in her coat, though the room was nearly warm from the brazier's strange crystals.

How many languages can you read?

She squinted, making a mental count. "Well, my own tongue, Numanese, and some of its earlier predecessors . . . um . . . classical Stravinan, Belaskian of course, and the Begaine syllabary of my guild . . . general Dwarvish and one of its formal variants . . . Elvish—modern and ancient scripts, including the Êdän, though I have not fully grasped the variation used by the an'Cróan. Some Sumanese, but not much of its older derivations or the desert—"

Wynn! Chap lowered his head, snout pointing to the hide pages. *What is written here?*

She held the crystal closer. "This page is very old Sumanese—Iyindu, I think—and the handwriting does not match what is written on the walls. I learned a bit of the modern dialect, but I have little grasp of the lesser-known desert dialects."

Wynn placed a hand on Chap's shoulder. "The passages are not signed, but this one mentions a name. 'Volyno,' in the past tense, so I would guess he was no longer present when it was written. Wait . . . here is another . . . a Sumanese name—'Häs'saun.' Perhaps the author of this passage, but I could be mistaken."

She sat back, lowering the crystal into her lap, and Chap huffed, wrinkling his snout in frustration. A flicker in the archway drew their attention.

The translucent outline of a shadow wolf showed against the lighter dark in the corridor. The entire animal was soot black, even its eyes. All thoughts of language fled from Wynn's mind.

The wolf remained in the doorway, but something pale approached behind it—and walked straight through the beast into the small chamber.

Wynn clutched the fur between Chap's shoulders at the sight of their returned captor.

Slender as a willow and barely taller than Wynn herself, the woman's white body was lightly tinged with orange from the brazier's glow. Shining hair hung like wild black corn silk across her shoulders and down over her small breasts. And where Wynn had sometimes seen a trace of brown in Chane's eyes, she now looked into irises like hard quartz. Even the woman's small mouth was as pale and colorless as her skin.

Wynn's gaze caught on the tips of metal around her neck. They peeked out through the separation of her hair.

"Chap, those knobs and the metal," Wynn whispered. "It looks just like Magiere's *thôrhk*."

The woman lunged a step at these words, and Wynn ducked behind Chap as he rumbled in warning.

The deceptively frail undead stared at Wynn. She traced her own lips with narrow fingertips, never looking at Chap. Then her gaze dropped to the pile of hide sheets opened on the floor.

Her strangely shaped eyes narrowed, and her lips parted in a silent snarl over clenched teeth. She began to shake as her fingers hooked like claws.

Say the name! Chap shouted into Wynn's head. *Her name!*

Wynn floundered in panic, not knowing what he meant.

From the column of words beside the door!

"Li . . . kun . . . ," Wynn whispered.

The woman froze, and her feral expression softened.

Wynn tried to find her voice. "Li-kun!"

The woman's eyes opened fully. Confusion washed anger from her face.

Her gaze flitted over the walls, wandering among patches of black scribbles, until she appeared to grow dizzy and stumbled. When she turned fully around, her back to Wynn, she stopped—and threw herself at the wall beside the door.

She crumpled, her delicate hands dragging down the column of a name written so many times. When she reached the floor, she twisted about to squat with her knees pulled up against her bare chest.

Do not move, Chap warned. *Do nothing to disturb her for the moment.*

Wynn flinched as the woman began weakly hammering at her head with limp fists, like someone trying to dislodge a forgotten memory. She sucked in air over and over. But undead did not need to breathe, and the corners of her mouth kept twisting, stretching.

Was she trying to speak? If so, her voice did not come.

"Volyno?" Wynn whispered. "Häs'saun?"

Enough! Chap warned.

Strands of black hair tangled over the woman's face as she lowered her head. Her crystal irises fixed upon Wynn.

In their frightening depths, Wynn saw anguished hunger for . . . something.

Chap remained poised before Wynn.

In this castle of Magiere's dreams, he had hoped to learn more concerning what memories the Fay had stolen from him, and why they had done so. He also believed he might find answers to questions concerning Leesil and Magiere, and their future—and the forgotten conflict and an enemy of many names.

Now all he could do was watch this ancient monster crumple into her insanity.

This place was old—older perhaps than any stronghold in the world. He felt how devoid of life these walls had been for centuries or longer. And this white thing might be older still.

No longer trying to speak, the woman watched Wynn.

Your voice . . . spoken words shocked her, he told Wynn. *Perhaps that is why she did not kill you.*

Wynn looked down at him.

He was only guessing, and yet he loathed the notion of dipping into the crazed thing's memories.

She has been alone for so long that she had forgotten the sound of words. It seems she knows only what is written.

Wynn's face brushed his ear as she whispered, "What now?"

Talk to her . . . and I will try to catch any of her memories.

"Are you sure?"

Do it . . . while she remains sedate.

Wynn inched forward on her knees and pointed to herself.

"Wynn," she said. "And you are . . . Li-kun?"

The woman tilted her head like a crow, or perhaps more like a hawk.

Chap cautiously slipped into her mind. He saw nothing, as if she had no memories at all to rise in her thoughts.

Try the other names again.

"Who is Volyno . . . or Häs'saun?"

At the second name, a wild barrage of broken images erupted in the woman's head.

Flickering white faces passed among other sights—cold peaks, an endless desert, a cowering goblin hammering at stone, massive iron doors, a pale headless corpse on a stone floor . . . the maelstrom made Chap sick.

Her name . . . again!

Wynn pointed to the woman. "Li-kun . . . is this your name?"

The woman's mouth gaped. She lunged forward onto all fours, and her black hair dangled with stray ends brushing the floor. A hoarse rasp issued from her throat. Something in the sound mimicked the way Wynn had pronounced the name.

"Li'kän?" Wynn tried, altering her pronunciation.

The undead studied the sage in fascination and crept forward across the floor.

Chap shifted, ready to lunge into the woman's face, but she slowed, hesitating. She lifted one hand and reached out to Wynn. Chap trembled.

The undead stretched out one narrow finger, the digit slipping through the side of Wynn's wispy brown hair.

To the sage's credit, she did not flinch, remaining frozen in place—even as the finger pulled down over her lips. When it passed her chin and retracted, Wynn swallowed hard and turned toward the wall beside the shelves.

"Are these your writings?"

Calm sanity vanished once more from Li'kän's face.

She clutched her own arms, scratching herself with hardened white nails. The wounds closed so quickly that barely any black fluids seeped out. Harsh, rapid hisses poured from her throat. But no matter how fast her small mouth moved, her voice would not come. Chap could not make out what she tried to say.

Li'kän thrashed in frustration, turning circles on all fours like a dog.

Wynn shrank back, but Chap stood his ground.

He feared the undead no longer possessed real memories, or that after so long alone, they had faded beyond her mind's reach.

Chap steeled himself and slipped again into Li'kän's mind.

Wild blurs of images, lacking any sound, passed through a mind that was no longer rational. Then a flash of something massive, with coils of black scales, rolled and slid in a dark place. Behind it, he saw a brief glimpse of natural stone, as in an underground space. Then the image vanished, replaced by one of Chap himself.

No, a large wolf—but it had the strange crystal sky-blue eyes of a majay-hì.

An ancestor of the breed from long ago, exactly like those Chap had seen in Most Aged Father's memory. Li'kän remembered one of the original born-Fay, who had come into the world during the forgotten war.

"Il . . . sa . . . mar . . . ," she rasped, and then her grating hiss trailed on.

Il'Samar—the only word of her voiceless gibberish that Chap could catch.

Why would she think of born-Fay—or any Fay—and then the enemy of many names?

Chap recoiled, pulling from the undead's mind, but he still wondered that she had no memory of anyone speaking—until Wynn.

Li'kän, this walking shell of death, could write, though not coherently. But spoken language had been lost to her for so long that she had forgotten even the sound of her own name.

· · ·

Magiere felt an undead's presence all around her, but not like ever before. It seeped from the rocks and snow and air, with no origin she could fix upon—and the pull within her pressed her to go on, upward.

She smelled blood in the cold air's light breeze.

Osha leaned into the black space in the cliff's wall and cried out, "Sgäilsheilleache!"

Sgäile ran past Magiere. She took off on his heels with Leesil close behind. Before they reached Osha, he collapsed, his knees sinking in the snow.

A rocky chute rose up through the gully's stone wall, and at its bottom lay a still form slumped against one side.

"Kurhkâge!" Sgäile whispered.

The corpse of the tall elf had only scar tissue for one eye, and the other was still open wide. A light scattering of snow had collected on his tan face, and a white cloth partially covered his open green-gray cloak. But the chest of his tunic was dark with frozen blood around a gaping hole where the ends of shattered ribs protruded.

Leesil hissed something under his breath, and Magiere spun about.

He'd stopped short on the gully's open floor, and the trail he'd broken in the snow ended where he stood. But something more had rolled ahead of his feet, something that he'd accidentally kicked from under the snowfall.

Blood on the head's ragged neck stump had frozen into red ice crust from the clinging snow.

"A'harhk'nis!" Sgäile exhaled the name and shook his head in disbelief.

"How?" Osha moaned, and then slipped into Elvish.

Sgäile weakly waved him into silence.

Magiere barely noted their shock and grief. She was too focused on keeping her dhampir half from rising. If she went near Sgäile, she'd try to force answers from him. Why were other anmaglâhk in these mountains, so close to her destination?

Leesil joined Sgäile, and his expression was hard to read. "You knew them?"

"Yes," Sgäile whispered. "Kurhkâge spoke for Osha when he first requested acceptance to our caste."

Osha stared at the corpse's one eye and didn't blink until his own eyes began to water.

"What were they doing up here?" Leesil demanded.

The low threat in his voice made Magiere's own anger quicken. Shock faded from Sgäile's face, replaced by wariness.

"I do not know."

"Then guess!" Leesil snapped. "How is this connected to us?"

Sgäile turned on him. "What are you suggesting?"

Leesil didn't answer. He just stood there, glancing back at the head lying in the snow.

The scent of blood sharpened in Magiere's nostrils.

"I swear, I do not know," Sgäile insisted and looked away. "I know nothing of this. Kurhkâge's hands . . . he did not even pull a weapon."

Leesil pushed past Osha and crouched before the dead anmaglâhk.

Magiere's eyes fixed on the head. Its face, half-covered in clinging snow, still held a frozen hint of outrage.

"Could there be more?" Leesil asked, though he sounded far away in Magiere's ears.

"No," Osha answered in Belaskian. "Our caste not leave them . . . perform rites for dead. We do it now."

Leesil's voice grew louder. "Not until we find Wynn and Chap!"

Magiere scanned the snow-filled gully. Not far back she spotted a long oblong mound.

She knew the headless body must lie there beneath the snow, and she crouched to pick up the head. Frozen hair crackled in her hands.

"Magiere?" Leesil called.

"What is she doing?" Sgäile asked, voice rising in alarm.

Something she had not done since Bela, and the hunt for an undead who had been murdering nobles. Holding a dead girl's dress, she had accidentally stumbled into Welstiel's footsteps, where he had torn open the girl's throat upon her own doorstep.

Two dead anmaglâhk lay here, and she sensed a Noble Dead like no other she'd come across. Instinct and blood told her in part what had happened. And Chap and Wynn were still missing.

Magiere cringed at what she might learn—see—through the undead's eyes by touching its victim. But she had to know. She had to—

"Magiere!" Leesil shouted. "Don't!"

Darkness and the previous night's blizzard swallowed Magiere's world.

She looked down upon an anmaglâhk pinned in the snow between her narrow white thighs. Before he swung a long curved blade, she grabbed his face. Her white fingers slid up into his hair as she drove her teeth into his throat.

Skin, muscle, and tendons tore between her jaws. Blood flooded her mouth and seeped into her throat. She arched, whipping her torso back as she tore his head free, and stared at another bloody mass clutched in her other hand.

She felt no hunger to feed upon his life. She was already glutted, constantly fed by something she couldn't see. And suddenly, claws bit into her bare back.

Magiere whirled to find Chap snarling, with hackles raised and teeth bared. He harried her until she backhanded him. Part of Magiere shriveled inside as his body hit the gully wall and slumped motionless into the deep snow.

She wanted to scream. She wanted to run to him.

The small white body she existed within turned toward a figure standing in the chute's opening.

Magiere tried to stop herself, but her delicate white hand latched around Wynn's throat. And then she cringed and shrank away at the sound of Wynn's cry.

She didn't know why the words hurt her, frightened her . . . and then made her hungry to hear more of them. She ran up through the chute with Wynn gripped in her hand, and Chap's scrambling paws fading behind her.

She crested the chute's top, and something hammered the side of her face.

Hunger erupted in Magiere's belly.

She tumbled back in the snow as someone slapped the frozen head from her hand. Her jaw ached but not from her sharpening teeth. She tasted blood—real blood—

"What are you doing?" Leesil's voice cracked with hysteria. "You think dreams are the only things that mess with your head?"

He crouched over her, one hand pinning her chest and the other still clenched into a fist. Rather than anger, blind panic filled his amber eyes.

Magiere's eyes began to burn. The sky around him was brilliant, but not as bright as his hair around his tan face.

She grabbed the front of his coat, pulling herself up.

"Your eyes . . . ," Leesil whispered, "they're almost pure black!"

Sgäile and Osha stood behind him, wary hardness and fright plain on their faces.

Magiere wanted only to run for the chute.

Resisting the pull within her no longer mattered. It now led to Wynn and Chap—and the creature who had taken them. All her drives led upward. She gripped Leesil's jacket with both hands, tears running from her burning eyes.

"Have . . . to . . . go," she snarled, barely understanding her own mangled words. "Now . . . to Wynn . . . and Chap."

"What is happening to her?" Sgäile demanded.

Leesil settled his hands on her cheeks, holding her face, and she dropped her forehead against his chest.

She still felt as if she were constantly being *fed*, as when she'd been inside the monster who had slaughtered these anmaglâhk. But it didn't sate her body. She clenched her fingers so tightly they ground upon the rings of Leesil's hauberk beneath his coat.

"Please," she whispered.

"Go," he answered.

Magiere lunged around him, bolting straight for the chute. Sgäile ducked out of her way, but Osha froze. She slammed him aside with her palm and drove up the rock path, fingers clawing the stone walls she climbed.

Somewhere behind her, Leesil shouted, "Follow! And don't lose sight of her! She knows where Wynn and Chap have gone."

CHAPTER EIGHTEEN

Leesil bolted out of the chute's top and chased after Magiere. They raced on through late afternoon until exhaustion threatened to pull him down.

He couldn't find a trail in the fresh snow that Magiere was following, but her course never wavered. And he was still uneasy about what she'd done with the anmaglâhk's severed head.

Magiere had seen—relived—the moment of an undead's kill. She had not tried anything so reckless since Bela, and that had been by accident. It had served a purpose then, and perhaps it did now, but she shouldn't have repeated the experience.

He hadn't even seen her pick up the head until it was too late.

And how could a vampire exist here, with no life to feed on? The only thing clear to Leesil was that Magiere somehow knew how to find Wynn and Chap.

"Is she still sane?" Sgäile panted beside him. "Is she aware of what she does?"

Leesil wished he could answer. It wasn't that simple where Magiere's dhampir nature was concerned.

"Yes," he lied. "Just be quiet and follow."

Leesil hadn't forgotten what they'd found in the gully. Sgäile had questions to answer later. What were other anmaglâhk doing here—and why? Sgäile said he didn't know, but was he lying? Or was this more of Brot'an's scheming?

Magiere hit a steep rocky incline where snow thinned. She didn't even slow, but climbed on, with one hand clawing for holds.

"Move faster," Leesil panted. "Before she's out of sight!"

Sgäile passed him on the slope as Osha came up behind. Leesil raised his head, grabbing for holds with both hands. Magiere stopped at the crest and looked down at him.

Her enlarged irises were pitch black in her pallid face. She shifted nervously, head twisting back and forth, and she kept glancing over the ridge's far side.

"Wait!" Leesil called to her. "Don't move!"

Magiere thrashed about, pacing the ridge's narrow top, and an anguished whine escaped her mouth. It turned into a screeching snarl that echoed down the ridge.

Sgäile stopped cold and glanced over his shoulder at Leesil.

"Just get up there," Leesil urged.

Sgäile pushed on, and Leesil noticed a flattened roll of canvas strapped to his back, along with Magiere's sheathed falchion.

The jostle of running had shifted the bundle, and the winged tip of one of Leesil's old punching blades peeked out the bottom. Sgäile crested the ridge, and Leesil scrambled over the top, rising to his feet beside Magiere.

Her breath came in vibrating hisses between clenched teeth. Leesil followed her fixed gaze into the distance and his eyes widened.

A vast plain lay trapped in a ring of distant high mountains. Its snow was a pure blanket of undisturbed white. And resting amid that smooth perfection was the shape of a multitowered castle. Even at a distance, its size seemed impossible, like a gray sentinel guarding the empty quiet of the sunken plateau. The castle itself almost seemed an illusion, sitting in this barren place at the top of the world.

"Is that it?" he asked, finding his voice. "The one you've been seeing?"

"Yes," Magiere hissed. She back-stepped once downslope, watching him in anticipation.

Leesil scanned the plain for any movement, anything out there waiting to intercept them.

"There," Osha said. "Tracks!"

A broken trail led away from the rocky slope's bottom and out across the smooth white snow.

Magiere inched downward, with her eyes still on Leesil.

He flipped the straps on his new winged blades and pulled them.

They didn't yet *feel* as if they belonged to him. His gloves muted his grip on their handles. But the half-loops of metal, rising partway down the wings, made the blades settle solidly on his forearms.

"Everyone on guard. Whatever took Wynn and Chap"—Leesil glanced sidelong at Sgäile—"and killed your friends . . . just be ready."

Sgäile made no move to hand Magiere her falchion. He just stood there, watching her.

Leesil wondered if he'd have to put Sgäile down to get the sword back. When he turned to Magiere, her black eyes widened, and they fixed on his chest.

In the waning daylight, Leesil hadn't even noticed. The topaz amulet Magiere had given him was glowing.

He grew worried how the others might respond to this clear warning, but Sgäile didn't even flinch at the amulet's light.

"You told us about the guardian undeads before we left Ghoivne Ajhâjhe," Sgäile said, "and something here killed our caste brothers before they could defend themselves." He looked to Magiere. "But I am guardian to *your* purpose. We will find this artifact you seek—and your friends."

Sgäile's certainty didn't squelch Leesil's worry. He saw nothing but the castle, so what had sparked the stone and Magiere's inner nature from such a distance?

"Go on," he said, and Magiere took off down the slope. "But stay within reach!"

They trudged down and followed the trail of broken snow. The closer they came to the castle, the brighter the amulet glowed. It made Leesil even more nervous, and he tucked it inside his coat collar. He didn't want a beacon announcing their arrival.

They reached a bleached stone wall surrounding the castle grounds.

Leesil hadn't noticed it from the ridge. Magiere turned along it, no longer looking to the trail. Leesil followed farther out from the wall, glancing up over its snow-capped top. The castle loomed in the darkening sky. It looked so old, decrepit and decaying.

Magiere halted before a pair of tall, ornate iron gates. One hung slightly ajar at the bottom from a broken lower hinge, leaving an angled space between them. The snow trail led inward toward a wide rise of stone steps that were strangely free of snow.

"No . . . birds . . . ," Magiere whispered, and tilted back her head to stare at the high arched peak where the gates joined. "Dif . . . rent. Wrong . . . old . . . broken."

She gripped the rusted iron with both hands and peered through the gates at the castle beyond. Her shoulders hunched, as if she were about to tear the tilting gate from its one remaining hinge. Leesil quickly grabbed her forearm, as Sgäile hissed a warning.

"Do not announce our presence!"

Leesil shook his head. "Whatever is here likely knows someone's coming—it might even have taken Wynn and Chap just to bait us."

Magiere looked expectantly into his eyes, but her gloved hands remained clenched on the gate's bars.

"Push the rage down," Leesil urged. "You got us here . . . now clear your head."

Magiere's brow wrinkled, almost in a snarl, then smoothed again. She appeared to understand. Her jaw muscles worked, and her tongue passed briefly over her teeth. She inhaled deeply, and her breath hissed out, turning to vapor in the cold air.

"Yes," she whispered, and she straightened up, but her irises remained fully black.

Relieved, Leesil turned to Sgäile. "Welstiel used the term 'old ones,' but we don't know how many. Your stilettos won't help. Get out my old blades and give one to Osha."

"No, we have not trained with your weapons," Sgäile answered. He held up his left hand, exposing a garrote's handles, its silvery wire looped about his gloved fingers. "But we can still take heads."

Magiere looked at the wire and nodded in approval. "Good."

Rather than ripping the gate from its hinges, she shoved it, widening the space. Leesil slipped through behind her.

"My sword," Magiere said.

Leesil glanced back, and at Sgäile's hesitation, he growled, "Give it to her!"

Sgäile unstrapped the falchion, and Magiere took it and belted it on. Osha held out the long war dagger before she'd even asked. She slipped it into her belt at the small of her back.

The sun had dipped below the western peaks. Though the sky was still light, deep shadows filled the sunken plateau, enveloping the castle and its grounds. Leesil cursed himself again for losing Wynn in the blizzard. If not for his desperation to find her and Chap, he would insist they all return to camp and wait for dawn before entering this place.

The courtyard's smooth white was broken by massive stones fallen from above ages ago. The first step of the wide stairs sank midway along the seam between two of its stones. They all climbed to the top landing. The large iron doors were etched and discolored—but sound enough to be a problem.

Magiere set her shoulder to one door and shoved. It moved barely an inch.

She was stronger than any of them with her dhampir nature awakened. Through the opening crack, Leesil saw only darkness inside.

"I don't like this," he grumbled. "The door isn't even barred."

"It doesn't have to be," Magiere answered. "Help me."

Sgäile joined Leesil, and they put their own efforts behind Magiere's. And they both flinched at the squeal of rusted metal as the door opened wider. Magiere didn't hesitate to slip through before anyone else.

Leesil followed, with Sgäile and Osha behind, and paused to let his eyes adjust. The temperature was no warmer than outside.

He and Magiere had entered the lairs of Noble Dead before—first Rashed and Teesha's warehouse in Miiska, and then Ratboy's lavish home in Bela. Both times, Leesil had had a sense of *something* therein, by Teesha's needlepoint and the paintings in Ratboy's townhouse. These false impressions of "life" marked a presence. But as his sight adjusted, he saw no such things here.

Dim twilight slipping through the iron doors offered barely enough illumination for his half-elven eyes. He stood in a long stone corridor wider than the council hall in Bela. Paired rows of pillars the breadth of elven trees stood near to either side wall, and each broadened at the base where it met the floor. The open way between was wide enough for seven armed men to walk freely abreast, and it ran on toward the castle's hidden depths. The walls beyond the pillars were difficult to see, but sections of stone appeared deeply etched by age in random patches.

"You said it looked wrong," he whispered to Magiere. "Do you mean compared to your dreams?"

"Older," she answered. "What I saw was sound and clean, even in the snow and ice."

"Maybe you saw it from the past?" he asked. "Through the eyes of who . . . whatever guided you here."

Magiere closed on one pillar and sniffed sharply.

"Pull out the amulet," Sgäile whispered.

"It won't be much use for tracking this close," Leesil answered.

"For its light," Sgäile insisted. "There is something wrong with these walls."

Magiere's gaze wandered as she sniffed again, and this time her nose wrinkled.

Leesil pulled the amulet out. "What's wrong?"

She shook her head. "Something familiar but . . . I'm not sure. Thin— and all around."

Osha watched her intently. "Wynn? Or Chap?"

"No," Magiere answered.

Sgäile tapped Leesil's shoulder. "Come."

He stepped around the first left pillar toward the wall beyond. Leesil followed, and his gaze fell on a patch of stone etched by decay. The amulet's light spilled across it, but the roughened age didn't vanish.

It became a wild patch of worn and faded black writing scattered along the wall.

Some crude implement had been used for the rough strokes, and even so, Leesil couldn't make out what it said. Once or twice he spotted Belaskian lettering, or something like it, but the characters didn't spell out words he recognized.

"Elven . . . and some Sumanese, I believe," Sgäile whispered. He crouched low, his fingers tracing a wandering line. "Here . . . and again, but not words in my people's language."

"More here," Osha called.

Leesil spotted him near the next pillar down the wall. The young elf lifted his gaze up the stone wall.

"More above," Osha whispered, and he looked to a height no person could have reached.

Magiere pushed in beside Leesil, flattening her hand upon the writing. She sniffed again and shuddered in revulsion.

Sgäile watched her. "What are you doing?"

"Magiere?" Leesil whispered.

Her eyes moved across the gibberish on the walls. She pressed her face even closer to the stone and inhaled deeply.

Magiere spun away, choking as she stumbled in the open corridor. She reached for her falchion and cast about, as if looking for a threat.

"Blood," she whispered. "From one of them . . . written with its blood!"

Osha lunged backward into the open corridor.

"What nonsense do you speak?" Sgäile asked Magiere. "This is not blood."

Leesil grabbed Sgäile's tunic shoulder and pulled him up. "Not from the living—from the dead . . . undead . . . the ones we've fought, the vampires, their fluids are black."

Both he and Sgäile backed away.

"I can smell it," Magiere hissed. "Faint . . . but everywhere."

"Who do such sick writing?" Osha asked.

Leesil remembered that an'Cróan were repulsed by any mutilation of the dead. Even he didn't want to imagine how this demented practice had been accomplished.

"Is there harm in touching it?" Sgäile asked.

Leesil shook his head. "Not that we've experienced. But let's move on."

He turned down the long corridor with Magiere close beside him. They stuck to the center between the pillars.

Farther on, they spotted a massive archway straight ahead, shaped in a peaked echo of the iron doors and the outer gates. Its frame stones were rounded and smooth but unadorned, and through the opening lay a wide stone stairway leading to upper floors. As they stepped through the arch, narrow passages stretched into the dark on the left and right.

"No central hall," Sgäile said. "No main meeting or feasting place."

"What?" Leesil asked.

"Human fortifications usually have a main hall from the entrance, where visitors are greeted and formal meals are held. But not here—this place is strangely built."

"It wasn't made for the living," Magiere said, looking down one side passage. "The dead don't take in visitors or host feasts."

Leesil thought he saw a flicker in the dim side passage beyond Magiere. Then it was gone, and he turned away.

Magiere suddenly flipped the falchion between her hands. She ripped off her coat and let it fall.

A mute shape, darker than a shadow, sailed toward them through the dark air in the side passage.

Leesil quickly shed his coat. He'd barely separated his blades back into both hands when the darting shadow shot into the stairway chamber. It rose higher . . . and spread into a set of wings.

An enormous black raven wheeled in the chamber's heights. It tucked wings and began to fall. When it spread out again at the bottom of its diving arc, Leesil saw the landing of the stairs behind it—through it—in the amulet's light. He remembered Ubâd's ghostly guardians in the Apudâlsat forest.

The black winged shadow leveled straight at Osha.

"Don't let it hit you!" Leesil shouted.

Another shadow shot out of the passage, rising behind its falling twin.

He raised his blades out, fanning them in the air as he shouted, "Here!"

As Osha dodged away, the first shadow raven swerved toward Leesil. He dropped and rolled forward beneath the bird's dive.

It slammed into the archway's wall and vanished.

Leesil heard the flutter of wings out in the pillared corridor, and the second raven flew at Sgäile. At the last instant, Sgäile lunged aside, out of its way.

"Stay off the stairs and in the open!" Magiere shouted. "Don't get penned in."

An eerie caw sounded loudly, and Leesil saw the first bird coming in low along the pillared corridor. When it neared the peaked archway, the amulet's light seemed to shine upon its black feathers.

Magiere stepped into its path.

Leesil went cold with panic, but the raven stalled, wheeling up in a flutter of wings.

"We need light!" Sgäile shouted.

Leesil spun about, still uncertain what Magiere was doing. The amulet's light turned with him, spreading over the chamber and stairs. He spotted the second raven diving along the central stairway, straight for Sgäile's back.

"Down!" he shouted.

Sgäile dropped flat, and the raven passed an arm's length above him. It swerved suddenly, straight at Leesil's face.

He had no defense against something that could pass through solid walls and threw himself aside. His shoulder hit the floor, and his hauberk's rings grated along the cold stone. As he rolled, he grabbed the amulet's leather cord, trying not to stab himself with his own blade. The cord snapped, and he cast the amulet to the chamber's center for light. Then he saw Magiere.

She turned to face the bird swerving toward her and just stood there, waiting before the archway. Her arms opened wide, as if challenging the thing coming at her.

"Magiere!" Leesil shouted.

She whipped her arms together and under as the second raven darted for her chest. And her falchion swiped upward.

The tip's arc caught the bird, dead center. A screech filled the chamber as it exploded into smoke.

Trails of sooty vapors blasted around Magiere, driven by the bird's momentum. They collected beyond her, smoke gathering again into the raven's form. It shot out the peaked archway as its twin dove in from the corridor.

The first shadow raven slammed into Magiere's back.

She buckled as it shot out her chest and rose up the center stairs. Sgäile's eyes widened at the sight just before he had to duck away from the bird's passing.

A rumbling growl escaped Magiere's mouth as she straightened.

Leesil took a shaky breath. These things had no more effect upon her than did the ghosts of Apudâlsat.

"How?" Osha cried out from where he crouched by the archway's near side.

"She can't be hurt by such things," Leesil shouted. "But we can, so watch yourself!"

The first raven turned for another pass. Magiere couldn't get her blade up in time. She swung at it with her free hand as the amulet's light glimmered on the bird's form.

Feathers tore away in Magiere's hooked fingers, and a squealing caw echoed through the chamber.

Torn black feathers turned to vapor before they reached the floor.

The shine upon the raven's plumaged faded as it righted its tumbling body. Magiere whipped the falchion in the air, and it wheeled away out of reach.

Leesil didn't know what these creatures were, but he saw an advantage.

Magiere's falchion inflicted true injury on an undead, so these birds were something akin. And when they couldn't harm her in their shadow state, one had appeared to turn solid for an instant.

"Watch for light on their feathers!" he shouted as Sgäile rose and backed toward Magiere. "That's when they can be struck!"

Leesil reached for Osha to drag him clear of the wall.

The black shadow of a wolf's head thrust through the stone, its jaws spreading wide.

Wynn knelt upon the floor near Li'kän.

Her pity mixed with fear as she tried to read aloud from pieces of writing on the walls. Every word drew a cringe from the pale woman, though her eyes were filled with hunger for the sound. She had been alone for so long that she no longer recognized the wall writings as her own. Chap urged Wynn on, hoping to learn more from whatever memories flashed through the undead's mind.

He was able to gather that Li'kän had been one of three guardians who once existed in this place, perhaps as far back as its original construction. She was the only one left.

Though Li'kän had the attributes of a vampire, Chap sensed no hunger in her, at least not for the blood of the living. What sustained her remained a mystery.

Time and again, Wynn halted over a mislettered word she couldn't make out. A few times, Li'kän slowly mouthed something. Wynn tried to catch the woman's voiceless, breathy utterance, sounding it out as best she could.

Some writings described events Wynn could not understand, but most were incoherent ramblings. In the worst places, the characters grew haphazard, perhaps written after Li'kän's mind had deteriorated too much.

Wynn dearly wished to return to the iron sheaf's hide pages or any other texts she could lay her hands upon. The clearer prose might hold far more than the mad marks upon the walls. She grew weary from constant fear, and her throat was getting dry. And she wondered if she would ever again leave this place.

Li'kän's fascination with her voice, her words, seemed to be all that was keeping Wynn and Chap alive. But it also made them prisoners. If Wynn stopped talking too long, Li'kän became agitated.

Chap stayed close, but often, Wynn dared not turn her attention from Li'kän to ask what he learned.

He suddenly pricked his ears and looked to the doorway.

Li'kän rose fluidly to her feet, turning the same way.

"What is it?" Wynn asked.

From a distance, she heard a voice shouting, and then the hint of metal striking something hard.

Li'kän darted out of the study. Chap lunged for the doorway, halting to look about the outer corridor, and Wynn quickly joined him.

Outside, the passage had dimmed once more. Had they been in this chamber all day? But Wynn saw no shadows moving. How far had Li'kän brought them beyond the pillared corridor?

Stay behind me, Chap ordered as he trotted out.

Wynn hurried after him. Ahead down the corridor, Li'kän's white form turned right at an intersection.

Chap rounded the corner ahead of Wynn. When she followed, she caught a glimpse of Li'kän far ahead. Dim light from outside spilled through ice-glazed windows high along the corridor's right wall. Wynn shuddered as the undead passed through those shafts.

Li'kän did not even flinch as waning daylight slipped across her naked body.

The shouting ahead grew louder, and Wynn ran on behind Chap as one voice became clear.

"Watch for light on their feathers!"

Li'kän swerved left into the opening of a narrow passage.

"That was Leesil!" Wynn cried. She followed as Chap turned in behind the undead.

Li'kän raced out the corridor's distant end. The space beyond was lit by a soft amber glow. Chap bolted out, leaving Wynn behind, until she, too, skidded into the open.

Magiere stood in a huge chamber before a wide staircase, and shadow ravens circled high above. Leesil reached for Osha, crouching beside a broad archway.

A wolf shadow lunged from the wall, directly behind them, snapping at Osha's leg.

"More damned dead!" Leesil spit.

He jerked Osha aside, and the lanky elf tumbled away as the wolf's transparent jaws closed on air. Another wolf shot from the small passage on the chamber's far side, and it charged at Sgäile. For an instant, amber light glittered upon black fur and eyes.

Images of Li'kän mangling the two anmaglâhk flashed into Wynn's mind.

"Li'kän, stop this!" she shouted.

Leesil spun about at her cry, as Sgäile ducked around the stone banister, poised to strike the wolf coming for him. Leesil ran to Wynn, grabbing her coat and pulling her backward.

The ravens lighted upon the stairway's rail high above.

Both wolves came to a halt, poised as their heads turned toward their mistress.

Li'kän stood staring at Magiere.

Magiere's eyes were flooded pure black, and a livid snarl twisted her face. She lifted the falchion, gripping it with both hands, and closed on Li'kän.

"No!" Wynn shouted, for Magiere did not know what she faced.

Magiere looked into the naked undead's teardrop-shaped eyes. This thing had to be one of the "old ones" that Welstiel had hinted at. But the woman looked nothing like what Magiere had expected. Frail and small, too tiny to be a true threat.

Yet she had taken two anmaglâhk before they could fight back. And she had stolen Chap and Wynn.

Magiere wanted her head.

She swung the falchion back and up. Both hands gripped the hilt as it rose past her shoulder. When she charged, she faltered at a glint of metal.

"No!" someone cried.

Magiere saw the thick ends of red-gold metal with protruding knobs about the undead's slim throat. The white woman sprung forward with a silent snarl, and Magiere twisted aside, bringing her sword down. A frail white hand caught the falchion's blade, and the sword stopped without cutting through.

The impact shuddered through Magiere's arms and into her shoulders.

The little woman wrenched the blade aside, and it twisted in Magiere's grip. This only made her angrier, and her hunger erupted.

"Leesil, stop her—she cannot win against Li'kän!"

Magiere heard Leesil's name, and her eyes shifted once to find him. Wynn struggled, pinned in one of his arms as he held a winged blade before her. A flash of doubt passed over Leesil's face.

The woman's colorless eyes widened, mirroring Magiere's hunger. She shook, and her mouth gaped, exposing sharp teeth.

Magiere released one hand from the falchion's hilt and grabbed for the undead's white throat. More quickly, the woman latched her other hand around Magiere's wrist.

They stood straining against each other. Black fluids ran down the falchion from between the white undead's fingers. Magiere tried to press her blade forward but couldn't, and her boots started to slide upon the stone floor. One of her legs began to buckle.

She let one knee drop to the floor, then thrust upward with her whole body.

The white woman's narrow feet lifted sharply, but her grips tightened on Magiere's wrist and sword. Magiere pivoted before the undead could come down, and whipped the woman's small body in an arc.

Glistening black hair snapped wildly around the woman's white face, until her body slammed into the stairway's side. The stone railing shattered, scattering pieces across the floor.

The grip on Magiere's wrist broke, but the woman's momentum jerked Magiere off her feet. Her sword clattered from her hand as she hit the floor and rolled onto all fours.

The white woman scrambled to her feet amid bits of broken stone. A figure in gray-green leaped up onto the thick railing's remains. A long, glinting wire was stretched taut between his spreading hands.

"Wynn, stop it!" Leesil shouted, and then, "Sgäile! Don't!"

Sgäile hesitated, his amber eyes fixed upon the white woman below him. She lashed out with one hand, not even looking up at him.

Sgäile hopped up into the air. A grating screech of stone filled Magiere's ears as the undead's nails tore more chips from the railing. Magiere gained her feet and lunged with her bare hands.

The white woman charged to meet her—and then jerked to an awkward halt.

Magiere's whole body grew instantly weak.

A sudden sense of weight nearly crushed the hunger out of her, and the chamber turned dim in her sight. She wavered where she stood, and when her sight cleared . . .

The white undead shuddered with narrow muscles straining beneath her smooth skin. She lifted her sagging head, but her eyelids drooped as colorless irises rolled up. She swayed like a drunkard or someone caught in waking sleep.

Wynn appeared in Magiere's way. "Wait! She is more dangerous than you know . . . and we may need her."

Chap trotted over, pacing before Magiere as he watched the frail-looking undead.

Magiere held her place only because hunger had slipped from her, and she wanted it back.

Nothing was as Magiere had expected. All she wanted was to kill any undead in her way, find and take the object she'd come for, and silence her dreams once and for all. She felt weary.

Magiere grabbed Wynn by the arm and pulled the little sage back behind herself. Then she remembered the shadow beasts.

The ravens were perched upon the rail of the upper landing. The inky coats of both wolves glimmered slightly. Then they all turned to translucent smoke and vanished through the chamber walls.

"This is getting a little too odd," Leesil whispered, "even for us."

Magiere's relief doubled at the sight of him beside her. Beyond him, Osha hurried toward Wynn, but Sgäile still perched above the white woman, watching her coldly.

The white undead lowered her head, crystalline irises rolling down to settle upon Magiere.

Chap reached for Li'kän's memories.

Her forced breaths hissed out, twisted and broken, as her lips worked in a failed attempt to speak. She pressed a hand over one ear and appeared to whisper to herself. But she never uttered a sound.

Chap recalled a memory he had seen within Magiere—and once heard her recount.

When Ubâd had conjured Magelia's spirit, Magiere's mother had shown her memories from a few moons before her birth. Welstiel had wandered her father's keep's courtyard in the dark, whispering to a voice Magelia could not hear.

Chap saw nothing within Li'kän's mind.

Then something blinked through her thoughts.

Not an image, but a fleeting sound, like a whisper or a hiss.

Chap could not make out any words. About to pull free from Li'kän's thoughts, he heard the sound change.

Like a leaf-wing flutter?

That was how Wynn described hearing Chap communing with the Fay, but rather than the chorus she'd mentioned, he heard just one quick, soft buzz in the undead's thoughts.

Then it was gone, like a blink completed.

Chap watched Li'kän tilt her head with half-open eyes, as if listening. Her lips moved silently again, and he pulled quickly from her mind.

Perhaps he had only heard Li'kän's own voiceless whispers.

He studied this mad thing and reflected upon the "night voice" spoken of in the old parchments found by Wynn's guild. He felt like a pup lost in a dark room, wandering to find a way out.

Chane stared at Welstiel in disbelief as dusk settled in.

"What do you mean, 'she's lost'?" he demanded.

"Last night," Welstiel answered. "Sometime before sunrise."

They crouched in the tent, facing each other across the glowing steel hoop. The ferals sensed their tension and shifted restlessly.

Chane's mouth hung half-open. He closed it, teeth snapping together.

"You knew . . . when you returned before dawn? And you said nothing!"

"What would you have done?" Welstiel challenged. "Run off once more to save your little sage—in daylight? Spare me your outrage."

Chane slapped open the tent's flap. He was already ripping down the shelter before any of the others got out. Barely bothering to fold the canvas, he lashed the tent into a bundle as Welstiel sat scrying in the snow. When the undead stood, he appeared mildly surprised.

"What now?" Chane hissed, hating to even ask.

"Magiere may have gone farther than anticipated . . . or has not yet returned from the search."

Welstiel's continued reluctance to share information was infuriating. Chane finished packing their gear and motioned to Sabel.

"We go."

She took up the bundled tent, and the other monks reluctantly gathered the remaining gear to follow. This trek of ice and starvation wore on all of them.

Welstiel stepped off upslope as they followed, but Chane hung back to walk at the line's end. They trudged on, until spotting a crusted canvas pinned to a rock face across the slope.

"Their camp," Welstiel said. "We can track from here along their trail."

Chane had a fleeting urge to look inside the canvas, as he smelled no life nearby. Instead, he pushed past Welstiel along the clear path in the snow left by Magiere's people. He followed this for a long while—up to a place where the tracks broke in all directions. Many of them turned back atop each other, all placed around a gully that forked in two directions.

"Which way?" Welstiel asked.

Chane crouched in the snow. The thought of doing anything for Welstiel's benefit made the beast in him yowl. But he could not stop picturing Wynn lost out here in this frigid land.

"The right fork has no returning footprints," Chane rasped. "Wherever they went, they did not come back this way . . . as on the other paths."

The ferals crouched, sniffing about, but none seemed to catch anything of interest.

Chane stood up and pressed on. They passed through a saddle between the rocks, and he slowed at the sight of a boxed gully. As they moved inward, he found a wide split in one stone wall—and a frozen, stiff body just inside.

And a head tossed haphazardly near one gully wall.

The ferals sniffed wildly but did not rush in. Even Chane smelled no blood in the cold. Perhaps the monks were confused by the lack of scent when faced with a dead body—and no life to feed on. He glanced at the head.

A coating of snow crusted its face and open eyes.

"How many elves were trailing Magiere?" he asked.

"Uncertain," Welstiel answered. He stepped close to the corpse in the chute.

A fist-sized hole gaped in the man's chest. Chane studied it from where he stood.

"Could Magiere have done this?"

Welstiel leaned over the wound before answering.

"No . . . this is not the way an undead kills, even her." But he did not sound sure. "We press on. There's nothing more to learn here."

"Press on?" Chane hissed. "To where?"

But he followed as Welstiel turned up the rocky chute.

Hkuan'duv and Dänvârfij watched the pack of crouching humans and their two leaders approach Sgäilsheilleache's camp.

"Downwind," he mouthed, and they slipped south.

Dänvârfij's eyes narrowed as she took her first clear look at these people.

The dark-haired one with white temples led, while the younger brought up the rear. Both wore cloaks and heavy clothing and swords. Both looked grim and weather-worn and pale, but otherwise like any common human Hkuan'duv had encountered.

But the hunkered ones sniffed and grunted like dogs, often crouching on their hands and feet.

The taller man with red-brown hair took the lead, following the broken trail in the snow.

Hkuan'duv waited until the last of them vanished into the broken mountainside. He had expected Sgäilsheilleache to bring his charges back, but no one had returned to the camp. He began second-guessing his decision to wait.

What if Magiere had not assisted in searching for her small companion? What if she had already found what she sought, whether the others located the young female or not? And what did these other two and their hunched entourage have to do with any of this? Did they seek the artifact as well?

"Follow?" Dänvârfij asked.

Hkuan'duv finally nodded. They slipped out of hiding, trailing low and carefully in silence.

. . .

Welstiel did not need to scry for Magiere. Out the chute's top, he found a clear trail again. The strides of the footprints were long, as if Magiere and her companions were running, and Welstiel picked up the pace.

They traveled a long while until they reached a steep rocky incline narrowly breaching two tall peaks. Three ferals grunted in protest, but he drove them on to the top and stopped upon the crest.

Out on a vast white plain, couched between high peaks all around, rested the six-towered castle.

After so much effort, and so much planning and manipulation . . .

Welstiel looked upon the end of his search and the promised end of his suffering.

His night sight sharpened under the moon, and the relief inside him wavered.

Even in darkness, the castle was not the same as in his dreams. It looked old and decayed. The trail resumed at the slope's bottom, heading toward the fortification.

Magiere was already there.

Welstiel hurried down the rocky slope.

CHAPTER NINETEEN

Hkuan'duv and Dänvârfij followed from a safe distance, letting the pack of humans keep a good lead. But when they reached the boxed gully, Dänvârfij halted, still as the snow, and stared at Kurhkâge's frozen corpse in the chute.

A'harhk'nis's head lay uncovered where someone else had found it. Hkuan'duv knew that Sgäilsheilleache would be aware he had been followed, and his suspicions might grow.

Dänvârfij sank to her knees. "What could have done this?"

When Hkuan'duv had returned to camp last night, his need to suppress shock and pain had kept him from relating too many details. She had not pressed for more.

"I believe this white woman is one of the humans' undead," he began, and then faltered. "They had no defense against her . . . she was too fast and strong."

"But this," Dänvârfij said, looking at A'harhk'nis's head, "to one such as him . . . We cannot leave them untended."

"We will perform rites after our purpose is fulfilled."

Dänvârfij lifted her eyes to him and, for a moment, he thought she might argue. Then her expression flattened until no trace of anger or grief remained. Their purpose came first, even if it meant irreverence for their dead. Dänvârfij stepped up the chute as if she had seen nothing at all.

Hkuan'duv followed and suppressed his trepidation as he passed between the stone walls—past the place where he'd seen a white face with colorless eyes like ice.

They breached the chute's upper end and saw no one, but the trail in the snow was clear. They trekked in silence until the path led to a rocky slope through a narrow saddle between two high peaks. When they crested the top, they both halted above a wide white plateau between the mountains.

"Look," Dänvârfij whispered, pointing.

Upon the sunken plain stood an ancient fortification of pale gray stone, and the distant specks of the two male humans and their band drew closer to it.

Hkuan'duv hurried down to the plain's edge and crouched to wait and watch. There he spotted a paw print in the snow near the rocks.

The majay-hì had survived and traveled on in the night without the others. Hkuan'duv closed his eyes, considering what to do next.

If the dog had tracked the white woman, then she was inside as well. All tracks led to this hidden place—the journey's end—and more than likely, Magiere and Sgäilsheilleache were already inside. The deceptively frail monster might be a guardian for this ancient artifact that Most Aged Father wanted. A battle for the object's possession seemed inevitable, but Hkuan'duv could not see how anyone could get past the woman. And how did these other humans, now trekking across the plain, fit into the growing tangle?

"If A'harhk'nis and Kurhkâge could not best this undead," Dänvârfij said, "then Sgäilsheilleache and Osha will not fare any better. They are in danger."

"Sgäilsheilleache would never betray his guardianship through reckless-ness," Hkuan'duv replied. "He would not allow his charges to fight a hope-less battle. He may possess knowledge in this matter that we do not."

Even so, Hkuan'duv did not know what the object truly was or where it lay in the vast structure. He only knew that Magiere was to retrieve it, and he would procure it from her.

He looked over the pristine plain, waiting for the pack of humans to get closer to the castle. Once they were hard to separate with his elven eyes, he knew their limited human sight would not detect two followers. He and Dänvârfij slipped out across the snow.

They stayed within the broken trail to hide their own passing from anyone who returned. Halfway there, he spotted the snow-capped outer wall. They traversed its outside until tall iron gates loomed before them. All trails passed through the tilting gate, and they backed away along the wall to hunker against its stone.

"If Magiere succeeds, she will return with the artifact," he said. "We will find cover and see how many of her companions survive as well. Once they head back for their camp, we will trail at a safe distance and take them among the crags."

"But if Sgäilsheilleache survives and—"

"His guardianship must end, overridden by Most Aged Father's request. Sgäilsheilleache is loyal. He will do what is right."

"And if others, besides Magiere, resist?"

"Dispatch the small human, but only incapacitate the half-blood." He paused, still scanning the valley. "Then we will attend our dead and return the artifact to our caste's safekeeping."

Dänvârfij paused, absorbing his words. Her face looked thin and tired. They had both spent too many days and nights on half-rations in this ice world.

"I agree, but . . . ," she began.

"You have another option?" he asked.

"No . . . but I dislike leaving Sgäilsheilleache and Osha to face this alone, while we wait so close."

Her honesty was always admirable. Had she felt any other way, she would not be Dänvârfij.

"I know," Hkuan'duv answered and pulled his cloak tightly about himself.

Wynn breathed in relief at the sight of Osha hurrying toward her. He drew close but did not embrace her.

"Are you well?" he asked.

Sgäile crept down the thick stone banister and dropped silently off its end. He did not take his eyes off Li'kän.

"I am thirsty," Wynn said.

Osha dug inside his tunic and produced a leather-sheathed water flask. She took it gratefully, but kept watch on Magiere and Li'kän. Neither had moved.

Sgäile studied the white woman with revulsion, as if uncertain whether to attack or hold his ground.

"Why did she stop?" Leesil asked.

Magiere's falchion still lay on the floor, but her black eyes were locked upon Li'kän. She looked almost weary.

At first Wynn gave her behavior little notice, but then she remembered the times Magiere had come out of her dhampir state. She had often succumbed to exhaustion, but only after, never during.

Li'kän swayed in a half-aware state. Her small mouth moved as if whispering voicelessly to herself. Wynn gulped down three mouthfuls of water and crouched to pour some in her hand.

"Psst . . . Chap, come here," she whispered.

He glanced over and then backed toward her rather than break his vigil. When he had lapped away the water, Wynn poured more, but he ignored it.

"What is happening?" she asked.

I cannot make out her words. It is as if she is speaking to someone, but I do not know who or what . . . or why she holds back.

Magiere glanced down at Wynn with irises flooded black, then reached out and grasped Wynn's hand.

"Chap believes something is influencing her," Wynn said and stood up, still gripping Magiere's fingers. "What do we do now?"

They had all followed Magiere this far, and Wynn hoped she would somehow know what to do.

Magiere crouched and picked up her sword. She scanned the wide stairs and upper landing with three plain archways, and then glanced briefly to the narrow passage from which Wynn had entered. She stopped last on the left-side passage.

"That way."

At Magiere's first step, Sgäile quickly closed on her.

"You would turn your back on this thing?"

His tone worried Wynn, as well as the way he watched Li'kän with the garrote wire still looped between his hands. How long would the naked woman remain passive if she sensed a threat?

"Li'kän?" Wynn said. "Will you come?"

Magiere spun back, releasing Wynn's hand. Her features twisted with menace, but Li'kän stood listless and unaware. Then a shudder passed through the white undead. Her own face wrinkled in a mute echo of Magiere's.

"What did you call her?" Magiere hissed.

"Her name . . . ," Wynn answered, but the mimicked expressions of these two women left her frightened. "Li'kän has been here, alone, for a long time."

Wynn flinched as Magiere turned on her. More than once, Magiere and Leesil, and even Chap, had chastised her sympathies for certain Noble Dead.

"This place holds secrets," Wynn added firmly. "Chap believes we need assistance in deciphering them, if we are to retrieve what you seek . . . and more."

Chap wrinkled a jowl at Wynn, but he huffed once in agreement. Leesil, Sgäile, and Osha all looked more uncertain and wary.

"Will you come?" Wynn repeated to Li'kän.

The white undead ceased whispering. A sharp shake of her head tossed her black hair across her face. Her irises rolled down from beneath quivering eyelids, and she swung her head toward the sage. Wynn sidestepped just a little way behind Magiere.

Li'kän studied her, appraised her, trying to decide if she were prey—or at least that was how it seemed to Wynn. Then Li'kän stepped out unsteadily, as if reluctant at each footfall.

Magiere headed for the left corridor. Chap closed behind her, watching over his shoulder.

Must you share all my concerns whenever they pop into your head?

Wynn did not answer as she scurried after him, and Li'kän came behind her.

Osha tried to step in, but Sgäile pulled him back. Leesil waited as well. Once the undead had followed Wynn into the corridor, all three fell in behind her.

"I had to say something," Wynn whispered to Chap. "You saw Magiere's face—not to mention Sgäile's."

I could be wrong.

Wynn's stomach flip-flopped. Chap rarely second-guessed himself, at least as far as she knew.

Li'kän is undead and mad . . . and cannot be trusted. If she has been here since the forgotten war, then she was likely a part of it.

Wynn glanced back.

Li'kän paced close behind. Her white body turned deep gray in the tight passage's shadowy space. Somewhere farther back, the glow of Leesil's retrieved amulet silhouetted the undead in a dim orange aura.

Wynn was caught between two natural enemies: one of the undead, immeasurably old, and a dhampir—a hunter of the dead—but born to lead them.

Magiere led the way out the passage's end into a large room. At first, Wynn made out little in the darkness—only tall shapes, like freestanding walls, partitioning a wide chamber too long to measure. When Leesil stepped out, his amulet's dim light spread.

Shadow partitions sharpened into high stone casements, and Wynn stumbled mutely to the ends of the nearest two.

Shelf upon shelf of disarrayed texts rose above her. Some had crumbled and others were broken and decayed. Scroll cases of wood, metal, and bone or horn stood on end or lay toppled in heaps. Everywhere she saw bound sheaves, books, and cloth- or hide-wrapped bundles. And the row of tall, wide stone bookcases ran both ways along the chamber, uncountable beyond the reach of the amulet's light.

Wynn stood in an ancient library or archive, perhaps the oldest ever found by one of her guild. She could not begin to measure the wealth of knowledge here, built over unknown centuries. As she slipped between the nearest casements, and shadows thickened around her, she looked up to the shelves beyond her reach.

"Wynn," Osha called. "Come out and sit . . . eat."

She dug her crystal out of her coat. Dim light still emanated from it, and she rubbed furiously as she turned, looking for Osha. He stood just inside the passage's exit with bundled coats and cloaks in his arms. Then he was blotted from sight as Li'kän rushed in between the casements.

"Wynn!" Osha called louder.

Li'kän's urgent eyes sparked in the crystal's white light, and Wynn backed deeper between the shelves. The undead slowly crept in, delicate hands clutching low shelves on both sides. Wynn retreated again. But if Li'kän intended harm to her, why did she not come more quickly? The white woman stopped, craned her head upward, and snatched a dust-crusted book.

Her narrow fingers bit through the aged cover and pages.

Li'kän's perfect white face twisted in anguish. Wynn forgot danger and gasped loudly as the ancient book shattered into dust. Then she heard frantic panting and looked up.

Li'kän's wide-eyed gaze raced around the shelves, and she grabbed for an age-marred tin scroll case. A gloved hand snarled in the top of her black hair.

Wynn heard Magiere's growling voice. "Get away from her!"

Magiere jerked Li'kän by the hair, and the undead's head snapped backward. But she clasped the scroll case to her bare chest, as if keeping it mattered more than freeing herself. Magiere dragged Li'kän out, pivoted sharply, and threw the woman beyond Wynn's sight around the right bookcase's end.

"Wynn, get out of there!" Leesil shouted.

"Spread out!" Sgäile snapped, then vanished to the right.

Osha dropped his bundles, drew stilettos, and disappeared to the left.

Wynn rushed along the bookcase row. "No, stop—no fighting!"

The instant she stepped into the open, Osha appeared on her left. He flipped one stiletto into his other hand and grabbed her wrist, dragging her left along the row of casements.

Off the other way, Wynn saw Li'kän's back.

Beyond the white undead, Leesil half-crouched and slid in next to Magiere.

Magiere cocked up her falchion in a doubled grip. Li'kän charged, and Magiere took a lunging step, bringing her sword down—and then stumbled.

The blade never passed Magiere's shoulder. It wavered heavily in her grip as Li'kän lurched to a halt, teetering on her small feet.

Wynn saw only Li'kän's bare back as the woman buckled and hunched.

Magiere blinked twice, opening her eyes more slowly each time. She was breathing hard.

Chap circled around both women, and his admonishment lashed sharply in Wynn's head.

Do not move—do nothing, unless you tell us first!

Li'kän spun about. Fury melted from her petite features when her gaze found Wynn.

Osha jerked hard on Wynn's wrist, pulling her behind himself. Wynn did not resist, but peered around his side.

Li'kän grew almost manic. Her colorless eyes widened over her slack mouth, her lips trembling. She began to shake as if caught in overwhelming anxiety, and then she thrust out the scroll case toward Wynn.

Even in fright, a part of Wynn wanted to know what was in that scroll. She reached out to—

Do not even think of it!

Then Chap's ears pricked up as Li'kän's small mouth began to work and twist.

More words . . . more words . . . , he projected, and his multitongued voice in Wynn's head matched the movement of Li'kän's lips. *She wants you to read to her.*

Wynn took a deep breath and pulled from Osha's grasp. But when she echoed Chap's thoughts to the others, Magiere growled back.

"What do you think you're doing with this thing?"

Leesil held his place with one blade still raised, and Wynn jumped slightly as Sgäile appeared out of the very row she had run from. The garrote was stretched between his hands.

"Spoken words," Wynn said and quickly tried to explain how she had kept Li'kän occupied while waiting for them to come. She'd barely got out Chap's accounting of how long Li'kän might have been here alone, when Magiere cut her off.

"You . . . your sages . . . your damn Forgotten History! Or don't you remember what Chap found in Most Aged Father's memories? Undead by the hundreds—or thousands—slaughtering every living thing in their path. And where do you think they came from?"

Magiere pointed her blade at Li'kän.

"Look at this thing! One of those who brought everything to an end . . . and you want to read to it!"

An uneasy truce had emerged, and Magiere watched Li'kän crouch beside the passage's exit. Beyond, down the row of bookcases, Wynn sat with Osha. Sgäile stood over the pair as the sage ate sparingly from their rations. Sitting beside her, Chap snapped up a piece of dried fish.

Li'kän stayed put but never took her eyes off the sage. Wynn watched her in turn between eager glances at the shelves.

A vibrancy had grown inside Magiere, shuddering through her bones.

At the courtyard gates, when Leesil had told her to get control, she had pressed her dhampir nature down—and that shiver had emerged in her awareness. Or had it been there all along as they approached the castle, only masked by hunger, fury, and the longing that drove her to this place?

She tried to suppress the tremors, as she had within elven tree homes, with their forest's life threading into her. But here, only the castle's cold stone and the ice-capped mountains surrounded them. So what was it that . . . fed her?

Magiere studied Li'kän, one of Welstiel's "old ones." What fed this monster, alone for so long in this dead place?

"That circlet around her neck," Leesil whispered, "it looks like yours. What does it mean?"

"I don't know," she answered.

Magiere wanted to rend this white monster and leave nothing but ashes in its place. Sgäile approached, slowing with care as he passed wide around Li'kän.

"There is more writing on these walls," he said. "Wynn believes it was all written by this creature, who does not remember that the words are hers . . . and more of her kind once existed here, at least two others."

"What is she feeding on?" Magiere asked.

"Nothing could live up . . ." Sgäile began, then lifted his eyes angrily. "*Is* feeding?"

Leesil tucked in close to Magiere. "I doubt she fed on those anmaglâhk we found—by the way she mangled them. But we've never encountered a physical undead that didn't need to feed, somehow, on the living."

Magiere caught Leesil's worried glance. Had he noticed her shaking again or some other sign? She wasn't about to let Sgäile know what she'd suffered in his land, so she had no way to tell Leesil what she felt now. Yes, something in this place was sustaining Li'kän.

"Perhaps the same thing Welstiel hoped to find," Magiere said.

"Are we near it?" Leesil asked.

"Maybe," she replied. "I'll take the lead with Chap. Leesil, you and Sgäile keep that creature ahead of—"

"Not yet," Sgäile cut in. "I have questions."

"You?" Leesil hissed. "You have questions!"

Sgäile's eyes stayed fixed upon Magiere. "That creature is not the only one who stalled amid bloodlust. You halted in midswing . . . why?"

Magiere didn't know. She had felt suddenly weak, as if her strength had drained away for an instant.

She shook her head. "I just felt heavy, tired, and then it passed."

"That was not the only response you shared with the white woman," Sgäile said.

Magiere instinctively warmed with anger. Before Leesil could snap again, Sgäile went on.

"She echoed your fury. What connection lies between you?"

"What else would you expect?" Magiere spit back. "It's undead. I was born to kill it. And it's not going to just stand there waiting for me to take its head. There's nothing between her and—"

"No," Sgäile snapped, his voice barely above a whisper. "When she stopped and slipped into delirium . . . even then her expression echoed yours."

Leesil lurched forward, but Sgäile raised one finger at him.

"I know what I saw," he warned; then he walked away with a last hard glance at Magiere as he called out, "Osha, prepare to move on."

Magiere didn't know what to think about Sgäile's veiled accusation. Any denial of her strange reaction to Li'kän, or the other way around, would be a lie.

"Come on," Leesil whispered. "Let's finish this and get out of here."

Li'kän curled her lips back as Magiere walked past.

"Move!" Magiere hissed back.

She headed off along the bookcases, trying to clear her head. Her hunger had waned, and it was barely enough to keep her night sight widened. But the longing was still strong, and it pulled her onward.

Magiere did not get far. They all stopped short at the chamber's far end, facing nothing but a wall of ancient stone blocks. Or that was how it seemed.

A long and rusted iron beam stretched across the wall's length, resting in stone cradles, like a door's bar. And while the stone blocks overlapped in construction, Magiere spotted one seam at the wall's center that ran straight from top to bottom.

Leesil traced the seam with his fingers, from the floor up to the beam as thick as a man's thigh. Twin doors built of mortared stone blocked their way, and Magiere couldn't imagine what hinged mechanism might possibly support them.

The pull inside Magiere told her to pass through these stone doors, to hurry beyond them. But why were they barred from the outside? And how could she and her companions lift the enormous beam, let alone open this massive portal?

Leesil slid sharply away along the wall, his hands dropping to his sheathed blades, and Magiere half-turned, reaching for her falchion.

Li'kän stepped silently up to the doors.

The undead pressed her smooth cheek to the beam's metal, as if listening for something beyond. Then her eyes rolled up. Her small mouth began working again, mumbling mutely.

Chap watched Li'kän slip into another semiconscious state. He reached out again to catch memories surfacing in the undead's mind.

He saw only darkness—but he heard the low, distant hiss again, like a whisper—or was it more like a fire's crackle? The sound sped up, buzzing furiously like leaves or insect wings. Chap lost his concentration as Magiere whispered.

"It's here . . . behind the wall . . . these doors. I can feel it."

Something shifted in the dark within Li'kän.

Chap almost missed it. Not a memory, but an *awareness*. Did Li'kän feel him inside her mind? He panicked and began to pull out—too late.

Something cold struck at him from the dark of Li'kän's mind. It thrashed about inside his thoughts, trying to find him and coil about him . . . and it took hold.

Chap's yelp echoed in his own ears.

"Stop it!" Leesil growled. "Stay out of that thing's head."

"Wynn, what's wrong?" Magiere shouted.

Chap thrashed wildly, struggling to get free.

The chamber and door walls cleared before his eyes. The only thing holding him was Leesil's hands about his shoulders. Chap settled, still shivering within.

Magiere crouched behind Wynn. The sage sat crumpled upon the floor, one hand over her mouth. She shook uncontrollably as she stared wide-eyed at Chap.

"What . . . was that?" Wynn whispered. "That buzz from Li'kän's thoughts?"

She had heard it as well—but that should not be possible.

Chap could not think of a reason. She only heard him because a taint of wild magic let her hear when he communed with his kin, the Fay. He had learned to use this to speak to and through her. But somehow, as he was rooting about in the undead's mind, she had heard the same sound as he had. It made no sense.

"What happened?" Magiere demanded.

Chap blinked twice, jowls twitching.

It . . . something . . . sensed me, he said to Wynn, and she echoed his words with effort. *Something inside Li'kän knew I was there . . . and wanted me out.*

"You all right?" Leesil asked.

No, he was not. Chap remembered an unfamiliar voice in the dark that had whispered to Welstiel and to Ubâd. He had little doubt it was the same voice in Magiere's dreams. Now Li'kän was mumbling voicelessly to herself—or to something only she could hear.

And Wynn had heard it as well.

Somewhere in this old fortification—among the centuries of records or buried in Li'kän's fragmented mind—might lie an answer. But all Chap could think of now was a "presence" that toyed with undead, manipulated Magiere's dreams, and perhaps held sway over ancient Li'kän.

The "night voice," that ancient enemy of many names, Ubâd's sacred il'Samar . . .

It wanted Magiere to have the artifact her half-brother desired.

Chap did not want Magiere to go any further—but he did not realize that the feeling was more than just anxiety for Magiere. Not until she rose, jerked out her falchion, and glared back the way they had come.

Magiere's black irises expanded. She bolted back toward the passage entrance as Chap cut loose with a rolling howl.

"Undeads!" Leesil shouted, pulling both silvery winged blades.

A white flash passed Chap before he overtook Leesil and Sgäile.

Li'kän left everyone behind as she raced after Magiere.

Chap heard Osha and Wynn scrambling to follow as he ran after the white woman. If other undead had come here, and Magiere found them first, on which side would Li'kän stand?

· · ·

Chane followed Welstiel along the castle's pillared wide corridor and the feral monks clambered in behind him, anxiously sniffing about. He followed suit and caught a thin scent, barely noticeable. It reminded him of old, rancid seed oil, but where had he smelled this before?

Welstiel's eyes glittered with anticipation. He kept onward in silence, until they all passed through a tall archway shaped like the outer gates and front doors. Straight ahead, a wide stone stairway led to upper floors, and to the left and right, narrower passages stretched into the dark.

One feral screamed.

Chane whirled, backing away as he pulled his longsword. A shadow shot out between the hunkering monk's shoulder blades and arced into the chamber's upper air.

"Spread out!" Welstiel shouted, pulling his own blade.

Chane turned circles as the monks scattered, snarling and crying out, but he kept his eyes on the shadow above—like a pair of wings gliding on a wind, though no breeze flowed through the dark chamber.

"From the walls!" Welstiel shouted.

Chane spun away toward the foot of the wide stairs. Another shadow stalked in, low to the floor, coming from the archway, a silhouette of black paws stretching up to four narrow legs. As it drew closer, a head and long snout took shape.

A wolf. In two quick steps, it leaped at Chane.

He flinched, unable to dodge away, and it passed straight through his chest.

Chane stumbled as deep cold flooded his torso.

"They cannot damage you!" Welstiel called out. "They are only ghosts!"

"No," Chane rasped, clutching his chest. "They are something else."

Ferals thrashed about, clawing and screeching, as the shadows assaulted them. Welstiel swung his sword, and steel rippled through a shadow bird's flapping wing. But the translucent creature flew higher, unfaltering. Welstiel flung his pack aside.

Chane did the same but peered upward uncertainly. Steel had no effect upon these things.

The two younger monks lost all control, their twisted faces frantic as they slashed at empty air. Jakeb looked even less coherent, though he was silent. Only Sabel and Sethè remained calm and pulled weapons—her knife and his iron cudgel.

Cold pain spiked between Chane's shoulder blades.

He choked as a shadow darted out of his chest. It flew upward, but this time he clearly saw the shape of its head and tail—a raven.

An eerie howl filled the chamber.

Chane quickly scanned about for either shadow wolf, but the howl had come from somewhere more distant. Its dying echo rolled from the narrow passage to the chamber's left side. Yellow-orange light glimmered in the dark therein, and another shadow wolf bolted out of the narrow opening.

No, this one was silver-coated, and Chane recognized Chap.

The dog barreled into the room like a beast gone mad. And directly behind him came the blur of a white figure. Glistening black hair whipped about her naked body. Her wild, slanted eyes glinted.

Chap charged straight at Welstiel, and his howl twisted into raging snarls. A startled Welstiel barely ducked out of the dog's way.

"Assist me!" Welstiel ordered.

Chap wheeled about, charging again, and Jakeb threw himself in the dog's path. Chap snapped and slashed at the monk with fangs and claws, trying to get past. Chane looked back to the naked undead.

Her smooth, perfect face filled with confusion, until one young monk rushed her with hooked fingers. Before the monk landed a grip, she snatched him by the throat, flinging him away one-handed.

The young feral spun head over heels, until his body slammed into the chamber's side wall. He slid down to the floor in a twitching, broken heap, and then ceased moving at all.

Chane turned his eyes back on the woman—this illusory frail thing.

This was one of Welstiel's "old ones."

She could destroy them all effortlessly. Before Chane could look for a way out, another figure emerged from the narrow passage.

Magiere's eyes were black amid the yellow light behind her. She skidded to a stop with her falchion drawn.

Chane's throat tightened at the sight of that blade, but her attention was not fixed on him. Her eyes widened, unblinking, as they locked on Welstiel.

Leesil emerged behind Magiere, wearing a glowing amulet upon his chest. A tall blond elf in a dark tunic came next.

Escape was no longer an option.

Chane readied himself for an onslaught, not knowing who would come at him first.

Chap was still harrying Jakeb, trying to get past to Welstiel, and only three other monks remained on their feet.

"Chane!"

He twisted toward the familiar feminine voice.

Chane froze, staring at Wynn.

A second elf, taller than the first, stood at the passage's arch with his arm wrapped protectively around her. She leaned into the young elf, her cheek pressed against him, and the cold lamp crystal in her hand illuminated her round, olive-toned face. Her small mouth opened halfway at the sight of him, and she clutched the elf's cloak.

Chane went hollow inside.

And that emptiness filled with rage. It built on a desire to tear the elf's arm from its shoulder socket and rip his throat out—anything to take that offensive hold off of Wynn. He almost dropped his sword to free both his hands.

Sabel hissed as she rushed around Chane, straight toward Wynn. He could not grab her in time. Leesil charged out, shining blades in his fists, their outer edges running like wings down his forearms.

Chane snarled, ready to kill the half-blood or jerk Sabel back, whichever of them he caught first.

Sabel swerved, and swung for Leesil's face with her knife.

Wynn pressed against Osha, her emotions in a tangle.

Welstiel was here. How was this possible? And he was surrounded by robed figures casting about and screaming at shadow ravens and wolves. She had seen their tabards before and recognized them—the Sluzhobnék Sútzits, the Servants of Compassion. But they were horrible, twisted and savage. Her heart sickened at their pale skin, colorless eyes, and the misshapen teeth in their snarling mouths.

Only Li'kän stood staring about, as if lost.

And Chane . . .

Wynn cried out his name before thinking. Truth struck her like poison or sudden illness.

Chane had come with Welstiel . . . to get the orb.

Chap ripped into one robed undead, tearing the back of its calf, and then charged straight at Welstiel with his muzzle dripping black fluids. The silver-haired monk was too fast and twisted about, back-fisting Chap and driving him off. Chap's voice shouted in Wynn's mind.

Get Magiere away! She must reach the orb first . . . before Welstiel!

Wynn ducked from under Osha's arm, shouting as she reached for Li'kän.

"Magiere, go! You must find it now!"

Aside from Magiere, Li'kän was the only one who might know how to get through the stone doors. Wynn's fingers closed on Li'kän's chill skin, and the undead half-turned.

Li'kän's expression flattened at Wynn's touch.

And Wynn was suddenly aware just how foolish her action was.

Magiere faltered when she saw Welstiel.

He looked shabby and weatherworn, but the white patches at his temples still glowed. How could he have found this place, when she'd only learned of it in her dreams two moons ago? She could only see one answer.

Welstiel had trailed her, perhaps from the very day she and Leesil had left Bela, some half a year ago.

Magiere hadn't seen him since the sewers of Bela, but she'd learned much of him since then. Images of her mother surged up—Magelia lying on a bed, bleeding to death in a keep as Welstiel took away an infant Magiere.

They shared a father he had known and she had not, but which of them was better for it? A small piece of Magiere might have pitied her half brother. But the greater part longed to rip his head from his shoulders and watch his body burn.

Hunger came back, and Magiere's jaws began to ache. Tears flooded from her eyes as the room brightened in her sight. She clenched her grip tight on the falchion's hilt.

Sgäile flew past, shining garrote wire in his hands as he went straight at Welstiel.

Leesil raced toward a mad, robed female brandishing a crude knife.

"Magiere, go!" Wynn shouted. "You must find it now!"

Magiere barely heard this over the rage telling her to rend any pale-skinned thing in her way—and get to Welstiel. Turning her head with effort, she saw Wynn's small hand wrapped around Li'kän's forearm.

Fear welled within Magiere's bloodlust.

But Li'kän just stood there and made no move to strike the sage. The white undead twisted her head, her gaze falling upon Magiere.

Li'kän rushed Magiere before she could react. The undead's small hand closed on Magiere's wrist. She bolted for the corridor, jerking Magiere into motion.

Magiere's hunger and rage vanished.

"Go with her!" Wynn cried.

Magiere didn't look back. Only she could retrieve the orb—and only Li'kän could help. No one told Magiere this. No one had to. The pull to follow the white undead overrode everything else.

Li'kän emerged into the great library, and Magiere shook free of the undead's grip. Li'kän bolted on without waiting, and by the time Magiere caught up, the undead stood before the stone doors. Li'kän tucked one narrow white shoulder under the iron beam, midway along one door and just beyond its stone bracket. She wrapped her slender fingers around the rusted iron's bottom edge, waiting expectantly.

Magiere sheathed her falchion and set herself likewise at the other door's midpoint.

Li'kän's frail body tensed, and Magiere called hunger to flood her flesh as she shoved upward.

The beam's weight nearly crushed her back down, but Li'kän slowly straightened upward.

The frail undead's half of the beam rose steadily, until it cleared the stone bracket. But every joint in Magiere's body ached as she strained to follow. She pushed harder with her legs as Li'kän held her half up against the stone door.

Magiere was soaked in sweat by the time her end of the beam grated out of its stone bracket. She dropped it, stumbling away, and Li'kän released her end. The beam crashed and tumbled across the stone floor, and a metallic thunderclap echoed through the library.

Li'kän took hold of her bracket and began pulling. Magiere tried to do the same, but her side barely moved. When the space between was wide enough, the undead stopped and slipped in.

A strange sensation washed through Magiere as she stepped through the gap.

Not a strong one, but like the lightness that followed a heavy burden cast off, as if she might never feel fatigue or hunger again. Pain and exhaustion from nearly a moon in the mountains slipped away.

When Magiere regained her senses, Li'kän stood slumped in a downward-sloping dark tunnel of rough-hewn stone. The undead's features appeared to sag.

Rather than the release Magiere felt, some sorrow or loss seemed to envelop Li'kän. The white undead hesitated, back-stepping once, and shook her head slowly. Then her body lurched as if jerked forward, and she stepped downward along the tunnel.

Magiere followed Li'kän's dim form, but glanced back once, wondering if the doors behind should be shut. But the white woman kept going.

Far down the tunnel, along its gradual turn, Magiere saw pale orange light filtering from somewhere ahead. And by that dim light, she spotted strange hollows evenly lining both sides of the way.

As she moved on, her night sight sharpened.

A figure crouched inside each of those hollows. She stopped and peered into one.

Age-darkened bones almost melded with ancient stone, but the skeleton had not collapsed when its flesh rotted away ages ago. It was curled on its knees, almost fetally, with its forearms flattened beneath it. The skull top, too wide and large to be a man's or a woman's, rested downward between the remains of its hands. With its forehead pressed to the hollow's stone floor, its eyes had been lowered for centuries.

Like a worshipper waiting in obeisance for its master's return.

Magiere glanced back up the tunnel, turning about to look into hollows along the tunnel's other side. She saw only one occupant that had once been human. Others she couldn't guess.

Some of the crouched, curled forms were small, but one was huge, with an arching spine and thick finger bones that ended in cracked claws. A ridge of spiny bone rose over the top of its downcast skull.

The hollows stretched on, endlessly, toward the dim light down the tunnel.

Li'kän turned to move on. She never glanced once at the hollows, as if the occupants' endless vigil were only proper in her presence.

Through wide arcing turns spiraling down into the earth, Magiere followed. At every step, skeletons hunkered in their small dark hovels, their eyes averted from Li'kän's passing.

Leesil thrust and slashed at the dark-haired vampire, blocking her every attempt to get past him. She slashed back with her knife, hissing and twisting beyond the arc of his winged blades. Her jaws widened with small jagged teeth and protruding fangs. Beyond her, Chap harried a silver-haired undead and a younger male.

And then Chane rushed in and tried to duck around the woman.

Leesil shifted with a sharp slash of his right blade. Chane jerked up short, twisting away from the blade's passing tip, but the mad little female came at Leesil again. And a stocky man with an iron bar closed around her other side. Leesil panicked, facing three at once.

Chane lashed out with his longsword.

Leesil braced and deflected as the small woman hacked at him. He ducked away under the doubled assault.

Then the curly-haired one raced by him and disappeared from view.

Leesil was too overwhelmed to look back for Wynn, and then Sgäile flew past him, running straight at Welstiel.

Welstiel nearly cried out as the frail white undead turned and hauled Magiere down the narrow passage. Disbelief overtook his shock.

Was the ancient one assisting Magiere? But why—and where were the others?

Any guardians here should have turned on this dhampir intruder. His abandoned patron had whispered that Magiere would be necessary to overcome them—not be assisted by them.

Welstiel tried to rush through the skirmish for the passage.

A gray-green–clad elf stepped into his way.

He saw the booted foot an instant before it struck his temple. The chamber swam in swirling black. When he shook off the impact, the elf was gone.

A glinting line passed before Welstiel's eyes.

He dropped and felt the wire drag sharply over his hair.

Welstiel whirled and swung his longsword behind, faster than anything living could avoid. He had to get after Magiere.

The blade's tip shrieked across the floor, but the elf was not there.

Chap swerved between two undead, snapping at their legs until his jowls spattered black fluid every time he shook his head. He had to weaken one of them enough to pull it down—and soon—or he might not reach his companions before they were overrun. Yet nothing he did seemed to slow these undead. They cried out but never broke down.

The silver-haired male raked out with his fingernails but missed and stumbled. Chap took the opening and lunged up for his throat.

He might not take this thing's head off, but he could tear through to its spine and cripple it. As he bit down, cold fingers clutched his shoulders from behind.

Teeth sank through his fur at the back of his neck.

Chap yelped and lost his jaw-hold. He bucked and thrashed, trying to pitch off his attacker. The silver-haired male before him raked its fingernails along his muzzle.

He kicked back with rear paws, and felt his claws tear up the young one's thigh. It let out a muffled yelp but did not pull its teeth from his neck. Then Chap caught a glimpse of Wynn near the passage. She started to run for him with Magiere's old dagger in her hand.

No—stay back!

She faltered, and a rasping voice shouted, "Wynn!"

Chap twisted sharply under the teeth in his neck. And there was Chane.

Sgäile hopped clear of the white-templed undead's sweeping sword.

This one commanded the others, and it was best to take down a leader first.

But Sgäile was stunned by how quickly this undead had shaken off his kick and eluded his garrote. He stomped down on the sword to pin it.

The instant his foot pressed steel, the blade levered up sharply.

It lifted him as if he weighed nothing, and Sgäile let the force carry him up. He rose in the air, folding his legs as the sword slashed away, and then lashed out one foot the instant his other touched down.

His heel caught the undead in the face, but his leg ached under the jarring impact.

The man only spun and stumbled, twisting away, and Sgäile caught sight of Léshil.

Léshil held fast against two, as did Chap, but neither would last long. At least one undead had to go down quickly, or the odds would take their toll.

Sgäile's attention was pulled in too many directions, and his gaze flicked back to his opponent.

He never saw the undead's sword coming.

Its tip ripped through his cowl and across his collarbone.

Welstiel watched the elf topple backward. Before the man's back hit the floor, Welstiel snatched up his pack, searching for a clear path to the passage.

Wynn stood near its entrance gripping a dagger. Sethè made a snarling, headlong rush around Leesil, closing on the sage. The other elf beside Wynn stepped between them.

"Protect my way!" Welstiel shouted to his ferals and charged for the passage.

The lanky young elf grabbed Sethè's wrist as the iron cudgel came down. They both struggled closer to the foray, but Chane's little sage still stood in Welstiel's way. Her eyes widened, and she raised the dagger as he came at her. Welstiel swung his pack.

The metal objects within clanged as the pack slammed Wynn aside. Welstiel bolted down the passage.

Chap saw Welstiel flee and Wynn flop away under the swinging pack. He felt his blood draining in the younger undead's teeth, and its weight bore him down.

It wanted his life, and he had nothing left to try as his companions were failing. All he could think was to give this leeching thing what it wanted—and more.

Chap's paws struck stone. His legs buckled as the gray-haired one descended on him and sank its teeth into the side of his throat. He rooted himself in stone . . .

For Earth, and the chamber's Air, and Fire from the heat of his own flesh. These he mingled with his own Spirit. He bonded with the elements of existence—and began to burn, as he had in turning on his own kin, when they had tried to kill Wynn.

She would not see him with her mantic sight this time, as trails of white phosphorescent vapor in the shape of flames flickered across his form.

Both undead upon him began to quiver.

Chane heard Welstiel's shout and went numb as Wynn tumbled away under the swinging pack. Then Welstiel was gone.

Hate welled in Chane—all that mattered to Welstiel was his prize.

He saw the lanky elf grappling with Sethè. Wynn tried to rise—too close to the struggling pair. Sabel threw herself at Leesil, and then screamed, her voice reverberating off the stone walls. And Chane knew she had been wounded.

But for him, there was only Wynn, and his hatred for Welstiel.

As Leesil and Sabel tangled, Chane took two quick steps and snatched the back of Sethè's robe. In a half-spin, he pulled the monk from his startled elven opponent and away from Wynn. He whipped Sethè around into Leesil's back. Half-blood and feral toppled over the screeching Sabel.

Wynn looked up at Chane, and he froze—then she scooted frantically away from him. Her round brown eyes filled with fear—not startled surprise or welcome relief—as she pointed her blade at him.

Chane shuddered, as if she had already cut him.

But the path from the chamber was clear, and this might be his only chance. He turned and ran—fled—down the passage. Hatred kept the pain from pulling him down.

He had lost his meager existence in Bela so long ago and bargained with Welstiel for a better one. He would have done—had done—anything to be a part of Wynn's world. But piece by piece, Welstiel's scheming had eaten away his hope . . .

All the way to that fear in Wynn's eyes.

Chane burst from the passage into an immense library, as if he had run blindly into Wynn's world only to find it dark and hollow, without even one of her cold lamp crystals to illuminate a single parchment. Footsteps echoed from far off to the right, and he clung to the sound, following it. He tried not to look upon the mocking wealth of knowledge surrounding him and came to the chamber's far end.

An enormous rusted iron beam lay before two massive stone doors. The sound of the footsteps came out between them.

A strange sensation washed through Chane as he stared into the dark opening, as if he felt something beyond it reaching for him. It smothered his hunger, until all he had left was sorrow and hate.

But Chane would not be alone in his loss.

He stepped through the stone doors, hunting for Welstiel.

CHAPTER TWENTY

Leesil's new winged blades were so solid on his arms that he didn't have to think about them. They moved with his body and will. He'd agreed instantly when Wynn had told Magiere to go, for they each had a part to play in keeping the orb from Welstiel.

But at what price?

From the corner of his eye, he saw Sgäile sprawled on the floor, but he could do nothing to help. He had to keep the savage female and Chane at bay. Then Welstiel broke through and ran down the corridor as Osha grappled with a large monk wielding an iron rod.

Desperation drove Leesil to move faster as Chane tried to dodge around. The small woman with the knife threw herself at him. He couldn't turn and stop Chane.

Leesil stepped wide to the left, leaning low, and then shifted right, putting all his weight behind a swing. His right blade tip tore along the woman's waist, splitting her robe open.

Viscous black fluids spilled down her bared abdomen as shock filled her colorless eyes. She screeched and grasped her belly, trying to hold herself together. Leesil brought his left blade across and high when he shifted back to the left.

A heavy weight slammed into his back.

He toppled onto the gutted woman.

Leesil lost sight of the others in a tangle of cold bodies and limbs.

Wynn watched numbly as Chane fled down the passage. She barely even noticed the stocky undead he had thrown into Leesil's back.

So many times she had wondered where Chane was, if he was all right, and if he would finally stay far from Magiere. To see him in company with Welstiel . . . it was too much.

Wynn came to her senses.

Leesil twisted on the floor in the tangle of two vampires. Sgäile was down, and Chap was in trouble. Any one of them could die.

Wynn clambered to her feet with Magiere's old dagger in her hand as Leesil rammed his elbow back and up. The muscular undead with the iron bar lay atop him, back to back, and its snarl choked off in a grunt as the wing tip of Leesil's blade sank through into its ribs.

Osha tried to close on the muscular undead, his hooked bone knife now gripped in place of one stiletto. The undead rolled off Leesil to its feet and went straight at Osha.

Sgäile curled, trying to pull his knees under and get up. Beneath the warmth of spreading blood, pain spiked in his left shoulder and spread up his neck. He lifted his head, and saw Chap half-buckled beneath two undead, their teeth buried in his neck.

Sgäile cried out.

And then a tingling wave washed over him.

It was much like what he had felt when he fully opened his awareness of Spirit to the life of his people's land. This gift he had been born with, which his grandfather had wanted him to use to become Shaper, had once raised his startled awareness to a majay-hì like no other. He had stood upon a rooftop in Bela, with Léshil in the sight of his shortbow. Then his gaze had fallen upon on Chap for the first time.

As Sgäile kneeled on the chamber floor, the overwhelming sense of Spirit enveloped him.

It radiated from Chap's hunkered form.

Both undead clamped upon the majay-hì began to shudder, but Sgäile saw only death feeding upon what was sacred. He flattened one foot on the floor stones and dove as he stretched out his right hand.

His fingers closed on the younger undead's robe-waist. He tried to twist, pulling down and away as he fell, but the effort cost him. As he crashed to the floor and rolled, all he could do was hold tight.

He pulled the undead away more easily than expected.

Its shriek pierced Sgäile's ears as it tripped on him and fell. Sgäile rolled clear of its flailing limbs and snatched his hand away. He rose on his knees, looking for Chap.

The majay-hì stood braced on all fours.

But the silver-haired undead no longer clung to him. It lay upon the stone floor and began to convulse.

Chap slowly turned his head, torso heaving in strained breaths. His muzzle was nearly black, and his neck was matted in his own blood as he glared at the undead.

Sgäile's gaze fixed on dark lines spidering across the pale form's face and bare forearm.

Black fluids welled around its eyes and ran from its ears. The spidering lines ruptured into cracks that bled more viscous fluids. Steam rose from its wounds in the chamber's cold air, as if heat had suddenly filled this dead thing to bursting.

Then it went limp, as did the younger one. Both lay as still as corpses, steaming as if freshly dead in the frigid air.

Chap snarled once and snapped his jaws closed on the old undead's neck. He ripped and tore at it for an instant, then halted, looking expectantly at Sgäile.

Léshil and Magiere had spoken of how they hunted undead, and Sgäile knew what Chap wanted.

He pulled the tie holding Léshil's old blades to his back. As the bundle hit the floor, he ripped it open and gripped one winged blade.

Sgäile hacked down through the younger corpse's neck with all his weight. Chap released the old one, stepping back, and Sgäile took its head as well.

Leesil heard an angry grunt as the heavy vampire rolled off his back. Before he could twist and slash at its legs, the woman beneath him latched her hand about his throat.

Her mouth widened with lips pulled back from long fangs and sharpened teeth.

Leesil slammed his left blade point through her side.

Her head arched back, eyes clenching shut, but her grip on his neck didn't break. Leesil couldn't get any air.

He levered his blade through her torso, until the point ground through her to the stone floor. When he lurched upward, her arm snapped straight, and he raised the right blade and fell on her.

The blade's outside edge sank into her throat. Leesil shoved down hard.

Black fluids welled over his hand and forearm, and then his blade cracked through her neck bones. Her head rolled away to one side, and Leesil turned over, ripping her limp hand from his throat.

Leesil gasped in air—just as he looked up to see Wynn ram her dagger into the back of the stocky vampire grappling with Osha.

Wynn scrambled in as Osha caught the muscular undead's wrist.

He pulled the man's swing aside but barely avoided the iron bar. As he slashed the bone knife at the undead's throat, Wynn ducked in and rammed her dagger into its back.

The undead twisted sharply and jerked Wynn around by her grip on the hilt. A sharp crack sounded as something narrow and solid whipped down across her thigh.

Wynn's leg gave way, and she crumpled with a sharp whimper. She fell, and the dagger ripped downward a few inches.

Something rancid and oily spattered across her face.

Wynn tightened her grip, and the blade came out. She quickly turned over, pushing up with one hand. The dagger was coated in dripping black.

Osha slid down the wall near the passage.

Blood seeped from the side of his mouth below one clenched eye. Before Wynn could call to him, the large undead whipped around above her and raised its iron bar.

A long split ran from its throat down its upper chest. Osha's knife had struck true, but the undead did not even notice. Wynn shrank away, raising the dagger to shield herself.

A snarling howl echoed through the chamber.

The undead lifted its head and froze, staring beyond Wynn.

"Don't let it get out!" Leesil shouted from somewhere behind Wynn.

The muscular undead spun and bolted down the passage.

Magiere stepped out behind Li'kän into a landing hollow on the edge of a vast cavern.

The glowing orange light was strong in here, filling a space nearly as large as the underground plateau where the "burning" one had crawled from the fiery fissure. But the hot air was far more humid here. Vapors misted off the near and more distant walls, as if the snow and ice above seeped down through the earth to be eaten by the cavern's heat.

"I am here," Magiere whispered, but the cavern's silence made her voice seem loud.

She stepped forward to the landing's edge.

A long and narrow stone walkway stretched out over a round chasm, so deep that Magiere couldn't see the bottom. The orange glow rose from below.

That one bridge joined three others, all reaching out from the distant cavern walls. They connected at a center point and blended with a stone platform suspended over the chasm. Looking around, Magiere saw pock-marks on the nearer cavern walls.

No, not marks, but more burial hovels carved in the stone—and more bone figures so old they resembled the color of the surrounding rock. Skeletons crouched and cowered with their heads and eyes cast down. They filled the cavern walls halfway up to its domed top.

"Who are they?" Magiere asked.

She didn't expect any answer, but Li'kän let out a voiceless hiss that grew too loud in the cavern's silence.

Li'kän looked at Magiere, the same way she had at Wynn, as if fascinated that anyone spoke to her. But the white undead never glanced at the walls.

A trace of disdain crossed her pure features, like one who saw nothing of any interest. Not even for those centuries-old dead, who still bowed before this ancient one—and whatever it served.

"Did you lock them down here . . . once they finished making this place?"

Li'kän didn't respond.

Magiere felt no rage at such injustice. What more could she expect from a monster?

A lightening sensation had washed through her from the moment she'd stepped into the tunnel. The deeper she had gone, the more it had taken away her hunger, but it also kept her dhampir nature at its peak. Yet anger, the source of all her strength and will, felt smothered.

Even the loss of that did not matter.

Magiere looked to the meeting point of those narrow stone walkways—to the landing hovering above the chasm's depths. Something stood upon it, barely visible through the misty air.

Li'kän stepped onto the narrow walkway.

Magiere followed, and waves of humid heat rose around her.

In the long depths below, she saw clouds gathered above a glow of orange-red. Water trickling down the chasm's walls met with severe heat somewhere below, and vapor collected in thick mist, obscuring the depths.

Vertigo filled Magiere, and she quickly turned her gaze on the walkway's narrow stone.

What was she doing here, following a voice in her dreams and an instinctive pull she couldn't name? That visitor hidden in her slumber hissed its words, and all she'd seen of it were writhing black coils.

This same voice had whispered to Welstiel—and to Ubâd, instructing him in Magiere's creation using the blood of five races. But it had abandoned the necromancer.

Had it abandoned Welstiel as well? Was that why he'd never found this place on his own—and had tried in Bela to get her to join him?

Magiere knew she had followed the whispered urgings of some *thing* that couldn't be trusted. And now she was passively following a mad undead across a chasm to seek . . . what?

She saw the three other bridges leading off to three other hollows in the cavern walls. Perhaps above there were other barred stone doors. The burial hovels around the cavern and in the winding passage suggested that hundreds had labored here, perhaps hauling up excavated stone to build the immense fortification above.

Li'kän blocked Magiere's view of the platform, but when the undead reached it, she stepped aside.

A four-legged stone stand rose smoothly from the platform. A perfectly round opening had been carved through the center of its top.

In the wide hole rested a globe, slightly larger than a great helm.

It was made of a dark material Magiere couldn't name, as dark as char and faintly rough across its round surface. Atop it, the large tapered head of a spike pierced down through the globe's center—and the spike's head was larger than her fist. When she crouched to peer through the stand's four legs, she saw the spike's tip protruded a hand's width through the globe's bottom.

Magiere saw no mark of separation to indicate that the spike could ever be removed. Both spike and globe appeared to have been chiseled from one single piece.

Was this the "orb" she had come for?

All Magiere's doubts slipped away. It was trapped here, and she had to free it—protect it—keep it from all other hands. This was why she had come. And still all trace of her hunger was gone.

Magiere rose from her crouch and looked at Li'kän. "This is how you've survived. It . . . sustains you."

Li'kän just stared at the orb, as if she had not seen it in a long time.

Magiere saw grooves around the spike's head. Looking closer, she found that they ended in notches on opposing sides of the spike, and she glanced back at Li'kän.

The undead raised her slender hand, and her fingertips brushed the circlet around her neck. Like the one Magiere wore, its open ends were adorned with inward-pointing knobs.

Magiere's eyes widened as she looked down upon the spike's grooves and notches.

"How do I—"

"This is not what I expected," said a refined voice.

Magiere whirled about.

Welstiel stood halfway across the narrow stone bridge.

Leesil had barely crawled to his knees when Sgäile and Chap leaped past him.

But the last robed undead was already gone. Panic hit him as he scrambled up and grabbed the back of Wynn's coat.

"Come on!" he growled, pulling her up. "Welstiel and Chane are already after Magiere, and now that big undead!"

Then he saw the state of his companions.

Chap's neck was matted with blood, and a split in Sgäile's cowl collar and the shoulder of his tunic were soaked in dark red. Wynn favored one leg, though she stayed on her feet, but Osha was slumped unconscious against the wall. Blood trailed from his hair across his temple, and more leaked from the side of his mouth.

Leesil wavered, desperately wanting to find Magiere.

"Wait," Sgäile said.

He held one of Leesil's old blades in hand and looked to the first undead Li'kän had left broken near the wall. It did not move, but its body was intact. Without hesitation, Sgäile walked over and hacked the winged blade through the undead's throat.

A wet and muffled crack sounded as the blade severed its spine.

Leesil watched Sgäile with a flicker of surprise. Apparently the man had overcome his revulsion of dismemberment. Sgäile returned and gripped Osha's limp arm, and Leesil helped lift the younger elf over Sgäile's good shoulder.

"The library," Sgäile said.

Leesil took Wynn's arm, steadying the limping sage as they headed down the passage. When they reached the vast library and turned toward its far end, they saw that the iron beam now lay on the floor.

The stone doors were partly open.

Sgäile lowered Osha, and Wynn caught the young elf's shoulders, helping ease him onto the floor.

"I will tend him," she said. "Go after Magiere—hurry!"

"I can't just leave you here!" Leesil shouted in frustration.

"Yes," she insisted. "You heard Welstiel tell those mad undeads, 'Protect my way.' He commands them. That is why the large one ran to assist him when the others were destroyed. Now go!"

Leesil looked uncertainly to Sgäile, standing before the doors and cradling the arm below his wounded shoulder.

"I can still fight," he said flatly. "Now come!"

Chap loped past Sgäile through the space in the doors.

Leesil's instincts screamed for him to run to Magiere, but another part railed against leaving Wynn alone.

"What if . . . ," he began, but hesitated to say the name aloud. "What if another undead comes back past us?"

Wynn cocked her head at him. "No matter what has happened here, Chane would never harm me . . . and I will never allow him to harm Osha."

Her reckless confidence infuriated Leesil. "Chane's not the only one down there!"

Wynn turned her serious brown eyes on Sgäile. "Then make certain no one else gets past you."

He nodded to her. "We must hurry."

Leesil hated that Wynn was right. Gripping both blades, he slipped between the heavy doors, whispering sharply, "No one gets past us."

Magiere turned and faced her half-brother, his sword in hand.

As always, her dhampir instincts never picked up his undead presence.

In a somewhat tattered cloak and scuffed boots, his hair was slicked back from his forehead and his white temples were tinged ocher in the cavern's dull glow. He was still as poised as when she'd first met him in Miiska—and as arrogant as when he'd revealed his nature to her in the sewers of Bela.

He didn't look surprised to see her.

That should have puzzled Magiere, but it didn't.

Welstiel had followed her.

In all the years he had desired the orb, he'd never found it—never could—which was why he'd toyed with her. He needed her, and for more than just bypassing the guardians he'd believed were waiting in this place.

But he had nothing to say now that Magiere wanted to hear.

All his manipulations of her had left a trail of innocents, dead and butchered, in his path, from her own mother, Magelia, to the first owner of her Sea Lion Tavern, and on to Chesna, torn and bleeding to death on her father's porch. Welstiel was a monster, regardless of their sharing a father—who'd given neither of them a choice in what they were.

Magiere hesitated with a quick glance at Li'kän.

The white undead gave Welstiel no notice, gazing only at the orb with her fingertips poised on the metal hoop about her throat.

Magiere didn't care to face Welstiel out on the narrow bridge above the chasm. She had to either lure him to the platform or drive him back to the hollow of the cavern's entrance.

"No, not at all what I expected," Welstiel repeated.

"What didn't you expect?" she asked, hoping he might advance.

"I am moved by the sight of you." But his tone carried no such sentiment. "Your black hair, that old armor, and you . . . so determined that you actually found it. We are alike, you and I. We share the same blood."

Her welcome old anger finally came to her.

"I have blood—you don't. We're nothing alike!"

"No? But you can feel it, just as I can."

Welstiel held both arms out wide in a grand gesture, sword still in hand, and smiled softly.

Magiere did feel it—her hunger had become distant, like a vague memory. She felt all of the dhampir within her, yet her mind was clear.

Welstiel lowered his arms. "Take it, Magiere. Bring it to me. I understand it as no one else does, and what it can do . . . for us. It is freedom from what our father put upon us."

And Magiere saw the tactic she needed.

Her intentions for the orb didn't matter. Telling Welstiel it belonged with the sages would only keep him arguing. She was tired of his coy persuasion, always pulling her off balance or driving her where he wanted.

"I understand it," she hissed. "No more hunger, yes? No more hunger . . . for me!"

She settled a hand on the orb's spike, tilted her head down, and cast him a mocking glance.

"I don't share what's already mine!"

Welstiel's eyes flicked toward Li'kän, but the ancient undead remained enraptured by the orb. Magiere slid her falchion from its sheath, sweeping the blade up before her, and Welstiel shifted his gaze to it.

Magiere felt sickened for an instant. Her half-brother had made this weapon, connecting him to her. And still, he hesitated upon the bridge.

Did he wonder if he could survive against a hunter of the dead, the thing he'd helped create? No, his real fear was making the wrong choice and losing his prime desire—the orb, his obsession.

Magiere grew anxious. She'd never been good at manipulation. She met things head-on, the only way she knew how to win. And she couldn't wait any longer.

She took a step onto the bridge toward Welstiel.

A presence—another undead—expanded in her awareness, and she stopped.

Chane walked toward them along the narrow stone bridge, longsword in hand.

He too looked weatherworn, but his red-brown hair was cut jaggedly shorter than the last time she'd seen him—on the night she'd taken his head in Droevinka. As he drew closer, she saw the scar around his throat. Vapor rising from the chasm left a sheen upon his pale skin.

Welstiel never looked back; he simply smiled. The odds had changed.

But Chane's sudden appearance didn't make Magiere fearful for herself. She had left Leesil and the others to watch her back, and yet here was Chane. So what had become of her companions?

Where was Leesil?

"I have no need to kill you, Magiere," Welstiel said. "Just bring me the orb . . . and after I leave, you and yours can go."

Chane halted and flinched sharply. His gaze fixed on Welstiel's back.

Magiere had no time to ponder Chane's strange pause. She'd never faced Welstiel in a straight-up fight, not as she had with Chane. And Chane had nearly bested her twice. Her main advantage now became the bridge's narrow path. Only one of them could come at her at a time, if she blocked both from getting to the platform.

Even if Welstiel did get past her, Magiere didn't believe Li'kän would allow him near the orb. She shook her head slowly.

"You're such a coward," she said. "Always in hiding, killing the defenseless in the dark."

"I saved you!" he answered, and anger leaked into his voice. "I brought you to that village myself! I left you armor and my own weapon, and amulets that kept you alive, until you faced who and what you are."

"So selfless!" she spit. "Take my head then, and you can have it all back . . . along with your prize."

Welstiel suddenly half-crouched upon the bridge, clearing Magiere's view of Chane.

"Kill her," he said calmly.

Magiere tensed.

Chane swung his longsword back and forth like a pendulum. With glittering hatred in his eyes, he arched the blade back and up—and then lunged in behind Welstiel, dropping low.

Magiere went rigid, but Chane didn't leap toward her.

He grabbed Welstiel's left forearm and slammed Welstiel's hand upon the bridge. Welstiel fell to one knee. Before he could turn or jerk free, Chane brought his sword down.

The blade split through Welstiel's gloved fingers and clanged upon the stone.

Welstiel cried out in pain—and Magiere's instincts sharpened.

Welstiel's undead presence flooded Magiere's awareness, like a curtain ripped away from a window to expose the night outside. He dropped his sword, and it clattered on the bridge as he grabbed his maimed hand.

Chane snatched up Welstiel's severed fingers and backed up along the bridge.

"Kill her yourself!" he rasped and turned to run.

He reached the cavern's entrance hollow and vanished in a pocket of darkness beyond the reach of the chasm's light.

Magiere held her place in stunned confusion.

She watched Welstiel's pale face twist. Black fluids dripped from his fingerless hand as he stood up, looking after Chane. Then he whirled to face her.

Open fear flickered across Welstiel's features. He quickly snatched up his sword and backed along the bridge.

Magiere spasmed as another undead presence filled up her senses.

Beyond Welstiel, the muscular undead with the iron bar stepped into the chasm's dim light.

"Here!" Welstiel shouted. "Defend me!"

Magiere rushed onto the bridge to take Welstiel's head.

CHAPTER TWENTY-ONE

Chane stepped into the cavern's entrance hollow still clutching Welstiel's severed fingers—one of which wore the arcane ring of nothing.

He felt no hunger at all. Why?

Welstiel's pack lay against the hollow's near wall. He must have set it aside before facing Magiere. Chane grabbed it as he headed for the tunnel.

Running footsteps echoed from the entrance, and he stopped short.

Whether it was one of Welstiel's ferals or Leesil and the others, Chane was too weary for a fight. All he wanted was to get away from this place. He turned back to the chasm's edge.

Reaching around the landing's side, he felt for the lip of the nearest pocket in the cavern wall. When he found a secure hold, he swung out and into the pocket.

He landed face-to-face with a mound of slick stone, like a half-formed figure rising out of the rock floor. He wriggled past to crouch in the rear and began pulling the glove's remnants off Welstiel's severed fingers.

The second one bore the ring of nothing, slick with black fluids.

Chane slipped it over his own finger without bothering to wipe it off.

The pocket's walls wavered briefly in his sight.

Leesil ran down the arcing tunnel, followed by Sgäile. He slowed only once when he spotted the skeletons in their stone cubbies. Chap raced on, giving them no notice.

The dog's eerie hunting cry rolled along the tunnel walls an instant before Leesil burst out into a widened hollow.

Hundreds more cubbies pockmarked the vast cavern before him.

Vapor wafted up from the glowing chasm, partly obscuring four narrow stone bridges arcing out to a stone platform above the wide chasm's center. Magiere stood but one step off the platform along the nearest bridge—with Welstiel a few paces in front of her.

"Get to that one!" Sgäile shouted, pointing with Leesil's old blade.

The muscular undead stepped to the bridge.

Leesil didn't see Chane anywhere as he sprinted forward. Chap closed first and snapped his jaws on the hem of the undead's robe.

"Hold him!" Leesil shouted.

He grabbed the big undead's robe between the shoulders, trying to get a grip with his punching blade still in hand. From the corner of his eye, he saw Welstiel block Magiere's first swing.

Leesil heaved hard as Chap lurched backward with his jaws clenched. The undead's robe began to tear in the dog's teeth. The muscular vampire stumbled as Sgäile closed from behind, raising Leesil's old winged blade.

The undead set his feet and twisted sharply around, swinging the iron bar.

Leesil's grip broke as the robe tore in his hand. He teetered, and Sgäile barely ducked as the iron bar arced through the air. It came straight at Leesil's neck.

He had no chance to regain his balance and raised both blades.

The bar connected with a sharp metal clang. The sound vibrated through his forearms as he was thrown off his feet.

Leesil landed hard on the stone floor.

The bulky undead lunged again for the bridge.

Magiere willed rage to come, pushing everything but Welstiel from her mind. Fury, like an echo of lost hunger, flooded Magiere at her first swing.

Welstiel blocked her blow with his longsword and stroked it aside, but his maimed left hand spattered black fluids all around. He retreated another step, drawing her further out onto the bridge. Rising vapor dampened Magiere's hair and strands of it clung to her cheeks.

"This is not necessary," Welstiel nearly shouted. "I know *it* speaks to you and fills your head with deception. Do not listen to that thing hiding in slumber, toying with us both! Everything I have done is to protect the orb—"

"For yourself!" Magiere returned.

Mention of that whispering voice, the connection between him and her, only made fury grow inside her. She snarled and swung again.

Welstiel dipped his longsword, catching her heavier falchion.

Beneath the impact of steel, he faltered, and quickly shifted his block. Magiere's blade slid along his and spun away. Welstiel came about and slashed for her throat. She didn't have time to pull the falchion up, and had to drop low.

The longsword passed just above her head. She jerked her falchion back, slicing across his side.

Welstiel's mouth gaped beneath his widened eyes, and he retreated another step.

The blade he'd created to defend himself against their father was now used against him. He felt its searing touch just like any other undead.

Magiere flushed with pleasure at his pain—and wanted to hurt him more.

As her mother, Magelia, had lain bleeding to death in her birthing bed, Welstiel had taken her only child, born of rape by an undead father and the blood rite of a necromancer.

But Bryen and Ubâd were gone. Only Welstiel remained to suffer for all three.

Magiere reached behind with her free hand. She pulled the long silvery war dagger from the back of her belt.

Leesil flopped over and slashed for the undead's leg. His blade's tip sliced across its calf, splitting cleanly through boot cuff and breeches. The vampire whipped its curly-haired head around.

Maddened eyes fixed upon Leesil. It swung down with the iron bar, and he twisted the other way. Stone chips scattered over his face as the bar's end cracked upon the floor.

Leesil slammed his blade down atop the bar before the undead could lift it again. Chap lunged in, wrapping his jaws around the undead's other ankle, and Leesil saw the split where he'd struck its calf.

Thin trails of black fluids still ran down its leg—but no wound remained. It had already closed.

The iron bar lurched, squealing with sparks as it scraped free of Leesil's blade. He looked up as Sgäile kicked out hard.

The undead's head snapped back under the blow. Chap released his jaws and bit into the side of the man's knee.

"Over the edge!" Sgäile shouted. "Into the chasm!"

Leesil kicked into the undead's other knee as Chap shredded the one in his teeth.

Sgäile whirled. His foot lashed out and connected again.

Leesil caught a glimpse of Magiere.

Welstiel backed along the bridge. Magiere charged him with both sword and dagger drawn.

Magiere flipped her dagger, gripping it point down. The heavy falchion was slower than Welstiel's longsword, and she might not parry well with the dagger. But the silvery blade braced along her forearm might keep her from losing a hand if she had to block. All that mattered was stopping Welstiel's sword, just for one moment.

His tunic was split along the side. The fabric's edges were soaked dark with his fluids. But in place of an open wound, Magiere saw only a scar.

She'd seen the marks her sword left on the undead, but the wound couldn't have closed that quickly.

"I am bolstered . . . fed in the orb's presence," Welstiel whispered, "but you . . . you still live and breathe. No matter what you gain from it, I will not need to take your head . . . to kill *you*!"

Magiere hesitated. She didn't know to what extent the orb could affect her and wasn't about to test it. If he was right, she had to take his head before she was too wounded to go on.

Welstiel rushed with an upward whip of his longsword, trying to strike for her chest between her weapons. Magiere pivoted sideways and swept her left forearm down.

She caught the sword's end with the flattened dagger. Welstiel dropped low and thrust out, and the longsword skimmed along the blade.

The sword's point buried in the upper half of Magiere's sword arm.

Without hunger to block the pain, Magiere crumpled and dropped the falchion.

Chap saw Magiere drop to one knee. And he went cold inside as Leesil shouted, "No . . . no!"

Sgäile's foot cracked against the muscular undead's skull.

Chap sprang, clawing up the undead's body.

He didn't care what happened to him, so long as this vampire went down and someone got to Magiere. He sank teeth into the undead's throat and called up a memory from within Leesil's mind.

The large undead teetered and began to fall toward the chasm's edge.

Chap clung to it by tooth and claw, letting his weight bring it down.

Leesil rolled to his feet as Chap latched on to the undead's throat. Between Sgäile's last kick and the dog's sudden weight, the undead began to topple toward the edge.

Chap didn't lunge away.

Leesil threw aside one winged blade. He reached out wildly to grab Chap by the scruff, but his mind was still numbed by the sight of Magiere buckling under Welstiel's thrust.

A memory erupted in his head.

Downstairs in the Sea Lion's common room, he'd been alone in the dark—drinking—as Ratboy slipped in through a window. At the sound, he'd pulled a stiletto and hurled it. But the blade had stuck into a tabletop rather than into the little vampire's head.

Only Chap could have raised that forgotten moment, trying to tell him what to do—whom to save.

Leesil snatched a stiletto from his wrist sheath, breaking the holding strap. With one quick flip, he caught the blade and threw it.

Magiere gasped as Welstiel jerked his longsword out of her arm. Her fury held, but it wasn't enough to eat the pain—not like her missing hunger could have.

On withdrawal, Welstiel flicked the sword tip at her throat.

She barely blocked it with her dagger-shielded forearm. The longsword's tip slid off and scraped her hauberk's shoulder. It didn't cut her, but its drag on the leather pulled her off balance.

Welstiel swung his blade back, and it rose over his head. With no room to dodge aside on the narrow bridge, Magiere raised her forearm with the dagger and braced for the impact.

Welstiel lurched.

The longsword stalled and wobbled above him. His eyes widened, and his lips spread, exposing clenched teeth.

Magiere almost lost her opening in surprise. She spun the dagger in her grip and slashed fast and hard across his knee.

The blade cut through his breeches. He screeched in pain, and Magiere heard a sizzling hiss from the dagger. She started at both sounds.

Smoke rose from the severed cloth around Welstiel's leg. As he spun away along the bridge, Magiere saw the stiletto embedded below his left shoulder blade. She glanced at the dagger in her hand.

A red glow along its center hair-thin line faded quickly to its old charcoal black. Vapor thickened and sputtered softly as its moisture touched the blade—as if the metal had suddenly heated during her swing.

Welstiel came about. He fixed upon her in cold anger and advanced.

Magiere abandoned any notion of grabbing for the falchion. She came up, gripping the dagger's hilt hand over hand. Welstiel took a double hold on his sword as he brought it down.

Sparks scattered as weapons collided and then vanished rapidly in the humid air. Magiere let the dagger tilt upon the impact.

The instant Welstiel's sword slipped away, she slashed the blade back up across his face.

Welstiel whipped his head aside with a cry, and the stench of burning flesh filled Magiere's nostrils. She swung out, striking for his sword arm. Smoke erupted from his wrist as the blade slashed across. He shrieked as his grip on the sword's hilt went limp.

The longsword clanged upon the bridge and Magiere heard nothing more.

Welstiel grabbed for his wounded wrist with his fingerless hand. He tried to shield his smoking face with both arms, and one foot slipped off the side of the bridge.

"No!" Magiere screamed. "Not that easy!"

She grabbed for him as he fell, catching his forearm. Her knees hit the bridge as Welstiel's full weight dragged her down, and her grip slid up to his wrist.

Magiere held on to Welstiel and strained to pull him up.

She couldn't spend her life wondering if he'd truly died in the chasm's depths. She wouldn't live with that doubt. But she wasn't going to drop the dagger for a second grip.

Magiere slammed the blade down into Welstiel's chest.

He didn't even scream as smoke welled from the heated blade sinking into him. She heaved on the hilt, draging his torso halfway onto the bridge. She released his wrist, pinning him with her knee, and snarled her fingers into his hair.

Welstiel convulsed once as she jerked the dagger out.

The blade crackled as his black fluids burned off under its heat. Magiere pressed it to his throat.

A charred gash angled between Welstiel's eyes, running from the bridge of his nose and down through his cheek to the side of his mouth. Teeth and bone showed through smoking split skin. His eyes were filled with confusion and pain, as if none of what was happening could be real.

And it still wasn't enough for Magiere.

Not for all she had suffered or what so many others had lost because of him. She leaned close to Welstiel's mangled face, whispering, "Whatever waits for you . . . when you get there . . . give Father my *hate*!"

Magiere shoved the blade down.

Welstiel's face went slack as it split his throat. When she felt the dagger jam into bone, she ground it through.

The tip of the dagger grated on the stone.

Magiere let Welstiel's body tumble off the bridge.

Leesil hoped his stiletto had struck true. He rushed for Chap, but he wouldn't make it.

The large undead's back and head cracked against the bridge's side. He rolled off and fell.

Sgäile flung aside Leesil's old blade and bolted onto the bridge.

In midair, Chap tried to leap off the undead's chest. Only his forepaws hooked the bridge's edge. Sgäile reached out and grabbed for Chap, pulling the dog up. The yowling undead clawed at empty air, and fell into the chasm's clouded depths.

Leesil quickly closed on Chap and Sgäile, but then his gaze traced along the bridge.

Halfway out, Magiere knelt, staring over the edge, but Leesil saw no sign of Welstiel.

"Drop down," he said.

Sgäile buckled low, still holding Chap, and Leesil hopped over them. Before he reached Magiere, she lifted her face.

Her fingers were snarled in the hair of a severed head, and Leesil saw one white temple as he slowed. Magiere slumped and closed her eyes. Beneath her scowl, Leesil could see her pain. In the end, even killing Welstiel hadn't taken it away.

With her eyes still closed, Magiere flung the head.

Leesil watched it fall through the misty air, growing faint and small. It vanished altogether, though he never heard it strike in the chasm's obscured depths.

Magiere felt as if she'd awakened in one of those seven hells Leesil so casually spit out in his curses. Welstiel was gone, but it solved nothing—changed nothing—for her.

It didn't erase what she was, or change what might wait for her in the future.

Then Leesil crouched down before her.

Magiere gazed into his wild amber eyes, so faintly slanted beneath white-blond eyebrows. What might he say about all this? What was there to say? But the sight of his tan face and bright hair pulled her halfway from that hell.

"Where's Chane?" he asked, so softly, as if reluctant to ask anything of her.

The question shook Magiere fully back into the moment. "I don't know."

Leesil pivoted, and Magiere saw Sgäile and Chap near the bridge's end.

"Stay there," he called to them. "Watch the tunnel . . . Chane is still missing."

Chap spun about, and Sgäile followed the dog off the bridge. Leesil turned back and reached for Magiere.

"Let's see that arm."

She'd forgotten about the wound, and strangely, all the pain was gone. Leesil pulled apart the blood-soaked rent in the sleeve of her wool pullover.

He wiped gently with his fingertips, clearing blood from her arm, and then stopped.

Magiere saw no wound. Not even a scar.

"Even you don't heal that quickly," Leesil said, looking none too pleased. "I saw a wound on that big undead close too fast. What is happening here?"

Welstiel had claimed he was untouchable in the orb's presence, and she wasn't. Apparently he'd been wrong—not that it made Magiere feel any better. She spun on one knee, looking back to the orb. Li'kän stood staring at it, and nothing on the platform had changed.

"Come on," Leesil urged, "before we get any more surprises."

He grabbed her arm, hoisting her up.

Magiere paused only to pick up her falchion, but she didn't sheathe it or the dagger. As she stepped onto the meeting place of the four bridges, she kept her eyes on the white undead.

All her dissatisfaction settled on the notion of taking Li'kän's head.

This ancient thing—and whatever controlled it—wanted Magiere to have the orb. So why had Li'kän done nothing to stop Welstiel and his minions?

"What's wrong with her?" Leesil asked.

Magiere took a long breath. "I don't think she's been down here in ages—or longer than I can guess. She just froze at the sight of it."

"So what is it?" Leesil whispered.

Magiere had no answer. She was no mystic or sage, and doubted that even those who were would understand the orb. She was just a rogue, a charlatan grown tired of the game . . . and a tainted thing born in the worst of ways. But instinct told her this device was no longer safe here, and she believed the Chein'âs knew this as well.

They had given her the circlet, what Wynn called a *thôrhk*.

Without even thinking, Magiere sheathed her falchion and tucked away the dagger. She pulled aside her hair to lift the circlet from her neck. From the look of its open-end knobs and the grooves in the spike's head . . . was this *thôrhk* a handle for lifting the orb?

Leesil's brow wrinkled as Magiere fitted the circlet over the spike.

The knobs slipped along the stone grooves, until they settled in the notches on the spike's opposing sides. Gripping the circlet like a bucket's handle, Magiere lifted with both hands, trying to clear the orb from its tall stone stand.

She expected resistance. Whatever the orb and false spike were made of, the whole of it looked heavy. To her surprise, the circlet lifted easily.

A hum rose around Magiere, seeming to fill the cavern. Or was it inside her, running through her bones, gathering in her skull?

"No!" Leesil shouted. "Put it back in!"

Magiere felt water droplets gather on her face. She saw them on her hands as the air's mist seemed to pull in around her. A light spread from somewhere beneath her grip on the circlet, and she dropped her gaze.

The spike hung free, dangling from the circlet's knobs. Rather than lifting orb and spike together, her circlet had pulled the spike, separating it.

The orb, still resting in the stand, emanated light . . . was made of light. Its glow sparked within the drops upon Magiere's arms and hands.

Rainbow hues swirling through the orb suddenly bled into each other, until its whole form burned pure teal.

"Put the spike back!"

Magiere heard Leesil's shout, but she couldn't turn away, and her eyes began stinging from the light. Her vision blurred like snow blindness.

Only the orb remained crisp and real.

Magiere couldn't move, though she felt someone's hands close atop her grip on the circlet.

Chap turned back as the landing hollow's dark space filled with light. He cringed at the brilliance erupting from the platform.

Three hazy silhouettes were barely visible in the glare. Then a tingle crawled over Chap's skin, making his fur bristle.

Fay—he felt his kin manifested here.

Chap turned aside from the blinding light and saw Sgäile shielding his eyes. And beyond the elf, the hollow's walls began to bleed . . . water.

Globules welled from the stone and ripped from its surface, but they did not fall downward. Each glittering droplet shot toward the platform, like heavy rain falling inward from all around into the teal brilliance.

Chap felt a hint of connection to Earth, Fire, Air, Spirit . . . and an overwhelming sense of Water. He had not tried to root himself in the elements of existence, yet they sharply filled his awareness—and the last, primal Water, smothered the others.

He remembered being born.

Every pain and sensation flickered past in his mind. He drifted back further, almost remembering his existence among his kin, the Fay.

They—he—had mourned a loss.

No, a sin—from an instant before the first "moment" existed.

From when "time" came into being at the beginning of creation.

Chap inched forward in the blinding light, feeling with his paws for the bridge's edge. He cried out through his spirit to his kin.

What . . . was so horrible . . . in the making of this world? What did you . . . we do?

There was no answer.

Once, at one with his kin, "time" had meant nothing to Chap. Now he struggled with moments and days and years like walls built around his lost memories. But he felt the presence of a Fay in this place.

Chap lifted his head and tried to gaze into the light.

One? There was only one Fay here?

How could he sense one and not the many? There were no others like himself in this world that he knew of. The tingle across his skin sharpened.

A wordless hiss in Chap's skull drove cold into his bones. For an instant it almost shifted to a leaf-wing crackle in his head.

He felt it clearly—another Fay—a second, yet singular and alone. It wormed through him like winter's ache, the same one that had tried to coil around his awareness as he fled from Li'kän's mind.

The presence vanished from Chap's awareness. The tingle within him ripped away as he choked.

Within the painful light upon the platform, Magiere had done something to awaken or activate the ancient artifact.

He did not yet understand what or why, but there was a reason that the orb had been left fallow in the frozen mountains and burning chasm. Water droplets raced from the stone walls toward its light as vapors from the chasm twisted upward.

"What is happening?" Sgäile shouted.

Chap scurried forward with eyes down, barely making out his paws' outlines upon the stone floor. The glare broke away on both sides, leaving only a narrow strip running ahead. It had to be the bridge.

Chap padded blindly out, heading for the platform.

Leesil grappled for Magiere's hands, turning his face from the blinding orb. Though it burned with a green-blue glow, the light filling the air was searing white. He felt rain patter on his body. But it fell inward from all around, all directions. Droplets stung him and seemed to roll over his limbs, sucked away toward the orb.

He closed his eyes and shouted, "Let go! Damn it, Magiere, let it drop!"

No matter how hard he pressed on her hands, she remained rigid and unyielding.

Something grabbed the back of Leesil's hauberk.

Wrenching force heaved him backward, and his fingers tore from Magiere's hands. He landed hard on stone and flopped over once. He quickly flattened in fear of blindly tumbling over the platform's edge.

Leesil looked back for Magiere, and his eyes watered instantly in the glare. Tears beaded and ripped from his face. They joined a thousand droplets racing through the cavern toward the light beyond Magiere.

Her body shielded the orb, as if she stood directly in line with the sun, turning her into a darkly blurred silhouette. White light radiated around her, blurring everything else from sight.

Until another hazy silhouette closed on her.

Narrower and shorter, it reached out beyond Magiere, somewhere above the orb.

Leesil turned his face aside as he crawled toward Magiere. He could barely make out the open cavern. Vapors thinned from the air, and the far walls were lit up. The pocket cavities of the dead, not as bright as the open stone, were little more than oval blotches in his blurred sight.

He saw them begin to move.

Like shadows that the light couldn't smother, they shifted along the cavern walls and flowed in a slowly swirling pattern.

Leesil dragged the back of his hand over his eyes, trying to clear his warped vision.

The swirling of shadows undulated. They flowed together in turning paths like a snake with no beginning or end, and those huge shadow coils turned everywhere across the cavern's walls.

Leesil continued crawling toward Magiere. As he got closer, her body shielded him enough to raise his head and look at her.

A dim form rose above her silhouette.

More muted shadows joined into the shape of a head, growing larger . . . or closer.

At first, Leesil thought he saw the outline of the serpent guardian he'd faced before the burial ground of the elven ancestors. But it kept growing until its dull oblong took on more features.

Pale outlines of ridges . . . or horns . . . or spikes . . . ran back across its top from above lidless eyes. Those faint staring globes, set wide on its face, were surrounded by bulged and thickened scales that trailed in twined rows down a long snout.

Its reptilian head rose, mounted upon the end of the shadow coils worming along the cavern walls. The faint outline of its jaws widened.

Leesil scrambled up.

Within the beast's huge maw, Leesil saw rows of dark translucent shapes, like teeth as long as his legs.

It was no snake or serpent. He didn't even know what to call it.

He shut his eyes against the glare and sprang, throwing his arms around Magiere's torso when his chest collided with her back.

He opened his eyes once, looking up.

The scaled monster's jaws widened, as if it would swallow the whole platform, and it came down on them.

Leesil wrenched Magiere away with all his weight.

Magiere saw no cavern, felt no circlet. She saw nothing but white light. Then all the pure light snapped to blackness.

Enormous dark coils turned around her.

A whispering hiss surrounded her, as if she'd fallen asleep for the last time and slipped into that dark dream. But no clear words came from the hidden voice of the coils.

Hunger rushed through Magiere. If she'd had breath, she would have choked.

She felt an undead presence, as if buried in it—swallowed by it.

Only those coils—coils of an undead—and hunger rupturing her within remained in the sudden dark dream.

Something touched Magiere's hands—she felt her own hands once more—and her sight filled with a flash of brilliant white.

Small pale hands pressed down atop her own—and someone else squeezed tightly around her chest and heaved.

Magiere came to a stop, lying prone atop whoever had pulled her back.

All around her, the cavern had suddenly returned to its dim red glow.

For an instant, water droplets hung in the air. They all fell suddenly, and the patter of a rainstorm filled the platform. The cavern air became silent and empty.

Magiere looked toward the orb—and saw Li'kän standing beside the pedestal.

The white undead's hands rested atop the circlet and the spike had settled back into place. It had melded into the orb's dark rough form, the two parts once more a whole and unbroken shape. The teal light was gone, and the only glow came from the chasm's depths.

Someone shuddered beneath Magiere's back, and she spotted Leesil's hands clenched across her chest. She broke his grip and twisted over.

His eyes were shut so tightly that his features became a strained and wrinkled mask. Spattered water had soaked his hair and face. She clawed up his body and grabbed his head.

"Look at me!" Magiere shouted. "Leesil . . . open your eyes!"

His eyes snapped open, and he began breathing too fast. He shook his head free of her grip and craned his neck, looking wildly about the cavern.

"Leesil!" Magiere whispered, and took his face again. "Leesil?"

She'd never seen so much fear in his eyes.

Chap appeared beside them, rumbling as he paced around to watch Li'kän and the orb.

Li'kän hadn't moved or taken her eyes from the ancient object.

Chane watched everything as it happened. He saw water bleed from stone, droplets race inward, and vanish as if swallowed in the painful light. When the light grew too strong, he had to duck and cover his eyes.

In the brilliance that stung him, he felt his hunger return.

It churned inside him, unrestrained. He curled within the rock pocket as the beast inside him began to thrash.

As the glare piercing Chane's eyelids faded, so did hunger. It vanished into nothing—and the beast within him whimpered, cowering in the dark.

He opened his eyes to look out. The white undead stood before Welstiel's lost treasure, but Chane did not care.

He had only scorn for Welstiel, who had risked everything for something so powerful—even if the man had believed it would sustain him without feeding. Welstiel was a fool for all his knowledge, and had died for it. This thing—this orb—should have remained lost and forgotten.

But Chane had been a follower through all his short existence as a Noble Dead, from rising in servitude to Toret and then taking up with Welstiel. And freedom, now that it came, left him with nothing again.

Chane was uncertain what he felt at Welstiel's second death. A part of him had even wanted Welstiel to win—to finish Magiere instead. Or, better, wanted each to have taken the other over the edge.

He watched the wounded elf run along the bridge to join the others upon the platform. No one remained in the hollow of the tunnel's entrance.

But where was Wynn?

Perhaps Leesil had hidden her somewhere safe, up in the castle.

Chane kept silent as he slowly crawled to the pocket's front and reached around its side.

Neither Magiere's nor Chap's awareness of undead, nor even Leesil's strange amulet would sense him, now that he wore Welstiel's ring of nothing. But the last thing he needed was someone locating him by sight. He quickly swung into the landing hollow and crept along the wall to the tunnel's entrance. Once deep enough into the tunnel's upward turn, he ran.

The heavy doors at the tunnel's end were still cracked open, and Chane carefully leaned through.

The younger elf, who had held Wynn amid the battle, lay unconscious upon the floor. But Wynn was not there.

Chane leaned out enough to peer around the doors' edge, and he saw her.

She stood at the back end of the last tall bookcase, but she was studying the library's stone wall rather than a text from the shelves. She traced faded dark writing on the stones with her small fingers, silently mouthing what she read.

"Wynn . . . ," Chane rasped, and hated the sound of his voice.

She spun, backing against the wall.

Her liquid brown eyes went wide at the sight of him. Wispy brown hair tangled about her small, olive face—dirtier than in his nightly visions, but otherwise the same face he remembered. In place of gray robes, she wore loose, dusky-yellow pants and a long hide coat.

Wynn rushed toward him, or so he thought, but she stopped between him and the unconscious elf.

"I will not let you harm him," she said. "He is one of our protectors."

Chane went numb, not because she sought to protect this man from him, nor even at the way she looked at him in frightened suspicion. He could not blame her for either of these things. But it hurt that she was correct in both.

"I saw you die," she whispered.

"Did you mourn for me?"

The question came out before he could stop it. Even as he spoke, the words sounded so petty and self-centered compared to all they had not said to each other.

"Yes," she answered. "I wept that night . . . and many nights after."

He stood looking at her. No one in his lost life—not his mother or his companions of youth—had ever cared enough to cry for him.

"But I mourned the scholar I remembered," Wynn added. "Not the true Chane . . . the one who would help Welstiel murder . . . the Servants of Compassion and make them into mindless, savage beasts."

Beasts. Chane flinched, anger growing inside him. He wanted to shout at her, but she only spoke more truth.

He had deceived himself as much as her. When they first met, had he not tried to pass himself off as a young, gentle scholar seeking like-minded company? And later, had he not helped Welstiel destroy the scholars within that monastery of healing?

"I did not turn them," he rasped at her and then faltered. "But I did not stop him either . . . and have regretted it ever since."

Her gaze softened, but only briefly. "Are my companions safe?"

More suspicion—and still legitimate. Chane knew he did not have much time left.

"Magiere took Welstiel's head . . . and the orb he sought. I thought it would be a small thing, created by some forgotten undead who no longer wished to feed. But . . . it is much more. What is it, Wynn?"

Her small brows drew closer. "It was created in the time of the Forgotten. I have been trying to find pieces—hints and clues—written by one of its guardians on these walls. It may have been created by whatever made her and the other undead who first appeared in the war."

She was close enough for Chane to reach out and touch.

"The orb belongs with the sages," she added.

The sages. Once Chane had believed that he, too, belonged among them—and with her. She did not seem to fear him now, but she should.

What place was there in her world for such a beast?

One that would never stop hungering and straining at its bonds.

Chane stepped out, walking wide as he turned his eyes from Wynn's.

He tried to hide his expression by studying the texts upon the shelves. He should leave and get as far from her as possible. But he could not bring himself to go just yet and lowered his gaze to the unconscious elf.

Bitterness slipped out. "Who is that?"

"I told you. One of our guardians . . . an envoy of the elves. It is a long story." She glanced at stone doors. "You should go. If Magiere and Chap find you here . . ."

Chane shook his head at her wish to protect him.

Wynn Hygeorht the sage—and sweet, naïve little guardian of monsters.

"So, you will take the orb to your guild?" he whispered.

"Yes."

Chane closed his eyes, seeing the Wynn he remembered, clothed in gray robes and drinking mint tea in a warm study full of scrolls and books.

He would never be part of that vision. He had been lying to himself for too long. If she ever saw that feral beast inside of him, he could not bear to exist any longer.

"I will not follow you anymore," he said with back turned. "You will not see me again."

He did not mean to turn and look, but he did.

Wynn stood with tears running down her olive-toned face.

It was last time he would cause her pain.

Chane strode along the dark row of bookshelves, and it was hard not to look back. He almost reached the side passage when his boot toe kicked something across the floor.

It rattled like hollow metal, and he glanced down. In the dark, he spotted an old tin scroll cylinder rocking slightly where it had come to rest by the wall.

Chane stepped into the passage, and then paused. He turned and stared back at the dark casements.

So much was here upon the shelves. Perhaps Wynn would salvage what she could before leaving, though likely she would not carry away much. It would have been good to be there when she returned with her finds to Domin Tilswith in Bela, especially after all she had been through to reach this lost place.

Chane stepped back out and looked down at that lone scroll case, now motionless where it lay. He stooped and picked it up, then turned back down the passage.

When he reached the stairway chamber, with its archway to the wide corridor of columns, the bodies of feral monks littered the floor, headless and still. He found his pack and tucked the scroll away with the books taken from the monastery. He slung both his pack and Welstiel's over his shoulders along with a piece of canvas and a length of rope. He left everything else behind.

Chane kept his mind empty all the way down the long corridor of columns. But it grew harder to stay numb inside as he left, passed through the iron gates, and stumbled out upon the snow.

Magiere carefully removed the circlet from the orb's spike and hung it back around her neck. Then she gripped the top of the spike and tried simply lifting the orb from its resting hole in the store stand. Now it felt heavy, like an anvil, and she used both hands to lift it out. With the spike intact, it did not illuminate again, and remained dormant.

Li'kän just stood there, eyes locked on the empty stand. She glanced once at Leesil, and her face wrinkled briefly.

Magiere was ready to drop the orb and step into the undead's path. Li'kän's world had changed for the first time in centuries. How would she react?

Confusion passed over the white undead's face. She turned back to staring at the orb's stone stand, as if she couldn't understand what the empty place meant.

"Start heading for the tunnel," Magiere whispered.

"What?" Leesil asked.

"Just do it."

Chap and Sgäile had already gone to the cavern landing, and Magiere waited until Leesil was well onto the bridge before she turned to follow. When she stepped off into the landing's hollow, she looked back.

Li'kän stood before the bridge's far end. Mist began to gather once more in the cavern as the chasm's heat rose to warm the wet walls.

Magiere could swear Li'kän was glaring at her, and that she tried to step upon the bridge. A wafting curl of mist blocked the ancient undead from sight and drifted into the cavern's upper air.

Li'kän stood still as ice on the platform before the bridge.

Magiere backed away toward the tunnel.

The orb had sustained Li'kän for centuries, and without it, that ancient thing would soon hunger again. Magiere remembered Li'kän lifting the iron bar from the wall doors, her frail body barely straining with the effort.

"We haven't found Chane yet," Leesil argued.

"It doesn't matter—just go!"

Leesil headed into the tunnel. As Magiere followed, she saw blood matting the fur on Chap's neck and the dark stain on Sgäile's cowl and vestment.

"It is a clean cut," he said without slowing. "I will dress it later."

They couldn't stop, not with Li'kän still free behind them. Whatever held the undead back, Magiere wasn't about to wait and see if it lasted. She felt little relief when they passed the last skeleton-filled hollows of the tunnel and approached the parted stone doors. She desperately needed her strength to last for one more task. Magiere stepped out behind the others into the dark library.

Wynn was kneeling next to Osha but gazing blankly at the floor. Such sadness lingered on her face, but it vanished when she looked up at all of them. Her eyes locked on the orb as Magiere crouched to gently set it down.

Magiere turned immediately, throwing her weight into one of the stone doors.

"Leesil!" she grunted, and he came in beside her. Sgäile joined them as well.

The door barely moved at first, and Magiere wished she had her hunger again.

Finally, the bottom edge grated along the floor. It took longer to close the other one, and both Sgäile and Leesil's faces glistened with sweat by the time it shut.

The iron beam still lay on the floor.

Realization passed across both Sgäile's and Leesil's faces, followed by doubt. Sgäile had only one good arm and couldn't be doing well with his wounded shoulder.

"One end at a time," he said. "And you must get it off the floor before we can assist you."

Magiere took hold of the beam's end. In place of hunger she tried to find fury, remembering her mother dying in bed. She thrust upward with her legs.

"Now!" Magiere grunted, as the beam's end reached her waist.

"Where is Li'kän?" Wynn asked.

Leesil and Sgäile ducked in, bracing one shoulder each beneath the beam.

They all heaved, pushing up with their legs, and Magiere's arms began to tremble. As Leesil and Sgäile pressed upward, she poured all the strength she could summon into one last thrust.

The beam grated over the stone bracket of the closest door. As it crested the bracket's top, Magiere shouted, "Get back!"

Leesil and Sgäile ducked clear as she let go.

The beam dropped, and a dull clang echoed through the library as it settled. Leesil bent over, panting. Sgäile wavered on his feet and was breathing shallow and fast.

"Where is Li'kän?" Wynn repeated.

Magiere slumped against the stone door. When Li'kän's hunger returned, it would grow into starvation, and they couldn't let her loose into the world.

"She can't leave this place," Magiere panted. "Ever."

Wynn stood up, but Leesil cut in before she could speak.

"Did Chane come out?"

Wynn swiveled toward him. Her mouth opened, then closed as she glanced toward the path around the ends of the bookcases.

"Yes," she finally answered. "But he left. He is not in the castle."

Leesil groaned in frustration. "You don't know that. Chap, see if you can sense him."

Chap growled, loping off along the row of bookcases.

Magiere glanced toward the iron beam's other end still resting on the floor. Leesil and Sgäile were spent, and she didn't feel any better. But they had to finish.

Li'kän must never leave this place.

"What was that thing?" Leesil suddenly panted out.

Magiere shook her head, not because she didn't know, but rather that she didn't want to think about it.

"An undead," she sighed. "That's all I felt, but worse than any other . . . I could barely stand it."

"Not Li'kän," Leesil said. "In the light . . . what was that misshapen serpent . . . horned snake . . . whatever tried to swallow us?"

Magiere stared at him, baffled by what he said. Chap loped back into sight, coming up beside Wynn. The dogged huffed once for "yes."

Wynn's mouth tightened. "As I told you, Chane is gone."

Magiere turned back to Leesil in puzzlement.

"I didn't see anything in the light," she said.

Sgäile shook his head. "I saw nothing, just light too bright to look into."

Leesil straightened, his sweating face gone blank.

"How you could miss it?" He glared at everyone in disbelief. "It could've swallowed the whole platform. It had teeth instead of fangs, and rows of horns taller than you, and scales all over its face and snout. Its coils were turning all over the cavern!"

"Coils?" Magiere whispered.

She hadn't seen a serpent's head—just the coils in her waking dream, and the sense of an undead all around her . . . within her.

"Don't look at me like that!" Leesil snapped. "I know what I saw. Those coils were taller than two men . . . maybe three!"

"No," Magiere said. "I didn't see—"

"Fay?" Wynn whispered.

Magiere stared dumbly at the sage.

Wynn knelt beside Chap, looking into his eyes. "He says he sensed a Fay. Not all of them together, as when they come to him. Just one alone . . . cold . . . malicious."

"It was an undead!" Magiere snapped.

Wynn ignored her and frowned at Leesil. "You couldn't have seen . . . what you say. Maybe you heard or read something and the shadows played tricks on you."

"No!" Leesil snapped. "We were practically blinded, there was so much light."

Magiere was so tired, she didn't care anymore what anyone had seen.

Wynn shook her head at Leesil. "I can only guess, but it is not real—only a myth. Even less, just a metaphysical emblem, a *wêurm* or—"

"What are you babbling about now?" Leesil growled.

"It is Numanese, my language," Wynn growled back, "for a type of dragon."

Chap snarled and lunged between all of them.

Wynn flinched. "Stop shouting at me! We heard you the first time—a Fay!"

The sage's anger vanished when she spotted blood-matted fur on his neck, and she reached for him.

Sgäile's angry voice startled Magiere. "Enough talk! We must bar the doors!"

She turned wearily along the tilted beam to grab its other end. But Chap's and Leesil's claims of what they'd experienced below—what either had seen or felt—ate at her.

One had sensed a Fay, and the other had seen a dragon, while she had felt the presence of an undead.

It was nonsense, nothing but the madness of this place. Leesil and Chap were wrong.

Magiere called the last dregs of her strength and hoisted the iron beam's grounded end.

"Someone comes," Dänvârfij whispered and notched an arrow to her bowstring.

"Wait," Hkuan'duv warned in a hushed voice and belly-crawled a short way out from the wall.

His companion was having difficulty breathing the frozen night air, but they had to retain their vigil. In the moonlight, he saw the tall, auburn-haired man slip out of the castle gates and trudge across the snow. But he was alone.

Hkuan'duv waited, but neither the man's white-templed companion nor their robed followers came out.

The man kept on with two bulky packs over his shoulders and a large folded canvas in his arms. He paused to look back.

Hkuan'duv let the hood of his white-covered cloak drop low and peered under its edge, watching.

The man closed his eyes, sagging where he stood. He looked lost and defeated when he gazed listlessly about the white plain. The man turned and pushed on, never looking back again.

"Should I fire?" Dänvârfij whispered.

Hkuan'duv considered having Dänvârfij bring the man down. But they would have to move into the open to retrieve him, risking exposure, and then hide a body once they had finished questioning him.

Only the artifact, and dealing with Magiere, mattered to Hkuan'duv.

"He is nothing to us," he whispered to Dänvârfij. "Let him go."

CHAPTER TWENTY-TWO

Magiere explored the castle's near reaches with Leesil and Chap, while Wynn tended to Sgäile and Osha in the library. They had all agreed to wait out the night and return to camp after dawn, but their efforts quickly became pointless.

They found no beds, blankets, kitchens, or sculleries. Either no furnishings had been brought to fill this place, or they had long ago decayed and been cleared away. They gave up and returned to the library, finding Osha awake.

As they entered, Wynn went still for a moment as if listening. "Since you did not find anything, Chap says we should move to the study that he and I first occupied. Though small, there is a heat source there."

Magiere nodded and heaved up the orb. "All right."

Sgäile and Leesil supported Osha as Chap led them through the varied passages to a tiny room. Neither Chap nor Wynn understood anything about the floor brazier filled with glowing fist-sized crystals, but Magiere didn't care. Without fuel for a fire or a place to burn it, any heat was welcome. The castle had grown colder as the night stretched on, and they had all slept in worse places.

Then again . . .

Not with madness written upon walls in an undead's fluids. Not with an ancient undead, perhaps impossible to kill, locked in the depths beneath them.

Doubts nibbled at Magiere. More so as she set the orb with its deceptive spike in the study's back corner. Still far too close for her peace of mind.

"Will Osha be all right?" she asked.

"I believe so," Wynn answered. "And Chap's neck appears to be healing."

Magiere ran her hand over the dog's head. She hadn't forgotten Chap's claim that he'd sensed a Fay in the cavern. It was harder to dismiss than Leesil's claim from half-shadows glimpsed within the orb's glare. Then again, she'd seen coils in her dreams.

"Sgäile's wound is the worst," Leesil said. "He may have chipped his collarbone, but I dressed it as well as I can."

"At least we're all alive," Magiere said, but didn't add *for now*.

Whatever had led her here and toyed with Li'kän—and by whatever name anyone called it—their three separate perceptions of what had come to the cavern didn't match up.

Undead. Fay. Dragon.

Magiere didn't want to know the answer to that puzzle. She didn't like thinking that the voice Chap had heard in Li'kän's mind was the same one in her own dreams. And when she looked at the orb in the corner, she didn't even want to stay in this room.

In another life, another time, could she have been just like Li'kän?

"I need privacy," she muttered. With her dagger and falchion, she shoveled in the floor brazier, pincered a glowing crystal between the blades, and headed for the door. She paused there, looking to Leesil.

"Are you coming?" she asked.

He picked up their coats to follow.

"Stay within calling distance," Sgäile advised.

Magiere headed for the closest opening along the corridor's wall. The door was long gone, and she stepped into a bare room, dropping the hot crystal in the rear corner. Leesil laid out one coat near it and began stripping off his hauberk. Magiere considered stopping him.

She didn't want him dropping his guard in this place. But by the time she finished second-guessing, he'd already slumped tiredly against the wall and reached out for her.

Magiere knelt down and collapsed against his chest. Leesil pulled the other coat over both of them as she shivered, but not from the cold.

Many pieces of an ancient mystery had been unearthed in the last half year. The few that made any sense suggested that this "night voice"—il'Samar—had planned her birth. Welstiel hadn't seemed to know even that much, and certainly not that she'd been made to master a horde of undead and serve as general for the return of an ancient enemy.

But it didn't matter. She wouldn't be pushed onto any path but the one she chose.

And as to the rest, all the fragments of the Forgotten they'd stumbled onto, which Wynn's sages so desperately wanted . . .

"I know what I saw," Leesil whispered. "Maybe it wasn't real. I mean, wasn't really there . . . but I couldn't have come up with that out of pure fancy."

Magiere tilted her face up. "I believe you, but something isn't right, especially about Chap's claim."

"I'm sick of it all," he whispered and closed his arms tightly around her.

Magiere closed her eyes and just listened to Leesil's slow sigh, feeling his chest rise and fall beneath her cheek.

Leesil was a different story. His birth and training had been planned by dissidents among the Anmaglâhk, so that he might fight this coming "enemy" that Most Aged Father feared. Even the an'Croan ancestor spirits had tried to enforce his destiny.

Unlike her, Leesil refused to even talk about it—but denial wouldn't help.

No one could avoid something they wouldn't acknowledge. That was no better than raising one's eyes to the sky and denying that a chasm lay but a few steps ahead in the path. Leesil had to recognize the forced destiny that others were trying to press on him. If not, it might take him anyway in his blindness. At some point, Magiere had to make him see this, if they were to have any chance at all in going their own way.

But for tonight, he'd been through enough—they all had.

The room was empty but for a high window barely within reach of the hot crystal's glow. The light of Leesil's amulet had faded the moment they barred the library doors to the tunnel. Li'kän's shadow animals never reappeared, as if their presence depended upon hers, or upon the white undead's awareness and focus.

Magiere wondered if some unnatural barrier existed between castle and cavern. How else could this place remain so cold resting above that misty chasm of heat?

How long had it been since she and Leesil had had a moment alone?

"I've been thinking," he said suddenly.

She tilted her head back. "About what?"

"Once we get home, we might add Wynn's herb and lentil stew to the menu . . . maybe her flatbread to serve with the fish chowder. We'll have to move the Faro table closer to the hearth by next autumn. It's too cold by the front window—"

"What?" Magiere grouched, playing along. "We're not blocking half the patrons from getting near the fire."

"They can sit down and play a hand," he countered. "How else am I going to earn any winnings come winter?"

Magiere closed her eyes, listening to him prattle and imagining home and hearth on nights where the most vexing question was what to offer patrons for dinner and why the latest ale shipment was late. She slipped an arm behind Leesil's waist beneath their cloaks.

The headless bodies of undead still lay in the stairway chamber. Below them in the depths, that ancient white thing still waited, though imprisoned in solitude. And its master had somehow wormed into Magiere's dreams.

But all Leesil wanted was to hold her and talk of their tavern—their home—as if nothing had happened at all.

And she let him.

Wynn finished checking Sgäile's dressing, though he grew impatient with her ministrations. The wound was clean, but she still suspected Welstiel's blade had chipped his collarbone.

"No lasting muscle damage . . . I would guess," she said, "but it will take some time to heal."

Osha leaned against the wall. She had cut off the hem of her elven tunic and used it to bandage his head, but she could do nothing for his pain. At least he was awake and alert, and this was a good sign. Chap's neck was healing, though she worried about infection, considering he had been deeply bitten by two walking corpses.

Sgäile looked directly into Wynn's face.

"I thank you," he said.

She rocked back from knees to her heels and sighed. "I wish I had salve. If we were back at the guild, I could make a poultice against infection."

Sgäile shook his head. "Do not be concerned. It is a clean wound."

She expected a harsh reprimand for running off and getting lost in the night, but Sgäile leaned his head back against the wall and closed his eyes. Perhaps he was just too tired to bother.

Wynn got up and went to the doorway, peering along the dark hallway. A low orange glow spilled from the next doorway ten paces away. She glanced back to Osha.

"You rest," she told him. "I want to check on Magiere and Leesil."

He started to get up. "You cannot go alone."

Strangely, Sgäile did not even stir. Wynn went to push Osha back down. He did not resist but began to argue again.

"Wynn—"

"Chap will come with me—now rest!"

By the time she reached the door, her stomach rolled slightly.

We should leave Magiere and Leesil in peace.

She looked down to find Chap on her heels. "I know."

Where do you think you are going?

Wynn sighed in exasperation. "I cannot leave here without more answers."

She pulled out her cold lamp crystal, rubbed it sharply, and headed off the other way along the corridor. Chap trotted out ahead and stopped in her way.

"Do not tell me you have not thought the same," she whispered. "We cannot leave without knowing what might lie within reach in the library! Who else here, besides me, could find anything of importance in that place?"

Chap's jowls wrinkled, but he finally turned about and headed down the corridor.

We cannot spend all night searching . . . and you cannot carry much more when we leave, so be judicious in your choices.

"Domin Tilswith would never forgive me if I did not try to bring some of it back."

With what? You do not have your pack, and I doubt the others will want to return here again before we leave these mountains.

"We are not the only ones who came," she answered, "and others brought packs and gear as well."

Chap slowed but did not stop as he glanced back at her with narrowed eyes. By the time they reached the stairway chamber, Wynn knew he was fully aware of what she had in mind.

Black ichors covered the floor around four headless bodies. On their

way to the study, Leesil and Sgäile had tossed the heads off down the col-
umned corridor, thinking it best to separate the heads from the bodies. They
had no lamp oil with which to cremate the corpses.

Wynn swallowed hard.

Well . . . get on with it.

She shot Chap a seething glare and swallowed again.

Wynn hooked her boot under the headless corpse of a small woman.
The body was so heavy that she struggled to roll it over. A crude, half-
flattened fold of canvas was strapped to the corpse's back with lengths of
rope. She set aside her crystal as she knelt and pulled Magiere's old dagger.

She cut the canvas free, preserving as much rope as possible. Black fluids oozed from the stump of the woman's neck when she jostled the body.
Wynn turned her eyes away, but her gaze fixed upon the dark robe and blue
tabard. She tried not to imagine what had happened to these people when
Welstiel and Chane first found them.

Wynn pulled cut rope from under the corpse, and oily black fluids
smeared over her fingers. Her stomach rolled.

Finish up!

Bile and dried fish welled in Wynn's throat.

"Be quiet!" she gasped and then gagged. "This is bad enough without
you in my head, making it worse!"

Chap grumbled and traipsed to another body, clawing it over onto its
chest. He tore at its rope harness, trying to pull more canvas free. Wynn
closed her eyes but still shuddered as she wiped off her hands on the body's
robe.

When her eyes opened again, Chap stood before her with a mouth-
ful of canvas. He turned away for the far passage in the chamber's corner.
Wynn grabbed the crystal, rope, and canvas, and scurried after him. As they
stepped out into the library, the crystal's light spilled over the ends of the
tall stone casements.

Chap dropped his canvas by the corridor's arch, as did Wynn. But
when she stepped between the nearest shelves, she could not help a shiver
of thrilled anticipation. She and Chap were alone and unobserved in a place
that would have taken years—or decades—for her guild to catalogue. But
her awe passed quickly when she remembered how all this knowledge had
come to be here.

She was surrounded by decaying texts penned by ancient undeads, like Li'kän.

Chap lifted his muzzle, turning as he scanned the upper shelves.

Wynn felt overwhelmed by the task she faced. There was so much here, and this was only one row among many, so how could she choose what was most important to take? Her stomach rolled again.

Look first for languages you can read. Second for those you at least recognize. Focus mainly on the books. Bound texts will be older, made with materials that later grew scarce.

"Yes," she said, nodding. "But books will be the weakest, worn down with time. Pages might fall apart if touched—unlike the scrolls that have been protected by their cases."

This thought raised uncertainty. All this should have been done by her betters—the most skilled of cathologers among her guild. She was barely a journeyer, let alone a master or domin among that order of sages. But she was the only one here.

And if you spot any mention of "night voice" in any language, take that text over any others . . . and those of tongues that appear to predate our current era, even if you cannot read them. Translation might be possible when—

"Could you make this any more daunting?" Wynn asked.

Chap glanced up at her. *Sorry.*

She followed him deeper into the row as they both peered among scroll cases, books, sheaves, and even small boxes by the light of her crystal.

And so, while Magiere, Leesil, Sgäile, and Osha rested unaware, Wynn hurried in her search, scanning for anything that hinted at secrets of a lost past.

Anything that might unlock the mystery of events that had shattered the world so long ago.

Magiere stood on the castle's front steps at dawn with large snowflakes drifting down from a white sky.

They had fashioned a makeshift hammock for the orb with cut-up canvas and rope, and scavenged leather as well from the baggage of a robed undead. With the latter, they rolled up two heated crystals from the floor brazier. Though the leather smoldered and smoked a bit, at least they needn't worry about dried dung for fires.

Wynn looked bleary-eyed and exhausted as she dragged out two canvas-wrapped bulks too heavy for her to lift.

Magiere turned a suspicious glance toward Chap, and the dog quickly looked away. It wasn't hard to guess what the two had been up to while the rest of them slept. Still, what else could she expect?

The library contained so much more than Wynn's selected burden. Who else might ever find this castle again, anytime soon? Perhaps what the sage had gathered would uncover something worthwhile.

Magiere looked out across the white courtyard to the iron gates. One still stood ajar where she'd left it. The prospect of another journey weighed her down, but it was better than staying here even one more day.

She and Leesil had whispered far into the night, turning from hopes for the future to planning their route home. They had no maps, but as long as they traveled due west, they should emerge somewhere over the Everfen, the vast swamplands south of Droevinka. From there, they could head north-west toward the coast, skirting the swampland's northern edge.

Leesil thought if they stayed along Droevinka's southern border, they could pass into southern Belaski without hindrance, but Magiere had her doubts. If Droevinka's noble houses were still warring over who would put their own on the throne of the Grand Prince, no corner of her homeland was safe. Outsiders might be cut down by any side as a potential threat—or just for convenience.

And though desperate for word of Aunt Bieja, Magiere knew her home village of Chemestúk was too far off any sure path.

Leesil had left Bieja money and a letter in the hope that she'd head for Miiska. Aunt Bieja was as stubborn as any woman in Magiere's line, but she was no fool.

Magiere sighed, tired of worrying. Once they reached Miiska, Wynn could send word to Domin Tilswith in Bela, and Magiere would find some way to track Bieja, if her aunt wasn't waiting there. Then they could all rest in peace while deciding how best to safely deliver the orb in the hands of the Guild of Sagecraft.

The wind picked up and snowflakes began to slant in their downward course.

"Another blizzard brewing," Leesil muttered.

"Yes," Sgäile agreed. "We must move quickly and reach camp."

The two crouched, and each pulled one of the orb's hammock loops over his shoulder. Leesil also grabbed the rope sling holding the leather-wrapped fire crystals.

"Wynn, put your hood up," Magiere said as she turned about to heave up one of the sage's bulky bundles.

Wynn scowled but did as she was told, then suddenly slipped back through the castle's cracked doors.

"What are you doing?" Magiere called.

Wynn emerged once again, stumbling awkwardly under the weight of a sheaf bound between mottled iron sheets. Magiere remembered it sitting on the study floor.

"Enough!" she said. "You can't bring every parchment in the place."

"This must come!" Wynn insisted. "It may be a journal . . . written by the others who were once here with Li'kän."

Magiere didn't care for that idea and wondered what had happened to those others. Why had they left Li'kän behind? And how had they managed to leave at all, when the white undead had remained leashed by her hidden master through the centuries?

"Oh, give it to me," Magiere grumbled, taking the iron sheaf.

She almost dropped the sudden weight, and Wynn gasped. Magiere managed to tuck it safely under one arm.

Osha heaved up Wynn's other bundle from the library. The young elf managed well for one who'd taken an iron bar to the head. He frowned and spoke softly in Elvish to Sgäile.

"I know," Sgäile answered.

"They have rites to perform," Wynn explained, "for the caste members that Li'kän killed."

Leesil frowned, glancing sidelong at her. "To camp first . . . then we'll see how bad the weather gets."

Sgäile looked beyond the gates to the open plateau. "Yes, our purpose comes first."

Magiere headed down the steps and through the crusted snow toward the iron gates.

Hkuan'duv could barely breathe by the time he heard voices. He and Dän-vârfij had sat vigils before in bad weather. But the thin air in temperatures well below freezing left him stiff, even with his training in controlling and conserving body heat. Snow was falling again, and the wind had picked up. He had difficulty moving his arms and legs as he crawled away from the wall for a better view of the gates.

"Sgäilsheilleache and Osha."

Hkuan'duv glanced back at Dänvârfij's whisper. Her face and lips were so pale. When he turned forward, someone stepped through the gates, and he flattened in the snow.

Magiere led with a square bundle under one arm and a larger canvas bulk strapped to her back with rope. Behind her came Léshil and Sgäilsheilleache, and something heavy swung in a canvas sling swinging between them. The majay-hì ranged nearby, and Osha came last with another canvas bundle like Magiere's. When he took a long step, the small human female became visible, trudging beside him.

Hkuan'duv's gaze shifted quickly over the procession, skipping between the two canvas bundles and whatever swung between Léshil and Sgäilsheilleache. More complications—he could not be certain who carried the artifact.

"It appears she was successful," he whispered.

"Do we take it?" Dänvârfij asked in a weak voice, though she gripped her bow firmly in hand.

"Not here," he answered. "When they are farther from this place . . . and its guardian."

He did not see the white woman, but it was better to wait. He did not care to risk dealing with her again.

"We wait until they are out of sight," he said.

When the procession had passed halfway across the white plain, he crawled back to Dänvârfij.

Her tan face was drawn and pale, and beneath the cloak's hood, strands of her hair had turned brittle with frost. Her pupils were small.

"Are you well?" he asked.

"Of course," she whispered.

He still opened his cloak and pulled her in against his body. She did not resist, and in truth he did not feel much better than she looked.

"Not long now," he said.

She leaned against him in silence. By the time the procession reached the distant rocky slope, the falling snow had thickened and the wind was blowing harder.

"They cannot travel far in this," he said. "They will remain at camp."

Dänvârfij said nothing as he got up. When she tried to do the same, the bow slipped from her fingers. It sank in the fresh snow an instant before she fell.

Hkuan'duv quickly dropped, rolling her over, and brushed clinging snow from her face.

Dänvârfij eyes were closed. Her breathing was shallow, barely leaking any vapor between her lips.

The wind sharpened as he disassembled her bow and stowed it behind his own back beneath his cloak. When he hoisted her over his shoulder and took his first step, his legs shook. The long night had taken more from him than he had realized. He stumbled across the white plain.

By the time he crested the rocky slope, he no longer heard Dänvârfij's breaths over the harsh wind. He climbed down with one hand clawing for holds on the loose, cold stones.

With their purpose so close to an end, he should have left her behind and finished what they had started—but he could not. Perhaps he had grown too old in service, and his dedication now faltered. But she would never survive alone in the coming storm.

And Hkuan'duv could not survive the loss of Dänvârfij.

He tilted his head down and pressed onward. Even when he passed through the chute, he barely glanced at Kurhkâge's snow-dusted corpse. When he reached their campsite, the tent was half-buried. He laid Dänvârfij down to knock off the caked snow, then quickly pulled her inside and found the bag of dung.

He built a smoldering fire at the tent's mouth, hoping it would keep going for a while, and then crawled beneath the layered cloaks beside Dänvârfij. He pressed in against her, and between the smoky fire and her closeness, a hint of warmth grew between them.

Hkuan'duv closed his eyes for a moment, trying not to let exhaustion take him.

He opened them again and raised his head. He heard no wind, and it was dark inside the tent. Dänvârfij shifted beside him.

"Where are we?" she murmured.

He crawled to the tent's opening. Snow pinned the tent's flap shut. He began digging to free it, and then emerged into a silent dark world covered in a fresh blanket of snow.

The blizzard had passed. In exhaustion and the welcome warmth of Dänvârfij's body, he had fallen asleep. The day was gone.

Hkuan'duv crouched to find Dänvârfij staring out of the tent. Her wide eyes mirrored his panic.

"Stay here!" he ordered, and he hurried out through the drifts.

When he reached a vantage point, and saw the canvas-covered depression, he knew he was too late. No light filtered out through the crusted fabric, and he closed quickly, not bothering with stealth. Why had they left the canvas behind?

He stepped forward, pulling the canvas back.

The bodies of Kurhkâge and A'harhk'nis lay inside the stone depression. With their hands upon their chests, Hkuan'duv did not need to look further.

Sgäilsheilleache had performed rites for their fallen brethren.

At least their spirits, if not their flesh, would return to their people and the ancestors. Without a way to bring home the bodies, the next choice would be to burn their remains and carry the ashes back. With no way to accomplish even that much, Sgäilsheilleache had done the best he could for them.

Hkuan'duv crawled out of the depression to scan the craggy mountainside, but he found no hint of a trail in the pure unbroken snow. The storm must have weakened after he fell asleep. His quarry had moved on, their trail covered by the day's lighter snowfall. He hurried back to his own camp to find Dänvârfij gathering their gear.

"I have lost their trail," he said flatly, crouching beside her.

She still looked pale and drawn. Her hood down, her thick hair fell around her shoulders. She leaned on her hands, close to his face.

"If they wish to deliver the artifact in Belaski, they will head straight across this range, trying to reach the western coast. Even if we cannot find them in these mountains, we can track them once they leave the snowy heights. They must come out above the Everfen, and I know that region well."

Hkuan'duv calmed at her words.

"Of course," he answered. "It is only a delay."

CHAPTER TWENTY-THREE

Magiere lost track of the days and nights as their supplies rapidly dwindled. By the time they reached the range's western side, Chap spent nearly half of each day hunting with Sgäile or Osha for anything to eat. Roasting mice and squirrels ferreted from hibernation became the low point in their scant and meager meals. But as the air grew warmer and any snowfall became rain in the foothills, they fared a little better each following day.

One day, spouts of light green wild grass appeared along a muddy path. And then spring greeted them as they stood upon a high crest looking down over the Everfen.

The marshlands stretched west beyond sight. Magiere began descending quickly, until Wynn took a step, and her boot was sucked off in the deep mud. Leesil helped retrieve it, as Wynn teetered on the other foot, and then everyone trod more carefully.

Even when the rain broke for a short spell, the constant drip from the trees soaked them. But the air was no longer frigid.

"If it was not so wet, I would leave my coat behind," Wynn joked.

Magiere was glad to see her in better spirits. The journey down through sharp foothills had been grueling for little Wynn. At one point, her limp was so severe that Sgäile suggested carrying her on his back. Wynn adamantly refused, though Osha took away her pack, slinging her heavy bundle of books over his shoulder.

Sgäile had changed since the night he and Osha had placed the dead anmaglâhk in the cave. He would have preferred to cremate the bodies and carry their ashes home. But Magiere felt that something else was troubling him. He'd become cautious in covering their trail whenever possible, and often looked anxiously back along their way.

She asked him about his strange behavior, but he only said she read too much into his vigilance. Perhaps this was true, and in any case Magiere had other concerns.

Her dreams had ceased completely—a relief on one hand, and yet disturbing on the other.

She never wanted to hear that hissing voice again, but felt this was only a reprieve—it might come again. And having reached the Everfen, they would soon have to find a way to cross it.

So far, they'd found adequate solid ground, but Magiere had heard accounts of this region. As they crossed its eastern end toward Droevinka, the dry islands and ridges would grow sparse, and then vanish for leagues beneath the swamps.

Sgäile led with Leesil, Chap trotting beside them, until the day grew late. Magiere wasn't sure why, but Sgäile had become even more laconic than before, had been withdrawn and preoccupied since they'd come out of the foothills. She knew she'd never get an answer out of him and didn't try.

Chap pulled up and barked once.

Leesil stumbled under the orb's swinging weight as Sgäile halted. "There is a dwelling up ahead."

"Who would live out here?" Leesil asked.

Wading through the last few yards of mucky water, they stepped up a dry knoll to a small, thatched shack. Its hint of a garden had long gone fallow and an empty chicken coop rotted away along its side. One soggy, aging willow tree stretched up over the roof.

Chap sniffed about the chicken coop as Leesil knocked on the door.

"Hallo?" he called halfheartedly.

Barely waiting for an answer, he shoved the door open, dragging Sgäile along as he entered. Magiere followed and quickly covered her nose and mouth. A fetid stench filled the shack's one room.

"What is that smell?" Wynn said.

Leesil pointed. "Over there."

An old man lay in a ramshackle bed beneath burlap blankets pulled to his chin. He was clearly dead, and his sallow skin had shriveled upon his face beneath thinned, straggly hair.

"He must have died here alone, in his sleep," Wynn said, gasping for air. "A sad thing."

Magiere guessed the man had been dead less than a moon, and she agreed—it would be sad to die alone.

"Oh, thank goodness!" Wynn exclaimed.

Magiere spun about. The little sage looked upward in exhausted relief.

Burlap sacks hung from the rafters and down the walls to keep them free of excess moisture and scavengers. One high shelf above the hearth held tin canisters and an unglazed clay jar. Wynn went straight for the hearth and began digging through the odds and ends. Her brow wrinkled as she inspected a blackened iron pot.

"No rust that I can see," she reported. "Let us hope there are oats and grains or dried peas in those sacks."

She set down the pot, grabbed the clay jar, and lifted its lid.

"Oh," she groaned as if finding a lost treasure. "Honey . . . honey for biscuits!"

Leesil shook his head. "Just get some water boiling, while we find a better place for the owner to rest."

Magiere looked over at the old man. "We'd better scrap the bedding as well."

Though it felt wrong to invade a dead man's home, no one balked at the prospect of sleeping inside and eating something besides wild game. Leesil and Sgäile rolled the old man up in his bedding and carried him out back to bury him. Magiere shifted the orb to the back corner, then sat on the floor while Osha played assistant to Wynn.

"Go look for rain barrels outside," Wynn told him pointedly. "And do not bring swamp water in its place."

A scowl spread down Osha's long face. He looked thoroughly snubbed as he headed out the door, pot in hand. After some time, Sgäile and Leesil returned, but Sgäile hesitated in the doorway.

"I should scout the area," he said. "So we may choose a final path."

"Forget it," Leesil said, settling beside Magiere. "Just rest, and we'll do that in the morning."

But when Magiere looked back, Sgäile was gone.

. . .

Most Aged Father lay deeply troubled in the bower of his great oak. Half a moon past, he had received word from Hkuan'duv, the first in a long while. But the report was worse than expected—beyond displeasing.

Magiere had indeed acquired the artifact.

But A'harhk'nis and Kurhkâge were dead, and Hkuan'duv and Dänvâr-fij had lost her trail. The Greimasg'äh and his favored student guessed at Magiere's most likely route and were in pursuit. There had been no further word from Hkuan'duv, and Most Aged Father was left wondering. How did a reckless human woman and her companions continue to elude two of his best anmaglâhk?

Perhaps it was Sgäilsheilleache's intervention.

Not that Most Aged Father blamed him. He only held to his oath of guardianship and sense of honor. No, the blame lay with the deceitful Brot'ân'duivé—not the misled Sgäilsheilleache.

If Magiere reached these human "sages," it would be harder to retrieve the artifact, and the consequences could be dire. Something so ancient had no place in human hands.

Most Aged Father grew agitated in anticipation of better news.

A soft hum rose in the oak's heart-root surrounding his bower chamber, and he leaned back, closing his eyes in relief. Hkuan'duv had finally called to report.

Father?

The voice threading through the oak into Most Aged Father's mind did not bear Hkuan'duv's cool dispassion. Lyrical but strained, it made Most Aged Father's frail heart quicken.

"Sgäilsheilleache?"

A brief pause followed. He had not heard from Sgäilsheilleache since the ship had sailed from Ghoivne Ajhâjhe.

Father, forgive my long silence . . . much has happened.

Most Aged Father's first instinct was to rebuke him for his lack of contact. His second was to order Sgäilsheilleache to seize the artifact and return. But this was a precarious situation, and he heard pain and doubt in Sgäilsheilleache's voice. Whatever had kept him from contact, the dilemma clearly troubled him.

This anmaglâhk was balanced on the edge of a knife. He needed reassurance.

"How do you fare, my son? Are you well?"

I am well, Father. . . . His voice broke off and then returned. *I still travel with Léshil and the humans. Brot'ân'duivé felt they would fare better on our ship with an interpreter, and I have . . . continued my guardianship. But so much has happened . . . now my thoughts turn circles.*

In the mountain peaks, I found A'harhk'nis and Kurhkâge slain. I could neither transport nor burn their bodies. I could only ask that the ancestors reach out and guide their spirits home.

Another pause, and a strange edge filled Sgäilsheilleache's words when he spoke again.

Do you have knowledge of their mission in that region?

Most Aged Father took his own moment of hesitation. He preferred not to lie outright to one of his own.

"Your news will bring mourning to Crijheäiche. My heart is heavy at their loss. Perhaps your brothers tried to pass over the range and veered off. Kurhkâge often coordinated efforts with Urhkarasiférin. They had discussed plans to scout the Ylladon States for potential ways to complicate the Droevinkan civil war. I will speak with Urhkarasiférin, as he may be able to enlighten us."

Yes, Father. Relief filled Sgäilsheilleache's voice. *That would be appreciated.*

"How does your journey fare?"

Magiere has succeeded . . . but a good distance remains before we can deliver her find to its destination.

Most Aged Father stifled frustration.

Osha and I will travel on to Bela. I will contact you then, on the chance that one of our ships might be near. If not, it will take us longer to return home.

"Ah yes, you have taken young Osha as your student. I was surprised, but you often see promise and potential where others do not. How goes his training?"

He has faced harsh times but remains unwavering in duty and purpose. What he lacks in aptitude, he counters with devotion. I believe, in the end, he may find a place of value among us.

Sgäilsheilleache sounded glad to speak of caste matters and the everyday trials of tutelage. It reassured Most Aged Father that he had taken the correct approach.

Sgäilsheilleache was fiercely loyal to the caste, but between Brot'ân'duivé and that half-dead human woman, he followed a misguided path. Someone else needed to step in and relieve him of his burden.

"I am pleased to hear you fare well, my son," Most Aged Father said warmly. "And what is your current location?"

Our location?

"To gauge the days until you reach Bela . . . and if possible, dispatch a military vessel to meet you."

That would be most welcome, Father. We are southwest of the mountains below Droevinka . . . at the inland end of what the humans call the Everfen.

"In the swamplands? That will not be pleasant going. How far in?"

Barely a morning's travel due west. We were fortunate to find an empty dwelling and will pass this one night in better comfort.

Most Aged Father could not extend his awareness beyond his people's forest. But he could feel a sense of place when one of his caste spoke to him through word-wood. In touching such to a living tree, the speaker's voice was altered subtly by what the word-wood pressed against.

"And you call me from a willow tree?" he said. "In the middle of that swamp? Ah, a hardy tree it is."

He played this little game with a few of his oldest or dearest children— to see if Most Aged Father could name the caller's tree.

Yes, Father, you rarely miss. Another pause followed. *It is so good to speak with you again.*

"And with you, my son."

I will contact you again when we reach Bela.

"I look forward to your return . . . and will do what I can to hasten it."

In silence and in shadows, Father.

The connection faded.

Most Aged Father had put Sgäilsheilleache's troubled mind at ease, and this situation would soon be over. He clicked his fingers against his bower, waiting a long time, until another voice threaded through the oak's wood.

Father, I fear that I have little—

"Wait, Hkuan'duv . . . and listen carefully."

The next morning, Leesil had barely stepped outside to stretch when Sgäile called from around the shack's rear.

"Léshil . . . Magiere . . . come!"

Magiere emerged behind Leesil, rubbing her eyes. "What's he yelling about?"

Leesil shrugged and walked off around the dwelling with Magiere on his heels. When he saw Sgäile holding up the edge of a tarp, he stopped. Magiere nearly stumbled over him.

Sgäile crouched beside a narrow longboat pulled up the knoll. It looked sound and in good shape.

"This must be how the old man gained his supplies," Sgäile said, far more cheerful than he'd been in days, "which means there is a settlement somewhere within reach."

Leesil glanced at Magiere.

She raised one eyebrow. "He's in a rare mood."

When Sgäile had returned from his short evening scout the night before, his demeanor had altered drastically. He'd checked on the orb, nosed in on Wynn's cooking, and Leesil could have sworn the dour elf almost smiled at the aroma rising from the blackened iron pot.

But in any case, the boat was a welcome sight. Leesil trotted forward to inspect it.

"Well, a settlement might not be so good," he replied. "Not if Droevinka is turned upside down in a civil war."

"True enough," Sgäile agreed. "But it is an opportunity to renew our supplies . . . and make the rest of the journey more tolerable."

Leesil looked up at him. "Did you find a flask of rum you didn't bother to share?"

"A flask of what?"

"Never mind."

Magiere stood with folded arms, quietly looking over the boat.

Leesil knew her feelings were mixed. She was desperate to reach Miiska but not eager to pass through her old homeland during a civil war—and neither was he, for that matter.

Wynn and Osha came around the side of the shack, erupting in excited chatter at the sight of the longboat. Chap came last, tail in the air. Magiere just rolled her eyes at them. She gazed around the marshes and cattails, moss-laden trees and murky green waters. Frogs croaked and enormous dragonflies sailed past.

"Never thought I'd miss this country," she said, "but after so long in those mountains . . ."

"Oh, we must be mad!" Leesil returned with exaggerated drama.

Magiere half smiled at him as she headed back inside.

They had all passed a pleasant night, and what remained of dinner, from flatbread and honey to chickpeas and smoked-cured beef, was still welcome for breakfast. As they began gathering their gear, Magiere retrieved the orb herself.

Soon, everyone had coats or cloaks with weapons strapped on. All their belongings were piled at the knoll's edge as Leesil helped Sgäile slide the longboat into the murky water.

"Store goods both ends—better balance," Osha suggested.

"I forgot the rest of the flatbread," Wynn said and ran for the shack. "I will be right back."

Sgäile spun the boat slowly, pulling its side in against the knoll. Leesil grabbed the pack Osha held out and tucked it in the bow.

"Magiere . . . ?" Wynn called out.

Leesil looked up.

The little sage stood at the shack's corner just beyond the half-collapsed chicken coop, and then she backed up without turning.

"Sgäile!" Wynn shouted.

Chap bolted toward her as Leesil took off past Magiere. He grabbed Wynn, a freed stiletto already hidden in his hand, and pulled her back. Magiere raced around him to the shack's front, hand on her falchion's hilt. Leesil saw the source of Wynn's warning as Sgäile came into the open.

A man and a woman approached through the shallow water at the knoll's north side. Leesil went rigid at the sight of their gray-green attire.

Anmaglâhk.

Both weatherworn, the woman held a shortbow drawn with an arrow nocked. But Leesil focused on the man.

Cowl down, his hair was almost white and cut short, standing up in un-washed bristles. His amber eyes were flat and emotionless, and even trudging out of shin-deep water, his steps barely left ripples. He didn't look down once, as if he'd never missed a step in his life. His gray-green cloak was tied up, and he held no weapon.

"Sgäile?" Leesil said, tearing his gaze away to glance at his companion.

Sgäile remained silent as the newcomers crested the knoll, stopping ten paces off. Then he nodded once to the older male.

"Greimasg'äh."

"I have a purpose from Most Aged Father," the man said in perfect Belaskian, and his tone was as emotionless as his gaze. "You will turn both the artifact and the dark-haired human over to me."

Magiere ripped the falchion from its sheath, as the female anmaglâhk turned the bow on her.

Hkuan'duv had not seen these humans this close. It was unsettling.

He did not blink when Magiere pulled her weapon.

Somehow, her black hair with the strange red glints, her white face and dark eyes, made him feel tainted. The proximity of the shabby half-blood, the deviant majay-hì, and even the small woman in rolled-up pants did not affect him the same way.

This half-dead thing with the defiant face and unnatural color sparked revulsion.

Most Aged Father had warned Hkuan'duv about her, ordered him to eliminate her.

In spite of his discomfort at her close proximity, he was relieved to finally reveal himself to Sgäilsheilleache and Osha, no longer skulking behind them. He had openly given his purpose, and it superseded all others. This entire matter was over.

Sgäilsheilleache stepped out and raised a shielding arm before Magiere.

"I do not understand," he said in Elvish. "My oath of guardianship is not completed . . . and cannot be broken."

"The word of Father outweighs all," Hkuan'duv answered flatly.

"With respect, Greimasg'äh . . . nothing outweighs my oath."

Hkuan'duv stared at him.

Sgäilsheilleache was openly questioning the will of Most Aged Father and the needs of his caste and people. Hkuan'duv studied him more closely, as Sgäilsheilleache's gaze shifted wildly back and forth.

"We serve!" Hkuan'duv snapped. "It is our place to put the hope and safety of our people above our own concerns. You will turn the artifact over at once!"

Sgäilsheilleache's eyes stopped shifting and locked upon Hkuan'duv.

· · ·

Sgäile's stomach clenched.

In the night, Most Aged Father had spoken to him like a son, asked after Osha, and expressed relief at the prospect of their homecoming. Now Hkuan'duv, one of the revered Greimasg'äh, had arrived by the next dawn— demanding that Sgäile revoke guardianship and turn over the artifact . . . and Magiere?

Chap lunged out before Hkuan'duv with a threatening snap.

The Greimasg'äh held his ground, but Dänvârfij backed a step, visibly uncertain of turning her bow on a majay-hì.

"Wait!" Léshil called, and the dog pulled up short. "What's this about?"

"He will not listen to Sgäile," Wynn whispered. "They want Magiere and the orb."

Sgäile flinched as Magiere took a threatening step forward, trying to push past his arm. He grabbed for her, but she slapped his hand away. Sgäile shook his head sharply, holding up his open hand, and she stopped.

"Relinquish the artifact," Hkuan'duv repeated, and his eyes narrowed. "Or I will take it."

The tightness in Sgäile's stomach released.

Hkuan'duv could not relinquish his accepted purpose. And Sgäile would *not* break his guardianship—to Magiere or her promise to the human sages. He stood opposed to two of his own caste.

He stilled his emotions and shook his head slowly at Hkuan'duv.

"I am my people," he said in clear Belaskian, "their ways and the protection of them . . . and I will not break a sacred oath!"

Leesil couldn't follow anything said in Elvish, other than what Wynn had translated in a whisper—and one Elvish term.

Greimasg'äh.

How had these two anmaglâhk found them on the edge of the Everfen? He quickly calculated who he'd have to take down first. Between a master anmaglâhk and the woman with a loaded bow, it was even odds which was more immediately dangerous.

In truth, only Osha's loyalties struck Leesil as uncertain. The young elf appeared confused and frightened by what was playing out before him.

Sgäile would never break his word, and he'd proven that more than once. But Leesil didn't truly understand the shifting authority in Anmaglâhk hierarchy. Who would Osha follow—his teacher and Sgäile's oath, or a revered master of his caste, sent by Most Aged Father?

Leesil shifted his eyes to the woman with the bow aimed at Magiere. It was clear which one he had to take down first.

Sgäile spoke a final reply, clear for all to hear.

At the quick flick of the female elf's eyes, Leesil snapped his hand forward.

Her bowstring released as the stiletto spun from his hand.

Sgäile shoved Magiere aside as Leesil pulled the catches on his punching blades. The arrow grazed Magiere's arm and flew out into the swamp. The woman crouched swiftly, and the stiletto passed harmlessly above her.

Leesil pulled both winged blades as she came up.

She never paused. By the time he'd readied his blades, she'd notched a second arrow. Chap charged as the woman pulled back the bowstring.

Sgäile slipped into the master anmaglâhk's path, bone knife in hand, and shouted, "Osha, do not interfere!"

"No!" Wynn shouted. "Stop, all of you!"

No one listened to her.

Wynn's late cry accomplished nothing, and her mind raced for a way to stop this confrontation. But Chap did not even slow in his attack.

He snarled savagely, but the female anmaglâhk changed tactics before he closed. She hopped, folding her legs an instant before he snapped at her knee. One foot lashed down and struck the side of his head. Chap's muzzle bit into wet earth as he twisted off his feet.

Wynn flinched, stunned that any elf would strike a majay-hì.

Magiere came back from Sgäile's hard shove as Leesil went at the elven woman with both winged blades.

Osha jerked Wynn back, pinning her to the shack's side. But she saw his stricken profile as he watched Sgäile and the Greimasg'äh in horror.

They slashed and feinted so fast that each time Wynn flinched another strike was already in motion. She counted half a dozen attacks. What would happen if one of them spilled the other's blood?

"Stop them!" she shouted at Osha. "You must do something!"

Magiere rounded the older elf's flank, cocking her falchion in a double grip. Osha blocked Wynn with his body, as if he didn't know what else to do.

The female anmaglâhk ducked Leesil's first strike as Chap hauled himself up.

A stiletto appeared in the woman's hand as she whirled and slashed for Leesil's face.

Magiere's mind went blank as the woman kicked Chap's head and the dog went down hard in the wet sod. Rage welled up inside Magiere.

Daylight burned in her widening sight. Her eyeteeth grew, her fingernails hardened, and then she saw Leesil charge the woman. The last of her wits turned her toward the male elf, hoping Leesil and Chap could deal with the woman.

The master anmaglâhk was the worst threat before Magiere. When reason overrode rage, she went at him, but she caught one last glimpse of Leesil.

The elven woman whirled away from his blade's reach and slipped behind his first slash. The tip of her stiletto sliced down Leesil's cheek to the corner of his mouth.

"No!" Magiere tried to snarl, but the word slurred.

Blood spattered from Leesil's face as he twisted his head aside.

Magiere veered around Sgäile and the Greimasg'äh, charging at the elven woman. Chap struggled up as the female elf came about.

The woman faltered at the sight of Magiere and hissed something in Elvish.

Magiere ground her rear heel in the sod. Chap dodged out of the way as she brought the falchion down with both hands.

The woman vanished, and Magiere's falchion only split wet earth. Her knees buckled suddenly, and her feet ripped from under her.

Magiere slammed down on her back, driving a grunt between her teeth. She saw the female anmaglâhk rise from a low spin, bow tossed aside, and a blade appeared in each hand. Magiere rolled away to one knee, whipping the falchion around to shield herself.

Leesil flashed into view as he leaped over Magiere's head and landed in front of the woman.

Blood trailed down the side of his face, spreading into his mouth. Magiere could see that he wasn't moving fast enough as the woman shifted for his flank.

Panic overran rage as Magiere pushed off to her feet.

Chap rounded Magiere's far side, trying to flank the female anmaglâhk.

In the span of a few blinks, the woman had wounded Leesil and put Magiere down. Leesil faltered as blood ran into the corner of his right eye, and Magiere would not close in time.

Chap's head ached, but he charged low at the woman's legs rather than leap to take her down. She would either dodge or simply slash at him, but he had no other choice to keep her off his companions for a moment.

Leesil tried to strike, and the woman twisted away. He turned his head and seemed to lose sight of her with blood smeared in his eye. The woman wormed inside his guard, driving a stiletto up.

Chap slammed headfirst into her left leg.

Sgäile cleared his mind of all thoughts, even his oath of guardianship. He let silence fill him and clear away distraction.

Hkuan'duv lashed forward with his curved bone knife.

Sgäile spun low, sweeping with his leg, but Hkuan'duv hopped sidewise as Sgäile barely achieved his crouch. Before the Greimasg'äh's feet touched earth, Sgäile was up again, but he did not close on the master among his caste. He stood his ground, maintaining a defensive posture. He knew he could not win on pure skill against Hkuan'duv's experience and skills.

Hkuan'duv charged again, and his lunging foot slid forward along the ground.

Sgäile took a wide step left, folding his trailing leg, and kicked down at Hkuan'duv's face. The Greimasg'äh hit the ground in a straddle and slapped Sgäile's foot aside without pause. Sgäile swung that foot back, trying to pivot on the other one.

He twisted with both stilettos inward, shielding his abdomen. Hkuan'duv simply leaned out in his straddle and hooked Sgäile's grounded foot with his free hand.

Sgäile could not get his other foot down, and the Greimasg'äh's stab came an instant later than anticipated.

As Sgäile began to topple, a stiletto sank to the hilt in the side of his chest.

He choked, not out of pain or even fear of death, but from shame at failure in his oath.

He slashed out with his bone knife just before his back hit the earth. The impact drove the remaining breath from his lungs.

Sgäile felt blood choking him from within and could not breathe. All he could do was roll his head, searching for his opponent. Hkuan'duv had frozen, staring back in startled denial—and his free hand was clamped about his own throat.

Blood welled between his fingers.

Sgäile watched as if through someone else's eyes as Hkuan'duv fell over. The Greimasg'äh crumpled limp upon the wet sod.

Sgäile heard Osha's cry, and then blood welled in his throat, filling his mouth.

The world was already dark when Sgäile closed his eyes.

Wynn shuddered as Osha shouted, *"Jeóin!"*

The female elf froze and half-turned.

"Sgäile!" Leesil yelled.

Magiere charged the elven woman but never reached her target. Chap slammed into the woman's legs and both tumbled down the knoll. They hit the water and thrashed free of each other.

Wynn shoved Osha's arm aside, and ran out in the middle of them, screaming, "No more!"

The elven woman stood shin-deep in the murky water as she saw her fallen comrade. Osha reached Sgäile before Leesil and dropped to his knees beside his teacher. Magiere turned, ready to lunge downslope at the elven woman.

Wynn grabbed Magiere's sword arm with both hands, not knowing what else to do. Before she shouted another word, Osha's voice rose in Elvish.

"Is this the way of our caste?" he cried, pointing to the Greimasg'äh as he gripped Sgäile's still form. "Is this what Most Aged Father would want?"

The elven woman's blank gaze slipped from her fallen companion—but not to Osha. She glared at Wynn—and hatred overran her shock. She turned that hate on Magiere as she backed farther into the water.

"Kill her!" Magiere snapped. "Bring her down, Chap!"

Chap stalked after the woman, paws hammering through murky water.

"No!" Wynn shouted.

"Get off of me," Magiere snarled, and tried to shove Wynn away.

Wynn slipped her arms tightly around Magiere's waist and hung on with all her weight. "Chap, let her go!" she called.

She will tell her kind where we are! I will not allow this!

"They found us—they already know!" Wynn shouted back. "More killing will not change that!"

Chap slowed to a halt but did not turn. His whole body appeared to shake under his rumble.

Wynn saw horror spread over the elven woman's face.

The female anmaglâhk shook her head once in denial or disbelief as she stared off toward the Greimasg'äh's limp form.

"Go!" Osha shouted, and his voice broke in pain. "Tell Father that the Greimasg'äh is dead . . . because he demanded Sgäilsheilleache break his oath of guardianship . . . break with our people's own ways!"

Osha choked out these words as Magiere ceased struggling, and Wynn turned her head to look at the young elf.

Osha and Leesil knelt to either side of Sgäile. But as Leesil took Sgäile's face in his hands, Osha reeled, hanging his head over his teacher.

"Sgäile?" Leesil hissed. "Sgäile . . . look at me!"

Sgäile did not move, and Wynn stopped breathing.

"Tell Most Aged Father . . . ," Osha went on with head bowed, his voice turning steady and low, "tell him how we spilled the blood of our own . . . and see what is left for us because of it!"

He swung his downcast head toward the elven woman but only raised his eyes to her. There was something on his face that Wynn had never seen there before.

Pure and naïve, desperately longing to be Anmaglâhk, Osha had never shown hate to anyone. But that was how he looked at the woman of his own caste and people.

"I will care for them both," he said to her. "Go, and wash your hands of our own blood . . . if you can!"

The woman turned and fled.

Chap made one lunge to follow but pursued no farther. Magiere lurched toward the knoll's shallow slope, dragging Wynn halfway before stopping.

"Let her go," Leesil said. "It's over."

Wynn let go of Magiere and ran to crouch beside Osha.

Sgäile's eyes were closed. Blood seeped from his slack mouth over Leesil's hands. A stiletto was buried to its hilt in the side of Sgäile's chest. Wynn put her hand on him.

"Sgäilsheilleache," she whispered.

Osha's arms wrapped around her, pulling her away. She felt his tight, rigid body against her back as she watched Sgäile's face for any flutter of eyelid.

Leesil jerked the stiletto out, casting it blindly into the marsh. The gash on his face dripped blood off his chin. Like red tears, they struck the dank ground and vanished.

Wynn wished Sgäile would berate her for foolishness—just once more.

Leesil sat numbly within the shack, ignoring Wynn dabbing the blood from his face.

Sgäile was gone. So superstitious and stubborn, with all his blind faith in spirits and codes and customs . . . he was worth so much more than his oath of guardianship.

Leesil's wound wasn't deep, but with nothing to fully close it, Wynn could only wrap his head in a bandage from another shredded shirt. The wound would leave a marked scar, but she said he would suffer no permanent damage.

At least not in flesh, and he cared little about scars.

One more meant nothing, though this one would be prominent compared to the faded marks that Ratboy's fingernails had left on his jaw. By the time Wynn finished, Leesil heard someone hacking at wood outside of the shack.

He pushed Wynn's hands away and stepped out beneath a clouded sky.

Chap sat out front, still watching where the elven woman had run off. The dog turned as Leesil emerged and headed silently toward the shack's rear. Leesil followed and found Magiere and Osha there.

They had slashed away at the underbrush until both were soaked to their elbows and knees from the wet vegetation. In the cleared space's center, near the old man's fresh grave, lay Sgäile's body and that of the other anmaglâhk. The two rested upon a pallet of the firewood taken from behind the shack.

"You don't wish to bury them?" Leesil asked.

Magiere began covering the bodies with brush. Osha halted but didn't look at Leesil.

"We bring body home when can," he said in broken Belaskian. "If cannot, then ashes . . . and if not ashes, then leave behind in hiding. But not bury."

Osha had cleaned their weapons and set these aside. Magiere halted suddenly, looking about with weary eyes.

"Not enough wood," she sighed. "Even green wood might help once the blaze gets going."

She headed for the shack's far rear corner and the willow rising above the structure. Before she could take a swing with the falchion, Osha seized her raised arm.

"No," he whispered and looked into the tree's branches. "Find other . . . not this one."

Magiere nodded, though she frowned in puzzlement and glanced to Leesil.

He had no idea what had spurred Osha's strange request.

"I will find some lamp oil," Wynn said, startling Leesil.

He hadn't even heard her approach, and turned as she headed away around the shack. Leesil pulled one winged blade, trying to find the driest reeds and brush.

When they'd made the best pyre they could, Wynn returned and poured oil from an old jar. She held out a burning brand taken from the stone hearth.

Osha shook his head. "Not yet."

Without knowing what to do, Leesil just stood with Magiere and Wynn as Chap settled beside them. Osha closed his eyes, speaking softly in Elvish.

"Hkuan'duv gan'Träi'éarnneach, Greimasg'äh, d'mé âg ahârean eólhasas'na . . ."

Wynn began whispering in translation.

"Blackened Sea of the Iron Shore clan, Shadow-Gripper, whose parents I do not know . . ."

". . . ag'us Sgäilsheilleache á Oshâgäirea gan'Coilehkrotall . . ."

". . . and Willow's Shade born out of Sudden-Breeze's Laugh of the Lichen Woods clan . . ."

Leesil lifted his eyes and looked to the sagging willow tree as Wynn continued.

"Mothers and Fathers of our people, seek them, siblings of the Anmaglâhk and protectors of your descendants, the an'Cróan—Those of the Blood . . ."

Leesil's mind filled with memories as Wynn went on.

". . . Find their spirits and honor them, as they have honored you in a life of a service."

It seemed so long ago. Leesil had stood with Sgäile in the dark woods as they headed for the burial ground of the ancestors. He'd asked about the strange an'Cróan obsession with seeking a second name in that place. He was only passing time in their brief pause to eat. And when he'd questioned Sgäile, concerning his name supposedly given by these ghosts, Sgäile had never answered completely. But the conversation now stuck in Leesil's mind.

"So you had some other name before Sgäile?" Leesil had asked.

"Sgäilsheilleache," he'd corrected. "It means 'In Willow Shade or Shadow.' "

When Leesil had pressed for more information concerning Sgäile's vision before his ancestors, all the man had said was . . .

"Something far off, far from this land . . . in the shade of a willow."

At the crackle of fire, Leesil lowered his eyes from the willow tree.

Smoke billowed as oil-sparked flames fought to catch on wet wood. Osha tossed the brand he'd used to light them atop the pyre and continued whispering the same words over and over.

"I call, my voice for theirs," Wynn softly translated. "Ancestors . . . take them home."

Leesil tried not to think of . . .

Sgäile's own name-taking vision, hinting of when and where he would die . . .

Or a ghostly image of some other Leesil, standing in the ancestors' clearing, cowled in the gray-green of the Anmaglâhk.

Leesil . . . Léshil . . . whose taken name was Léshiârelaohk—Sorrow-Tear's Champion.

Visions were lies, nothing more. Not fate. Not ever.

. . .

Magiere watched the flames fighting to consume their fuel. They needed to move on, and soon. She didn't trust that the one fleeing anmaglâhk would simply give up. As much as she hated to ask, she did.

"How long?"

Osha breathed deeply and exhaled with an effort. "Until ashes."

Magiere nodded and kept quiet. When Wynn looked at her sadly, she regretted saying anything at all.

Leesil gazed into the flames.

His brow wrinkled. His eyes narrowed and turned hard, like stones baked in the fire's heat. The muscles at the back of his jaw bulged, and she heard the creak of leather. His gloved hand closed in a tight fist and wouldn't release.

Magiere stepped behind him. She slipped her hands under his arms and around his chest, and rested her chin upon his shoulder.

"In Willow's Shade," Leesil murmured. "That's what Sgäile's name meant."

One of his hands closed down hard on Magiere's against his chest— until her fingers ached—but she didn't pull away.

"We won't forget him," she whispered.

CHAPTER TWENTY-FOUR

Days of rowing carried them north through the worst of the Ever-fen. Although Magiere wasn't sure, she believed they were inside Droevinka's southern edge. Chemestúk, her home village, was many leagues away. But for much of the trip, her thoughts drifted to Apudâlsat as well.

Her mother's bones lay unattended in Ubâd's cave near that abandoned village. Coming so close, and not returning to retrieve Magelia's remains, weighed on Magiere. Even more so when she looked at the two small jars Wynn had cleaned for Osha to bring home the ashes of Sgäile and the Greimasg'äh.

But Magiere kept all this to herself.

They couldn't linger in her homeland. Not when they carried the artifact from ancient times hidden away beneath canvas.

They spoke little along the way, especially Osha. His thoughts were on Sgäile, his lost teacher, or *jeóin*. Or was there more behind the new coldness in his eyes?

The marshes grew shallow and small islands denser, and it was time to travel on foot once more.

"Everyone keep your wits," Leesil cautioned, dragging the emptied boat up a bank. "We don't want to run into conscription squads, let alone a military detachment."

Osha looked warily about. "I know some . . . of political here."

Magiere glanced at him. His grammar hadn't improved, but his vocabulary must have expanded, if he grasped the word "political." Living day in and day out among humans had rubbed off on him, that and Wynn's badgering that he keep practicing his Belaskian.

Osha turned to the sage. "Which house . . . is rule now?"

Over the past days, Wynn had interacted the most with Osha, and this began to concern Magiere.

"What?" Wynn said, rising from her own thoughts. "Umm . . . probably the Äntes, headed by Prince Rodêk, but there is no telling who has power now—if anyone. News was scarce, and we have heard nothing since leaving Soladran to cross into the Elven Territories."

Magiere took the lead, watching all around as they moved on. If open fighting was still taking place, most would be farther north between Enêmúsk and Kéonsk—the home of the Äntes house and the capital city.

Growing up as a peasant, she knew little of her homeland's history of internal struggles.

Divided among noble houses, each was headed by its own prince in a bloodline claimed to be noble. Most descended from peoples who'd migrated here or invaded this territory in the distant past. But all acknowledged the rule of the Grand Prince—or claimed to.

Every nine years the conclave of the noble houses chose a new leader. Seemingly more democratic than a monarchy, this practice had also led to civil war more than once. During Magiere's time in Venjètz, and then the elven forests, she'd learned how Most Aged Father had used the Anmaglâhk to seed discord within human nations. Whether the Anmaglâhk had had a hand in this recent war was beyond her guess. She wasn't even certain which houses were now vying for the throne.

"Keep your hood up," she told Osha.

He drew his brows together. His hood was up.

"Most people here have never seen an elf," Wynn explained.

Magiere still regretted letting that female anmaglâhk run off. Osha had assured them that she would go directly to Most Aged Father over the failure of her "purpose." Magiere didn't understand what made him so certain. At this point, she had little choice but to hope he was right.

Dangling moss beards hung from the old trees thickening overhead, blotting out most of the sky. Even in spring, the air was chill and damp. Beneath the scents of wet loam and wild foliage lingered a thin odor of decay and rot. They traveled through this for most of the afternoon.

"Is that a dwelling?" Leesil said, and quickstepped up beside Magiere.

She had already seen it. "And there's another . . . a village, perhaps."

Magiere counted about twenty dwellings, something like a common house, and even what appeared to be a smithy with smoke rising from its scavenged-stone chimney. All of it looked surprisingly well maintained.

At the village's nearer edge, an old woman with two small children turned and saw them. Her expression grew cautious, but not openly frightened, and Magiere guessed that the fighting had not reached this far southeast.

"Hello," Leesil called in a lazy tone, and he smiled with a quick but exaggerated bow.

He could put people at ease no matter what he felt inside. Magiere sometimes wished she possessed such a talent.

The woman nervously half-turned and called into the smithy. "Cameron, you there?"

A barrel-chested bear of a man, with brown sweat-matted hair and a leather apron, stepped out, wiping his hands on a scrap of burlap.

"What now, Mother?"

Then he spotted the strangers. He quickly tossed the burlap back inside and stepped in front of the old woman and children. His gaze settled longest on Chap and Wynn, and his suspicion softened slightly. Osha wore his cloak loose with the hood up over his hair and ears, but he still looked far too tall.

"Can we purchase supper and a night in your common house?" Leesil asked.

At the word "purchase," Magiere set the bundled orb between her feet and swung her pack off to dig inside. It felt strange to take the purse out. How long since coin had been useful to them?

The enormous smith stepped a bit closer, still cautious.

"I am Cameron," he said. "This is Katrina, our village elder." He looked at them in surprise. "You came from the Everfen?"

"We're passing through on our way to Belaski," Leesil answered, side-stepping the question. "Can you offer a roof for the night?"

"We can pay," Magiere added, pouch in hand.

Coin wasn't common here, but was still useful for taxes or purchases in the larger cities. Magiere frowned. They had some silver among their gold, but little of it was in small coin. No pennies or groats, and even shils were a bit flashy in these backwoods.

"Come with me," Cameron said and turned down the path.

As they followed, Magiere noticed Osha hanging back, and she realized this was his first time in a human settlement. Hopefully Wynn would keep an eye on him, but the large smithy didn't seem to give much notice. With the sage's knack for languages, she'd picked up some Droevinkan, but Osha spoke none at all.

Katrina reached the door first and opened it, shooing off more children who'd gathered at the sight of strangers—most especially to see the large silver-gray dog.

"Off with you all. Go on home!" she said, then stepped inside, waving for the guests to follow. "Not many pass this way, but I can find some oatcakes and goat cheese."

"That would be fine," Magiere answered. "Thank you."

Chap trotted around, sniffing the floor. The place was dry, and a decent mud and stone hearth rested in the back wall. Three rough-cut tables accompanied by stools filled the room.

"We heard talk of fighting," Wynn blurted out. "Is it safe to pass through?"

Abrupt as this was, Magiere watched Cameron, eager for his answer.

"No fighting here," the smithy said in his baritone voice. "But we hear things . . . it is bad north of here, near the capital . . . and has been for a long while."

"What have you heard?" Magiere asked.

"Bits and pieces, whenever our own go elsewhere for trade. The Väränj accused the Äntes of murdering one of their barons. They demanded restitution, as well as the surrender of those involved. Prince Rodêk denied knowledge of it. Rumors claim his brother accused the Väränj of carrying out the deed themselves. Fighting broke out inside the walls of Kéonsk, the capital. After that, we all kept out of the way. We heard hundreds died the first day, not all of them soldiers. The last I heard, the Väränj had laid siege to Enêmúsk."

"What about Chemestúk?" Magiere asked.

Cameron frowned. "I think I've heard of it. To the north, across the Vudrask River, yes? I've never traveled that far. No one here has."

"I have family there," Magiere said, fighting to remain calm and steady. "Have you heard anything at all?"

The big smith shook his head. "If it's where I think, then it's well within war's reach. Anyone with wits would've run long ago or ended up dead . . . or conscripted."

Magiere's first instinct was to bolt and keep running, to reach the capital and grab any barge or boat headed for her village. Anything, at any cost, to make certain that Aunt Bieja had gotten out alive.

Leesil grabbed her hand. When she turned, her gaze landed on Wynn. The little sage leaned tiredly against Osha's side.

"What about a safe route?" Leesil asked. "We just need to get through to Belaski."

"Head west," Cameron counseled. "Don't veer north for at least six days. The forest is thick and the roads are bad, but I doubt any house will have soldiers that far out. It's mostly minor houses out there, and they can't afford to be dragged in between the major princes."

Magiere breathed deeply. Common sense quelled some of her fear. Aunt Bieja could be in Miiska already, long gone in the past season—Magiere had to believe that.

Osha reached his arm around Wynn.

Magiere did not begrudge either of them a companion's comfort. Far from it, but she worried about something Brot'an had once told her. She had to speak with Wynn at the first opportunity.

"I'll go find that cheese for you," Katrina said and slipped out.

Magiere turned back to Cameron. "Our thanks, and I hate to ask, but might you have a packhorse or mule we can purchase?"

Beasts of burden were dear in this land, but Cameron nodded.

"There's an old horse I'd planned to take to the next market fair. Long past his prime, but he'll do all right . . . even as far as Belaski. Might as well sell him to you as anyone else."

Magiere handed Leesil the pouch. "Would you take Chap and Osha to go see about the horse? Wynn and I will settle our gear."

Leesil raised one eyebrow at her. For one thing, she had just handed him all their money, relinquishing her tightfisted ways to his openhanded ones. And two, she'd suggested he take Osha out into the village.

But in true Leesil fashion, he waved Osha along and then smiled at Cameron. "Lead the way."

The last thing Magiere wanted was to speak to Wynn alone about matters of the heart. But she had to.

. . .

Wynn was confused when Magiere sent Osha off with Leesil and Chap, but not curious enough to ask why. She was too tired—in body, mind, and spirit.

Since Sgäile's death, she had been wrung out with exhaustion every day beneath the canopy of the Droevinkan forest and its perpetual false dusk. Now all she could do was try to comfort Osha, but the pain of effort left her weary. She did not even want bread and cheese, only sleep.

"Wynn . . . ," Magiere began, then faltered.

"What is it?" Wynn asked.

Magiere pulled out two stools at the nearest table. "Sit with me a while."

She ran a hand through her black hair as Wynn settled across from her. Twice Magiere opened her mouth then closed it again, dark eyes blinking rapidly as if she had no idea how to begin.

"Are you in love with Osha?" she asked suddenly.

Wynn flushed in embarrassed shock and sputtered, unable to get a word out.

"It's important," Magiere said, and her voice grew firm. "Do you remember the night in Crijheäiche . . . when Brot'an tossed you and Chap out of the tree dwelling, so he could speak privately with me?"

Wynn remembered quite clearly.

"He told me something about . . . about his people," Magiere added, squirming upon the stool. "When they choose a mate, it is for life. If they lose that mate, they suffer. Some don't recover—ever—and some even . . . it's part of what they are. They are different from us . . . humans."

Wynn was dumbfounded, not even sure what Magiere was trying to say. Then she remembered Osha's speaking of his father, who had died young for an elf. His mother had not risen from her grief—and had not lived her full span.

Wynn looked wide-eyed at Magiere. "What are you saying?"

"Leesil is everything to me," Magiere went on. "I'm sometimes afraid, thinking of what I've done to him, and that he'd suffer if anything happened to me—but I'll never leave him. I want to see his face every day of my life and just before I close my eyes each night. Can you say the same about Osha?"

Wynn swallowed and closed her eyes, finally catching Magiere's meaning.

She envisioned Osha's kind, long face. Then she thought of the days ahead, studying what texts she had saved from the castle's library.

Osha's face changed to a pale and narrow one, with red-brown hair and eyes almost colorless. Chane's image faded as Wynn opened her eyes.

"I cannot," she finally whispered.

Magiere reached across the table, gently gripping Wynn's small hand.

"Then don't give him false hopes. I know you'd never hurt anyone on purpose, but you could harm him just the same . . . and far worse than you'd care to imagine."

Magiere took a long breath, as if what she'd said cost more effort than trudging through the Everfen. She released Wynn's hand and stood up.

"Let's get our beds ready."

Wynn's legs trembled as she got up. "Magiere?"

"Yes?"

"Thank you."

A day across the western Droevinkan border, well inside Belaski, Chap barked as he saw a good-sized town ahead. Following Cameron's advice, they had kept due west without incident and only turned northwest after six days. It took longer to work their way into familiar territory.

They had all been surprised to find Belaskian cavalry patrolling the border—and then Chap realized he should have expected such with Droevinka in a state of civil war. But he and his companions passed through easily after answering a few questions about their destination.

Now, finally, they were nearing their home. If they maintained their direction along Belaski's inland roads, they could gain the coast soon enough, perhaps six or seven days in good weather.

He looked back at his companions, leading the old packhorse Wynn had named Aspen. Its coat was a mix of grays and browns, and Leesil had lashed the covered orb and Wynn's bundles of texts onto the animal.

Everyone was much improved physically, and Chap's relief grew by the day. Since leaving Droevinkan territory, they had been blessed by regular stays in villages and better food.

Wynn stumbled, eyes wide, and came running past him. "A town . . . an actual town!"

"Maybe we can buy horses," Magiere suggested. "And ride the rest of the way."

"Not for all the dead deities," Leesil grouched. "After all this, I'm not risking my neck on some half-mad bag of bones—not again."

"Fine, we'll buy a wagon," Magiere snapped back, "since horses frighten you so much."

Leesil scoffed. "You'd never part with that much coin . . . not before you got us thrown out of the town with your endless haggling and insults."

Magiere slowed, and her voice dropped to grating growl. "What did you say?"

Osha listened with startled interest, plainly baffled at this couple who never tired of their little battles.

Chap shook his head and scurried after Wynn.

Would Magiere never learn when Leesil was baiting her, or that making her angry gave him a thrill? But Leesil only prodded Magiere when he was happy—and he was happy to be going home. And Magiere only squabbled with him this way when she felt safe, for even a moment.

And they both believed they would stay within the Sea Lion Tavern, finally returning to the life they wanted.

Chap wanted to believe it as well.

But he could not—not since the wide cavern and chasm, when Magiere had mistakenly opened the orb. He had spent the passing days since watching over his shoulder.

They entered a bustling little town, and few townsfolk even looked their way. That in itself was another relief. People passed through the towns and cities of peaceful Belaski every day, and no one gave them much notice.

"I need to find a courier," Wynn said. "Or at least some place where the caravans stop. I want to send word to Domin Tilswith now, and not wait until we reach Miiska."

"Chap, go with her," Leesil said. "Meet us at that stable up the way. One of us will find an inn before you get back."

He grabbed Magiere's waist.

"Almost home," she said tiredly, and Leesil tucked his head in close to her.

Chap did not hear what was said, but Magiere turned a scowl on Leesil.

"Not until you've had a bath," she growled.

Leesil swatted her on the rump and took off before she snatched hold of him.

Wynn looked to Osha. He nodded to her, and she headed off.

Chap followed Wynn, wishing at heart that they could simply go home and stay there.

CHAPTER TWENTY-FIVE

Magiere fell silent as she walked into Miiska.

She quickened her pace, not wanting to be seen by anyone they knew just yet, not until they reached the Sea Lion Tavern. They'd arrived from the south, so the tavern was just ahead beyond the trees. All she wanted was to see her home. By the time she reached the sloping road's bottom, and stepped from the forest into the edge of town, Leesil had to jog to catch up with her. The others were left behind, but Chap bolted headlong around Magiere, racing toward the dockside of Miiska.

And then she saw it.

Leesil's hand-painted sign hung above the narrow door, and the whole place looked so much the same, as if she'd been away but a few days.

The Sea Lion—and Chap was turning in pinwheels by the time Magiere squeezed the latch and shoved the front door inward.

Everything inside still looked brand new, from the polished bar to the two-sided hearth in the common room's center. Rashed's sword hung above the hearth on the room's bar side, marking the tavern's rebirth from ashes. Beyond the bar's far end, narrow stairs climbed to the second floor and bedrooms.

Leesil pushed around Magiere, casting his hungry eyes over everything. At first he couldn't speak any more than could Magiere. Then he sighed as his gaze fixed on the corner beneath the front windows.

"My Faro table!" he whispered.

Chap squeezed between their legs and made a hurried circuit around the hearth.

"Caleb, you deaf old hog!"

Magiere's throat tightened. The loud, gruff woman's voice came from behind the kitchen's curtained doorway.

"How many damn times have I told you—don't put onions in the soup when Karlin is coming! You know he can't abide the taste!"

"I already put his serving aside," came an answering shout from up the stairs. "Leave me be, woman!"

A stout form in an old purple dress and stained apron burst through the whipping kitchen curtain. She turned, heading for the stairs like an irate captain hot after an errant soldier. But she halted halfway and turned quickly about. She almost dropped the long wooden spoon she wielded as shock washed away the ire on her round, wrinkled face.

"Aunt Bieja," Magiere whispered.

Bieja barreled along the bar and nearly cracked Magiere's ribs in a fierce embrace.

"My girl . . . my girl!"

Her aunt's hair smelled musky, and it took all Magiere's effort not to weep in overwhelming relief. Bieja had come, just as Leesil had insisted she would.

Magiere's aunt released her, and with tears on her gruff face, she spotted Leesil. Before he could duck, she grabbed him as well.

"Ow," he grunted. "Go easy! It's good to see you, too."

Bieja stepped back, wiping the back of her hand across her eyes, as Chap snuck out between table and chair legs.

"Ah, so the troublemaker is still with you." Then she noticed Wynn and Osha in the doorway.

Magiere reached back, pulling Wynn in. "Auntie, these are friends. This is Wynn and that's Osha."

Bieja crossed her arms, taking stock of the tall, hooded elf.

"Osha," Leesil mumbled, "better keep your ears covered."

Beija whacked him in the gut with her spoon. "Shut that mouth, imp."

Then a commotion began on the stairway. "Leesil!"

Little Rose nearly flew down the stairs.

Caleb descended quickly behind the girl, and his eyes widened at the newcomers. "Mistress Magiere?"

Rose ran straight for Leesil and jumped at him. Leesil hooked her underarms and lifted her with an exaggerated grunt.

"You're getting heavy!"

In truth, Rose had grown, and her muslin dress looked a bit small. Her auburn hair was thick and long—she was becoming quite pretty. Aside from her aunt's presence, this was the first mark of just how long Magiere had been gone. Little Rose ran her small fingers down the closed wound along Leesil's cheek.

"What happened to your face?"

"Fierce battles," he said in a haughty tone and hefted her higher. "I'll tell you stories at dinner."

"No, you won't!" Magiere warned.

"Just the suitable ones," he corrected.

Caleb joined them, his back slightly bent, and he grasped Magiere's hand. "Welcome home, Mistress."

She gripped his hand with another breath of relief at that one word—*home*.

"Domin Tilswith?" Wynn blurted out in surprise.

She pushed past everyone as Magiere spotted someone else descending the stairs. He was slight-built and silver-haired, and his old gray robes sagged on him a bit.

Domin Tilswith stepped into the common room with a smirkish grin. His green eyes sparked at the sight of his apprentice.

"I received message . . . came right away."

Wynn hurried to meet him, but they did not embrace. They only clasped hands with mutual smiles.

Osha still hung in the doorway with the two jars of ashes in his arms. He looked about in complete loss. A pang of guilt hit Magiere for ignoring him, but Aunt Bieja closed on the young elf first.

"Oh, I don't know where my girl keeps finding your kind," she said and grabbed him roughly by the arm. "You best come have supper. No one that tall should be so skinny."

Even an anmaglâhk stood little chance against the will of Aunt Bieja. Osha forgot to duck, and his forehead smacked the top of the door frame.

Magiere clasped the back of Leesil's head, pulling his face close, little Rose still in his arms. She settled her forehead against his and whispered.

"We're home."

Near midnight, Leesil finally succeeded in sending Bieja, Caleb, and Rose off to bed. Osha settled the jars of ashes atop the hearth.

Leesil didn't want the homecoming celebration to end, but Domin Tils-with had been "smiling" patiently all evening. The old master sage awaited a more serious discussion, particularly when Leesil returned with Magiere from unloading their packhorse, and Wynn had returned from taking Aspen to the local stable.

They gathered in the kitchen around the canvas bundle on the prep table, and Magiere unwrapped the orb.

Leesil suddenly wondered where any of them would even begin to tell their story.

Chap appeared to study Tilswith's face, which grew dour and puzzled as the old man leaned over the artifact.

"This what Welstiel sought . . . where you find?"

"Do you know what it is?" Magiere asked bluntly.

"Where you find?" the domin repeated.

The old man's Belaskian hadn't improved any more than Osha's had, perhaps less. Magiere, Leesil, and Wynn in turn each told him varied parts of their journey. Osha only listened, and Chap continued watching Domin Tilswith.

Leesil wondered suspiciously at the dog's fixed attention. Hopefully Chap wasn't messing about in the old man's head.

Tilswith's mouth opened slightly at Magiere's mention of Li'kän, of the circlet that had removed the spike, and of water droplets rushing madly toward the orb to vanish in its searing light. But Magiere never mentioned their differing impressions of the presence that had risen in the cavern.

"Eô, âg-léak!" Domin Tilswith sputtered in his own guttural tongue. "Wynn, what we done?"

Wynn's olive face flooded with alarm. "Do you know what it is? Where it came from?"

He shook his head, seeming suddenly older. "No. . . . But is more than simple tool, even for it power. The place found . . . so guard and protect it was. And secret so long. May . . . be . . . we should left it there."

Leesil flushed cold with disbelief. "After all we've been through? Sgäile died trying to help us bring this back! And you think we should've left it?"

Domin Tilswith's forehead wrinkled. "I did not understand—"

"You cannot safeguard this?" Osha asked abruptly.

Wynn turned her startled gaze to his face.

Leesil followed her and found the young elf watching the domin as carefully as Chap was.

"Osha, it is not that . . . ," Wynn began. "I am sure the domin meant—"

"I believed . . . your sages offer safeguard," Osha cut in. "I complete my teacher's guardianship because you said sages give . . ."

He struggled a moment and finished in Elvish.

Wynn looked at Leesil. "Security. He thought the sages could provide security, and truly they can—"

"Not from Anmaglâhk," Osha said flatly.

"What?" Leesil asked.

"Most Aged Father wishes much for this thing," Osha continued. "So much, he set caste brother against brother. He will not stop."

"We let that woman back in the swamps get away!" Leesil nearly shouted. "You said she wasn't a danger anymore."

"Dänvârfij make no difference!" Osha snapped back. "Her life, her death, no difference. Most Aged Father send others. Two moons, not more, and he will send my caste."

Osha turned equal anger on Domin Tilswith.

"Sages cannot give . . . security from Anmaglâhk. They scholars, not guardians. They die and my caste take the orb."

Leesil looked to Magiere for any support.

She stood leaning with her hands braced upon the kitchen table. Her eyes went dark, and Leesil felt as if the floor had shifted suddenly under his feet.

Magiere whirled away for the back door. She slapped it open with her palm, stormed out, and the door swung shut behind her. Leesil rushed after her.

When he stepped out, she was gone. He peered along the back of the tavern and adjacent buildings, and jogged to the tavern's corner, looking about, and he still couldn't spot her. When he turned back, he caught a glimpse of white in the forested neck of land behind the tavern that shot outward into the sea.

Magiere stood there, the sleeves of her white shirt rustling in the sharp breeze.

Fresh salt air blew against Leesil's face as he wove through the birches and evergreens.

Magiere just stared out to sea with one hand over her mouth, as if too overwhelmed to breathe. She took it away as she glanced at him, and he ached inside under her lost eyes.

"What are we going to do?" she whispered. "Tilswith would take it if we asked him . . . but that's like tossing fresh meat into a sheep's pen to draw in the wolves."

Leesil wanted no more of this. They'd been asked too much already, and he couldn't—wouldn't—struggle for an answer right now. He slipped his arm around Magiere, gripping her shoulder, and tucked his head next to hers until their cheeks met.

"Not now," he said. "We just got home . . . I don't want to talk about orbs or sages or Anmaglâhk. I don't want to think about any of this!"

When he lifted his head, that lost look faded from Magiere's eyes. She glared at him, her face filled with that familiar accusation for whenever he took refuge in denial.

"What *do* you want to talk about?" she asked.

He lifted his hand to her cheek, fingers combing up into her black hair.

"Getting married."

Five days later, and loaded with trepidation, Leesil followed Karlin Boigiesque to the newly constructed dockside warehouse.

"Karlin . . . Magiere thinks it's a fine idea," he grumbled, "but it's not what I had in mind."

"It's the only building in town that's large enough," Karlin insisted. "You just wait, lad. You'll see."

The stout, balding baker with kind eyes was their closest friend in Miiska, and now chairman of the town council. The previous summer, Leesil had burned the town's main warehouse, trying to cover his heels as he and Brenden raced to save Magiere and escape a trio of vampires. Later, he and Magiere had earned enough coin in Bela for its reconstruction.

Made of stout pine, from the outside it was impressive—for a warehouse. But it was hardly where Leesil had expected to be married. Magiere seemed satisfied with the idea, claiming they'd come full circle. But at least the celebration afterward would take place in the Sea Lion.

"Go on, take a peek," Karlin said, and slid open one huge dockside door.

"We had it cleared yesterday. Aria, Geoffry, and Darien's mother worked on the rest all morning."

Leesil stepped around the baker and his jaw dropped. "Ah, dead deities in seven hells!"

"Watch your tongue," Karlin admonished with a chuckle. "This is now a sacred place."

The high bay doors used for loading the lofts sat open, and afternoon light streamed in wide shafts to the floor. All the crates had been removed and only barrels lined the walls, but garlands and bushels of wild blossoms and spring roses were carefully woven around them and up the walls.

Clean muslin sheets hung at the front in a half-moon backdrop. To either side of this stood a linen-draped barrel supporting a decorated white vase filled with roses. Dead center between them, before the backdrop, stood a small linen-draped table. Upon it waited three white candles, an incense stick and brazier, and a long, neatly coiled strip of white silk ribbon.

"That's where you'll stand for the ceremony," Karlin said and dropped a thick hand on Leesil's shoulder. "Guests start arriving soon . . . too late to run now, lad."

Leesil breathed the perfume from hundreds of flowers caught in the variegated light spilling into the wide space. He couldn't wait for Magiere to join him.

Magiere hid in a back room of the warehouse. She'd relented to Aunt Bieja's insistence that it be turned into a dressing area, but now doubted her decision.

Between Aria and Bieja rushing in and out with hot irons to curl her hair, she felt . . . exposed. But the dressing ordeal finally ended, and Aria and Bieja went off on some last-minute task. Magiere stepped in front of the large oak-framed mirror in a welcome moment of solitude.

She hardly recognized her own reflection.

Magiere possessed only one gown—of dark blue—which her mother had worn and left to her. It fit her well and offset her pale complexion. Before donning it, she had bathed and washed her hair; and she'd allowed her female "attendants" to not only curl it but also weave in bits of white lilac.

"Beautiful!" someone proclaimed from the back door.

Magiere tensed as if trapped, then turned to find Wynn staring at her with a soft smile.

"I don't know," she said, scowling at herself in the mirror. "I look . . . strange."

"Well, you cannot be married in a hauberk and sword."

"Why not?"

"Because Leesil will swoon when he sees you," Wynn answered and stepped in.

It was Magiere's turn to stare, for the little sage had been transformed as well. Wynn had agreed to stand as Magiere's second during the ceremony.

Her wispy brown hair had been pinned up with curling tendrils framing her small face. A light green dress blended well with her olive complexion, reminding Magiere of fragile creatures in children's tales about to take flight on dragonflies' wings.

"Where did you find the dress?" Magiere asked, suddenly happy for the first time since being hauled into this back room.

"Your aunt bought it for me," Wynn said with some embarrassment. "There was no time to have anything made and it was the only finished one we could find that fit. Is the color all right?"

"It's fine." Magiere nodded.

They stood together before the mirror, Magiere tall and pale with dark hair and blue gown, and Wynn so small and olive in her light green.

"Like fine ladies going off to a noble ball," Wynn whispered. "So long as no one saw us a few weeks past, crusted in snow and starving for anything besides dried fish."

The mention of dried fish brought Sgäile to Magiere's thoughts. And Wynn's as well, judging by the way her smile quickly faded.

"Is Osha ready?" Magiere asked, as Leesil had chosen him to act as second.

"Yes"—Wynn let out an exasperated sigh—"but he would only wear his own clothes. So I had them washed, and brushed out his cloak. . . . He looks fine. The guests are gathered inside, and Leesil is waiting to walk you in. We should go."

Magiere had wanted this—the whole ceremony—to celebrate joining with Leesil. Now that it was upon her, she wondered if something more private might have been better. She took several quick breaths.

"Just keep your eyes on Leesil," Wynn said, "and you will be fine."

They walked out and around the warehouse's front to find Leesil waiting with Osha and Chap.

Wynn's advice was sound, and Magiere forgot everything else the moment Leesil turned, looked at her, and his mouth fell open. She'd never been vain, but his expression was worth all the primping.

"M . . . Magiere?" he stammered.

"Close your mouth," she said, "before you swallow a mosquito."

He made a handsome sight himself. Aunt Bieja had managed to sew him a loose white shirt, just in time, that he wore tucked into black breeches. He'd polished his boots and tied his white-blond hair back at the nape of his neck.

Magiere took his arm. "Ready?"

He nodded, still looking into her eyes.

Osha fidgeted awkwardly. Wynn hurried over to him, and the young elf looked her up and down as if he'd never seen her before.

"See how Magiere has Leesil's arm? They will walk in first. We wait and then follow with Chap."

Chap whined with ears perked. Wynn had completely brushed out his coat the night before, ignoring his growls. She hooked her arm into Osha's, having to reach up a bit.

Magiere turned into the warehouse with Leesil, and her breath caught at the hundreds of flowers in the streaming light. She kept her poise and moved steadily forward on Leesil's arm.

Domin Tilswith waited before the muslin backing in his long gray robes. A thin trail of smoke drifted up from an incense stick in the brazier. Magiere had no idea their friends had gone to so much trouble.

The cavernous room was filled to the walls with people.

But a clear path was left for her and Leesil, and faces blurred by as she walked.

Karlin and the constable, Darien Tomik, stood with young Geoffry and Aria. Even Loni, the elven owner of the Velvet Rose Inn, watched with interest. So many had come to share this day.

Magiere and Leesil came together before Domin Tilswith. Chap settled right behind them, and Wynn and Osha, as their seconds, stepped off to each side. Domin Tilswith's voice carried in accented Belaskian, but he never missed a word, as if he had studied every one most carefully.

"We come together to celebrate the joining of Magiere and Leesil in a life bond."

Magiere's heart began to pound as he leaned over and picked up the silk ribbon.

"Hold out your hands," he instructed.

He lightly tied Leesil's left hand to Magiere's right. "Magiere, do you swear to love Leesil, to stand with him, honor his heart, and care for him above all others for as long as you live?"

Magiere looked at Leesil and answered, "I swear."

"Leesil, do you swear to love Magiere, to stand with her, honor her heart, and care for her above all others for as long as you live?"

Leesil held her eyes with his. "I swear."

Domin Tilswith removed the ribbon and took up the incense. Blowing its tip to a coal, he lit the two outside candles, their wicks lightly dipped in clear oil.

Magiere picked up one candle and Leesil the other, and together they lit the center candle. They blew out the candles they held and set them aside.

"Two lights are now one," Domin Tilswith proclaimed. He held up the single candle. "Leesil and Magiere are one."

The warehouse filled with cheers.

Wynn kept stumbling sideways every time she took a step. Maybe the common room had not been built on level ground.

The celebration in the Sea Lion Tavern had broken into . . . well, a celebration. She had never taken part in anything like this.

Bieja had outdone herself with the feast, and now poured wine straight from a cask into large mugs and tankards, passing them around like water. Domin Tilswith had finished two already, and even Osha held a mug.

Wynn had tasted wine before, on special occasions and in small amounts, but she most certainly was not drunk. Besides her, Leesil was the only one sober, as he sipped on spiced tea.

The common room had been half-cleared of tables and chairs, and Bieja had abandoned the bar to dance with Karlin. The pair dominated the floor with their girth and energy, until Leesil pulled Magiere out to join them. After that, Wynn tried to teach Osha a few steps, but she did not know much about dancing herself. She stumbled into a chair, nearly taking him with her. The floor was definitely uneven. Yes, that was the reason.

The Sea Lion was packed with people, who all seemed affectionate with Leesil and Magiere, but Wynn hardly knew anyone. She noticed Osha's wary glances at the only other elf present, but oddly, these two avoided each other.

"Magiere said his name is Loni," Wynn shouted to Osha over the din.

"He is not an'Cróan," Osha answered.

Loni's hair was light brown, and his eyes were amber brown. He was not as tall as Osha, but his facial structure, slanted eyes, and oblong pointed ears clearly marked him as fully elven. He seemed just as determined to ignore Osha. But his differences from the an'Cróan left Wynn wondering.

She had heard Leesil and Magiere speak of Loni once or twice, but in seeing him for the first time, Wynn thought he looked much more like the elves from her own continent. So what was one of them doing here, so far from home?

"At least people here are so accustomed to him that they do not find you strange," she said to Osha.

Or she thought she had said it. Some of the words did not sound right, but that was because of all the noise. Before she could repeat herself, she noticed the room's awful tilt and felt as though the chair beneath her might fall over.

It was too hot in here.

Wynn had tried not to dwell on the conversation in the kitchen with Domin Tilswith, especially the part after Leesil ran out after Magiere. She had promised herself to wait until after the wedding before telling Magiere or Leesil the domin's unsettling news.

Today was about them, their day of joy, and she would not spoil it for anything.

"Let us go outside," Osha said. "It is too warm."

Thank goodness someone else noticed, thought Wynn, and she followed as he waded through the crowd for the front door.

The night outside was better—cooler. Rather than stand about before the tavern windows, they walked as far as the nearby stables. Osha half-crouched, leaning back against the stable's outer door, and Wynn stood before him, watching him weave a little before her eyes.

"I am . . . dizzy," he said and wiped his brow.

He had fallen back into Elvish. Obviously Osha could not hold his wine. Wynn giggled before she could stop herself.

"I fear the Anmaglâhk would not approve of a single thing you did today."

His slanted eyes grew serious. "No, they would not, and that thought is sad."

Wynn lost her own humor.

"Today was good," Osha went on, "and humans are nothing like I was taught. Even Sgäilsheilleache, who spent so much time in these lands, knew little of them. . . . Then you came." He glanced away. "Sgäilsheilleache should have stood with Léshil today—not me."

"No, Osha," Wynn said. "Leesil mourns Sgäile, but he was glad to have you with him."

He looked at her, his face intense—lonely—and hungry in moonlight.

Wynn teetered so much she stumbled. She grabbed the stable door near his shoulder. With his face so near hers, Wynn's muddled head flushed with a new heat.

She wanted to feel what Magiere and Leesil had, to know that closeness with someone she cared for. Wynn realized, standing there, that she could make Osha fall in love with her. Just kiss him on those soft . . . thin . . . tan lips.

She shoved off the stable door, growing too warm again.

With all they had been through together, she loved Osha—but was she *in love* with him? Their paths would soon diverge, and perhaps that was best. She took another step back.

Osha studied her until she could not bear it anymore.

"We should go back inside," she said. "Magiere will wonder what became of us."

His mouth tightened in puzzlement, or was it disappointment?

He stood up. "Yes, we go back now."

Chap lay by the hearth watching everyone around him drink, dance, and laugh. More than once he had quickly scooted aside before someone stepped on his tail.

Wynn slipped in the front door, flushed and staggering as she looked about.

When she spotted him, she wove among the crowd and dropped a bit too hard beside him. She buried fingers in his fur, rubbing his back, and it felt good. He wondered why she was no longer joining in the festivities.

Osha came through the front door.

He scanned the room and spotted Wynn. Before he could make his way over, Aunt Bieja hauled him off to where Karlin had collapsed into a chair. Osha seemed happy enough, or perhaps even relieved to sit with them.

That young elf will never be Anmaglâhk, Chap projected.

"I hope not," Wynn mumbled, still rubbing his back. "Though he wants it so much. Osha knows more about humans than most of his caste. Perhaps that will make a difference."

She sounded so sad—and drunk—that Chap raised his head. *What is wrong?*

"You, Magiere, and Leesil . . . cannot stay here . . . long, will you?"

He sighed through his nose, settling his head on his paws once more.

Tonight is for them, but tomorrow . . . no, we cannot stay. We must leave and get as far from Most Aged Father's reach as we can. Even that will only be a delay.

Wynn took her hand away.

"Domin Tilswith was . . . overwhelmed by the texts we brought back. Translation at our barracks in Bela is not possible. We do not have the reference materials needed—and he cannot leave. There is still too much to be done in Bela in starting that little new branch of our guild."

Her silence was too long and too easy to read on her sad face.

You are going home . . . taking your find to Malourné, and the guild's founding branch.

Wynn did not seem surprised that he knew. "Someone must take the texts to them . . . to those more experienced in translation. Domin Tilswith thinks this best, as I will be needed for what I learned on our travels."

Chap shifted closer to her. In truth, he had known this day would come. And now he worried again for Wynn's safety . . . from those who might seek the texts to learn more of the orb Magiere and Leesil bore—and from his own kin.

You are part of this now—and no safer than any of us. It is best that you leave this land as well.

"What am I to do without you?" she whispered.

Tears formed in her bleary brown eyes. But Chap knew she would be safest in one of her guild's communities, though not safe enough.

Once you arrive, stay where many are around you. My kin do not want to be known by mortals. They will shy from manifesting where they might be noticed.

"You know something dark is coming," she said. "Is it your kin . . . from what you sensed in the cavern? Are they behind all of this?"

He had no answer.

No . . . something more, beyond them. And I have made other . . . arrangements, which I hope will come through, in the interest of your well-being.

He cared for Leesil and Magiere—they were his charges and deeply woven into the path he followed. But Wynn was the only one to whom he could "talk." Before her, he had never understood how much such a companion could mean.

Chap laid his head in her lap.

Almost instantly, Wynn flopped heavily atop him. Even over the ruckus, Chap could hear her snore.

Long past midnight, Leesil lay in the warmth of their upstairs bedroom, holding Magiere against his chest.

"A good day," he whispered.

"The best," she agreed. "Right before the ceremony, I panicked a little. But everything was perfect. I'm glad we waited to come home for this."

He tightened his hold on her. He didn't want to say more, but it finally slipped out.

"You know we can't stay."

She was quiet for a moment. "I know. We can't give the orb to the sages. We can't risk Most Aged Father's anmaglâhk coming for it . . . here or in Bela."

"I've thought about that, too," Leesil answered.

Magiere pulled away and propped up on one elbow. The last remnants of white lilacs still clung in her black hair.

"So now what? I'm not giving up on our life here."

Leesil shook his head. "Me either. I overheard Tilswith talk about getting Wynn's texts to his guild's home, but he also mentioned plans for the new guild branch in Bela. I don't think he's going to deliver the texts himself."

"You think he's sending Wynn back?"

Leesil shrugged. "We'll find out in the morning, but getting the orb off this continent would go a long way to masking our trail, wherever we end up."

"We'll have to catch a ship out of Bela," Magiere added with a sigh.

Leesil nearly groaned at the notion of more seafaring. "I've been thinking a lot about the idea of home lately."

"And?"

"Home is just wherever you are."

Magiere rose on her hands and knees, like some pale predator next to him, and looked him right in the eyes.

"No, it's right here . . . where we want it!" She leaned so close that Leesil felt her breath on his mouth. "But it'll have to wait . . . again."

Magiere pressed her mouth hard over his.

Nine days later, Wynn stood beside Osha on the south end of Bela's vast docks, and they watched the variety of ships throughout the harbor. They had all taken a schooner from Miiska to the king's city, but Magiere, Leesil, and Chap had stayed behind at their inn.

Osha was going home, but not by any of the ships in the bay.

Wynn had asked few questions, and he only told her what he'd heard from Sgäile. Most Aged Father would have the nearest elven ship come, and Sgäile and Osha were to watch for it.

Far out off the harbor's northern point, the glint of silken sails sprouted high above the waters. It was larger than any elven ship Wynn had ever seen, especially the one that had carried her south and died for it.

Somewhere out near the woods of the northern point, a skiff and crew would be waiting for Osha.

Wynn could not bear to say good-bye at the inn and just let him leave, so she had come down to the shore with him, but this was hardly easier. Gray-green hood up covering his head, she could still see his large slanted eyes, anxious and desperate. He did not wish to go, and yet he longed for his homeland.

Perhaps Osha feared what waited there, or hated it and was all the more eager to face it. His innocence had died with his teacher. But Wynn needed him to do one more thing when he got there.

She pulled out a small paper-wrapped package and held it out.

He looked down at it, and before he could ask, she was explaining.

"When you reach home, find Brot'an and give him this . . . to him and no one else."

Osha's eyes widened. Wynn had stayed up half the night in the inn, writing the small journal wrapped in that paper. It contained everything she had learned or guessed concerning what had happened on their journey.

"Do not let anyone else see this," she warned. "If you cannot reach Brot'an, then take it to Nein'a and Gleann, as I think they may know how to find him. But never let it fall into anyone else's hands . . . even if you have to destroy it before you find Brot'an."

Osha slowly took the package, and Wynn understood his reluctance. What she asked leaned hard against his oath to his caste. She only hoped he had learned enough from Sgäile, his teacher.

Not of the ways of the Anmaglâhk, but rather the ways of his people that Sgäile had held dear above all else.

Osha nodded and tucked the paper bundle into his tunic.

Wynn wanted to embrace him but could not. "I will not forget you or all that you have done for us."

"I . . . I . . ." Poor Osha had always had difficulty expressing himself with words.

"I know, it is all right," she said. "Go."

He turned, heading along the bustling docks toward the city's north side.

Wynn watched until Osha was barely a tall spot of gray cowl above the heads of dockworkers, hawkers, and merchants too busy to notice him. And when the last glimpse of him vanished among the crowd, she panicked.

How many times had he come for her, stood between her and harm? Simple Osha was not so simple. Even next to Sgäile's unshakable honor, only Osha among his kind and his people had learned to look at her for who she truly was—and not some savage human to be feared and hated.

Wynn broke into a run, shoving her way along the crowded dock. At the sight of swinging gray-green fabric, she reached out and grabbed hold.

Osha turned suddenly at the tension on his cloak and dropped his eyes.

Wynn clawed up to throw her arms around his high neck, and she buried her face in his shoulder as he crouched down.

"Do not forget me," she whispered.

His long arms wrapped about her.

It was foolish, stupid, and something she could not stop. Magiere's warning meant nothing against the pain. Wynn lifted her head and thrust her face into Osha's.

Clumsy and awkward, she found his mouth with hers, and pressed hard.

Chane and Osha . . . and she would never see either again.

Wynn was crying before she pulled back and lost the wet warmth of Osha's mouth. She could not even look at him as she fled. She ran away through the streets of Bela, but it was a long while before she returned to the inn.

Magiere faced into the wind as the captain called to leave harbor. Leesil was already hanging on the rail like a dying man. The seasickness was all in his head, since they hadn't even set sail, and she knew the worst of it wouldn't hit him until tomorrow.

The orb was locked away in their cabin below.

She was determined to protect it, but was still repulsed by its effect upon her. And Leesil would've been in his bunk already, but he didn't want to be near it either.

Chap latched forepaws on the rail beside Wynn, and the two watched the bustling docks of Bela.

News that Wynn would return to Malourné had brought mixed feelings for them all, especially Chap. At least for now, the little sage remained under his protection. But nothing was predictable, and nothing stayed the same.

Magiere had no idea where she, Leesil, and Chap would take the orb. All they could do was get out of Most Aged Father's reach. So parting from Wynn was inevitable—but not just yet.

Leesil staggered over to join Wynn and Chap as the ship slid away from the dock.

A rush of memories filled Magiere's head, from the day she and Leesil had first set foot in Miiska, first saw the Sea Lion . . . to the first time in Bela when she'd felt Leesil's mouth on hers.

She remembered Chap crouched beneath a table in the sage's barracks, growling as Wynn pushed Elvish letters at him, trying to show that he was far more than just a dog.

She remembered Wynn once angrily facing her down, insisting that they give all their food to a village of starving peasants.

She remembered Chap running along a burning rail to throw himself at Leesil amid the fire aboard the elven ship.

She remembered Sgäile's body under a willow tree.

And Leesil's face at their wedding when he said, "I swear."

Magiere turned from the wind to join her companions—and her husband. As she ran her fingers through the back of Leesil's hair, she didn't know what the future held—only that she had to protect the orb and trust in those she loved.

The ship sailed out toward open sea.